CW01080248

Randy Bastard

Randy Bastard

Simon Craig

Black Fountain

Published in 2004 by Black Fountain

Copyright © Simon Craig 2004

Simon Craig has asserted his right under the Copyright,
Designs and Patents Act 1988 to be identified as the author
of this work.

A CIP catalogue record for this book is available from the
British Library.

ISBN 0-9547909-0-1

Printed and bound in Great Britain by Antony Rowe Ltd,
Chippenham

Black Fountain
PO Box 47121
London W6 9XJ
www.blackfountain.co.uk

Mere fame is just luminous obscurity

Clive James

One

Senior staff only

You may well be aware that we have been conducting clandestine negotiations with the Indian Government over the purchase of a small island in the Arabian Sea. The deal has now been done, and it is therefore time to let you know exactly what is going on.

Thus far, we have allowed the rumour to circulate that we want the island for TV reality game shows. This we can now confirm, but the show we have in mind is something special. It will be called *Predator*, and the competitors will be required to kill or be killed. It will be broadcast by SEXITEL, and the sole survivor will win the $1,000,000 prize.

Our reason for buying rather than leasing the island is of course that no government on earth could allow such an event to take place on its sovereign territory. The purchase has been made possible in part by the generous sponsorship of UK arms manufacturer BOMZIZUS, whose executive chairman, Rab McGeddon, is taking a hands-on interest. All staff are asked to treat him with courtesy: it is essential that we maintain good relations with our sponsor.

You should be aware that our ownership of Predator Island will be absolute. Certain details remain to be resolved before we can declare independence, but from that moment, neither the company nor any of its employees need fear adverse legal consequences over what happens there. Nothing in international law can stop us doing whatever we wish on our own territory. As for moral scruples, bear in mind that all competitors will be volunteers, and will be fully aware of what they are letting themselves in for.

Do not be concerned that we might fail to get contestants: we have researched the matter carefully, and it is clear that there will be no difficulty. While the prize will be a significant factor, it seems that for most if not all applicants, fame will be the spur.

In order not to reveal details of the show too early, the selection process will be discreet. We shall present it as sheer chance that all successful candidates turn out to be under the age of 35 and physically attractive, but it will not damage our viewing figures if people guess otherwise. Sexual contact between competitors will be openly encouraged.

We have been singularly lucky in avoiding leaks to the media thus far, but as of now it is virtually certain that rumours will circulate. The best response to enquiries, whatever their source, is 'No comment', but a flat denial would probably do no harm. All staff are, however, requested not to reveal the truth. We want the official announcement to have the maximum possible impact.

The show may be up and running in as little as seven weeks, but three months may be a more realistic target.

Two

'My name is Dan Grabbitall, and I fucking know you Brits. That's where I'm different. I'm not scared of you. You may not believe it, but most Americans are. They're never quite sure if you mean what you say, or if it's some fiendishly clever piece of fucking irony, so they're terrified of making fools of themselves whenever they talk to you. I'm different, and don't you ever forget it. I'm different because my mother's a Brit, and I lived here as a kid for eight years. I know you.

'When Americans do business over here, they try to adapt. They compromise. They think it's the only way. Well, they're wrong. I know them, I know you, and I know you're both wrong. I'm here to make you all American, because that's what counts in today's world. There's America and there's failure. And I will not let you fail. You don't intimidate me, because I know you. Don't ever forget that. Don't ever make the mistake of thinking that I'm just a brash young go-getter from the wrong side of the pond and the wrong side of the tracks, and I'll learn my lesson soon enough. I could play the game by your rules if I wanted. But – and get this if you get nothing else I'm saying – I don't want.

'Let me tell you a little story. You know *University Challenge*, don't you? Well, do you? Come on, you bastards, I'm not here to talk to my fucking self . . . Okay so you do, most of you anyway. Well, listen to this. A million fucking years ago, there was a challenge match between the Brit winners and the American winners – oh yes, the Yanks copied you, like we always do if you come up with a good idea by some amazing fucking accident . . . Ah, a few self-satisfied titters. Well, I'm sorry to disappoint you, but I was lying: the Americans invented it because they'd long since given up expecting any amazing fucking accidents from you

3

bastards. They called it College Bowl. Never mind. Guess who won the match between the Brits and the Americans.

'Don't bother. I'll tell you. The Brits won so easily, it was embarrassing. And then twenty years later, somebody had the idea of checking up on the contestants. All bar one of the Americans was a millionaire, the other was a billionaire. Of the Brits, two were academics paid a fucking pittance and living in terror of losing their jobs, one was an undischarged bankrupt living in a bed and breakfast, and the other was in a cardboard box under the arches at Charing Cross. That's you Brits all over: fucking brilliant at anything that doesn't really matter.

'And all Americans know that. Even if you make them nervous from time to time, when it comes down to it they can't help despising you. That's when they bother thinking about you at all. Listen. Have you guys ever heard of the special relationship? Have you? Well, bully for you. Because your counterparts on the other side of the pond certainly haven't. Or if they have, they think it's another name for fucking somebody up the ass.

'Oh, don't think I don't know what's going on in your tiny little brilliant fucking brains. *Who is this nasty little upstart? These Yanks really are so brash! Did he really say eff? In a staff meeting? At Over & Dunwith? If he thinks he's going to push us around, he'd better think again.* But the fact is, you're scared of me. You're scared of me, because the past is always scared of the future. Did you get that? I said the past is always scared of the future. The present is at least prepared for it, but you're not even the present. You're the dinosaurs of the publishing world, that's what you are. You're looking around in fucking bewilderment at a world you don't understand, full of creatures you can't even eat, because you're too slow and stupid to catch them.

'Well, you've been caught yourselves. Bound to happen, of course. Fucking amazing it took so long, do you know that? The last serious independent publishing house in Britain. So everybody says nice things about you. Bet you all read your profile in *The Times* three weeks ago. All about your style, your spirit, your independence, your insistence on publishing good literature in a world where nobody else cares and blah blah blah. Well, get this. I sat in my office – my huge, plush office in New York – and my secretary, who is stunningly beautiful, who addresses me as Mr

Grabbitall, and who I fuck whenever I feel like it, brought me a copy of the article hot off the Web. Jesus, I laughed like a fucking drain. Because I was already closing in for the kill, even then. Of course, you Brits knew nothing about it. You never know about anything until it's too late. It's just the way you are. Well, all the qualities that the guy who wrote the article – what's his name, Cecil Squirm, or something? – went bananas about, are all the qualities that you lose as of now. Got that? And if you don't like it, then you can leave. I don't owe you a fucking living.

'Spare a moment or two to think about the top entrepreneurs in this country over the past couple of generations – since the world's gone international, that is. Remember Robert Maxwell? Tiny Rowland? Rupert Murdoch? Mohammed Fayed? Here's a general knowledge question of the kind you Brits are all so brilliant at: how many of them were Brits? . . . Precisely. Any foreigner with balls, energy and any kind of brain at all can't fail over here. Christ, I'm surprised you're not all fucking dead. I'm surprised some clever bastard from Rurifuckingtania hasn't done experiments on you all and fucking killed you. It wouldn't be hard. Just explain to you that it's for the good of humanity, and everybody's going to think you're all jolly good chaps and jolly good sports and jolly I don't know what the fuck. Just hit the right tone, and it'd be a piece of piss. Might try it myself sometime, now I come to think of it.

'Tell me something. What's the greatest Brit virtue? Forget it, I'll tell you. Fair play. And no fucking country on the fucking planet ever had a stupider idea than to put fair play at the top of their wish-list for national characteristics. Fair play? Listen. Did anybody ever tell you that nice guys finish last? Did they? You thought it was the title of some book, didn't you? Well, get this. It's just a statement of fact, that's all, a statement of fact.

'You're fucking amazing, you know that? What other country in the whole fucking world would let Youssuf Al-Majnooni roam its streets? Know who I mean? Islamic fundamentalist in west London. Jesus Christ, he actually *says* he wants to destroy your society, and everybody knows he's done kidnappings and murders. You think he respects you for letting him do and say whatever the fuck he likes? Fuck me, he *despises* you! And you even get people like that Salvation Army guy – whatsisname, General Pius Oldgit – bending over backwards double to say what a great guy he is. It was when I saw Youssuf Al-Majnooni on TV in the States that I just knew this place was for me. I just knew I'd be a fox among chickens over here.

'Never mind. For now, I need you. Even you just might be useful if you listen and try to learn something that matters for once in your jolly decent stiff-upper-lipped hypocritical fucking lives. I'm going to tell you about publishing. I'm going to tell you everything about publishing that you've never fucking learned.

'That guy Squirm . . . sorry? . . . okay, Smarm, Cyril Smarm. I don't give a fuck what his name is, but why not get it right. If he's got any influence, I'll probably have to get to know him sooner or later. Well, he practically blubbed about the way you bastards decide what to publish. Christ, I nearly fell off my fucking chair, when he said that at Over & Dunwith it's editorial that decides. Is that really true? Jesus. Well, not any more, it isn't. From now on, it's sales and marketing, just like at a real publishing house. Which, as of now, is what you are. Get this. Editors don't make decisions like that. Money people make them, because they understand books, and editors don't. Editors *pretend* they decide, of course they do. Fact is, they learn to self-censor.

'They begin to understand that their personal opinions are irrelevant. They've got some book that they think is fucking brilliant, but they know it's not going to get the nod, so they don't even try. They used to, but not any more. Time was when editorial would say this is the biggest bestseller since the Bible, and the money men would say this is the biggest fucking disaster since Goliath reckoned he'd be too hot in a helmet. I tell you, there could be blood on the fucking walls and on the fucking ceiling, too. But as soon as the big beasts – people like me – took control of publishing, editorial didn't stand a chance. There's people under the arches at Charing Cross today who would be fucking great important editors at Fuckface and Cuntballs if they'd taken a reality check early enough, and learned not to fight any more.

'Everybody knows now. Except you, that is, and you're going to have to learn. The money people in publishing understand risk. They know that for every risk that comes off, three or four won't. If you think you can survive in publishing today without minimising risk, then you're too stupid to be in the business. You'd better learn that. If you want to survive. If *I* decide on some whim that you're going to publish something, that's different. I own you, and I can do what I like. Otherwise, decisions will be made by committee, and it's a committee run by sales and marketing.

'So what do editors do? I'll tell you. They burn the fucking slush pile. We don't need one. We'll publish the fact that we accept no unsolicited manuscripts and never return them, even with postage included. Stop fucking pretending. Nobody bothers with the slush pile any more, nobody. When some publisher boasts about having discovered a fucking genius in the slush pile, it's a marketing ploy. Truth is – even you must know this – that it's the work of somebody they know but the public don't. That's not slush pile, and it's a fucking lie to say it is. The slush pile – and we'll still get one even after we say we've done away with it – is made up of all the crap written by people you've never heard of and not on any agent's books. That's the slush pile.

'And I don't care if once every million fucking submissions, there's something bigger than the Bible and Harry Fucking Potter. What you do with the slush pile is spend one point three eight minutes looking at each piece of shit before you throw it out. And if you do miss the latest Harry Fucking Potter Bible and somebody else gets it and I find out you rejected it, you'll be out of here so fast you'll break the fucking sound barrier.

'So that's the first thing that editors do. Next, you come up with ideas. I want the Fuckchester City scandal written by their hottest player. I want the truth about Cliff Richard and Mother Teresa. I want to know that he fucked the ass off her ten times a night throughout the seventies and eighties. I want . . . I'll tell you what I want. I want ideas that will sell. Do you know what sells in today's world? Do you? I'll tell you. The four esses, that's what. Sex, Scandal, Sport and Celebrities. That's what sells, that's what I want.

'Now listen carefully. I'm going to tell you the biggest bestseller there's ever been, and if you can come up with it, I'll give you a jelly baby, or whatever you spineless Brits expect as a reward for being clever. The biggest bestseller is the inside story of the up-the-fucking-ass relationship between a prince of the blood – because royalty are the biggest celebs of all – and the biggest soccer star in the fucking world. Changed my mind. Two jelly babies for that one.

'Oh, don't get scared. We'll still publish novels, and we'll even publish good novels if they make money. But if they don't make money, we won't publish them. You're going to go through your rapidly diminishing list of writers – oh, don't look so shocked, I know the rate at which you're haemorrhaging talent, I know everything about you, whatever Cyril fucking Smarm might say – you're going to go through that list, and you're going to ditch anybody who isn't making money and isn't going to. The rest you're going to fucking market properly so that they do fucking sell. And then you're going to bring in some big names. If you can't do that, you're no good to me, and you'll be under the fucking arches at Charing Cross along with the fucking genius from *University Challenge*.

'And when I tell you we're going to get rid of anybody who's not profitable, don't think it's a fucking joke, because it's not. Any writer we get rid of is finished. Nobody else is going to take him, not the way things work today. In a year or two he'll probably be dead of a heart attack – or cirrhosis of the liver, more likely. So if you can't face that kind of responsibility, you'd better fuck off out of here and go and work for some bleeding-heart charity where you belong. The secret is not to give a fucking fuck. The moment you give a fuck, you're finished in this line of business.

'What else do editors do? Can't remember . . . Nothing very important, then . . . Oh yes, you work with writers because they're tender flowers, especially if they're Brits. You wipe their eyes for them when they cry, you wipe their asses for them when they shit themselves. You do that because the people that really matter – the people that see to making money – don't have time. You fall down on that part of the job – you lose some serious money-maker to another publisher – and it's the arches. Don't ever forget it.

'And that's about it . . . Jesus, you Brits have an amazing way of looking shocked. You should see your own faces. No expression whatever. You could just've been listening to some guy reading the weather forecast. Americans would be climbing the fucking walls by now, Wops would be throwing their fucking arms about, Frogs would be looking down their superior fucking noses trying to pretend they despise me, but *you* . . . Never mind.

'There's just one more thing. Don't ever think I don't know what I'm talking about. Don't ever forget that I already own a real

8

publishing house, of which Over & Dunwith is now a part – not much of a part, but my foot in the European door, anyway. Not only that, but I started out in publishing as an editor. Little known fact, but true, I do assure you. I'm not proud of it, but there it is on my record. You can check if you like. Would I lie to you? Yes, I would, but as it happens I'm telling the truth on this occasion.

'Oh, I know what you're all thinking. You're thinking, *Jesus Christ, this Grabbitall person has actually been an editor, and he just despises literature! Disgraceful!* Well, I don't give a fuck what you think. And as it happens, I do not despise literature. If it makes money, I fucking worship it. And that's the secret of my success. If it doesn't make money, it's not literature at all. It's fucking crap, and I won't publish it. Being an editor is what did it for me. Seeing all the crap that was once published and that nobody ever read.

'Get this. I have never read a book in my life. Understand? Never. En ee vee ee fucking ar. Ah, a reaction at last! Disbelief. So Brits are human. Sort of. Listen, if a fucking bomb lands on this place in the next few moments, archaeologists are going to have an interesting dig a million years down the line. They'll find a lot of the old model of homo sapiens alongside a representative of a more advanced species altogether. They'll wonder how the fuck you and I could have lived at the same time. They'll write learned articles trying to explain it away . . . Never mind.

'I was saying. I've never read a book in my life. Oh, Jesus, I wish I couldn't read your minds. It's so fucking depressing. *But he must have read hundreds of books, for God's sake! He was an editor, wasn't he?* You think editors need to read books? Well, get this. They fucking don't. I was the hottest editor in New York, and that was because I didn't waste my fucking time reading. Oh, I'd look at a page or two now and again, I'd ask a reader what he thought now and again. But mostly, I wouldn't even do that. You know what I'd do? Do you? I'd *smell* a book, that's what I'd do. And I'd smell an author, too. I'd find out what other people thought. I'd find out what the movers and shakers might say about the thing. I developed the finest nose in the world for a book that would really sell. And I did it without ever reading one. I promise you. I could – a couple of times I did – go on air to talk about some fucking brilliant novel, and why everybody should buy it. Jesus, I didn't have to read it to be able to do that!

'And then I got bored with it. It was just too fucking easy, and anyway, I wasn't going to be somebody else's pet fucking monkey for the rest of my life. I wanted money and I wanted power, the only two things in this world that are worth having. So I made a move into marketing. And that's where I learned what it's really all about. Not just publishing. Life in general.

'The most important thing I learned is that most people are so stupid that there's nothing they wouldn't believe. Tell them something is free for instance, and they believe you even after they've paid for it. Seen the latest way to sell an orange? Double the price, and tell the poor saps that the bit of tissue you give them with it is a free hand wipe. I tell you, I'm sorely tempted to sell steering wheels at thirty grand a time, with a free car thrown in.

'Another thing I found out was that if you want to reach the top, it's a good idea to own one big publishing house, and at least two big newspapers – one each side of the Atlantic. I haven't got there yet. The US titles I own just aren't big enough, and I don't see the opportunity over here yet. But I'm looking, and when I shoot, I don't miss. Stay with me and you'll do well.

'Come to think of it, I'd better tell you what's in this for you, I suppose. You might even be wondering why I want to keep you on at all if I have such fucking contempt for you. Well, I don't think much of you, it's true. But it's easier and cheaper to stay with you than to fire you all and try to fill your places with the sort of people I really want. So I'm going to give you the chance to show me you're capable of learning. I'll know the picture soon enough, and any of you that don't make the grade will be out. Those of you I reckon I can use, you can expect to get richer. Even a lot richer. But you're going to have to learn to work, and work my way.

'You won't, as it happens, see very much of me from now on, because I've got plenty of other things to do on both sides of the pond. In fact, I'm going to be in New York for the next month, in which time I'm going to leave the running of this place mostly up to you. That's going to be your chance to prove to me that you're not as fucking useless as I think you are, your big chance to show me that, despite overwhelming evidence to the contrary, you can handle business. Because business is what matters.

'You have to have a nose for it . I said that celebs sell. Whatever you're doing in today's world, you'll do it ten times better – I mean you'll make ten times as much money out of it – with celebs on your side. So when I'm not buying *The Times* and *The Washington Post* – and the biggest TV franchise I can get, I should have mentioned that – I'll be looking after my new PR business, Rich & Famous. That's something I'm not going to delegate – not yet anyway – because when it comes to a new enterprise, I always start off with total personal control. Get the show firmly on the road, then find some pygmy who can just keep it going. Foolproof.

'Anyway, my PR business, as it happens, is good news for you, because it means you're not going to have to do all the work when it comes to getting celebrities to write for us – or pretend to write, which is what it really comes down to. I'll push the celebs your way, and all you'll have to do is find the ghosts to write their autobiographies, their cookbooks, their gardening books and so on.

'And don't give me any crap about conflict of interest. The celebs in question will be free to take on a different agent or a different publisher if they want to, but the fact is that they'll do better with me as both. It's in my interest to maximise their sales, and that's exactly what I'll do. Publishers don't pay the huge advances they used to, but if somebody tries offering one of my clients something special, I'll think about it.

'I've hit the ground running, like I always do. Heard of Letzgetcha Nickersoff, have you? I shouldn't have to ask, but it's incredible how ignorant you Brit intellectuals can be. Decent tennis player, and gorgeous with it. Now that's rare, because almost any good female tennis player you can name is a lezzie, and butch as fuck. Which is a major disappointment to all the dirty old men who'd like to get off on sweet little girls running around in their undies, isn't it? So I've signed her up. Fucking weird, if you think about it, because she should be with some big sporting agency, shouldn't she? Well she was, but ten minutes with me convinced her she shouldn't be, even though I told her I know fuck-all about tennis. She just knows a good thing when she sees it, so she's with me now. And that means that Over & Dunwith will be bringing out her autobiography and her cookbook and her gardening book before you can say get 'em off. All you have to do is find some jerk to write them for her.

'Personal feelings do not come into it. If there is one person on this earth that I hate more than any other, it's that fucking bitch

Cassandra McRaker. All that's worst in gutter journalism. And she hates me. Took a few pot-shots at me when she was based in New York – like, "Dan Grabbitall is to literature what Adolf Hitler was to racial harmony" – and I'll bet she's not done yet. But she's a big-name columnist now, and I've heard that she's working on the autobiography which she always said she'd never write – and fuck me, she's only 35. But I don't care. If it's true, I want it. See the point I'm making? Business is business, and nothing else matters. Personal feelings are irrelevant in business. Correction, personal feelings are fatal in business. See you leave them at home, and never bring them to work.

'And if you start feeling enthusiastic about anything except the success of the business, take a cold shower. Look at sports commentators. Think they're really interested in what they have to talk about? They're bored out of their fucking minds with it, but it's their job to sound interested. You know what happens when a player's won his Wimbledon semi-final? If he's interviewed before he knows who he'll play in the final, then he answers one set of questions for one potential finalist and one for the other. Or look at what happens when some oldie kicks the bucket – a royal, for instance. The obituaries are already recorded. So you get your rentabores all dressed up in black, weeping crocodile tears for some old fart who might live for years yet. Call that cynical? I call it realistic. That's how it goes. To make it big in today's world, you've got to be genuine about everything except sincerity. That's got to be fake, because you just won't make the grade if you let yourself feel anything. Stay in control and fake it. That's how it's done. You won't make it if you can't fake it.

'And I'll tell you what else is fatal in business. High moral principles. I'm thinking of *Predator*. And don't be fooled by denials. The lid is off now, and the thing will be announced officially in the next few days. Disgraceful, isn't it? A TV reality show in which the contestants actually kill each other. Tut tut, what is the world coming to? That's a question, in case you hadn't noticed . . . No offers? . . . Well, I'll tell you. Its senses, that's what it's coming to. If you can get enough people prepared to kill or be killed just to be on TV, then do it and you'll make a fucking fortune. The winner will be the biggest celeb in the world the moment it's over, and every agent in the world will be after him –

because it's not going to be her, is it, even if little girls are allowed to play. But I'll get him. Promise. And then he's going to do tricks for me for just as long as he's marketable, and one of the tricks he's going to do is write books, starting with his autobiography. That's how you're going to get the world's biggest celeb. I'll do the work for you.

'Personal feelings and moral principles, then, are a big no-no. Just to bang it home with a sledgehammer, you've heard that another businessman was kidnapped today, haven't you? Rab McGeddon, by name, chief of BOMZIZUS, arms makers and sponsors of *Predator*. It's an open secret, isn't it? Islamic militants after a fast buck so they can get nuked up as quick as possible. Well, if Youssuf Al-Majnooni's behind it, as I would very strongly suspect, then there's nothing I'd like more than to sign him up for his autobiography. Or maybe an Islamic fundamentalist cookbook . . . Yes, good idea, I might just follow that one up. You know, that's the only good thing about talking to a bunch of losers like you. Sometimes I get ideas that way, and this could be a good one. Let's see . . . *Cooking for God* maybe, or *Kitchen Jihad* . . . I'll think about it.

'Anyway, I'll say it again. Do things my way and you'll be okay. And that's about it. For the rest of today, I'm going to go around familiarising myself with this place. Tomorrow night I'm flying back to New York for four weeks, but before that I'll be here to see all senior staff individually. Just wait till I call you – and when I do, see that it takes you no more than 45 seconds to get to my office. Now fuck off back to work.'

Three

Clement Dormatt was a worried man. For a start, he was on his way home, and that was always worrying. But now there was more. Even if home had never been much fun, at least he had always enjoyed his job. The great advantage in working for an independent publisher was that you were always something more than a tiny cog in a vast machine. You knew what people thought, and all voices were heard: where everybody knows everybody, nobody can be completely ignored. Dormatt knew all about the giant conglomerates which had taken over every other significant publisher in the land, and they scared him.

Hammersmith Bridge shook and rattled beneath him. He liked the eastern walkway, which he always took in the mornings, but not the western, which he was on now: the western walkway meant he was getting near home.

He knew editors who actually claimed to enjoy working for a giant firm. They were all younger than Dormatt, such people, and he was made uneasy by their Newspeak: it made him feel like a Neanderthal meeting Homo sapiens for the first time, and dimly sensing that this was his nemesis. These people talked of 'the bottom line', they said 'k' when they meant thousand, they said 'Ciao!' and 'Enjoy!' and they glittered with a hard sheen that frightened Dormatt.

They told him that publishing wasn't a charity any more (which they wrote as 'anymore', just as they wrote 'alright'), and that writers had to learn that. It was tough, they said (although they didn't seem to find it tough at all) but you couldn't 'carry passengers'. If it wasn't profitable, it had to go: the bottom line.

Dormatt had often wondered how he would react if Over & Dunwith were ever to be devoured by one of the big beasts, and he

14

had feared that it would destroy him. If work became as bad as home, he would be finished. But it was never going to happen. Dodo Dunwith, as he frequently reassured his staff, wouldn't let it. They were always talking about it, though, because, while Grabbitall had exaggerated in saying they were haemorrhaging talent, there was nonetheless a steady drain of big names to bigger publishers. Dormatt would sigh, and say 'Enjoy it while you can, because it can't last. We all know that. It can't last.' But he hadn't said such things because he believed them. He had said them in an almost superstitious way – as if disaster predicted was disaster forestalled.

He looked out over the Thames to his right, noticing for the thousandth time as he did so a weathered brass plaque set into the bridge's handrail. For the hundredth time, he promised himself that he would stop and read it sometime. He looked down and shook his head.

His great hope was that Dodo Dunwith would last. Dodo, at 56, was just eight years his senior, and, provided his health held up, could surely see Dormatt into retirement – his father, after all, had remained at the helm until he was 81. Yes, the great thing was that Dodo would have nothing to do with the giant conglomerates. Dodo valued Over & Dunwith for what it was – England's last significant independent publisher – and would not let it go.

The irony was that, after reading the profile which Cyril Smarm had written for *The Times*, Dormatt had never felt so sure that Over & Dunwith's future was secure. All right, it was the sort of thing you expected of Cyril Smarm, but even so . . . 'oasis of literary virtue', 'the reassuring smell of leather armchairs', 'the only publisher not obsessed with the size of its manhood', 'the standard-bearer for values otherwise lost', 'almost hear the scratch of quill on parchment' . . . Dodo would never have allowed such a piece to be published just as he was negotiating an end to it all.

But he had. Dormatt closed his eyes and shook his head again. He felt such a fool. All those times he had assured everybody that it couldn't last, that they were bound sooner or later to go the same way as all the other independents; all those times he had assured himself secretly that it would never happen. True, their most profitable writers were being lured away by firms able to pay advances which, though smaller than they would once have been,

Over & Dunwith couldn't match; but their list was still viable, if only just.

Perhaps it wouldn't have happened if he hadn't taken Cyril Smarm so seriously? Maybe that was it. Maybe it was because he had dropped his guard. Maybe Dormatt's crossed fingers really had been to Grabbitall what garlic was to Dracula. Maybe Grabbitall had planned it all: 'Okay, Cyril, here's what we're going to do. I can't get in while that bastard Dormatt has his fingers crossed, so . . .' 'Yes, Dan.' Oh God.

He was over the river and into Barnes now. Nearly home. Except that it wasn't really home at all. Over & Dunwith was home, but now it was changing, and he didn't know if he could take it. Of all the times for such a thing to happen, it had to be now, just as he was about to strike a blow for the values he really believed in. Oh God. Just as Dormatt was about to do the unthinkable, and publish a novel from the slush pile.

Even Over & Dunwith, last of the old school of publishers, didn't publish real unknowns any more, especially middle-aged unknowns. A good novel from the slush pile might still very occasionally rate a mention at an editorial meeting, but everybody had known for years that this was no more than a pious nod in the direction of old-fashioned literary values: everybody knew that it would never in fact be published. An unknown who made it was never really unknown: it was always somebody's nephew, or someone who had been to university with somebody, or someone who had joined a publishing house and impressed with a display of wit or knowledge.

But this time, Dormatt really had something, and he wasn't letting go. Boris Fartleby, as Dormatt knew from the covering letter, was middle-aged – just a couple of years younger than Dormatt, in fact – and he was a teacher, a schoolteacher. Now everyone at Over & Dunwith knew perfectly well what that meant. At Over & Dunwith people did not actually say it (as they did at the big publishing houses), but they still thought it: teachers were *thick, ignorant and boring* – because if they weren't, they wouldn't be teachers, would they? Everybody knew it. English teachers couldn't spell or punctuate, History teachers didn't know the Duke of Marlborough from the Duke of Wellington, Geography teachers thought Walsall was the capital of Poland. None of this would have mattered had it not been for the most distressing thing of all about teachers: *they were incorrigible writers of unpublishable novels.*

And now Dormatt had found a schoolteacher – and a middle-aged schoolteacher at that – who had written a novel so good that it had to be published. Not only was it a novel by a middle-aged schoolteacher; it was a quiet novel, set in bourgeois suburbia in the 1990s. It didn't start with a bang, the sex was never explicit, there was no violence, there were long descriptive passages, there was a dearth of dialogue. It was, in other words, utterly unpublishable. And it was brilliant: a subtle satire on a society which had lost its soul. It had to be published.

Alexander the Great: son of Philip of Basildon was, like Joyce's *Ulysses*, an updating of the tale of a hero of antiquity. Fartleby's clear intention was to lay bare the shallow values by which we live today. Alex, the hero, was tall, blonde, handsome, brilliant, athletic . . . and entirely empty. He was so perfect that he was characterless; all things to all people. Everybody envied him, everybody admired him, nobody really liked him. It was a wonderful book, and Dormatt was going to see that it was published. There would be strong opposition, but Dormatt was a senior fiction editor, and for once he was going to make his seniority count.

And now this. Dormatt was miserable. There was just one compensation: at least he hadn't contacted Fartleby to express his interest. His first reaction on reading *Alexander* had been to get on the phone immediately, in order at least to be first in the queue. But no: even if Fartleby had had the sense to submit his manuscript to a dozen publishers simultaneously, there was still no possibility that anyone else would be remotely interested. No, he could safely leave it until he had at least run it past an editorial meeting, and been given the go-ahead, however grudging, to express official interest. Thank God he had decided to wait.

He had been looking forward so much to one of his rare great moments – and one of Over & Dunwith's great moments, too. It was to be the moment at which Clement Dormatt finally asserted himself as a significant figure in the world of fiction publishing, and the moment at which Over & Dunwith asserted its status as a truly independent house, prepared to buck even the most powerful publishing trend of all, the trend which said that *nobody publishes nobodies.*

He stopped, waited for a gap in the traffic, and crossed the road. How could this have happened? Grabbitall's tirade had hit him like a train coming out of a tunnel at top speed, its lights doused and its engine silenced. The real world had suddenly arrived at Over & Dunwith, and nothing would ever be the same again. One thing was clear: he wouldn't dare even mention the name of Boris Fartleby at a firm owned by Dan Grabbitall. Almost home.

Dormatt wouldn't survive this. He was going to become just another functionary in a huge American multinational. If he stuck with it, he might well become richer, he might well gain in status, because Dormatt was very good at delivering what people wanted. Intelligence and application, together with a pathological loathing of confrontation, made him in many ways the ideal employee. Yes, he could very easily dance to Dan Grabbitall's tune. And hate himself for doing it.

But what was the alternative? Resignation? Clearly the only honourable course of action. But what then? What publisher would be interested in a middle-aged fiction editor who had just proved that he could no longer function in the world of publishing? Even if someone was prepared to take a chance on him, who would it be? With the exception of Over & Dunwith, Dormatt could not think of a single publisher that he would wish to work for. Oh, they all pretended that they cared about literature, but they didn't. Grabbitall at least was honest. What was Dormatt to do? With the usual sinking feeling, he turned left down his street. Just another half minute . . .

There was no hope. He tried to imagine himself standing up to Dan Grabbitall when they met the following day, and he knew he couldn't. If he dared even to mention the name of Boris Fartleby, that would probably be the end of him. The fact was that Dormatt was already terrified of Dan Grabbitall, and there was nothing he could do about it. There was no point in trying to stand up to someone in every way more powerful than you. What could a mouse achieve by defying a snake? The admiration of stupid mice, the contempt of intelligent ones, and the satisfaction of the snake's appetite.

Distracted by the image of Mouse Dormatt impaled on the fangs of Snake Grabbitall, he stopped, opened his garden gate and walked up the immaculately clean path to the front door. Clearing his throat he inserted his key in the lock, turned it gently, and walked quietly into the house.

Dormatt's Wife appeared from the kitchen, as she always did. And she stood staring at him, hands on hips. 'You are absolutely unbelievable, did you know that? Did you? I simply do not believe you're real. I tell people about you, and they think you're mad, did you know that? *STOP!!*' Her voice suddenly became very quiet. 'What have you got on your feet?'

Dormatt looked down in bewilderment. 'My feet? Shoes. Black shoes. What . . .' And then he remembered. His slippers were at the door.

'Every single day I have to tell you. I mean, what *is* wrong with you? Listen, and for the last time: YOU . . . DO . . . NOT . . . WEAR . . . SHOES . . . IN . . . THE . . . HOUSE. Have you got that? I tell people about you, and they can't believe that anybody could possibly wear shoes in the house, did you know that? Grit, mud, dust, chewing gum . . . I mean, I don't know how you do it, but you seem to walk through all the filth in all of London, you do. Have you the remotest idea of what you do to the carpets in this house, you and your filthy feet?'

Dormatt sighed. 'I'll remember next time.'

'You'd better,' said Dormatt's Wife, and returned whence she had come.

Obediently, Dormatt changed his footwear before entering the kitchen to make himself a cup of tea. His Wife was sitting at the table, staring at the advertisements in a glossy magazine. 'Have you seen next door's new car? Have you? I mean, I feel quite ashamed of ours, I really do. How old is it now?'

'Two years.'

'Two years? Two years?? You say it as if it just doesn't matter. What sort of people drive two-year-old cars today? Honestly, I feel quite ashamed in company. I mean, anyone would. I can't think of any of our friends who drive a car as old and shabby as ours, really I can't.'

Dormatt looked at her with distaste. Why on earth had he married her? What could he possibly have seen in her? She had been quite good-looking – still would be, if her face hadn't soured permanently – and had not been as obviously mad then as she was now. And that was it. He could never understand how someone who had worked in publishing – a job which she gave up the moment they were married – could possibly have so little interest in books. He had not seen her open a book in all the 23 years of their marriage.

Children. At the beginning she had wanted children, but the first signs of impending madness had been her insistence that they should 'get the house right first'. And every spare penny had gone into the house. New wallpaper in every room, new carpets throughout, fitted kitchen, fitted bathroom, double glazing, new furniture for the dining room, new . . . But why go through the list? It just went on and on, and it would never stop. There was always something else, and there always would be. She redecorated the house as they used to – did they still? – repaint the Forth Bridge: started at one end, got to the other, then went back to the beginning and started all over again. Her latest thing was loft conversion – utterly pointless since they already had more rooms than they needed.

Anyway, the children (who had never greatly interested him) gradually faded, and, about ten years into the marriage, disappeared altogether. Dormatt could see it, even if she couldn't. The house was her baby: she was forever cleaning it, dressing it up, seeing that it behaved in a way which would make her proud of it. And of course, if the thought of children ever had occurred to her after that first decade, so would the thought of the mess they would inevitably have created. They would have scuffed the furniture, they would have dragged dirt into the house, they would have spilled things. They would have been even worse than Dormatt, and that was saying something. So there had never been children.

The evening progressed as evenings always did in the Dormatt home. Always. Dinner was all right. Dormatt's Wife could cook quite well, but bitterly resented doing it unless they were having guests, an increasingly rare occurrence. Dormatt had never been all that sociable, and Dormatt's Wife had become less so as time went on. Dinner was all right; it just wasn't any fun. Then they watched television, Dormatt marvelling as ever at the slack-jawed intensity with which this once-intelligent woman studied the commercials. The programmes which interrupted them interested her far less.

'We should really have one of those water filters,' she said. 'Thames water just isn't safe, you know. You can get all sorts of things from it. People wonder what's wrong with us when they see that we don't filter our water, did you know that? People look at me in the street, and they're thinking, there's that woman that just doesn't filter her water.'

Dormatt grimaced. 'Neither of us ever seems to get sick.'

Dormatt's Wife shook her head despairingly. 'You never notice anything, do you? I'm tired all the time. I am. And I notice it. It's such an effort to get up in the morning, and I'm so weary during the day that I can hardly get through it. Look at all the things I've got to do. A house like this doesn't look after itself, you know. Did you know that? Did you? It's got to be hoovered every day, or it just gets completely out of control, especially when you go charging through it in those incredibly filthy shoes you always wear. So when you're there in your office, drinking cups of coffee and putting your feet up, here I am slaving away. And seven days a week, because I don't get two days off every week, like you. I . . .'

'I've never seen you hoovering on a weekend.'

'Haven't you? Haven't you? Well, maybe that's because I'm just too considerate. Had you thought of that? It makes a lot of noise, hoovering, and I don't like to disturb you when you're here. But do you know what it means – that I can't hoover on Saturdays and Sundays out of consideration for you? Do you?'

Dormatt sighed. 'No.'

'It means that on a Monday, I've got to do twice as much . . . no, three times as much, that's what it means. Do you think that's funny? I'd like to see you try to do my job, I really would. You know, I think Viraga Hateman's got it about right. The feminist movement hasn't made any difference, except on the surface. The plain fact is that women are still just the servants of men . . . slaves, I mean. Viraga Hateman . . . You have heard of Viraga Hateman, haven't you?'

'Everybody has. Even me.'

'Yes, well she says that everything . . . Oh God!' She reached for the remote control, and switched channels. 'Now look what you've done. The news has begun – I mean it's nearly finished now – and you know I always watch the BBC news, but did you remind me? Did you? Oh no, not you. Now, what was I saying? Oh yes, I was saying that I don't hoover on weekends, out of consideration for you. Well, can you imagine what it's like on Mondays? Can you?

Mondays are the worst of all, because it hasn't been done on Saturday or Sunday, and of course you've virtually ruined every carpet in the house. I have to go over them all three times, that's what I have to do. All because of you. And I have to wash dishes every day. Every single day. I . . .'

'We have a machine for that.'

'Oh, a machine! Oh, how wonderful, we have a machine! And who do you think puts the dishes in it? Who do you think puts in the detergent? Who takes them out? Who . . .'

'As it happens, I usually do.'

Dormatt's Wife turned away from him. 'Oh, God, why do I bother? I mean . . . And the windows need doing again, did you know that? And then there are the sheets, which of course, you never notice. Threadbare, that's what they are, and all of different colours. We've got yellow sheets and blue sheets and white sheets, and I don't know what. You have no idea how unpleasant it is for someone with an eye and a bit of sensitivity to have things that just don't match, that just don't go together . . . God, the way you used to dress! Did you know that that was what I first noticed about you? Did you? The incredible way you used to dress? People used to think you were mad, did you know that? You would wear jackets and trousers that didn't match, and you'd wear . . .'

'I thought you wanted to watch the news.'

'Don't you dare interrupt me! Don't you dare interrupt me!! I decide what I want to watch on my own television, and don't you ever forget it. What was I saying? Oh yes, your appalling dress sense. I remember once you wore a patterned tie with a patterned shirt. Nobody could imagine what was wrong with you. And your hair was always all over the place, you didn't even notice that, did you? Well, did you? I'm not talking to myself, you know.'

'No, I didn't notice that.'

'You don't have to tell me. I know you didn't. But everybody else did. Everybody. Every single person in the entire world noticed how bizarre you were. People in Japan and China and Chile knew all about you, did you know that? People in . . . in Tahiti would say oh God, what's that strange Englishman wearing today? What weird thing has he done with his hair today? You think I'm joking, don't you? Do you know why I married you? Do you?'

'I can't think.'

22

'You never realised, did you? I married you because I was sorry for you. I saw the way that everybody looked at you, and I heard the way that everybody said how odd you were, and I felt sorry for you. Did you know . . .'

Dormatt stopped listening to her, and turned his attention to the television. The news was over, and *Spotlight* was beginning. '. . . and the fact is that, whatever the tabloids might think, there are people who take an interest in topics other than *Predator* and Letzgetcha Nickersoff, in topics which, at least arguably, are more important than *Predator* or even Letzgetcha Nickersoff.' Clive Sneersly looked, as ever, as if there was a particularly bad smell just under his nose. 'One of these is certainly the state of the nation's schools. It's a hardy annual on *Spotlight*, but I would never make any apology for returning to it.'

'Things just don't seem to get any better, do they?' he went on, with what had become known nationally as the Sneersly Sigh. 'Politicians can't be trusted. When seventy per cent of Cabinet ministers are sending or have sent their children to private schools despite the Government's supposed commitment to the state system, what are the rest of us supposed to think? We begin with this report from Justin Poser.'

Only Clive Sneersly, Dormatt mused, could look macho behind a pink shirt and yellow tie. His mind wandered. What was his life coming to? Home was controlled by his Wife, work would now be controlled by Dan Grabbitall. Was this even survivable? . . . And then, as the voice of Dormatt's Wife grated on and on and on, he saw what he had to do. If he was not to disintegrate completely, he had to make a stand. Not at home – that wasn't even possible any more. He had tolerated his Wife's bullying for so long that he could no more resist it now than he could resist breathing. But Dan Grabbitall didn't yet know him; at work, it might still be possible for him to turn and fight. And that was exactly what he would do. Dormatt was going to make a stand. When he met Dan Grabbitall, he was going to tell him about Boris Fartleby; he was going to tell him that they would be publishing *Alexander the Great*. And he wouldn't take no for an answer.

Having for the moment run out of complaints, Dormatt's Wife rose with a growl, picked up her coffee cup and his, and carried them ostentatiously through to the kitchen, from which soon issued the sound of clinking crockery and running water. They weren't going into the dishwasher: Dormatt's Wife was Making a Point. But it was wasted on Dormatt, who was now deep into his agreeable reverie. Grabbitall would storm and bluster, that was inevitable. But Dormatt would insist. Quietly and determinedly, he would insist. And his insistence would finally overcome Grabbitall's rage. Clement Dormatt was going to stand up to Dan Grabbitall, and Dan Grabbitall would respect him for it. Yes, Dormatt was going to make a stand. He was. With a nod of satisfaction, he turned his attention back to the television.

Sober-suited and with matching face, the figure on the screen was standing in the middle of a venerable quadrangle. '. . . and more and more Muslims,' he was saying, 'will line up behind the militants. If we continue to neglect the education of all but a small minority of our young people, what sort of future can we expect? This is Justin Poser, reporting from Eton College.'

Back in the studio, Clive Sneersly sighed. 'Here with me to discuss this sorry state of affairs I have journalist Cassandra McRaker and General Pius Oldgit of the Salvation Army. Cassandra McRaker, herself a former teacher, has written extensively on the problems of our educational system, while General Oldgit has frequently emphasised his anxiety to reach out to the youth of the world.

'Cassandra McRaker, if you were secretary of state for education, what would you do to turn things round?

The woman he was addressing was in her mid-thirties, good-looking in a slightly severe way, with a face which had been around – a face which had come through some tough times.

'As education secretary, there's very little I could do. The main problem is simply one of funding. If I were prime minister or chancellor, then I might be able to do something. I might be able to double the amount of money we spend on our schools, and put the education secretary in a position to make a real difference. As long as we refuse to fund schools properly, these problems will not be solved. To take just one example, Bogsworth Community School in west London used to be highly regarded, but years of underfunding have taken their toll. I have this from the headmaster himself. The fabric of the school is disintegrating, and the problem of discontented ethnic minorities is particularly serious there because of the school's proximity to Youssuf Al-Majnooni's Farootkaik Mosque. We . . .'

'Well, let me stop you there for a moment. Money might indeed help to solve some of the problems mentioned by Justin Poser, but it will surely do nothing to discourage the activities of those like Youssuf Al-Majnooni who are implacably opposed to the whole British educational system. Pius Oldgit, let me turn to you. What would you do about the likes of Youssuf Al-Majnooni?'

General Pius Oldgit was nearly seventy, but seemed at once ancient and ageless – an effect probably heightened by his uniform.

'What we must understand, Clive, is that God cares deeply about education, and in this respect, perhaps we should give some credit to Youssuf Al-Majnooni. At least he and his congregation at the Farootkaik Mosque are committed to securing for their children an education which . . .'

'Do you know there's a crack in the kitchen wall? Never noticed it, have you? Well, go and have a look at it now. Oh God, I don't know how this house is still standing, the way you neglect it, I really don't. It's going to come crashing down one of these days, and when it happens, just don't tell me I didn't warn you. Come on, up. You're going to have a look at this crack whether you want to or not.'

Four

(From the *Daily Shocker*)

Betjeman returns from the dead
Viraga Hateman

Tell me, does anyone remember John Betjeman any more? Been dead a long time, I know, but he was a big name in his day, he really was.

'Sir' John Betjeman (I'm afraid so) was a poet. If, that is, you're prepared to extend the definition of poet to cover writers of pure doggerel, because it was doggerel that Betjeman wrote. It was phenomenally popular because it was so easy to understand. The one thing Betjeman never never did was to tax his reader's intelligence. As an example, let me just quote the first couple of verses of his best-known 'poem', entitled *A Subaltern's Love-song*:

> Miss J. Hunter-Dunn, Miss J. Hunter-Dunn,
> Furnish'd and burnish'd by Aldershot sun,
> What strenuous singles we played after tea,
> We in the tournament – you against me!
> Love-thirty, love-forty, oh! weakness of joy,
> The speed of a swallow, the grace of a boy,
> With carefullest carelessness, gaily you won,
> I am weak from your loveliness, Joan Hunter-Dunn

No need to hurt you any more. You get the idea, I'm sure. But however awful this drivel might be as poetry, I want to consider it not from a literary but from a moral standpoint.

Did you watch Justin Poser's news report from the Durtapuran capital Corupcion the other night? I don't suppose anyone was especially surprised to learn what a hellish place it is. Name me one black African city which isn't pretty desperate. And there was the usual depressing tale of downtrodden women just about holding together a society being torn apart by violent or feckless men. (Justin Poser, predictably, chose to blame this on Islam, as if it would be any different if the Christians ran the country.) All pretty ghastly, but nothing you wouldn't expect. And then he grabbed my attention. What a place like Corupcion is doing hosting a women's tennis tournament, God only knows, but there it is – something to do with putting the place on the map, if Poser is to be believed. (As it happens, Corupcion is already on the map. Check an atlas if you don't trust me.)

Now the whole thing has gone predictably pear-shaped, because in a city which is sixty per cent Muslim, women's tennis is bound to be controversial. So, in this desperately poor place, we had the interesting sight of a hugely expensive indoor arena guarded by armed police and soldiers against furious demonstrators ready to put their lives on the line in order to stop a sports event. Bizarre or what?

Bizarre enough even to impress Justin Poser, but what really made an impact on the great reporter was the early exit from the tournament of Letzgetcha Nickersoff. For the benefit of those lucky enough not to have heard what he said, I quote – look away now, if you're the squeamish type – 'Without the gorgeous Letzgetcha Nickersoff, the women's singles has lost much of its savour, even for those who have nothing against women's tennis. As one smitten young spectator told me: "Without her breasts, her legs, her smile, what is women's tennis?" I could see his point.'

Now if that doesn't make you want to throw up, then you've got a stronger stomach than I have. Tell me something. Why is it that women can watch men's tennis without hot flushes, yet men are reduced to an erotic frenzy by any reasonably attractive woman player? My postbag is always full of letters from those of you who think that I take things far too seriously, but they never convince me. Why, for a start, are they always written by men? As long as men in general watch men's tennis for the tennis, but women's tennis for erotic thrills, there is something deeply wrong with our society. Believe me.

But we've all got so used to this kind of thing that you may wonder why I should even bother drawing attention to it, yawn yawn. Well, I'll tell you why. Justin Poser's report was followed by an item on Bogsworth Community School, which is under fire from Youssuf Al-Majnooni. The Islamic firebrand is up in arms over – well, over just about everything, to be honest – but especially over girls' sports. There is a strong Islamic presence in the area, many pupils are Muslim, and Youssuf says that scantily-clad girls should not be seen in public. Well, for the very first time, I think I might be in agreement with him.

You see – and I mean this as a guilty admission – hearing about local opposition to women's sport in an African country is one thing, but hearing about such opposition here in England is quite another. It makes an altogether greater impact. It shouldn't, but it does.

I've been highly critical of Youssuf Al-Majnooni in the past, and have always been suspicious of a religion which, whatever the theory might be, frequently represses women. But I'm beginning to think that Islam might not be altogether wrong when it comes to relations between the sexes. Islamic societies keep men and women apart as much as possible, and they see that women cover themselves up. If I understand anything at all about men, it is that they will always be excited by the sight of women's bodies. They will always be excited by women tennis players. It's time that women began to wear loose-fitting shorts on the tennis court, and denied these perverts the thrills they seek.

But the news is bad. I have just heard that Letzgetcha Nickersoff has got herself a new agent. If you've never heard of Dan Grabbitall, you should have. Remember Robert Maxwell? Rupert Murdoch? Mohammed Fayed?

Well, Dan Grabbitall, still in his mid-thirties, is cast in the same mould. Having begun his entrepreneurial career in Australia and the US, he has now taken over London publisher Over & Dunwith, and his latest wheeze is a London-based PR business, christened Rich & Famous. Now why open a PR business when what you want is clearly a media empire? Well, Dan Grabbitall has worked out that access to celebrities is vital in today's fame-obsessed culture, and control of celebrities makes you invincible. So, despite his almost total ignorance of sport of any kind, he talked Ms Nickersoff into leaving IMG, *the* sports agency, and joining him. Now here's what's going to happen. I guarantee it. Grabbitall means to market Ms Nickersoff as a sex symbol, and her tennis will go downhill as her earnings from outside interests escalate. Will it make her happy? I doubt it. Rich, yes. Happy, no. But it will make Dan Grabbitall rich *and* happy, and that, from Mr Grabbitall's point of view, is all that matters.

And what ammunition do we have to use against him? Unless I'm greatly mistaken, virtually none. When moral principle goes out the window, and all we believe in is money, those who are best at making it will always triumph. But if Youssuf Al-Majnooni had his way, some of the worst excesses of rancid capitalism might at least be curbed. Women would be shielded from the eyes of dirty old men like Betjeman and Poser, and our whole society would be the better for it, I promise you.

For once, then, let's have two cheers for Youssuf Al-Majnooni and his beliefs. It's very easy to convert to Islam, you know. All you have to do is to recite the Muslim creed – which is very brief and to the point – in front of two reliable witnesses, and you're in. I could do it. I could very easily do it. Am I serious? Well, perhaps not entirely. But you see, I'm wondering where a society might end up when it replaces God with Mammon, and Mammon will tolerate no curbs whatever on the pursuit of profit.

If you don't think this is serious, then you've never heard of *Predator*, and that would be amazing. Yes, so out of control is Mammon now that, in order that rich people should become even richer, he would even have us watch human beings kill each other. And incidentally, if it really is Islamic militants who have kidnapped Rab McGeddon, that's another plus to them: McGeddon's arms company, BOMZIZUS, is sponsoring *Predator*.

But I was looking at the problem from a feminist perspective, to which I now return for a final word of warning. From the old perv Betjeman. In *Senex*, he writes of an old man who wishes he wasn't still sex-obsessed – not because he reckons it's not very nice, you understand, but just because it gives him grief. Perhaps, if you've got this far, you might manage a single verse:

> Get down from me! I thunder there,
> You spaniels! Shut your jaws!
> Your teeth are stuffed with underwear,
> Suspenders torn asunder there
> And buttocks in your paws!

Well, if you want to be made sick in the near future, just tune in to the next women's tennis tournament, and listen to the dirty old men drooling over Letzgetcha Nickersoff. Thank God Betjeman is no longer with us. And how unfortunate that Dan Grabbitall and Justin Poser still are. (If it's true that SEXITEL is trying to lure Poser away from the BBC, then the Beeb would be well advised to let him go to his natural home.) The sooner that Justin Poser and Dan Grabbitall go to join Betjeman in the only place where men pose no threat to women, the better.

Five

The Bogsworth bell rang with its accustomed harsh insistence. Boris Fartleby groaned, put down his cup of coffee still half full, and hauled himself to his feet.

The corridors were chaos between lessons. Boris had been one of those who had favoured allocating classrooms to classes instead of to teachers, but the arguments against had prevailed: teachers liked to personalise their rooms in keeping with their subject, and it was thought dangerous to allow pupils to think of a classroom as their territory rather than the teacher's.

Boris pushed his way along to his domain, which was at least on the ground floor so that he did not have to fight his way to a higher level in the midst of rioting pupils, who had been known – successfully on two occasions – to try to push teachers down the stairs. (In recognition of its similarity to the army practice of shooting an unpopular officer in the back, this was known in the school as fragging.)

Still, it was a long and wearisome trek to the opposite corner of the building, where Boris's class – fifteen-year-olds richly imbued with what he had learned to call attitude – were waiting outside his room. Like most of his colleagues, he kept it locked when he was not there, having found that instructions to remain outside till he arrived were otherwise ignored. Boris sighed as he pushed his way to the door, then turned to face his scuffling and squabbling pupils, hands on hips.

'When you are quiet and standing still, I'll open the door, and you can all come in and sit down.'

He had to wait several seconds for his words to take effect – which, even when it came, was in truth little more than a slight diminution in near-riotous behaviour, but Boris had long since

31

given up attempting to insist on complete peace and quiet. He nodded as if satisfied, unlocked the door, and preceded the class into the room.

'Here, somebody's taken my fucking pencil! That was you, that was! Give it back!'

'Fuck off, cunt, who'd want your fucking pencil? You'd get fucking AIDS or something off it.'

'Well, some fucker's taken it.'

'Hey, piss off to your own seat! That's mine!'

'It fucking isn't!'

'Oh yes, it fucking is! You . . .'

Boris opened his briefcase and took from it a book which he slammed down on his desk. The loud bang silenced the pupils momentarily. 'You can sit anywhere. All that matters is that everybody finds a seat, and sits there quietly. You will also moderate your language.'

'What's that mean?'

'It means stop swearing.' Boris began to write 'moderate' on the board.

'Fuck! A period with Boring Old Fart's all I fucking need!'

'You're fucking lucky. You don't know you're born. Last year we had a double period with him, last thing Fridays.'

'Fuck!'

Having finished writing on the board, Boris turned round and clapped his hands loudly three times. 'I'll take the register. Answer to your names.'

About average. Five pupils had not turned up at all that day, while two were now absent who had been present earlier, and three were now present who had been absent earlier. Truancy had been out of control for years, and no one had much cared unless the truants were engaged in criminal activity. Now it was different: now no one cared even if they were engaged in criminal activity. Bogsworth was a poor area, and car theft, burglary and shoplifting were part of life. You just had to put up with them.

'Hey, Fart!'

'If you want to talk to me, you can call me Sir or Mr Fartleby.'

'Sorry, Sir Fart. Listen, why do we keep getting supply teachers. I mean, seriously, we've had four different French teachers in three weeks. Seriously.'

Boris sighed. 'You all know the situation. There's long been a shortage of teachers over the whole country, and this school is no exception. Then we have staff members off sick from time to time. We have no option but to fill the gaps with supply teachers. It's regrettable, but there's nothing we can do about it.'

'That's because teaching stinks. That's what my dad says. I mean, who'd want to teach a bunch of cunts like us? I . . .'

'Speak for yourself, cunt! Mind who you're calling a fucking cunt!'

Boris banged his fist on his desk. 'Language, please!'

'Well, but, I mean, I bet you wouldn't do it if you had your time again, would you? I mean, my dad says that anybody who's got anything to him just wouldn't be a teacher. He says . . .'

'Oh yeah? And what does he do then that's so wonderful, your dad?'

'He's a bus driver, and . . . no, seriously, it's an okay job. Because you don't have people like us to put up with . . . No, I'm trying to be serious.'

'My uncle says that some guy once said that them that can do, and them that can't teach.'

'What the fuck's that supposed to mean? Them that can't teach. That's every fucking teacher in this shit-hole of a school, them that can't teach. Them that can't teach what? I mean what do they do, them that can't teach?'

'You're fucking thick, you are. Listen again. I said . . .'

'Fuck off! I heard you the first time. You . . .'

'Quiet! Enough! . . . It was George Bernard Shaw, and what he said was, "He who can, does. He who cannot, teaches." What he meant was that somebody who's good at, say, physics, becomes a physicist, but someone who's poor at it becomes a physics teacher.'

'Hey, that's all right, that is. True an' all.'

'That's like what Clive Sneersly said last night on *Spotlight*. He said . . .'

'Yeah, fuck, he was talking about *Predator*. Fucking fantastic. I just can't fucking wait. All these guys trying to kill each other. Fuck!'

'You're just fucking stupid. My dad says it's all a big con. He says it's like the Americans going to the moon. They never did.

He says they'll just get a lot of actors to pretend they're killing each other, and all the silly cunts like you will think it's real.'

'Watch who you're calling a silly cunt! I . . .'

'No, I was talking about the bit that came next. Clive Sneersly was going on about how we've got such fucking useless schools, and . . .'

'Clive Sneersly wasn't going on about it. He was just asking the questions. He's not the one that says what he thinks. He's the presenter, and . . .'

'All right, whatever. But he was talking to that cow . . . what's her name?'

'Cassandra McRaker.'

'Yeah, that's her. And I tell you, I'd give her one if . . .'

'You? You?? She wouldn't even fucking notice you! You haven't even got a proper dick. You . . .'

Boris Fartleby banged his desk again. 'Once more, mind your language. All right, so what did they say?'

'Well, Clive Sneersly said there had been a crisis in Britain's schools as long as he could remember, and Cassandra McRaker said it's not surprising, because teachers are so fu . . . so useless. She said they don't get paid enough. She said that if you pay peanuts, you get monkeys. That's like what that guy said, the one you just mentioned, isn't it?'

'Shaw. George Bernard Shaw. Well, I suppose it's the same sort of thing.'

'Well, I mean did you see it? I nearly fell out of my armchair when she said that this is one of the worst schools in the fucking country. I mean, I wasn't surprised to hear it, but . . .'

'Then why the did you fall out of your chair, you daft cunt?'

'Fuck off, you! I mean, I was surprised that she knew about us. I was.'

Boris shrugged. 'Well, there you are. At least we're famous for something.'

'I mean, it's good that people know about the broken windows and all that. Then there was the bit about that weird guy Youssuf Al-Majnooni. He . . .'

'I once saw that guy from the Salvation Army, just walking down the street. What's his name again?'

'General Pius Oldgit.'

'Yeah, well I reckon he's just scared of the Muslims, because . . .'

'My mum says it's Youssuf Al-Majnooni that's kidnapped that guy McGeddow, or whatever his name is. She says he's dead clever. He kidnaps these rich bastards, and he lets them go when he gets a big ransom. And then he uses the money to buy bombs and things. She says that he's making his enemies pay for his war against them.'

'Why doesn't Youssuf Al-Majnooni like us? I mean, the school.'

Boris grimaced. 'Youssuf Al-Majnooni objects to many things in our educational system, especially religious studies and girls playing sport in public. He thinks girls and women should be covered up at all times when men might see them.'

'That's fucking mad.'

'Oh no, it fucking isn't. You only say that because you don't know the truth. The truth is in the Holy Koran! The Holy Koran tells us that women should always be covered up!'

'That's balls!'

'No it fucking isn't! The Prophet Mohammed, peace be upon him, told us that . . .'

Boris banged his fist again. 'Be quiet everybody! And sit down.' He glared round until something resembling order prevailed. 'You've brought up the subject of Youssuf Al-Majnooni and Islam. Well, in that case, I might be able to interest you for once, because today we're going to talk about Christianity and Islam. This is because we're going to study the Crusades, and the Crusades, as you may already know, were a long-running war between Christianity and Islam. Now . . .'

'They're still going on. Christianity is still making war on Islam today. We . . .'

'That's balls! What it is, is that there's all these terrorists, coming over here and living off the state and bombing everybody. They . . .'

This time, Boris used both fists. 'Quiet! What we are going to do today is to talk about the differences between Christianity and Islam, so that we understand what lay behind the Crusades, and what lies behind some of the tensions in the world today.'

'Will Struglor says we're not to talk about religion because it gets too hot when we do.'

Boris gritted his teeth. 'I've discussed this with Mr Struglor, and he is in agreement with me. These things can't always be swept under the carpet. If we're going to talk about the Crusades – and we have to, because it's part of the syllabus – then we have to talk about Christianity and Islam. We . . .'

'My dad says I'm not to talk about Islam to teachers, because you can't discuss it. It's true and that's all there is to it. He . . .'

'My dad says it's just a load of crap. I'm an atheist.'

'You'll go to hell, you will. That's where atheists go. I was . . .'

'Quiet, everybody! Now just listen for once. I am not going to try to convert anybody to or from any religion. We are simply going to talk about factual differences between Christianity and Islam, so that we understand what was going on during the Crusades. Which ended many hundreds of years ago. We . . .'

'What do you mean, ended hundreds of years ago? It's still going on. America invades Afghanistan and Iraq and everywhere, and you say the Crusades aren't still going on. How . . .'

'ALLAHU AKBAR!' The cry, loud and insistent, came from outside. It was echoed excitedly by several of the pupils. Boris looked puzzled.

'That was Youssuf Al-Majnooni! He's taking the battle to the enemy, just like he said he would.'

Everyone looked out to the playground. Scores of people, all adult males, were streaming in through the gate, pushing aside a bewildered janitor who had evidently attempted to bar their way. Some were dressed in robes, most were bearded, many were carrying placards. Some of these were in Arabic, but others were readily comprehensible to Boris and all of his pupils: 'PROTECT OUR WOMEN', 'GOD IS GREAT', 'DEATH TO THE ENEMIES OF GOD', 'NO SPORT FOR GIRLS'. There was a cacophony of yells of Allahu Akbar.

The classroom was out of control. Everyone was crowding to the windows to see what was going on. The janitor was trying again to intervene, but without success. In the end, he gave up and retreated, at the maximum speed consistent with the maintenance of minimum dignity, into the relative safety of the school building. Then a figure was produced, resembling a guy. The white moustache made clear that this was intended to represent headmaster Will Struglor. The effigy was hung from the netting which separated the playground from the pavement, doused in petrol, and burnt. There were loud cheers from a crowd which now numbered at least a hundred.

Youssuf Al-Majnooni, a large man with a limp, his portliness somewhat concealed under a long white robe, produced a loudhailer. 'Take a good look, Will Struglor,' he said through his luxuriant black beard, 'and be relieved that this time, we're only burning you in effigy. It will be different next time, I promise you. We are . . .' He was interrupted by loud cheering. 'We are not playing games, even if you are. Teaching that Islam is no different from any other religion is wrong. And allowing girls to expose their bodies before men is an affront to God, and must stop now!' More cheering. 'Islam is the one true religion, and infidel teachers will not discuss religion with our children!' The remains of the blazing effigy fell from the netting, and lay smouldering on the ground. The cheering was still louder.

Boris clapped his hands. 'All right, now would you all go back to your seats. We have work to do.'

Hardly anybody even bothered to turn and look at him. Boris gave up. He had lost them, and there was no way of getting them back as long as the demonstration continued. It wasn't as if anyone else could have done any better. It was just the way things were.

Six

'Come in! Ah yes, Clement Dormatt, I believe. Last and least of my senior staff. That's why I'm meeting you last, in case you were wondering. Been here fifteen years, I see, senior fiction editor for four. Jesus, Clem, I'd have put my head in the gas oven before now.' Dan Grabbitall shook his head and stared at Dormatt as a responsible adult might at a dirty and disgusting small child.

Dormatt, who was carrying a large and bulging jiffy bag under his left arm, looked anxiously at the chair in which Dan Grabbitall had not invited him to sit. Was it an oversight, or was Grabbitall making a point? Should he sit down anyway, just to make his own point? Would Grabbitall respect him for it, or would he sack him? Or would he just not notice?

'Now you already have some idea of what it's going to be like here from now on, but it's my policy always to see senior staff individually. That's the way you make sure of people. Tell them once publicly, once privately, and you've got them. That's how it works. You understand that from here on in, it's the bottom line that matters, and no crap about literary values, yes?'

Dormatt gulped. 'Yes,' he said.

Grabbitall opened a drawer in his desk, took from it a piece of paper, and held it up. 'This,' he said, 'is a list of *Predator* competitors. Finalised yesterday, distributed to a very few people today. It's supposed to be top secret, but I've managed to intercept the copy that was on its way to Rab McGeddon.'

Dormatt looked perplexed, and adjusted the position of the jiffy bag under his arm. 'But he's been kidnapped.'

Grabbitall shrugged. 'Then he won't be missing his copy, will he? And if he ever gets set free, I'll see that this one finds its way to his office and he never knows anyone else has seen it. Well worth the trouble I took to get it, because I mean to sign up the winner of *Predator*, and advance knowledge is always worth having. I was in the US Army once – special forces – and they taught me that time spent on reconnaissance is never wasted. Well, neither is money spent on reconnaissance, which is why I was prepared to shell out five grand on just a list of names. And yes, I'm trying to impress you.

'You see what I'm saying? The winner will be worth a fortune, and I'll do whatever it takes to get him. That's how I work, and as of now, it's how you work. Got it?'

Dormatt coughed. 'You mean you try to predict . . .'

Grabbitall's vertical palm commanded silence. 'I never predict, Clem. Not the future, anyway, because it can't be done. Answer me this. A hundred years ago, who could have predicted that today the poor would be fat and idle, and the rich would be thin and overworked? Nobody. Fucking nobody. What I do is to spot the future when it comes, because I see the straws in the wind. The trick is to see them before anyone else does.

'Being proactive is what it's all about. Being original. You know the worst thing about you Brits? Do you? You tell some Brit businessman that he'd double his profits – or halve his losses, more likely – if he made some change or other, and you know what he'll say? "But I've always done it this way and it's never worked. Why should I change now?" Jesus fucking Christ.

'Every original business idea that's worth anything has to come from the States. You know how American TV networks get newsreaders now? They've got plenty of people on their books already who could do the job, or they could poach somebody from another network, but they don't. Instead, they advertise nationwide and have a fucking great competition. That way, they get the poor saps they call viewers to pay for staff recruitment. Perfect. Trouble is that people get the idea that just about anybody can be a newsreader, and so the buggers who already do it lose a bit of their mystique. But that's just it: anybody, within reason, can do it. The notion that you've got to be some kind of fucking genius to read the news is so fucking stupid that you've got to be a newsreader to believe it.

'Forget about that. The point is that the idea is dead simple, and highly profitable. The viewing figures show it. But it took the

Americans to think of it, and still the Brits don't want to do it. It's time to join the real world, Clem, and if you won't do that, there's no hope for you.

'Now let's talk books. Whatever it is, we'll take it if we're rock solid certain it's going to make a serious profit. If not, we won't. Money is power, Clem, and power is what matters in this world. Show me somebody who says he's more interested in . . . I don't know . . . Beethoven's late sonata quartets than in power, and I'll show you a fucking liar. What he means is that he can't hack it in the real world, so he needs consolation. He knows he can't ever have power, so he listens to fucking Beethoven to try to soothe his wounded vanity.'

'Well er, I'm sure there are people who have power *and* love Beethoven.'

'So what the fuck? Every poor sod has a weakness somewhere. Except me. I have none, as you will definitely learn. Now here's what I want you to do for Friday. Like I said yesterday, I'll be in New York for the next month, but you can use e-mail. Give me the list of novelists we publish or have published, and exactly how profitable they are or have been. If you don't know, find out. And then give me a list – and I don't care if you're telling me things you think I already know – of big-money novelists we just might be able to poach from their present publisher. And then give me a list of big-name celebrities, with an idea of the sort of novel they might like to write. See what I'm getting at? Letzgetcha Nickersoff might write a novel about tennis, that kind of thing. It's all got to be feasible. Don't waste my time with ideas you know won't work. I want the three lists by five o'clock Friday. Okay?'

'Yes,' said Dormatt. The jiffy bag was becoming heavier and heavier.

'For the next four weeks, this place will have to keep going without me. Just carry on fucking things up the way you always have done, but keep in mind everything I've told you, and be ready to jump the moment I get back. Got that?'

'Yes.'

'Good. Now listen. Don't think I don't know what's going on in your mind, because I do. You think I'm a philistine and a bully, and you despise me for it. Don't say anything. That's how I want it to be. I exercise maximum control at all times, and maximum control

40

demands fear, not respect. Now I'm going to ask you a question, and you'd better give me an honest answer. Do you think you can work for me? Or will your aesthete's fucking brain explode if you have to take any more of this? What do you think? Can you hack it?'

'Well er . . .' Dormatt couldn't think what to say.

Dan Grabbitall began drumming the fingers of his left hand on his desk. 'I haven't got all day.'

'Well, I'm er . . . certainly prepared to give it a try.'

'Good. Now here's a nice surprise for you. I want to know if you have anything to say to me. Everybody tells me yes sir, no sir, three bags full sir, anything you say sir. Of course I don't respect you for it, but it's what I like to hear, so it keeps you in a job. We both get what we want out of your grovelling. But if I ever ask you what you think, you tell me. Because I don't ask if I don't want to know. It's like if I say "How are you?" It means I'm concerned about your health because it might affect my bank balance. I say "How are you?" and you tell me, because I must want to know. Well, I'm asking you now if there's anything you want to say to me. Anything on your mind. Because I want the decks cleared for action before I leave this shit-hole today, and they're not clear as long as any senior staff have things on their minds that shouldn't be there. Shoot.'

Dormatt gulped. There *was* something he wanted to say, and he knew that Grabbitall wouldn't want to hear it. But he had to say it. Everything he believed in, over all of which Dan Grabbitall was enthusiastically urinating, depended on his making a stand. Oh God. Sitting at home in front of the television, ignoring the rantings of his wife, it had seemed such an easy thing to do. It didn't any more.

Grabbitall was drumming again. 'I'm waiting.'

'Well, yes, there is something. Now I'm not sure you're going to like this, but I just ask you to hear me out. It's er . . .'

'Listen, Clem, this isn't the way I do things. Just tell me what's on your mind, using the smallest possible number of the shortest possible sentences containing the simplest possible words. Think you can do that?'

'Okay. I mean all right. Well, of course you're correct about the slush pile. I mean you said yesterday that we just ignore it. Even as things stand, we haven't published off it for years now. But on our slush pile I've just found the finest novel I've seen since I first came here.' Dormatt stepped forward, and placed the jiffy bag in front of Grabbitall, who surveyed it with manifest distaste. 'I haven't contacted the author yet – his name's Boris Fartleby – but he's written a novel which will sell, I promise. It really is something out of the ordinary. This one will sell – at least steadily – for . . .'

'Steadily? You said steadily?' Grabbitall had not touched the jiffy bag.

'Well, yes, it . . .'

'Steadily, hmm? Steadily. Listen Clem, I want novels that'll sell in fucking millions tomorrow. I don't give a fuck what they're going to do in ten years time. By then I'll probably have moved on. What the fuck is it to me what this little sideshow is doing when I've conned some no-hoper into buying it for a million times what it's fucking worth?'

Dormatt had to stand up for what he believed in. He just had to. 'You did say that if anybody missed something really good from the slush pile . . .'

'Stop there. What you mean by good isn't what I mean by good. Good to me means profitable. Got that?'

'Yes er . . . But I still feel . . .'

'Don't push me. Just don't push me . . .'

Fight, Dormatt told himself, fight. 'I . . . I don't mean to push you. I'm only saying that this man is good. He . . .'

'How old?'

'What?'

'How old? Come on, how fucking old is he, this man Fart?'

'Well, he's er . . . he's in his forties. He . . .'

'IN HIS FORTIES? *IN HIS FORTIES??* A COMPLETE UNKNOWN IN HIS FORTIES? WELL, GET THIS. PUBLICATION ISN'T *FOR* THE LIKES OF HIM! JESUS FUCKING CHRIST! I'D FUCKING *KILL* ALL WRITERS OVER FORTY IF I COULD! THEY JUST GET IN THE FUCKING WAY! HOW THE FUCK ARE YOU GOING TO MARKET SOME MIDDLE-AGED NOBODY? . . . Listen,' [Dan Grabbitall's voice suddenly dropped almost to a whisper, and Dormatt had to lean painfully forward to hear him] 'if she's in her teens, has tits

42

like Mount Everest, a face like Helen of Troy and a voice of liquid gold, then I *might*, just *might*, be interested. Otherwise no. NOW FUCK OFF OUT OF MY OFFICE, AND NEVER PULL A TRICK LIKE THIS ON ME AGAIN!!'

Seven

(From the *Sunday Screamer*)
Us & Them: Cassandra McRaker tells it like it really is!

New kid on the block: Dan Grabbitall

My guess is that half the population of this country know very little about Dan Grabbitall, and the other half have never even heard of him. A straw poll among friends and neighbours tells me that, in so far as he is known at all, it is as just another big entrepreneur. Well, believe me, there's a lot more to him than that, and *Screamer* readers should know that this man is set to make or break more famous names than anyone ever. From now on, if you want to know who's hot and who's not, you'd better pay attention to Dan Grabbitall.

Hitherto, he has been well known only on the other side of the Atlantic, but his purchase of London publisher Over & Dunwith – the name will survive, but only as an imprint of Sledgehammer – is going to change all that. Still more significant is the fact that he has now set up a PR firm, Rich & Famous, a move which indicates that he has grasped the importance of celebrity in amassing power and money in today's world.

I have to admit to an interest here. I have never met Dan Grabbitall, but I have followed his career, and have even written about him. It was only last year that I returned to this country after three years in New York, during which time I drew attention to him as one of those publishers who pursue profit to the absolute exclusion of all other considerations. In response, he has said publicly that I am 'just a bitter brainless bitch consumed by envy of those more successful than herself.' Charming.

A quick glance at his career to date might be of interest. His early years are, as they say, shrouded in mystery. What is certain is that, born of an American father and an English mother, he was brought up partly in the US and partly in this country. It is equally certain, although he has been known to deny it, that his father served at least one prison sentence in America, for embezzlement. He has given different stories about his education, and it would take a more dedicated digger and delver than me to look into these claims and try to sort them out. He has asserted more than once that he attended Rugby School, but this is certainly false. More likely, he went to some other school in Rugby, but even that is uncertain.

After completing his formal education in America, he went into the US Army. He served less than a year, during which time he acquired a reputation as a misfit – determined, regardless of rank, always to give orders and never to take them. His early departure, which the Army refuses to discuss, was apparently greeted with relief all round.

He then undertook a course in hotel management, and obtained a post in a hotel in Rhode Island. This time he survived rather more than a year, but seems to have been little missed after his departure. The impression given by those who knew him at the time is that he made it very clear that he considered himself too large a fish for so small a pool.

Anyway, Mr Grabbitall's failure to make much of his life in the States may explain his decision to emigrate to Australia, where he began to take a serious interest in the acquisition of power and money. It isn't easy to determine in detail what he did, because the man is adept at covering his tracks, but – again, in spite of denials – he most certainly worked at one time with a businessman so shady that even his real name is elusive. When Grabbitall was his partner, he was calling himself Ernest Deeler, and was selling cruise holidays. The firm went into receivership after running up enormous debts, and I have been unable to discover what happened to Mr Deeler.

Dan Grabbitall, however, was on the wrong end of an official investigation into the company's affairs, his passport being withheld until its completion. He was eventually found to have acted 'unwisely and perhaps naively', but was never convicted of any offence. There are those in Australia who say that he was very lucky to avoid a lengthy jail sentence.

There was in fact some talk of a possible civil action against him, but this came to nothing: very soon after the end of the investigation, he left the country. Whatever his business ethics, he had done well financially, and returned to the States a wealthy man.

This was five years ago, since when he has made quite a name for himself. His first move – onto the editorial staff of New York publisher Sledgehammer – may seem odd. Had he not already found his métier in business? For once, I think we can take Grabbitall's word for something: he had decided that publishing was for him, and wanted to see how it looked from the bottom before trying the view from the top.

Whatever his motivation, it was not long before he branched into marketing, and before three years were up he had a seat on the board, eventually acquiring a controlling interest in the firm. He has presided over the removal from Sledgehammer's list of many literary names, and the addition to it of many celebrity names. I have not been the only hack publicly to deplore his influence on the literary scene, but there is no disputing the result: Sledgehammer's profits have rocketed.

And Dan Grabbitall's stock has risen with them. He now owns two American newspapers and has very recently acquired a TV franchise. None of these is especially noteworthy, but this is a man who is quite happy to get his foot on any available rung of the ladder. This is a man who knows how to climb.

And now I must admit to an even closer personal interest. Bearing in mind that Dan Grabbitall knows exactly what I think of him, you can imagine my surprise when he telephoned me just a few days ago – the first time we have ever spoken. He had somehow discovered that I was working on an autobiography, and said that he would like to publish it. (This is good news: if Dan Grabbitall thinks it worth publishing, it should make a packet.) I told him that I already have a publisher, and expressed my surprise that he of all people should wish to publish anything of mine. To cut, as they say, a long story short, he reminded me of my vow never to write an autobiography, and said that if I do not let him have the book, he will let it be known what my word is worth.

Well, pardon me for not collapsing in terror, but, bearing in mind that people are going to find out about the thing anyway just as soon as it's published, his threat isn't worth much. I admit that I'd have preferred to keep it secret until just before publication, but it was always possible that news would leak out. Let me just say at this point, that I will explain in due course why I have changed my mind.

For the present, I simply want to alert everyone to the fact that Dan Grabbitall is now over here, for this is not a man to take lightly. Look how far he has come by the age of 34, and try to guess how far he may yet go. If you are old enough to remember Robert Maxwell, you may have some idea of what to expect.

I've already mentioned his new PR business. Dan Grabbitall knows that celebrity sells, and he's going to sell it for all it's worth, I can promise you. He sees that celebrities are now the biggest brand names of all, and I'm prepared to bet that, despite the obvious conflict of interest, he will frequently act as agent and publisher, giving himself almost total control over his clients' image.

What will tell most in his favour is that he himself is quite indifferent to fame. Dan Grabbitall values power and money, and is single-minded in their pursuit. Most PR people are star-struck, whatever they might publicly claim, and that gives their clients a significant advantage over them. Dan Grabbitall, you may be quite sure, will never show such weakness. What others think of him concerns him only in so far as it affects the success of his business.

He has hit the ground running, having Letzgetcha Nickersoff signed up for Rich & Famous even before he had officially opened the business. And she's only the first. There will be many, many more. So once again, I warn you: if you want to know what's what and who's who in today's fast-moving world, keep an eye on Dan Grabbitall. The sight you see will not be pretty, but I guarantee that it will be informative.

Eight

Boris Fartleby wished he was somewhere else. Boris Fartleby wished he was anywhere else. Bogsworth Community School had never been much fun and teaching had never been much fun, but both, it seemed, were about to become a great deal worse. Boris and his colleagues were getting a pep talk from the new head.

'Well, good morning, everybody, good morning. And a very warm welcome to . . . What am I talking about? It's me who's new, isn't it? Ha ha, yes, it certainly is, so perhaps it's you who should be welcoming me. Never mind, let me begin by introducing myself, just in case anybody is in any doubt as to who I am. Well, my name is Marshall Mallow, and I'm your new head – although, as you'll find out, that's not a term on which I'm very keen. In fact, it's not a term I intend to use at all, but more of that in due course.

'Well, instead of my welcoming you, let me simply say how delighted I am to be joining you at The School of the Torch of Learning. Ah, I notice some surprise on the part of my audience. But yes, you did hear correctly. As of now, Bogsworth Community School no longer exists: The School of the Torch of Learning – I would guess that people will come to call it the Torch School – has taken its place.

'And this seems to be a good place to begin. Why a new name? Well, I don't intend to dwell on unhappy matters, but you all know how things have been going of late, because you've experienced it at first hand. I'm not going to begin by quoting sensational media reports, but with something a lot more objective, namely the Ofsted report which you have just been given. Please don't think that this means that I like inspections, because I don't. It's just that the *Screamer* and the *Shocker* probably have even less of value to tell us than do Ofsted.

'As it happens, I dislike inspections intensely. Far too prescriptive, in my opinion. In nearly twenty years in teaching, I have seen that the chief characteristic of the teaching profession is dedication. Dedication to the kids, dedication to the school, dedication to education. And more than that, dedication to humanity. And I make no apology for sounding emotional.

'Inspectors, it seems to me, ignore all of this. They come into schools with their little check lists and they tick things off. They see that a window is cracked, that's a black mark. They don't know, of course, that a teacher placed his – or her – body between the window and that of a charging pupil in order to prevent the pupil from suffering serious injury. They see a class in which pupils seem to be listening to each other rather than to the teacher, and that's a black mark. They don't realise that the teacher is deliberately giving the pupils free rein to express themselves in that lesson. They see a teacher make a slight spelling mistake on the board, and that's a black mark. Never mind that the teacher is one of the finest servants the profession has ever seen, and that he – or she – cannot be blamed for suffering from dyslexia. They see . . . but I think I've made my point. I think the present inspections régime is a brutal infringement of the rights of teachers and pupils.

'So please don't think I'm one of those heads – oh dear, oh dear, that awful word again – who is not on the side of his staff. I stand shoulder to shoulder with you, and I always will. I stand shoulder to shoulder with you and with every pupil in The School of the Torch of Learning!

'However, we must work with reality as we find it, and not as we might like it to be. And even if we ignore the inspectors' report, even if we regard the whole concept of inspection as intrusive and negative, we have to admit that things are not as they should be. No doubt many of you saw the *Spotlight* discussion of our schools three weeks ago, when Cassandra McRaker singled this school out for criticism. Well you already have some idea of what I think of sensational media reporting, but we can't simply ignore everything she said. Run-down state of the building and fittings, breakdown of discipline, rising rates of truancy, truants responsible for rising crime rates in the area . . . Well, it was pretty damning.

'And it has been followed up by lurid press reports which I don't need to go into. These, of course, have frequently featured Youssuf

Al-Majnooni's campaign, but I'll come to that in due course. The sad fact is that it has all been too much for Will Struglor, from whose brave but failing grasp it falls to me to pluck the banner. I did go to see Will in hospital yesterday, since he is now finally permitted visitors, and I'm pleased to say that he may yet make a partial recovery from his suicide attempt. He has not yet spoken, and the drip feed is still in place, but the doctors say that, all going well, he may at some stage even be able to return home and live there with a package of help from social services. I know that we all wish him well.

'Now it is not for me to say that I am made of sterner stuff than Will, but let me just say that I think I can take the pressure. I said that I've had nearly twenty years in teaching, and the last four of those have been as deputy head. I know that it didn't prove easy to find a successor to Will Struglor at short notice, and in fact my application was, strictly speaking, received after the deadline. However, I was lucky – perhaps in part because two of the other three applicants had criminal records, while the other was over eighty years old. Not that anyone could ever accuse me of being ageist, far from it, but . . . Well, if the octogenarian applicant had been the most suitable, I would of course have been the first to congratulate him – I believe it was a him – on his success.

'But . . . well, no, perhaps I should also make clear that I do not believe we should discriminate against criminals either . . . I mean, people with criminal convictions. Who are we to judge? Was the man – or the woman – even guilty? Who is to say? And even if he or she was guilty, what are prisons for if not for rehabilitation? I am confident that the rejection of the two applicants with criminal records was based solely on an assessment of their suitability for the post, with no heed paid to a past which they have no doubt put safely behind them. I wish them both every success in future. Oh, and of course, the more mature applicant. I wish him every success too.

'Where was I? Ah yes, I was about to explain why the name of the school has changed, wasn't I? Well, as I said, the school has taken a bit of a battering from the inspectors and the media, and so perhaps a new image is a good idea anyway. But when I met the governors on Friday, we had a long discussion about our philosophy of education, and the one thing on which we could all

51

agree was that a school is, first and foremost, about learning. Now the problem that many schools have is that they emphasise teaching. Sounds all right, doesn't it? But what is teaching? If you remember nothing else of what I am saying, please at least remember this: teaching which does not result in learning is bad teaching.

'So when the inspectors come into a school, what they see and assess is teaching. Because clearly they can't stay long enough to see what the learning is at the end of the day. But if the pupils have learned, then the teaching has been good, however it might have appeared to an inspector with his little check list. So the governors and I decided that this should, above all, be a school where learning takes place. Because if that happens, then we know the teaching has been good. And we also wanted to be an example to others. We wanted to light a path that others might follow . . . Not that I am suggesting that other schools are not doing a very good job, far from it. But I'm sure you see what I'm getting at, and I'm sure you wouldn't disagree with me.

'That, then, is why we are now The School of the Torch of Learning. Better get used to it, folks! But I also mentioned my title. I have no wish to be headmaster, or head anything. Who am I that I should be the head? Who am I that I should be anybody's master? Am I better than you? No, I want nothing to do with élitist titles. They are divisive, and I want them to go. We will be a community of equals, pupils as well as teachers. That is the way ahead.

'As it happens, it is also a most appropriate philosophy for a school with a large Muslim intake. Almost all of the Muslim families around here are Sunni, and Sunni Islam is one of the most democratic religions there has ever been. Sunni Muslims do genuinely believe that all men are created equal. And women, of course. Now what this means . . . And of course, all children. Goes without saying. Now I might not . . . and Shia Islam, I should say, is also a wonderful religion, with rich traditions and a moral code which might be the envy of the world.

'But I was about to say that, while I might not agree with everything said by Youssuf Al-Majnooni just down the road, when he says that no Muslim child should ever be part of a Christian hierarchy, I am with him. My position is pretty well that of General Pius Oldgit of the Salvation Army, whom you might have seen on

Spotlight with Cassandra McRaker. Indeed, the only point on which I might take issue with him is that of his own commitment to the Christian religion. It goes without saying that I have the very highest regard for Christianity, but no higher than my regard for other great religions. And small religions too, of course. Our school will be multi-ethnic, multi-faith, and as far as possible a community of equals.

'With this in mind, my new title – since unfortunately, it seems that I have to have one of some kind – will be Staff–Parent Interface Coordinator, or SPIC for short. Now the title doesn't even begin to express all the different tasks I mean to perform, but I had to find something short and snappy, and so I simply went for one of the most important functions and settled for that.

'As for what you – and the pupils – will call me, well, I want no formality. Did you know that there are schools in this country where the head is addressed by all as *Sir*? Did you? Oh, dear me, dear me! Well, I don't expect you to call me SPIC, you'll be relieved to hear! No, and I don't expect you to call me Mister Mallow, either. I will call you by your first names, and you will do the same with me. But not even Marshall, if you don't mind. I'm Marsh to my friends, and that means I'm Marsh to you. And, of course, to the pupils.

'We must also . . . Ah, but if you look outside, you'll see something interesting. Those of you on this side of the room anyway, will see that the school sign is coming down . . . Yes, well, no need to get up. Just take my word for it. Or if you're not ready to trust me yet, take the word of people on this side of the room that you feel can trust. Yes, the sign is coming down, because clearly a new one is needed. It will tell everyone the school's new name, my name and title, and the school motto. Yes, that's right, I said school motto.

'Now this was something else that the governors and I worked on quite hard. Took quite a bit of thrashing out, I can tell you. You know the sort of thing, don't you? "Working hard to get it right", "Trying hard to serve you right", that sort of thing. Gone are the days when schools had mottoes in Latin, which nobody ever understood. Remember them? Oh dear, oh dear! I remember that my primary school had the motto "Per Ardua Ad Astra". Through hardships to the stars. Dear oh dear! Sounds a bit like Captain Kirk

53

and the Starship Enterprise, doesn't it? Well, those days are gone, and good riddance, say I!

'As with the school's new name, as with my new title, we were very anxious to hit on something that really expresses just what it is that we are all about. Well, I won't go into detail about the very intense discussion that we had, but what we came up with was "Working hard to bring out the best in everybody". You see, we were determined to have nothing that seemed to emphasise competition over cooperation, and nothing that might seem to imply that teachers and pupils are not exactly the same. So that's our new motto, and I hope we can all live up to it.

'Perhaps I should emphasise that I really am serious about this. Please don't think that our motto is just a pious platitude. Far from it. In a world in which competitiveness seems to be everything, I want us to be a little haven of cooperativeness. I don't want competitive sport in which any pupil who isn't a winner is made to feel a failure. I want . . . But that reminds me, back for a moment to Youssuf Al-Majnooni. There has been so much public interest in his campaign against religious education and girls' sports and so on that I think I have to address the issue.

'So where do I stand? Well, when it comes to religious education, my belief is that children should be taught about all the world's great religions, in order that they can choose which, if any, they wish to follow. I would reassure Youssuf and all Muslims that there will be no religious indoctrination. And I think I might safely say that no one could possibly object to such a policy.

'As for girls' sports, I've told you that I dislike all competition, but that doesn't mean that I am against sport entirely, only that I am against competitive sport. I believe in a healthy mind in a healthy body, and I will not allow pupils to be withdrawn from sport without good medical reason. Nonetheless, I intend to take Youssuf Al-Majnooni's concerns seriously, since he is quite right in saying that the Koran forbids women and girls to expose their bodies in public. I have no doubt that a compromise will be possible. If even Viraga Hateman – I don't know if any of you read what she wrote about Youssuf in the *Shocker* recently – if even Viraga Hateman thinks he may have a point, then he must be taken seriously.

'In the article I'm talking about, Ms Hateman draws attention to the way that men see women's tennis. And I think anyone might be made uneasy by the sort of attention that Letzgetcha Nickersoff draws wherever she goes. So I repeat, I will take the concerns of Youssuf Al-Majnooni seriously. I deplore the demonising of anybody, and I will make it clear to Youssuf that I am prepared at any time to meet with him to discuss the issue.

'Now where was I? Oh yes, I was talking about replacing competition with cooperation. It strikes me that in the news at the moment there is an excellent example of competition gone mad. You've all heard all about *Predator*, I'm sure. We will soon be able to watch on our TV screens a reality show in which the contestants are actually required to kill each other. Need I say more? At the Torch School, we will cooperate, not compete.

'Did you know, incidentally, that Rab McGeddon's company BOMZIZUS is sponsoring *Predator*? Well, I don't say I'm sorry that he's been released, but I have to say that if any pupil of this school were to become an arms manufacturer, I would feel we had failed. What I want to produce is well-rounded human beings who have a genuine respect for others, and who deplore the sort of mindless violence which BOMZIZUS represents – anybody can have horrific weapons who can pay for them. In other words, I do not measure success in terms of power and money. I hope that this is something on which we can all agree.

'Now . . . Oh, and by the way, if it's true that his kidnappers were Islamic militants, can I point out that these monsters have released him totally unharmed?

'What else was there? Let me see, now . . . Ah yes, school uniforms. I know that the present uniform isn't compulsory, but even so, I see that a lot of the pupils wear it. Well, they are of course entirely welcome to continue doing so, but it ceases as of now to have any official status whatever. I want our pupils to be able to express themselves through what they wear just as you and I are free to express ourselves through what we wear.

'In general, I want no rules which apply to pupils but not to teachers. Why should we expect the pupils to keep rules which we are not ourselves prepared to keep? This is not something which the governors and I had time to look at in detail, and so I would welcome suggestions from all of you – and indeed from all pupils – as to which rules should go, which should stay, and even which new ones we might like to consider. But not too many in the last category, please, because I prefer to do with the bare minimum of formal regulations.

'What was next? . . . Oh yes, morning assembly. I've always had mixed feelings about morning assembly. I've seen assemblies – as I'm sure have all of you – which have been ultra-formal, boring, and of almost no practical use. And so I had considered doing away with them altogether. But the fact is that there are always things to say to the entire school, and morning assembly is simply a very convenient time to do it.

'But it is going to be a much more democratic affair than anything you've known before. In the first place, it will not always be me who takes it. There is no member of the school who will not be given the chance to take assembly. This goes for all of you. It goes for the janitor – Bert, isn't it? – and for every pupil, down to the very smallest in the school. Shocked? Are you? Well, I can only tell you that you'd be surprised at just how much even a 12-year-old can be capable of if you just give her – or even him – the chance.

'Yes, well, I think that's all I had to say – and I dare say you've had just about enough anyway! – so . . . Oh no, there was just one more thing. I . . .'

At the back of the room, Boris Fartleby closed his eyes, shook his head, and suppressed a yawn.

Nine

'. . . and you're listening to *Cometh the Hour* with Cyril Smarm. My guest in the studio today is a man you had probably never heard of a month back. And then he was kidnapped by – well, by whom? We still don't know. But certainly he was kidnapped, and was released on payment of a substantial ransom just a couple of days ago. Meanwhile, his weapons company, BOMZIZUS, has become notorious as sponsor of forthcoming TV reality show *Predator*. And I don't think I need to go into any details on that one, do I?

'But even if Rab McGeddon wasn't exactly a household name a month ago, he was still a very substantial figure, a man who has rated a mention in several lists of Britain's most successful businessmen. And he has come up the hard way. Born into a poor family in Glasgow's Govan district, he left school at 16, and, after what he describes as three fallow years, went into the armed forces. As a member of the Parachute Regiment, he saw service in Northern Ireland and the Falklands before retiring with the rank of major, and going into business.

'As he himself admits, whatever his success today, it hasn't all been plain sailing. There were a number of business failures, and near-bankruptcy on two occasions, before he founded his arms manufacturing company BOMZIZUS. That was eight years ago, since when the man and his business have gone from strength to strength. To quote an admiring profile in *The Economist*: "Rab McGeddon's success rests on a foundation of solid rock – the rock of a personality inured to hardship and capable of shrugging off massive disappointment and even disaster as if they were minor setbacks." Rab McGeddon, welcome to the programme.'

'Thank you Clive, I can honestly say I'm very glad to be here.'

'Yes, it's er . . . Cyril . . . actually.'

'Oh. Sorry.'

'Never mind, just thought we'd clear that up. Now first of all let me say that it genuinely is a privilege and a pleasure to have you in the studio. A privilege because of your extraordinary achievements, a pleasure because you might still have been enduring a miserable captivity.'

'Thank you.'

'Before we talk about your recent and terrifying experience, a word about *Predator*. What is the point of an arms company sponsoring a TV programme? This must be a first.'

'Aye, a first, but probably not a last. You see, there are so many very rich individuals in the world now that even some private citizens are buying submarines, warplanes and so on. Almost as toys, you might say. Then you get one or two multinationals developing their own weapons divisions. Their representatives, as well as representatives of governments round the world, will be watching *Predator*, you can be sure of that. We're pretty sure that our sponsorship will bring rewards, otherwise we wouldn't be doing it.'

'All right, we'll see if any callers want to follow up on that one later. But let's move on to recent dramatic events. It's just over three weeks now since you were kidnapped. You're said to be one of the richest men in the land, and that, presumably, is why you were thought worth holding to ransom. Describe for us the conditions in which you were held.'

'Aye, well, first of all, Cyril, let me correct you on one small point. I don't think I was kidnapped because of my personal wealth, because no demand was ever made of my family. The demand went to my company who, I deeply regret to say, coughed up the money. Speaking as a dour Scot, I feel very strongly that when ransoms are . . .'

'Now just let me stop you there, Rab, if I may. Shortly before we open the lines for listeners to talk to you directly, we'll come back to your opinion – entirely admirable, I might say – on the payment of ransoms. For the time being, let's return to the conditions of your captivity. What was it like?'

'In a word, hell. I was kept chained to a radiator in a room that was cold, bare and dirty. Not what I'm used to. But I survived. I come from the mean streets of Glasgow, and on those streets when I was young, you grew up fast or you never grew up. I learned to look after myself, I learned to be tough physically and tough mentally. If I hadn't learned in a hard school, I could have found my weeks in captivity hard to take.'

'Did you have any contact with the outside world? Did you know, for example, that General Pius Oldgit of the Salvation Army had offered to take your place in captivity?'

'I had no access of any kind to information except what my captors told me. They certainly never mentioned Pius Oldgit's offer. It was a wonderful gesture from a wonderful man, but I have to say that I would have refused to allow him to suffer in my place. I don't know if a man of nearly seventy could easily have survived what I went through.'

'But I mean, look at you, Rab. Well, of course, this isn't the sort of thing that comes across on radio, but you look to me to be in pretty good condition. The sort of man, if you'll forgive me for saying it, that women might describe as a hunk. You must at least have been given enough to eat.'

'Hmh! I suppose you could say that. But I wouldn't have fed a pig on the sort of food that I was given. Many's the time I dreamt of a good plate of haggis. But again, I come back to having learned in a hard school. I knew I was in trouble the moment I was kidnapped, and my first thought was that, whatever happened, I would eat everything I was given, just as I had to when I grew up in a Govan tenement. If you left food on your plate in Govan when I was young, you went hungry.'

'Exactly the sort of tough and practical attitude one might expect of you. But even if you managed to keep your strength up, there was very little you could do with that strength, was there? I mean, chained to a radiator all the time.'

'True. But I was ready if the chance had presented itself. My kidnappers were always careful to see that I was never one on one with any of them. Much of the time I was just left alone, and if anybody was with me – to feed me, for example – there were always two. But if I'd had just half a chance, I'd have taken them on. I would.'

'And perhaps I should just say, for the benefit of our listeners, that Rab McGeddon is a big man. I've never thought myself a wimp, but I wouldn't readily pick a fight with him, even if he *was* chained to a radiator. But you were saying, Rab, that you are very disappointed that a ransom was paid for you at all. Secretly, weren't you relieved?'

'Absolutely not. In fact, I seriously considered sacking the man responsible for the decision to pay up. Do you know that poem by Rudyard Kipling, called *Danegeld*? It's about the protection money that Saxon kingdoms used to pay to the Danes. Kipling says that "If once you have paid him the Danegeld, You never get rid of the Dane." Well, there have been several kidnappings of businessmen recently, and Danegeld has been paid every time. It has to stop.'

'Do you really mean that? I mean, could you honestly have taken longer of that awful captivity? Would you have been prepared to die just for that principle? Because who's to say it wouldn't have come to that?'

'My captors told me several times that it would. They said they'd cut my throat if the ransom wasn't paid. And I believed them. But when it comes to a point of principle, I yield no more than did my great countryman William Wallace when fighting for Scotland's freedom. That ransom should never have been paid.'

'Well, I take my hat off to you, I really do. You've drawn attention to the fact that your kidnapping was only one amongst several recent abductions of wealthy businessmen. As you know, there are strong suspicions that this is the work of Islamic fundamentalists, who are deliberately asking for relatively modest ransom sums that they are pretty sure will in fact be paid, in order to fund terrorist activity. Did your experience give you any idea of whether or not this might be the case?'

'My kidnappers were always masked, and very seldom spoke. Certainly, they never said anything that might have given me a clue as to their identity or motivation. For what it's worth, a couple of them might have had Arab accents, but I wouldn't even be sure of that.'

'There's another theory, which says that you were kidnapped by a Western urban guerrilla group who simply wanted to hurt a major arms manufacturer, or perhaps to hurt *Predator* through its sponsor.'

'Who's to say? I can only say that nothing has been said that might give credence to that idea. Surely you would have expected some propaganda statement from such a group. In the absence of any propaganda statement, I suppose you have to say it could just have been common criminals.'

'All right, let me hand over to our listeners now. In the studio with me I have BOMZIZUS chief Rab McGeddon, talking about his recent kidnap and still more recent release. You're free to talk to him about that, about his business, or perhaps about his sponsorship of *Predator*. The lines are busy, but you might still get through if you're quick. Our first caller is Jim from Hackney in London. Jim, what question would you like to put to Rab McGeddon?'

'Hello?'

'Yes, hello. Cyril Smarm here. You're on air now.'

'Oh, right . . . Well, I'm a first-time caller, and I want to thank you for having me on the show. I . . .'

'Yes, thanks, Jim, but could you just put your question to Rab McGeddon?'

'Er . . . yeah, right. Yeah, hello, Rab? Are you there?'

'Yes, I'm here.'

'Right, well, I just wanted to say, it's great to see you . . . well, hear you, anyway, and you know, congratulations on er . . . you know.'

'Thank you, Jim. That's good to hear.'

'And I just wanted to say, that, you know, it's great, what you said about coming from the mean streets of Glasgow, and I just wanted to say, I mean, if you'd come from some sort of, you know, lah-di-dah background, you know, do you think you could, you know, do you think you could have survived like you did?'

'Briefly if you would, Rab, because I think you've already told us something about that one.'

'Well, Jim, I think it would have been a lot more difficult for me. It was tough growing up the way I did on the mean streets of Glasgow, but I wouldn't change that upbringing. It's made me the man I am.'

'Thank you, Jim, for that. Next we have Sheila from Torbay in Devon. Sheila, you're through to Rab McGeddon.'

'Oh, thank you. Well, first of all, Mr McGeddon, it's a great privilege to speak to you. I think it's wonderful that you're taking a hard line against paying ransom to kidnappers. I just wanted to ask,

61

though, do you think you could keep to that hard line, if, say, your own son was kidnapped – God forbid – but you know what I mean.'

'I do know what you mean, Sheila, and I would keep to exactly the same line. Who am I that I should endanger other people's children by paying a ransom for my own? As I said before, it only encourages future kidnappings. We have to stop paying the Danegeld, whatever the circumstances. And that's all there is to it.'

'Thank you Sheila. Our next caller is Graham from Glasgow – your own city, Rab. Graham.'

'Right, well, I'm not going to tell Bill McGeddon how bloody marvellous I think he is, because I don't. I'm a socialist, and I never admire rich businessmen. Now I don't suppose Bill McGeddon . . .'

'Graham, it's Rab McGeddon. I'm not going to cut you off, but the name is Rab, not Bill.'

'Whatever. I just wanted to say that some people seriously suspect that you staged the kidnap yourself just for publicity. What do you say to that?'

'Oh, please! Who let this call through? Never mind, I'll let Rab answer if he wishes, but you don't have to, Rab.'

'I'll answer. If you believe that, Graham, you'll believe anything. I've never sought publicity. Publicity for a man in my position is not especially good for business, and I go out of my way to avoid it.'

'Then what are you doing on national radio? See, people like you, you just . . .' The voice of Graham from Glasgow faded away, to be replaced by wallpaper music.

'Yes, well, that's enough from Graham. And we won't have you back on the show, Graham, so don't bother trying. Tough debate we welcome, abuse and bad language we do not. If you want a fight, turn up here with your boxing gloves, and I'll sort you out. Next on the line to Rab McGeddon we have Terry from Cardiff. Terry, you're through to Rab McGeddon.'

'Hello, Cyril. How are you?'

'Fine. Your question to Rab McGeddon?'

'Right, well, first of all, I'm really pleased that Rab has been released unhurt, even if he thinks he shouldn't have been ransomed. But I want to talk about something else. Rab's firm BOMZIZUS is sponsoring *Predator*, the new TV programme, on which contestants will actually kill each other live on television. Well, isn't this worse than anything that happened to Rab? I mean how you can justify sponsoring this bloodbath I just don't understand. There's only one word for it, and that's genocide.'

'Well, Rab, I think a lot of people have a problem with this one. What do you say?'

'All right. First of all, Terry, let's get our facts straight. The rules haven't been made public yet, but I understand that nobody will be killed live on television, because the programme won't be transmitted live. Highlights – including any killings, of course – will be broadcast every day worldwide, between midnight and one in the morning GMT. The programme makers have made the very responsible decision not to broadcast live, in order to be able to edit out any particularly distasteful aspects of a killing. That's the first point.

'But the main thing is this: everybody who appears on *Predator* will be a volunteer. The programme makers have vetted all contestants for their mental stability, and have gone very carefully into their family circumstances. These people know exactly what they're letting themselves in for, and so do their families. They want to do it, and they will give us, I don't doubt, an inspiring display of courage and resourcefulness. I'm looking forward to it, and I think it might even be good for us. It might remind us of a few tough virtues which in our soft affluent society, we are in danger of forgetting. I know that some people have a problem with it. I don't. When I was kidnapped, I didn't volunteer for anything, and there was no possible advantage for me in it. That's why my kidnapping was wrong, but *Predator* is fine.'

'All right, Terry, I hope that answers your question. Our next caller is Linda, who is in Somerset. Linda?'

'Oh, hello, Cyril, great to speak to you. Great show, I listen to you every morning, I just wanted to say that.'

'Thanks, Linda. What's your question to Rab McGeddon?'

'Oh, yes. Hello, Rab?'

'Hello Linda.'

'Hello. I just wanted to say that I belong to the Temple of the Magic Twilight here in Taunton, and we pray to the Eternal Spirit for one good cause every week, and last week we prayed for your release, and look what happened. But I have to say that we also prayed that you will have been changed by your experience and that you'll be reborn to new life as . . .'

Ten

(From the *Daily Shocker*)

A TV Reality Show Too Far
Viraga Hateman

I had meant to hold my fire on *Predator* yet awhile. Everybody talks about it all the time, and it gets a bit tedious. Anyway, I thought I'd wait a little just to see how things pan out when it actually gets under way in a few days' time.

And then I saw the picture on the front of Saturday's *Morning Filth*. Oh God. Sharon Wonnaby, it seems, is Australian, and she's the face of *Predator*. And the tits and the bum. We know she is, because this is a *Filth* exclusive, and exclusives are very hard to come by these days. It's safe to assume that SEXITEL and the *Filth* agreed on it.

In other words, *Predator* is being marketed as yet another sleazefest for dirty old men. Never mind that nine out of the ten competitors will be dead within a month. Never mind that their families will be devastated. Never mind that the whole world will be cheapened by this disgusting piece of 'entertainment'. The important thing is to get the raincoat vote out. That's where the money is.

Well, thanks to the *Filth*, now we know it all. Several days before kick-off, we know the identities of the competitors, we know the rules, we know where it's all going to happen. Of course, there have been rumours galore, and I admit that I was taken in by one or two of them. Weren't we all? But SEXITEL and the programme makers have been so clever. They've leaked the truth here and there, they've leaked lies everywhere. They've ensured that we all have our tongues hanging out waiting for hard official facts.

I said that we know where it's going to happen. A small island in the Indian Ocean of the kind often referred to as a tropical paradise. Well, as of now it's going to be a tropical hell, isn't it? But did you know – well, you hardly would, since the *Filth* didn't bother to tell you – that this island was inhabited until a couple of weeks ago? Yes, nearly two hundred people used to have their homes there, and now they don't. I've been in touch with the programme makers, you see, and they've told me. Under pressure, you may be sure. They insist that the islanders have been 'relocated' to the mainland, where they will live in better houses and enjoy a much higher standard of living than they ever knew before. They are all – wouldn't you just know it? – delighted.

But let's get back to the gorgeous Sharon Wonnaby. Her with the face. And the tits and the bum. Well, she's one of five gals who are up against each other and five guys. Now don't get me wrong. I have no doubt that Sharon and the other females are tough as old boots, whatever they might look like. But it would make no sense to allow men and women to compete against each other in the Olympics, and it makes no sense to have them compete against each other on *Predator*. Just check the vital statistics of the competitors, which the *Filth* has obligingly given us.

And quite apart from the physical discrepancies, all the really useful experience is with the men. To take just one example, American Paul Nekred is 28, a former Marine and a martial arts expert. Now the competitors must do their killing either with the knives which they will be given or with whatever weapons they can make from what they find on the ground. Honestly, what chance does Sharon Wonnaby have against Paul Nekred?

Or what about our own brave boy, lauded by the *Filth*? Basil Wrigley will apparently have us all out on the streets waving our Union Jacks, and the *Filth* reckons he's in with a great chance. He hasn't had Nekred's training, but he is said to be very strong and very fast. The bookies are taking an awful lot of money on him, it seems. Not surprising, really, when you recall that of his nine opponents, one is the gorgeous Sharon, and a further four share her gender. (For what it's worth, my money would be on Nekred, but I don't bet.)

Now it may well be that neither Nekred nor Wrigley will win. My point is simply that the women don't have a chance. And the pompous hypocrisy with which the programme makers announce their belief in 'equal opportunities' makes me sick. The plain fact is that all of the females are as nearly as possible certain to die. The men, on the other hand, should all have a serious chance of survival, and of the rather measly (if you ask me) million dollar prize.

This whole show is to be a celebration of the very worst male values. When I rang the programme makers, I asked if there was a woman in authority to whom I could speak. I was told there wasn't. So it's all pretty clear. A bunch of rapacious men run the show, with a few cute little tits and bums answering telephones and typing out documents.

And what this ferociously male world wishes to offer us is three weeks of mayhem in which the camera will dwell lovingly on the tits and bums of Sharon and the other females, while the men get on with the killing. Best of all, of course – get your very oldest raincoat out for these – will be the killings of the gals.

You know, don't you, that the whole disgusting bloodfest is being sponsored by BOMZIZUS, the arms company run by Rab McGeddon? Well, if you heard him on the radio yesterday, interviewed by Cyril Smarm, then you will be in little doubt as to the arguments in favour of *Predator*. McGeddon (Oh why did they have to let him go?) sees it as a celebration of all the male virtues which his own firm embodies. We're in real trouble.

He actually said that he thinks the world will be a better place for *Predator*. Can you believe it? There is, it seems, too much peace in the world, and a bit of mayhem does us good now and again. His main point, however, seemed to be that all the competitors are volunteers, going into this thing – going to their deaths, remember, in nine cases out of ten – with their eyes wide open.

But even if they can see, Rab McGeddon clearly can't. The fact that these people are volunteers makes it all worse, not better. If they were forced to do it, then it wouldn't say anything quite so dreadful about our society. It would only mean that the wrong people are in charge, and we might be able to do something about it. But if ordinary people are prepared to volunteer to kill or be killed for the entertainment of the world, what is happening to us?

This horror would be impossible outside our Tantalus society. In Greek mythology, the sinful Tantalus spent the afterlife tormented by hunger and thirst, with the bunch of grapes above his head and the water of the stream in which he stood, both moving tantalisingly (yes, you've got it) beyond his anguished mouth whenever he tried to reach them. Today, it's the urge to be famous that tantalises, and on which all reality TV is based. In truth, 99.99 per cent of hopefuls will spend their whole lives yearning for what, contrived appearances notwithstanding, was never meant to be theirs in the first place.

At least the gladiators who fought in the Roman arena two thousand years ago were forced to do so. (And no letters, please, from pedants who have heard that a handful of free men chose to become gladiators.) Gladiators always wanted to escape from the arena if they possibly could, and they frequently tried. Under Spartacus, they almost destroyed Rome in their determination to be free. In other words, unlike their present-day counterparts, Rome's gladiators were at least free in their own minds.

And I would point out that virtually every gladiator who ever fought was a man. All right, there were a very very few women, but at least they fought only against other women. At least they were given a chance. And at least the rest of the world didn't have to watch. You actually had to turn up at the arena if that was to your taste.

I'm well aware that you have to tune in to the correct channel on your TV if you want to watch *Predator*. But how many of us will be able to resist at least a peek now and again? It's just too easy to access. My great fear – and the great hope of SEXITEL and the programme makers – is that we'll all be tuning in in huge numbers. Could this be only the beginning? Please God, no, but it might. If I were a Christian, I might go along to General Pius Oldgit's mammoth marathon anti-*Predator* pray-in at Hyde Park. But I'm not, so I won't. I fear that the only thing we can do against *Predator* is absolutely refuse to watch. If nobody watches, then it won't happen again. That's our only defence.

Eleven

'Wimmin, wimmin!' Eartha Muvver looked pained. 'Why must our discussions always turn into shouting matches? Is this the spirit of the Goddess? No, this is the spirit of war. Go off to the Falklands and fight for Thatcher, if that's what you want. Here we must respect the views of others. We . . .'

Marcia Mugger was on her feet, pointing dramatically at Jack Ladd. 'I do respect her fucking views! I do respect her fucking views! It's her that doesn't respect my views, the fucking slag!'

Jack Ladd too found it impossible to remain in her chair. 'Fucking slag yourself, you fucking slag! I've always respected your fucking stupid views, because that's . . .'

'Wimmin, please!' Eartha Muvver stamped her foot. 'Now sit down both of you.' Eartha's voice carried real weight in the commune, and Jack and Marcia did as they were told. There was trouble whenever a meeting was called, which was often. The problem was that they were trying to abide by the principle that they had no leader. Thus they never allowed anyone to chair a meeting or to foreclose discussion – with the result that, unless everyone was in clear agreement virtually from the start, meetings always degenerated into shouting matches.

The truth was that they did have a leader – had had from the very start. Eartha's word, like her body, had always carried more weight than anyone else's, and it was only the tacit acknowledgment by everyone of her authority that prevented the commune from breaking up completely. As long as Eartha was there, and everyone regarded her almost as an oracle, a line could be held. But her preeminent status was never openly acknowledged.

She rose ponderously and lifted both arms in a characteristically hieratic gesture. Her brightly-coloured poncho spread out on either side of her until she looked like a gigantic and very gaudy bird. She closed her eyes. 'O Goddess, our Mother, teach us the ways of gentleness and peace. Teach us to respect each other, and not to give way to the evil masculine part of our natures. Goddess, we beseech you.'

'Ah wimmin!' they all said in hushed voices, this being their accepted variant of Amen. Exactly who the Goddess was had never been made plain. She was, however, invoked frequently, and her precise identity seemed not to be a matter for concern.

'Now,' said Eartha, when everyone was calm again, 'we are going to discuss this properly.' She eased herself back into her chair. 'Let's remind ourselves where we stand exactly. We have a vacancy because Harridana has left us to join the women of Greenham Common.' Here she paused, and led a sober round of applause.

Marcia did not join in. 'All right, so she's off to demonstrate against Reagan's missiles, but she was still a fucking bitch. Her bastard son took that money, and she defended him.'

'Come on,' said Jack, 'we don't know that.'

'Oh yes we fucking do! The whole fucking tin of petty cash! Everybody knew who took it, even her, the selfish bitch. Probably took half of it herself.'

It had been a most unfortunate affair altogether. Harridana, whose real name was Mhairi O'Mahony, had been in the commune less than a month, during which time things had never quite gone smoothly. There had been problems from the very start: the meeting at which Mhairi had been proposed for membership had been especially heated, largely because Mhairi had a son, Joseph. Now the rule of the commune was that no men might ever cross the threshold. (In fact, the wimmin had found it necessary to make certain exceptions, since electricians, plumbers and others still had a nasty habit of being male, but the exclusion was observed as strictly as was practicable.) The acceptance or rejection of Mhairi had turned, therefore, on the status of a nine-year-old boy: was he to be considered a man?

The meeting split into two factions: half the wimmin declared that the term man covered any male human of any age; the other half that a boy became a man at the age of eleven, at which point

Joseph would admittedly have to leave. What swung things in favour of Mhairi and Joseph was that she was Irish and he was black: centuries of British oppression, it was affirmed, entitled an Irishwoman to special indulgence, while all black males were to be considered at least part female because of the oppression they too suffered in a world dominated by white men.

The final decision, carried largely because of Eartha's unspoken authority, was that Mhairi and Joseph could stay, but that Joseph was to be treated, as far as possible, like a girl (or 'pre-womin', to use the term favoured in the commune). When in the house he would wear girl's clothes, and would be required to pee sitting down. Mhairi had bitterly resented the restrictions placed on her treatment of her own son, but she needed a place to stay.

It hadn't worked out. Mhairi, who did not in truth share the feminist perspective of her housemates, had let her son wear boy's clothes and choose his own peeing position. She was far more interested in Irish republicanism, and frequently deafened everyone late at night when she came back drunk and bawled out rebel songs. She had never really fitted in, and Marcia in particular had resented her greatly from the first.

The last straw had been the petty cash. No one in the commune had much money, and it was a point of pride that a tin of petty cash as they called it, could be left freely accessible for emergencies without anyone ever taking selfish advantage. Men, it was generally agreed, would never have been able to maintain a system based on honesty alone. When the tin was one day found unaccountably empty, Marcia had immediately blamed Joseph, and Mhairi's impassioned defence of her son – 'a God-fearing Irish Catholic who wouldn't know how to steal, you Prod bitch!' – had led to a fight which had culminated in Mhairi's decision to leave the commune and move to rural Berkshire. All she knew of Greenham Common was that it was full of women, and that they were opposed to the British government. That was enough.

It was against this background that the debate on Virginia's candidature for commune membership was taking place. Jack, who had never got on with Marcia, was enraged by the latter's aggressive insistence on Joseph's guilt and Mhairi's complicity in the petty cash affair. 'Fuck you!' she screamed, 'Fuck you! You . . .'

Eartha was up again, right arm raised like that of a ponderous policeman on points duty. 'None of this is relevant. That somebody took the petty cash is all we know. Nobody's admitted to it, and the matter is closed. The point is that Harridana's departure leaves a vacancy, and Marcia is proposing Virginia to fill it. Well, it's a week since I found Virginia at King's Cross and brought her back here, so you've all had time to form an opinion. Now Marcia will tell us why she thinks we should elect her to the commune, and then Jack will tell us why she thinks we shouldn't. And we haven't got all night. Virginia will be back in half an hour to get the decision. Marcia, you first.'

'Well, er . . .'

'Why don't you stand up?' said Eartha, as she sat back down. 'You can make your case better if we can all see you clearly.'

Marcia stood and cleared her throat. 'Well, the thing is that this place is a fucking tip, and everybody knows it. I mean, look at Virginia's room – where that bitch Harridana was before with her bastard. I mean, it was like a fucking midden before, wasn't it? And everybody else is the same. No offence, and maybe your room's not so bad, Eartha, but look at the rest of us. All right, so we all hate housework and we never want to do any again. But that's no excuse for living in fucking filth, is it? I mean, look at the kitchen now. It's fucking sparkling, and people aren't sick every day. That's because we've got a bit of hygiene at last. And Virginia says she'll do this room next, just as soon as we let her. And er . . . and I think she's all right. And er . . . that's all.' She sat down, looking somewhat deflated.

'Thank you, Marcia. Jack, your turn.'

Jack stood. 'Look, the main thing in any commune is that everybody should fit in. You just can't have fucking misfits, or the whole thing goes fucking pear-shaped. See, Harridana, well, maybe Marcia didn't like her, but she got on well enough with everybody else. She was . . .'

'Oh no she fucking didn't. Pig didn't like her, did you . . .'

Eartha Muvver sighed. 'Marcia, sit down. You've had your turn. Now it's . . .'

'Oh, come on, Eartha! You're on my side. Jesus Christ, you like Virginia, don't you? I mean, it was you that brought her here in the first place.'

73

'Marcia, be quiet!' Eartha spoke much more sharply. 'I've listened to what you had to say. Now I'm going to listen to Jack before I make up my mind. That's what we're all going to do. She didn't interrupt you, so please don't you interrupt her. Carry on, Jack.'

'Right, well, I was saying that I reckon that Harridana fitted in well enough, but Virginia just doesn't. I mean, look at her. Totally wet behind the ears. We'd never get her dry, she's so fucking sodden. She's so fucking prim and proper and bourgeois. And I mean, she's fucking pregnant! What happens if she has the kid, and it's a boy? Now, see, I'm easy about it for a few years, but it's only going to cause the kind of trouble we had with Joseph. If it didn't work before, why should it work now? We . . .'

Eartha cleared her throat. 'Just a couple of points there, Jack. One, we don't even know the sex of the child yet, and two, she's seriously thinking of having an abortion. Being pregnant can't exclude her. But carry on.'

Jack gave a contemptuous snort, but did not dare take issue with Eartha. 'Yeah, well, whatever. There was something else . . . Oh yes, she's not only pregnant, she's still a fucking man-lover, too. And er . . . I mean, we just don't have anything to do with men here, and we don't allow them in, and er . . . that's it. She just won't fucking fit in, and I don't want her here.' Jack sat down.

'Thank you, Jack. But what do you say to Marcia's point about keeping the place clean and tidy?'

'Well, I mean, like I just said, she's just fucking bourgeois, that's all. You've all heard her – *Mister* Reagan, *Misses* Thatcher. And as for her housework, see how long it lasts. What she's doing is, she's just making herself useful – or she thinks she is, I don't care what the fucking place looks like – just so as to get herself in. Cos she's got nowhere else to go, has she? I mean, I bet she won't be the perfect Mrs fucking Mop once she gets in. She'll just breathe a fucking great sigh of relief, and never do a stroke again. Sticks out a mile.'

Hands hitched to the shoulder straps of her dungarees, Marcia was looking sullen. But Eartha was in control. 'Now Marcia, what do you say to Jack's point that she's just too bourgeois to fit in? And that she's a man-lover. Because that could be a problem, couldn't it? We couldn't let her bring men in, could we?'

74

Marcia was not letting go. 'Look, she's only nineteen. She still doesn't know the fucking world, does she? I mean, I agree with Jack, up to a point. She *is* wet behind the ears, it's true. Has she ever told you about her fucking parents up there in Newcastle? Has she? I mean, I've never heard anything like it. Church every Sunday, never a drop of alcohol, never any kind of life of her own at all. As for being a man-lover, well, I mean, it's a man that's made her pregnant, then fucked off and left her. Just give her a little time, and she'll see things more clearly. She'll see what men are really all about. Just give her chance.'

'Fuck!' Jack was angry. 'I bet she fucking won't! I bet she'll just – if we let her in, I mean – I bet she'll just wait until her little bastard is born, and then she'll fuck off. Sticks out a mile. She just reckons she's on to a good thing here. The only real reason for letting her in seems to be that she's Mrs Mop, and even if she is, and even if she never changes, we've never cared about that kind of thing, have we? I mean, what does it fucking matter?'

'Look,' said Marcia, trying to sound ultra-reasonable, 'this place was just a fucking tip before Virginia moved in. Now look at it. After just one week.'

'Piss off,' said Jack Ladd, who had no interest in physical cleanliness whatever. 'All the little slag's doing is trying to make herself useful so's she'll get in. If we let her in, then it'll all stop. She's fucking useless. Sticks out a fucking mile.'

'Fuck you, you fucking slag!' yelled Marcia, all pretence of reasonableness abandoned.

'Fucking slag yourself, you fucking slag!' shouted Jack in reply. 'You just . . .'

And this time, even the ponderous rise of Eartha from her armchair had no effect. Everyone joined in, and a real physical fight seemed likely. Such things did happen in the commune from time to time.

It was Pig Wozzel who saved the day. 'Shut the fucking fuck up, all of you!' she screamed, hurling a cushion in the general direction of Jack Ladd. 'Listen, I don't know if she'd fit in either. And I don't know about her kid. But Jack's got her wrong. She's a fucking charlady by nature, and that's what this place needs.'

Pig had earned her new name (her old one had been Sally Scroggins) for she was the filthiest person in the world. Quite simply, Pig could never be bothered cleaning or tidying anything at all. Everyone thought admiringly that this showed her rejection of bourgeois values, it showed how determined she was to defy the male image of woman as the eternal housekeeper. The truth could hardly have been more different. The truth was that Pig absolutely hated living in filth, but was fantastically lazy. She had a secret vision of herself as a princess living in a gorgeous palace. She saw herself reclining on an enormous bed covered with snowy white linen. She was eating an orange, and as soon as she threw a bit of peel on the floor, a liveried flunkey would pick it up and bear it away on a silver salver. Pig had a recurring nightmare that Jack and the others might see inside her head, and turn on her in outraged anti-bourgeois purity, tearing her to pieces.

She needn't have worried. None of them could ever have suspected such values in one who lived in such awesome squalor. In fact everyone was utterly astonished by her defence of hygiene. So astonished that, for some moments, no one could say anything. But everyone was thinking the same thing: if even Pig reckoned it a good idea to have the place a bit less filthy, then how could anyone think otherwise?

As the mood of the meeting became clear, Jack took refuge in a sulk. 'Hasn't even got a fucking name yet,' she said, scowling. 'What about that?'

In one sense, this was true. Marcia had once turned up an unlikely piece of research done at a polytechnic in the early seventies, purporting to prove that, whatever the ostensible process, girls' names were always in fact chosen by their fathers. This meant that both family name and given name were an imposition of a patriarchal society which the wimmin of the commune utterly rejected. The rule was, therefore, that, within one month of acceptance into the group, a new member had to choose a new name. Under no circumstances could she keep any name by which she had been known on entry to the commune.

'She'll have a new name soon enough,' said Eartha.

It was over. Virginia Greenlove was about to begin her new life.

Twelve

(From the *Sunday Screamer*)

Us & Them: Cassandra McRaker tells it like it really is!

No one for tennis: Letzgetcha Nickersoff

Three weeks ago, in writing of Dan Grabbitall, I mentioned that he has signed up Letzgetcha Nickersoff for his new PR company Rich & Famous. Well, it strikes me that it might well be time for a look at Miss Nickersoff herself. As it happens, I have never profiled a sports personality before, having no interest whatever in sport of any kind. But I'm always up for anything new, and in the case of the gorgeous Letz, her place on Dan Grabbitall's list makes her much more of a celeb than she ever was before. (And much less of a tennis player, but I'll be coming to that in due course.)

So, I . . . No, I can't lie to you. There's more to it than that. On Friday, Youssuf Al-Majnooni, crazed imam of London's Farootkaik Mosque, publicly described Letzgetcha Nickersoff as a 'prostitute whom God hates'. Well, I'm not going to second-guess the Deity, but the pronouncements of His west London mouthpiece are never to be ignored. To have Dan Grabbitall as an agent is one thing, but to be publicly denounced by Youssuf Al-Majnooni is a cast-iron guarantee that you really have arrived. When the bearded nutcase finally gets round to preaching a sermon against me, I'll break open the champagne. Till then, I'm just another tired hack.

Back to Letz. Beyond what everybody knows about her – that she is a professional tennis player, and that she is very beautiful – who exactly is Letzgetcha Nickersoff? (And tennis fans will just have to bear with me. Mindful of my own annoyance when others take for granted that I know everything about subjects which are of no interest to me, I never assume knowledge in others.)

Letzgetcha Nickersoff burst onto the tennis scene three years ago at the age of seventeen. Having won a major tournament, reached the semi-finals of the American Open, and the ladies' doubles final at Wimbledon, she ended the year ranked number nineteen in the world. From being just another poor little Ruritanian girl who dreamt of being a rich little Ruritanian girl, she had in twelve months been transformed into a very rich big American girl.

And where is she now? Well, she has, for the first time since getting into it, dropped out of the world's top fifty, and the slide is beginning to look unstoppable. Sounds awful, doesn't it? But don't be too ready with the tears of sympathy, because Letz is by a country mile the best-paid sportswoman in the world, earning vastly more now than she ever did before. Bully for her.

The reason, of course, is endorsements. In addition to straightforward upfront commercial advertising, she makes a fortune simply from being seen to favour certain products, from tennis rackets to clothes to cars. The machinations of the world of advertising are far beyond me, but I can assure you that Letz is hugely marketable, and that, with Dan Grabbitall representing her, her full earnings potential will now be realised. The trouble is that Mr Grabbitall is no more interested in sport than he is in literature. He cares no more for the quality of Letz's tennis than he does for the quality of the writing he publishes.

Let me pause for a moment here to consider a name from the past. How many people today, I wonder, would recognise the name of Mary Rand? Unless you take a serious interest in athletics, you have to be of a certain age to remember her. In fact, you have to be old enough to remember the Tokyo Olympics of 1964, which is ten years before I was born. Never mind. I've taken the trouble to find out something about her, and I now give you the benefits of my research.

Mary Rand was a British long-jumper who broke the world record to win gold in Tokyo, and she was also – you've guessed it – very beautiful. So what happened to her? Well, she went on being an athlete, and disappeared completely from the public consciousness on her retirement.

The point I'm making is that times really have changed. By the time Anna Kournikova appeared on the tennis scene, while looks could already come between a sportswoman and her performance, she could still turn her back on the attention they drew if she really wanted (which Anna didn't). Not any more.

Just a generation back, Letzgetcha Nickersoff might well have been drooled over by lots of dirty old men (and dirty young men), but she would have been allowed to get on with her tennis, and would probably have made a pretty good living out of it. Instead of which, she is now fabulously wealthy, but clearly in serious decline as a tennis player. Envy her all you like, but my guess is that she would be happier trying to develop her talent to the full instead of letting others take advantage of looks which are a matter of pure luck. What bothers me is what all this will do for her self-esteem.

I've been wondering about the origins of the celebrification process of which Letz is a victim, and suspect you could date it to when Rupert Murdoch (remember him?) started buying up the world's media, and taking it all relentlessly downmarket. Sales and viewing figures became all that mattered, and media people began a desperate search for what would make people buy newspapers and watch TV. And what they came up with was celebs. The public couldn't get enough of them. Sex had always been hugely saleable, so you didn't have to be a genius to work out that a sexy celeb just had to be a winner. Of course, there had always been the film stars – Rudolph Valentino, Marilyn Monroe, and so on – but they had been sold as sex symbols from the start. This was different. Now you could take a tennis player, leave out the tennis, and still have a winner. Simple.

But back to the tennis player in question. It's not only that I reckon Letz's self-esteem might suffer if she allows herself to be Dan Grabbitall's milch cow rather than her own woman. There's something else that makes me wonder if she's wise to allow herself to be marketed as a sex symbol. One of the endless clichés used to describe her is 'ice maiden'. Why? Well, in part at least because her name has never been associated with that of any man. Why not? Now that would be telling . . . and I'm going to tell you.

When she's not actually playing – which is most of the time now – Letz divides her time between her Manhattan penthouse and her London mansion. And the interesting thing is that she shares both with the same companion, who always travels with her, but is kept carefully in the background. I can't even give you the name of this companion, but there is no evidence that she works for a living. Feel free to doubt me, but my source is unimpeachable.

Well, it may just be that she – Letz's companion, that is – inherited a great deal of money, but my contact thinks not. No, the truth is that Letz keeps her. Nothing wrong with that, of course, but it makes you wonder if it's quite above board to market Letz as every man's fantasy. I went so far as to check the facts with Dan Grabbitall, but he was not very forthcoming. In fact, he told me to fuck off.

Not very polite, but then, politeness never was Dan's strong suit. Back to his protégé. I would be prepared to bet that Letz (who is not yet 21), will have finished with tennis completely before she is 25, perhaps a long time before. And – and this is the point – I would also be prepared to bet that she would have been happier in an earlier era, when she could have been a fine tennis player, who just happened to have been blessed with beauty too.

So if, by some extraordinary chance, Letz, you ever cast your eye over this humble column, my advice to you is to tell Dan Grabbitall to fuck off. You could still, so those in the know tell me, be a great tennis player, and you wouldn't have to pretend to be something you're not. In the long run, I'm prepared to bet, you'd be doing yourself a favour.

Thirteen

'Good evening, and welcome to *Spotlight*.' Clive Sneersly's red and blue tie gleamed like a jewel against his cream shirt. 'Tonight we turn our attention once more to the TV phenomenon in everybody's mind. There has never been anything quite like it before, and many are praying that there never will be anything quite like it again. Literally praying in the case of the Salvation Army, with General Pius Oldgit leading a massive anti-*Predator* pray-in at Hyde Park. But if preliminary indications are anything to go by, they're going to be disappointed. Very.

'When the first dose of *Predator* was broadcast on SEXITEL last night, viewing figures internationally dwarfed anything seen hitherto. And the contest itself hasn't even begun. We have now met all ten participants, we have seen them arrive on the island. There are five men and five women, and already the bookies are overwhelmed. Everyone, it seems, wants to back a compatriot. In America, all the money is on Paul Nekred, in Australia on Sharon Wonnaby, in this country on Basil Wrigley. And so on.

'It's all set up. We now know exactly where the action will take place – that's been an open secret for the past couple of weeks anyway – we know the names and faces of the contestants, we know the rules by which they will play this deadly game. And those rules, of course, ensure more than three weeks of what SEXITEL is pleased to describe as entertainment. In general terms, the first four days will be bloodless so that we can get to know all contestants, then there will be a killing every two days thereafter, these to take place only in designated killing zones where cameras will be running twenty-four seven.

'Whatever your attitude to the show – and opinion polls suggest that the vast majority of people worldwide are bitterly opposed to it

– you can't fail to have been chilled by the long scene in which the anonymous former SAS man trained the contestants in killing techniques. Learning how best to slit someone's throat is not most people's idea of light entertainment.

'But those viewing figures give real food for thought. I've just said that opinion polls show an overwhelming distaste for the show worldwide, so why did so many people watch last night? Was it, as some have suggested, that we all knew that there would be no killing in that first instalment? Or will figures climb even higher once the bloodshed actually gets under way? We shall very soon know. But what gives most food for thought at present is that, for every three Britons who watched the show, only one is actually prepared to admit to it. This courtesy of a MORI poll in today's *Evening Perv*. Just what sort of hypocrites are we?

'Here in the studio to discuss that and many other questions arising out of *Predator*, I have publisher Dan Grabbitall and journalist Viraga Hateman. But before we hear what they have to say, let's have a look at the report filed with us by Justin Poser earlier today from somewhere in the Arabian Sea.'

Cut to a golden beach fringed by emerald palms; blue sea, and the sun dazzling out of a turquoise sky. Suave thirty-something man strolls into view, casually dressed for moderate heat.

'This' [waves elegant arm to take in surroundings] 'is the sort of place which travel companies like to call a tropical paradise. Not a very imaginative description, perhaps, but you can see their point, can't you? It really is beautiful. But of course, distance lends enchantment to any view, and when you get close, you find poverty and suffering among the people, and you find nature red in tooth and claw. You are also more than likely to get nastily sunburned, even at the end of September, and quite possibly stung or bitten by something very unpleasant – cobra or scorpion if you're lucky, dog if you're not. I'm serious about that. The prevalence of rabies among the local dogs, combined with the absence of accessible medical facilities, ensures that a dog bite is much more likely to kill you.

'But there's now an added hazard in paradise. As it happens, I am not at risk, because this, contrary to what you may be thinking, is not Predator Island at all. That's Predator Island over there. And if your eyesight's good enough, you'll be able to make out a red dot moving left to right across the middle of your screen just in front of it. That is a gunboat. There are in fact seven in all, and they are there to ensure that not even a BBC reporter can get on to the island. It would be pretty stupid to try. Remember that Predator Island has declared independence, and they have said they really will fire on anyone attempting an unauthorised incursion. Well, I'm not going to take that risk. I've come here instead.

'The programme makers did in fact look at this island, but finally decided that there were just too many people here: it was going to be too expensive to rehouse them. And remember that the relocation is expected to be permanent, because they have bought the island, and intend to go on making *Predator* there for just as long as there is a market.

'Now the Indian government has been roundly condemned for selling the place for such a purpose. They defend themselves by saying that *Predator* was going to be made somewhere anyway, and the money they received – the amount has not been disclosed – will be devoted entirely to humanitarian purposes, beginning with the relocation to the mainland of the island's population. Well, maybe so, but we have been quite unable to find the people who used to live there, and the government is being singularly unhelpful. They simply insist that the people – anything between sixty and two hundred, depending on who you believe – now live in substantially better conditions than they enjoyed before. We just have to take their word for it.

'Since we cannot find them, we can't ask them what they think about the whole business. Instead, we'll have to be content with the next best thing, which is talking to the people on this island . . .'

Five minutes later, Justin Poser, back on the beach, wound up his report. 'Well, make of it what you will, the fact is that the people of this island are mightily relieved that *Predator* is going on there and not here. Mightily relieved, that is, that they still have their own homes where they want them. Perhaps the most significant thing I have learned here is that, while rich people – which means Westerners generally – are almost obsessed with *Predator*, the world's poor people must concern themselves with more workaday, less dramatic matters. They have to till their fields, make bread, draw water. They have to work hard to stay alive. The short time that I have spent with them has been for me, in many ways, a humbling experience. I can't help thinking that their very poverty helps them to retain a humanity which we in the West may be losing.'

Back in the studio, Clive Sneersly paused for a moment, lips pursed. 'Justin Poser. Well, everyone, it seems, has an opinion about *Predator*, and my two studio guests are no exception. Viraga Hateman is a journalist whose column in the *Daily Shocker* is only one of many strings to her bow. She holds uncompromising feminist views, and has said in the *Shocker* that she believes that *Predator*, despite the equal number of male and female competitors, is a celebration of all that is worst in a male-dominated society. Dan Grabbitall is an Anglo-American entrepreneur, with fingers in many pies. Having laid the foundations of his empire in the US, he has now taken over London publisher Over & Dunwith, and set up a PR company, Rich & Famous.

'Dan Grabbitall, let me start with you. I might begin by thanking you for coming on the programme at all, because we had a very hard time getting anyone to speak in support of *Predator*. In the end, we had a choice between you and Rab McGeddon of BOMZIZUS, sponsors of the programme. If there's nothing wrong with it, why do you suppose we've had such difficulty?'

Dan Grabbitall sat back comfortably. 'You said it in your introduction, Clive. People are such hypocrites. Everybody watches *Predator*, nobody admits it.'

Clive Sneersly did not look convinced. 'I think it was Rochefoucauld who said that hypocrisy is the homage paid by vice to virtue – meaning, presumably, that when people's words belie their actions, you can take it that those actions are something to be ashamed of.'

'I don't think it's quite that simple.' Grabbitall was unfazed. 'When a bible-thumping puritan patronises a prostitute, he'll lie through his loathsome teeth about it. It's not sex that's wrong, just his attitude to it. Look at all those thousands of people at Pius Oldgit's anti-*Predator* pray-in at Hyde Park. I'd stake my life on it that half of them are tuning in just as soon as they get home, because we know that most of them aren't there twenty-four seven in spite of some claims.'

'Well,' said Clive Sneersly with a shrug, 'that would be difficult to prove either way. Viraga Hateman, let me turn to you. I have to say that you're honoured, because we had hundreds to choose from when it came to speaking *against Predator*. Tell Dan Grabbitall what's wrong with it.'

Viraga Hateman shook her head wearily. 'It's so obvious that it's a bore to repeat it, but here goes. What we're doing is turning murder into entertainment. Of course you'll always find people to watch such a spectacle. There were plenty of people happy to watch gladiators fighting to the death in the Roman arena, plenty of people happy to watch public hangings in this country until the late 19th century. But the fact that lots of people are prepared to do something doesn't make it right. Everybody knows that such a spectacle is degrading.'

'Degrading. That's the point, isn't it? Is it not the case, Dan Grabbitall, that everyone who watches *Predator* is cheapened by it?'

Grabbitall closed his eyes, and shook his head emphatically. 'The great difference between the Roman arena and public executions on the one hand, and *Predator* on the other, is that the contestants on *Predator* are volunteers. They are prepared to risk their lives for fame and fortune. If they were slaves who were forced into it, I would be the first to condemn the whole enterprise. But they want to do it, and if others want to watch them, then it's none of your business, or mine. Or Viraga Hateman's.'

As he finished speaking, Grabbitall turned in Hateman's direction. The scowl on her face might have withered a lesser man. Grabbitall simply smiled.

'Viraga Hateman, he's got something there, you can't deny. Forcing thousands of slaves to fight to the death in the Colosseum is not at all the same thing as allowing ten volunteers to fight it out on Predator Island.'

'Look,' said Viraga Hateman, 'if a bunch of no-hopers want to kill each other, that's fine by me. My only difference with Pius Oldgit is that I'll let consenting adults do whatever they like provided they're not corrupting others. Seems stupid to me, but as long as they don't hurt anybody else, let them. What I object to is trying to make money out of it by turning it into entertainment for paying spectators. Of course Dan Grabbitall thinks it's a great thing. He reckons that if there's money in it, then it can't be bad.

That's his twisted philosophy. The truth is that it's the money that *makes* it bad.'

Grabbitall laughed dismissively. 'So there we have it. Viraga Hateman can't really find any good moral argument against *Predator* – which is because there simply isn't one – so she decides that it's got to be bad because it might make a profit. Well, she's dead right when she says that I think it's a good thing to make money. Wealth is better than poverty.

'The show is sponsored by a company which makes money out of manufacturing weapons of war. Ask employees of BOMZIZUS if they think the money they make is bad money. Of course they don't. Ask their boss, Rab McGeddon, if he is ashamed of what he does. Unlike all the bleeding-heart hypocrites, Rab McGeddon and his workers know that it's people who can be bad, not the tools they use. And I think I'm right in saying that no company has refused on principle to take an advertising slot during the programme. In fact, they're falling over themselves to get in, and all because they know they'll make money.'

Clive Sneersly tried to intervene, but Viraga Hateman gave him no chance. Clenching both fists, she leaned aggressively towards Dan Grabbitall. 'That is just so typical of the predatory male in our civilisation! Two things matter: money and power. Jesus, if you could get some lunatic to agree to be publicly tortured to death, would it be all right if you could just persuade people to pay to watch?'

'Dan Grabbitall?'

The more excited Viraga Hateman became, the more laid back became Dan Grabbitall. 'Might be a bit boring, just watching someone passively being tortured to death. But to . . .'

'Oh God!' Viraga Hateman looked away in disgust.

'To be serious about it, Viraga Hateman talks of a lunatic giving his consent to being tortured to death. Well, of course that would be wrong, because a lunatic can't give informed and reasoned consent. If . . .'

Viraga tried to interrupt, Dan went on talking, and there were several seconds of cacophony as both refused to give way.

'All right,' said Sneersly, holding up both hands to indicate that he was still in charge, 'I think I get the picture. But Viraga Hateman, you mention predatory males. It would seem that there are predatory females around too. Half of the contestants are women. Isn't it a bit unfair to use this issue to make a feminist point?'

'It most certainly is not. These misguided women are simply falling into line with the masculine way of doing things. Throughout history, man rather than woman has been the aggressor. Men continue to exploit women as they have always done. All we have on Predator Island is five little Letzgetcha Nickersoffs, there to excite the dirty old men. It's disgusting.'

'Dan Grabbitall, that's an interesting point. Let's take Miss Nickersoff as an example. You're her agent, and it is frequently said that you are exploiting her as a sex symbol rather than as a tennis player. Is it the same sort of thing on Predator Island? The women are theoretically there to compete, but in practice there only to titillate?'

Grabbitall spread his arms in a gesture of innocence. 'Well, I don't accept that I'm not interested in Letzgetcha's tennis. Ask the lady herself. She's still playing at the top level. She . . .'

Viraga Hateman leaned forward again, and pointed accusingly at him. 'So why isn't she with a sporting agency, tell us that. How did you manage to poach her from IMG, who were already exploiting her earnings potential as a tennis player? You're just marketing her as a sex symbol. You should be ashamed of yourself. Anyway, how much interest has she ever shown in men? Her close friends are all women as far as I can see.'

Grabbitall suddenly looked very serious. 'If Viraga Hateman wishes to slander any client of mine, I can only say that I hope she has deep pockets. I . . .'

Clive Sneersly cleared his throat noisily. 'Yes, well let's not get into deep water on that one. I was simply taking Viraga Hateman's analogy between Letzgetcha Nickersoff's tennis and . . .'

Fourteen

It was all too much. At the end of the day – was it safe to leave at the normal time? would Dan Grabbitall, now that he was back in the country, make a surprise visit to the office at midnight just to check that he was still at his desk? – Dormatt felt like a drink. But a drink, he strongly suspected, would do him no good at all. He enjoyed alcohol only when he didn't really need it; when he did, it always made him feel worse. A particularly irritating application of sod's law. He put on his coat and walked glumly out of the building.

A month had passed since Dormatt's humiliation, a month which Grabbitall had spent in New York. Now he was back, and was about to take hands-on control; he was coming in to the office the next day, and Dormatt didn't think he could face it. The intervening weeks had felt like a phoney war, a period of strained normality which everybody knew couldn't last. The shooting was about to start.

He reached the tube station, paused . . . and walked on. He had rung his Wife earlier, to say that he might well be late. That was when he had thought that he might indeed work on, or might go for a drink before returning home. Instead, he would walk. He needed to walk. He needed to feel the rhythm of his footsteps on the pavement, he needed to calm his troubled mind.

Which was presently tormenting him with reruns of his recent humiliation. Whatever had possessed him to try to persuade Dan Grabbitall to publish Boris Fartleby? It had seemed like such a good idea at the time, but the moment he was inside Grabbitall's office, he had known that it was one of the worst ideas he had ever had. Why had he been such a fool as to go through with it? The surprising thing was that he hadn't been sacked on the spot. But might it not have been better if he had? The only tangible result of his pathetic stand had been to make him more abject than ever in the eyes of his new employer.

And then there was the jiffy bag. Like a routed army, Dormatt had abandoned his equipment as he fled the field: he had forgotten Fartleby's manuscript. When, in Grabbitall's absence, he had tried to locate it the following day, he had failed completely, Grabbitall's secretary pleading total ignorance of its existence. This wasn't good. Even the worst manuscript was the property of its creator, and should always find its way back to him. Dormatt hoped that Fartleby had another copy, or at least had the thing saved to disk. Not that anyone would ever publish it now, but even so.

Well, he had his story ready. When Fartleby got round to asking what had happened to it, Dormatt would say that, to the best of his knowledge, it was with his boss – which, after all, was not impossibly far from the truth. But Dormatt was as sure as it was possible to be of such a thing that Grabbitall would already have destroyed it. *Alexander the Great: son of Philip of Basildon* could be of absolutely no interest to Dan Grabbitall, who would have thrown it away without a second thought. Theoretically, of course, he might have returned it to its author, but . . . but Dormatt knew perfectly well that he hadn't. Oh God.

Something unpleasant began to happen, something that Dormatt had not previously experienced: he began to notice London. For eighteen years he had lived there, but it had never really got to him before. Now it was getting to him, and it was not nice. He had thought that the rhythm of his footsteps against the humming roar of the capital might calm him, might induce a mood of something like tranquillity. Instead, it was bringing him close to panic. What was going on?

It wasn't a humming roar that he was hearing at all. For the first time he was hearing not the white noise of a big city, but all of the myriad disparate noises of which it was composed. It was horrible. He heard each individual vehicle – some of them admittedly roaring or humming, but some whispering, some snarling, some screeching. And in place of the normal buzz of voices he heard the words and phrases. Somebody said fuck, somebody said piss off, somebody said that if Eric tried that again he'd know all about it, somebody laughed like a braying donkey.

And it wasn't only that he heard all; he saw all, too. A bright red bus with grim, strained faces at the windows; a car with a broken wing mirror, another with its green bonnet blistered brown with rust. An old man, grey-haired and with a stick, limping; two schoolchildren, faces supercilious and bored. A florist, with a bucket of white flowers; a clothes shop selling everything at fifty per cent below marked price . . . A woman with an eye-patch, a lorry grinding its gears, a man saying I'll tell you tomorrow, the smell of stale vegetables, the slap of leather on stone, the feel of his own feet on the pavement . . .

Dormatt's head was coming off. This was his city. This was where he had lived for nearly twenty years, and never before had he even noticed it. Near to panic, he crossed the road and approached a strange pill-box-like structure in the broad pavement. All he knew was that this was a public toilet (known as a hygiene unit), and that it might therefore offer at least a temporary refuge. And a refuge, if only temporary, he desperately needed. Just before he put his coin in the slot, he noticed a small plaque attached to the door at eye level: *SuperCleen. 'Caring for public hygiene'.* And just above it was another plaque, in powder blue: *This facility is brought to you by BOMZIZUS, the caring defence contractor.*

For some minutes, he simply stood in the white, curved, antiseptic interior, waiting for his overloaded senses to recover. When he felt a little calmer, he returned to the pavement and recrossed the road.

And it began again: cars and pillar boxes and shouting and plate glass and a dog barking and two men in raincoats, and . . . Turning his back on it all in despair, he looked into a shop window. Bad move. Bad bad move, for this was a window full of Mobile Phone. Dormatt hated mobile phones. They had been everywhere for almost as long as he could remember, but he had never himself touched one, never even seriously looked at one. But he had seen people using them. He had seen people cupping a palm to their ear and talking apparently to themselves. Now he saw the offending objects in all their sleek, miniaturised awfulness. They were horrible.

Many of the kids who used them had never known a world without them, and research had established that most people bought a new one every six months or so. Television commercials were as boring to Dormatt as they were fascinating to his Wife, but he now recalled one which had, nonetheless, made an impact. A bunch of yobs were laughing, not at the possessor of an out-of-date mobile, but at the phone itself. He had been struck by the deviousness of the advertisers: without alienating potential customers by directly suggesting that they themselves might be ridiculed for possessing an old mobile, they had managed nonetheless to convey the message that it was shameful to be seen with one.

Did they have to be so tiny? Were they not, in fact, inconveniently small? It was as if the manufacturers were engaged in some kind of competition – which, come to think of it, they probably were – to make the smallest phone possible, regardless of ease of use. And presumably the people who bought them valued miniaturism just as much as the advertisers doubtless told them to.

Dormatt went in. At least his mind had started working again, which meant distraction from the terrifying sensory overload. There were tiny mobile phones everywhere, all secured in place against those who might think of stealing them. Dormatt had not known there could be so many in the world. A horrible thought came to him. He would have to have one himself. Now that Grabbitall was about to take full control, he would give all his staff mobile phones, Dormatt just knew he would. He picked one up, and looked at it with fastidious distaste. He never had wanted one, he never would want one. Never would he feel the need to inform people that he was on a train or that they were breaking up.

'Can I help you?'

White teeth flashed at him. He had ventured too close to the water's edge, and a crocodile – female, young and sharp – had grabbed him. He was about to be dragged in and under, spun round and round till he blacked out and drowned. And then the croc would take him to its lair, and devour him at leisure.

He wrenched himself free. 'No thanks, just looking,' and fled back from the water's edge and out of the shop. The crocodile retreated disappointed below the surface again, waiting for the next careless wildebeest.

As soon as he was outside, the cars and the people and the lamp posts and the shop windows blazed and growled and rattled and hissed once more at his beleaguered senses, and he couldn't take it. A few yards further on, he ducked into another shop. It was one of those strange hybrids, caught somewhere between a small supermarket and a large corner shop, and which in less politically correct times would have been called the local Paki. The shopkeeper eyed him warily from behind the protection of his counter.

Everybody wanted Dormatt's money. Why had he never noticed before? It was as if he had lived in a vipers' nest all his life without even noticing the snakes. The crocodile – or viper, as you preferred – in the mobile phone shop had wanted to lighten him of hundreds of pounds. The Paki, or whatever he was, might be prepared to settle for the price of a Mars bar . . . Dormatt wondered if he shouldn't oblige him. Some chocolate might give him a boost. The rhythm of chewing might be good for him. There were Mars bars, there were Milky Ways, there were Crunchies and Aeros and Maltesers – the chocolates with the less fattening centres – there were Smarties and there were Treets and . . . and . . . and things he had never heard of before. Too many, too many, too many . . .

He looked away in despair, and his eye was taken by the newspaper shelves.

Predator: First killing today?
Poser for SEXITEL
Letz down and out
Torch school head gives ground

He picked up a copy of the *Morning Filth*, and flicked idly through it. Bare-breasted girls, bare-bottomed girls, garish headlines. And advertisements. Page after page after page. There were adverts for telephone sex lines ('Let me strip for you alone!'), there were promises to enlarge his penis ('How she'll gasp!'), there was a 'once in a lifetime' chance to acquire the Eternal Beloved Diamond Ring ('a breathtaking brilliant encircled by sumptuous rubies'). But far outnumbering all other types of advertisement, there were pages and pages of ads for unsecured loans. Everybody wanted to lend him money, and nobody cared whether or not he had any security to offer.

As he replaced the newspaper, he turned aside and saw jars: jars of coffee and jars of powdered milk and jars of peanut butter and jars of jam and jars of marmalade . . . There were tins, too: tins of peas and tins of beans and tins of condensed milk and tins of peaches and . . . and then he noticed something really strange. He noticed oranges which were being sold in their own individual blister packs.

Curiosity calmed him down, and he went over to look more closely at one. It claimed in fact not to be an orange at all but to be a 'citrus snack'. Citrus snack? Citrus snack?? Through the corner of his eye he could see a box of less pretentious oranges altogether – oranges that made no claim to be anything other than oranges. They had exactly the same look as the citrus snacks; they had the unmistakable look of oranges that would resist to the last any attempt to part their skins from their more edible parts. Aside from the extraordinary packaging of the citrus snacks, the only discernible difference between them and the oranges was that they were exactly twice the price.

Ah, but a closer look revealed that the citrus snacks came with a 'free hand wipe'. Just as Grabbitall had said. Dormatt had had enough. Pursued by a look still warier than before from the man behind the counter, he walked out again.

And the whole dreadful world was waiting to grab him, and he knew already that it would never now let him go. There seemed to be a sale on at almost every shop. 'EVERYTHING MUST GO', 'EVERYTHING AT HALF PRICE', 'CRAZY REDUCTIONS!', 'MASSIVE SAVINGS'. Did people really believe this kind of thing? In the window of a gift shop selling ionising lamps ('Can you afford to be without one?') was a large poster proclaiming 'CHRISTMAS IS HERE'. Dormatt checked the date on his watch. It was the twenty-ninth of September.

The very existence of this world had previously been concealed from him by the curtain of his own thoughts and attitudes. His Wife knew it intimately, and her knowledge of its overwhelming power had so unhinged her that she could no longer communicate with him. It was Dan Grabbitall who had contemptuously ripped the curtain aside and shown him what lay behind it, because Dan Grabbitall could look Medusa in the eye without turning to stone. But Dormatt had been happier looking at his curtain.

Dormatt's Wife. Her constant badgering of him to get more and bigger and better of everything had made home life very difficult. Now for the first time he could begin to feel, if not exactly sympathy, then a measure at least of understanding. If you let this awful world get to you at all, it would destroy you. Unless you were Dan Grabbitall.

He saw something extraordinary on the other side of the road, and crossed to have a closer look. It was a gym. *Fit for Anything*, it was called, and behind a huge plate-glass front of the sort normally associated with car showrooms, people could be seen working out on various pieces of equipment. There were bicycles that went nowhere and boats that went nowhere, there were skiing machines and running machines and walking machines and . . . It was the plate glass that Dormatt couldn't fathom. That people did such humiliating things he knew, but could they really want to be seen doing them? Evidently they could.

Dormatt walked on, shaking his head. It was all too much. Even if he didn't really understand it, he was at least beginning to see the world for what it was. What he did understand was that it was a world which had no place for him. His Wife, being crazy, fitted in without difficulty; Grabbitall was one of the very rare people who could bend it to his will. But there was no place in such a world for Clement Dormatt. There never could be. Fixing his gaze on the pavement in front of him, he trudged on.

He was surprised a few minutes later to find that he was already at Hammersmith Bridge, surprised to find that it was getting dark. He had been walking for longer than he thought. A chill wind blew little eddies of leaves about his feet.

Half way across the bridge, he stopped. He was at last going to read the old brass plaque past which he had walked a thousand times. Long ago, in an age when bicycles moved and telephones didn't, someone had done something notable on Hammersmith Bridge, and Dormatt wanted to know what it was. He read of the night in December 1919 when RAF Lieutenant Charles Campbell Wood of Bloemfontein had dived into the river to rescue a woman. She had lived, he had died. It was clear enough what had happened. The wretched woman hadn't fallen, not from the middle of Hammersmith Bridge. She'd jumped. She had wanted to die, he had wanted to live. Sod's law.

If he could, he would have gone back through time to that night, and warned Charles Campbell Wood not to bother. 'Don't do it! You want to live and she wants to die. It's all as it should be. Don't try to change anything.' Dormatt leaned over the rail, and stared at the black water swirling around the piers of the bridge below him.

Fifteen

Letzgetcha Nickersoff tossed a skein of blonde hair out of her eyes. 'I don't like the way you talk to me.'

Dan Grabbitall yawned. 'Fine. Off you go to your old agent. Of course, your income won't ever reach the heights I can take it to, but at least you'll have an agent who will treat your majesty with proper respect.'

Letz appeared to be controlling herself with difficulty. 'I want you to promise to be more polite to me in future.'

'No. I'm not going to be told how to behave by a little tart like you. If that's your attitude, you can fuck off.' Dan opened a drawer, took out a file and began to read.

'Bastard!'

'If you stay with me, you accept the way I do things. You already know the difference I can make to your earnings. But if you're more interested in the way people speak to you than in what you earn, then you can fuck off.'

Letzgetcha Nickersoff looked close to tears. 'Look, you're doing a very good job for me, and I still want you as my agent. I just want you to be a little more polite, that's all.'

Dan closed the file. 'Fine. I take notice of the fact that you want me to be more polite. Now let's get back down to business. You were wearing shorts last time out.'

Letz looked back at him, eyes flashing. 'So?'

'So you never wear shorts again.'

'It's my business what I wear on court.'

'Oh no it fucking isn't. Not as long as I'm your agent. As long as I'm your agent, what you wear on court – and off it, come to that – is my business. And I'm telling you that you never never wear shorts again.'

Letz banged her fist down on the table in front of her. 'You can't tell me that. I choose what to wear.'

Dan went on as if she had not even spoken. 'And it's not only shorts that you're done with. I don't want to see you wearing those bizarre long tight pants under your skirts either. Tell me something, Letz. Do you know why men watch women's tennis?'

Letz gritted her teeth and looked fixedly at the ceiling.

'Well, I'll tell you. They watch it for the panties – knickers as they call them this side of the Atlantic. And it's more true for you than for any other player on the circuit. You're going to have to make your money from sex-appeal, Letz, because you're never going to set the world on fire with your tennis.'

Letz had had enough. 'Oh yes, I am! Oh yes, I am! I've been in the world's top ten, and . . .'

'And that was nearly two years ago. You're never going to get back there because you're just not hungry enough. Or maybe because you're too hungry. How'd you get to be so fat?'

Letz banged the table again. 'I am not fat! Don't you dare say I'm fat!'

Dan Grabbitall was not fazed. Dan Grabbitall was never fazed. 'You look fat from where I'm sitting. Okay, I grant you, you may not be obese for the average female of your height, but for a tennis player, you're definitely carrying too much weight. You're not even in the world's top fifty now, and if you're going to rely on prize money for your income, you're in trouble. You've got expensive tastes, Letz, and with the money you can make from tennis, you're not even going to be able to keep yourself in sticky buns. Which might be a good thing, of course, as regards the weight problem.'

'Stop saying that! I am not fat! I . . . I was out with an injury for two months. You know that. Of course I put on a little weight.'

'You've been back five weeks.'

Letzgetcha pouted beautifully.

'Listen, what I'm saying is that you can make a living from tennis, but not the sort of living you want. For that you're going to have to take full advantage of your looks.'

'I already do,' said Letzgetcha. 'I see that I always look good.'

'You look all right,' said Dan, 'but not sexy enough. Like I said, you wear the wrong knickers.'

'How dare you!' cried Letzgetcha, whose English sometimes sounded a trifle old-fashioned.

Dan Grabbitall leaned forward threateningly. 'Listen, Letz, and listen carefully. If you want to make all your money from tennis, that's fine by me, but get yourself another agent. Doesn't matter who, because any fool can make you ten times what your tennis brings in. I can double or triple that, but if you want to stay on my books, you have to listen to me.'

'I'm the one who earns the money. People like you are just . . . just like little animals that live on big animals. You're a flea.'

'The word you're looking for is parasite. You're saying I'm a parasite. Well, I don't care. Why the fuck *should* I care? You're welcome to think I beat up grandmothers, and eat babies for breakfast. I don't care. All that matters to me is that you do as I say. That's because I know how to maximise your earnings potential, and you don't. I don't do it to make money for *you*, I do it to make money for *me*. If that makes me a parasite, that's fine by me. But remember that in serving my own interests I also serve yours. I only do well if you do well, that's how it works. If you think you can do better without me, that's fine. Off you go. Concentrate on your tennis. Lose a bit of weight and you might even get good again.'

'You bastard! I told you I am not fat!'

'No, honey,' said Dan sweetly, 'and neither is a tub of lard. Now listen, if you stick with me, you're going to get very seriously rich, but you're going to have to do as I say. And if you won't do as I say, then you can fuck off. If you want to be rich, you will play directly to a gallery full of dirty old men. You fucking well imagine them in dirty raincoats and with their hands somewhere inside them, and you'll get the idea. Alternatively, you can try to make a living from your prize money. But your income will nose-dive, and you won't last long.

'I was talking about what you're going to wear on court. No more shorts, no more long tight pants. Ever. From now on, you'll wear dresses and skirts that go up when you serve, and up in the wind. And under them, this is the sort of thing you'll wear.' Dan opened a drawer, and took from it a pair of plain white pants, short and tight, which he laid on the table in front of her. 'That's the colour, that's the style. Don't ever let me see you in anything else.'

'You are disgusting.' Letz took the pants and stuffed them into a pocket. 'Now have you finished?'

'Not quite. Tell me something. Are you a lezzie?'

'A what?' She looked genuinely puzzled.

'You heard. A lezzie. Oh Christ, I keep forgetting. You always sound so fucking American that I always forget that you're really a fucking foreigner. A lezzie is a lesbian – a gay woman. Prefers women to men. Well?'

Letzgetcha Nickersoff looked down at the table. 'No.'

'Hmm. You saw Cass McRaker's column in the *Screamer* on Sunday, didn't you? She said pretty clearly that you're gay, and in my experience that bitch usually gets her facts right. Sad but true. And she's crossed me once too often for her own good. Now for all I care, you can fuck kangaroos and elephants, but I have to know so that I can ensure it won't affect your earning power. Once again then, are you gay?'

Letzgetcha Nickersoff pouted. 'It's not your business.'

Dan sighed. 'I thought so . . . Look at me, Letz, because I want you to understand me. I don't give a fuck about your sexuality. As far as I'm concerned, you can stick your fat little tongue up any cunt that . . .'

Letz slammed the table yet again. 'I am not fat! Stop saying I'm fat!'

'Don't bang the desk like that, Letz. You might hurt your hand, and then where would you be? Just listen. This doesn't have to be a big deal. A male sex symbol has to be exclusively hetero, but a female can work okay as bisexual. But you've got to be careful. Don't you ever go around flaunting your sexuality, and don't you ever ever tell anybody that you couldn't get interested in men. Got that?'

Letzgetcha Nickersoff was sulking. 'Yes,' she said, like a child being forced to promise to behave better in future.

'Now here's what really matters. You know Viraga Hateman?'

Letz nodded.

'Well, bear in mind that the world is full of aggressive, self-righteous lesbians like her, and they'd just love to have you onside. You're their wet dream in just about every way possible. They'd just love to have you say publicly how much you hate men and how much you love women. If they had their way, you'd make

100

yourself as ugly as possible, and play tennis in a suit of armour just so's no man could ever see you. You ever line up with them, and you're finished with me . . . Well?'

Letz shrugged ill-naturedly. 'I wouldn't do that anyway,' she said angrily, not even deigning to look at her agent.

Sixteen

Above Rab McGeddon's desk was a large portrait of a man whose face seemed hewn out of granite. The resemblance to the real man sitting beneath was unmistakable, but the hair was thicker and darker, the jaw more firmly set, and there were no pockmarks. Among the more literate of his employees, the portrait was known as Ozymandias.

'One last thing.' Rab McGeddon's face was hard and cold. 'I come from the mean streets of Glasgow, and I learned at a young age that when the going gets tough, the tough get going. It was nose to the grindstone, shoulder to the wheel the whole time. And feet on the ground. If you can't stand the heat, get out of the kitchen. Think about it.'

His young employee, unsure apparently as to whether he should be looking at the man or his portrait, stood trembling in front of him. 'Thank you, Mr McGeddon.'

'The pleasure's mine. Out.'

Rab McGeddon turned to look at his computer screen, which displayed the website of the *Shocker*. 'Search: McGeddon. Hits: None' He tried *The Times*, then the *Filth*, then the *Screamer*, all with the same negative result.

He picked up the phone from the console on his desk. 'Jane? Have you managed to get Clive Sneersly yet? . . . Bastards. And you told them I could talk about the arms trade, I could talk about kidnapping, *Predator*, anything Sneersly wanted? . . . Well, that does it. And I'm not giving Cyril Smarm another chance. I gave him a good interview, I'm offering him another for nothing, and he turns it down. Bastard. Right, get me SEXITEL, they'll just have to do. Tell them who it is, and say I need to speak to someone in authority. I won't be fobbed off with some little bimbo of a receptionist. I'll stay on the line.' He drummed his fingers impatiently on his desk as he waited for a reply.

'Hello? Yes, this is Rab McGeddon, executive chairman of BOMZIZUS, sponsors of *Predator*. Who am I speaking to? . . . All right, you'll have to do. Now I've been following the show closely, and I'd say it's going well enough. But I believe viewing figures could be higher yet, if you were prepared to have a bit of plain speaking from the common man. You see, what's wrong at the moment is that you have all these fancy psychologists and behaviour experts and so on, and they're all trying to explain . . . Well, change your plans, then. I guarantee you that if you just did a straightforward interview before each episode, with a plain man from the mean streets of Glasgow, that would get people's attention. Now . . . Yes, I think it's going well, too. I just think it could go better yet . . . I see. Well I only hope you know what you're doing, that's all I can say. But I can make you one more offer. When we get our winner, I am prepared to fly out to the island to congratulate him in person . . . Look, did you get who I am? Well, people don't talk to me like that. If you . . . Hello? . . . Hello? . . .' Rab McGeddon snarled, and replaced the receiver.

For some moments, he sat in silence, then picked it up again. 'Jane. Get me Conservative Central Office. Now. I'll stay on the line.'

Rab McGeddon kept the phone to his ear, scowling. 'Hello? Conservative Central Office? Right, this is Rab McGeddon of BOMZIZUS. Now I'm prepared to do you a big favour. I'm prepared to be a candidate for a safe seat at the next election. I . . . Don't give me that. I wasn't born yesterday. Constituency parties do what they're told if Central Office twists their arm hard enough . . . Now look, I'm a natural Conservative. Always have been, always will be. I'm the sort of man you need . . . That's enough. Put me through to your boss will you? Anybody with a bit of authority . . . No, I will not ring back . . . I see. Well, I think I can safely say you'll regret this. Goodbye.'

With a snarl, he pressed a button on the console in front of him, keeping the phone to his ear. 'Jane. Get me New Labour. Quick.'

Again, he waited, mouth downturned in a determined scowl. 'Hello? Is that New Labour? This is Rab McGeddon of BOMZIZUS, and I've got a proposal to put to you. I'm offering

103

you a big-name candidate for the next election. A safe seat, it would have to be. Now . . . What do you mean who? I mean me, Rab McGeddon. Who did you think it would be? . . . Look, I wasn't born yesterday. If you want to tell a constituency party who their candidate's to be, you can do it. Just twist their arm enough . . . Well, I can assure you I'd have plenty to offer. I'm natural New Labour, a self-made man from the mean streets of Glasgow . . . Right, forget it. Just put me through to someone with a bit of authority . . . Is that so? Well, I think I can safely say that you'll regret this.' Rab McGeddon snarled again and pressed the same button on the console.

'Jane, get me the Lib Dems. Get . . . No, forget it. Socialist bastards.' He banged the phone down and sat back, brooding. Half a minute later, he picked it up again.

'Jane. What's the name of that American publisher and PR man. Represents Letzgetcha Nickersoff. Dan Garbit or something . . . That's him. Get him for me. I've had enough of this.'

This time he had to wait somewhat longer. 'Hello? I wanted to speak to Dan Grabbitall . . . Tell him it's Rab McGeddon, and if he'll speak to me now, then he has every chance of a highly lucrative contract. If not, I'll go elsewhere . . . Right . . . Hello? Dan Grabbitall? This is Rab McGeddon of BOMZIZUS . . .'

Seventeen

'. . . but now over to Clive Sneersly and *Spotlight*.'

Clive Sneersly was wearing his most serious and responsible expression. He was also wearing an unusually sober tie. 'Good evening. Sticking to our unique policy that there are subjects of interest in the world other than *Predator*,' [he curled his lip] 'tonight we are going to discuss a matter which presently affects one London school in particular, but which has implications for many others up and down the land. Where the curriculum followed in British schools conflicts in some way with the beliefs of an ethnic minority, which should take precedence?

'If you have, by some strange mischance, taken an interest in anything other than *Predator* of late, then you will have guessed that I'm referring to the School of the Torch of Learning in west London, formerly Bogsworth Community School. The controversy is essentially between Western liberalism and Islamic orthodoxy, the former being represented by new headmaster Marshall Mallow, and the latter by Youssuf Al-Majnooni, firebrand imam of Bogsworth's Farootkaik Mosque. Marshall Mallow' [clean-shaven, smart casual dress, self-deprecating smile] 'has said that the two of them should get together to discuss the matter, and is sure that some accommodation can be reached. Youssuf Al-Majnooni' [black-bearded, white-robed, grim-featured] 'seems much less confident, but we have at least managed to arrange the meeting suggested by Mr Mallow, because, as you can see, I have them both here in the *Spotlight* studio. But before we hear from them, Justin Poser brings us this report – his last for the BBC before he leaves to join SEXITEL incidentally – from the scene of the controversy.'

Justin Poser's white suit set off the most tremendous sun-tan. He was standing in front of a large, square and ugly 1960s building surrounded by a considerable area of asphalt. It could only have been a school.

'Two months ago, this building in west London's Bogsworth was little known outside its own area – though even then it was notorious locally.' [Justin Poser looked at once censorious and sympathetic.] 'Today it is something of a national scandal. Until very recently known it was known as Bogsworth Community School, and its headmaster was Will Struglor. The school's many problems so wore him down that he suffered a breakdown, culminating four weeks ago in a suicide attempt which very nearly succeeded. He will never fully recover. Will Struglor, whom I have visited in hospital, is a decent man of whom, quite simply, too much was asked.

'But life goes on, and his successor is giving the school something of an image makeover. Amongst other innovations, Marshall Mallow has renamed it the School of the Torch of Learning. Things have not all gone smoothly, as the state of the new school sign just over there might tell you. It was defaced in protest against another of Mr Mallow's new ideas, namely his decision to style himself Staff–Parent Interface Coordinator, or SPIC for short. Mr Mallow, it seems, was unaware that spic is an insulting term for a Latin American. Following an angry demonstration by some of those who felt insulted, he has apologised profusely and reverted to the old title.

'No one, least of all Marsh Mallow, denies that the school has had its problems. Cassandra McRaker highlighted some of these on *Spotlight* a month ago. Inspectors' reports have been poor, examination results place it in the bottom five per cent of schools in England and Wales, and high rates of truancy are endemic. Not long ago, the government would have designated it a failing school, and would have taken emergency measures to bring it up to scratch, with the threat of closure if these did not work. But such things seem not to be happening any more, and the suspicion is that so many schools are now failing that the Government dare not draw attention to the situation by making a serious attempt to tackle it.

'One problem is simply money: the school doesn't have enough, as you'll see from the state of it when we have a look inside. Marsh Mallow says he is addressing this issue as a matter of urgency, and already has ideas on how to raise cash. A few weeks hence, for example, there is to be a school fête, during which, amongst other entertainments, the head will stand for fifteen minutes in the stocks while pupils and others pelt him with wet sponges and other harmless – he hopes – missiles. He is keen to make the point that he would do almost anything to turn the school round.

'But while there may be ways of addressing the cash shortage and even improving academic performance, the Torch School now has another problem entirely, and an especially awkward one. It has a high percentage of Asian pupils, many of whom are Muslims, and a long-standing controversy over how they should be educated has recently come to a head. The two most intractable issues are religious education, and girls' sports.

'Youssuf Al-Majnooni, imam of the Farootkaik Mosque, the minaret of which you can just see behind the school, has said that only Islam should be taught to Muslim pupils. They should not be introduced to any other religion until they have a thorough grounding and unquestioning belief in Islam. This issue has come to a head of late over the teaching of the Crusades in some History classes. Marsh Mallow has tackled the issue head-on by removing the Crusades from the syllabus, but the Islamists say that they will not be satisfied until Muslim pupils are protected fully from what they regard as false religions.

'As for less academic parts of the curriculum, Youssuf Al-Majnooni says that it is entirely unacceptable for Islamic girls to take part in sport where they can be seen by men. The school's playing fields are, as you can see if you look over there, in full public view, and there girls take part in sports for which they are dressed in what the Western world considers to be an appropriate manner. According to Youssuf Al-Majnooni and his supporters, girls of secondary school age should not expose in public any part of their body except for the face and the hands.

'Feelings run very high, and police have advised Marsh Mallow that he should take seriously a number of death threats he has received, two of them advising him to concede the demands of Youssuf Al-Majnooni if he wishes to live. The imam, while categorically denying any responsibility for these threats, has pointedly refused to condemn their anonymous authors.

'Leaving all this aside for the moment, let's go in and have a look round . . .'

Several minutes later, Justin Poser was back outside. His expression had darkened still further. 'As ever, it is the innocent who are paying the highest price. The pupils of the Torch School have done nothing to deserve this, but it is their education that is suffering. What is our country coming to when children are used as pawns in deadly adult games? I have been deeply impressed by the courage of some of the children I have met here, and humbled by their determination, despite everything, to get the education they deserve. If we let them down, it is surely our whole society which, ultimately, will be the loser. This is Justin Poser at the School of the Torch of Learning, Bogsworth, west London.'

Clive Sneersly looked grim. 'Justin Poser, whose final BBC report that was. We wish him well in his new career with SEXITEL. Now to help me get to the bottom of this extraordinary business, I have with me in the studio both Youssuf Al-Majnooni and Marshall Mallow, this being the first time they have come face to face. We'll see if it might be possible to find common ground between them, and then, after Mr Mallow has to depart to honour a prior engagement, I'll have a few more questions to put to the imam.

'Youssuf Al-Majnooni, if I might begin with you, and deal first with the issue of girls' sports, Marsh Mallow says that he fully respects your views, but that girls have as much right to enjoy sport as boys. Is that not a reasonable point?'

Youssuf Al-Majnooni's bearded face gave nothing away. 'It is right that girls should be fit and strong. Otherwise, how could they bear children? But it is wrong for them to take part in sports in the view of men. The Holy Koran is very clear on the matter of women's dress. They may not flaunt their bodies in the way that they now do at the School of the Torch of Learning.'

'And presumably, at all other schools in the land. I take it that you would like to see an end to the playing of sports by Muslim girls wherever men can see them.'

'Of course, but the Torch School is in my area, and I consider it to be a test case.'

'Marsh Mallow, if an activity which goes on in your school is an affront to the beliefs of any group represented within the school, is it not right that you should give way and excuse from participation those who object?'

Atop his yellow jersey and open-necked shirt, the face of Marsh Mallow smiled carefully. 'First of all, let me thank you for having me on the programme. Since my appointment just a couple of weeks ago, I have looked forward to the chance to discuss this matter with Youssuf directly, and I'm grateful to the BBC for bringing us together. Of course it is not our intention to offend anyone, and it is surely possible to reach some sort of compromise. Islam is a truly great religion, and the Prophet Mohammed was one of the greatest moral teachers the world has ever seen. In the Koran, he tells us . . .'

Youssuf Al-Majnooni looked angry. 'Stop! The Prophet Mohammed, peace be upon him, did not write the Holy Koran. The Holy Koran was revealed to him through the Archangel Jibreel, and he recited it to others who wrote it down. The Prophet himself could not write. This is a very important matter to all Muslims.'

'Yes, I see. Well er . . . at least we can agree that the Prophet Mohammed was a very great man. I was saying that Islam is a great religion, and I myself would agree with most of its moral code. But of course, there are other great religions, too, and we must learn to coexist peacefully in a multicultural society. Christianity is a great religion, as is Judaism, and both are very close to Islam. And then there is Hinduism and also Buddhism, which are also very great religions. Now I am quite sure that Youssuf, like me, would fight to the death in their defence if . . .'

'There is only one true religion. Of course I would not fight for a false religion. Jews and Christians understand something of the truth, but Hindus and Buddhists live in total darkness. Their religions are idolatrous, and are an affront to God.'

Marsh Mallow cleared his throat and looked down. 'Well, er, I mean to say only that in my position, I have to respect all the religions represented in my school. And the pupils include Christians, Jews, Muslims, Hindus and Buddhists. There may even, for example, be Zoroastrians. Certainly there are also atheists and agnostics. I cannot, as I'm sure Youssuf understands, discriminate against any of these. I . . .'

'Already you discriminate against Muslims. You allow girls to play sports in public. You teach religious studies, and say that all religions are equal. They are not. Islam is the only true religion. When British . . .'

Clive Sneersly held up an admonishing hand. 'I really don't think that this is getting us anywhere. Let's just accept that Youssuf Al-Majnooni does not wish to see Muslim pupils made to take part in activities which, he says, conflict with their religious beliefs. Marsh Mallow, are you prepared to let Muslim girls off playing sport? Yes or no?'

Marsh Mallow cleared his throat again. 'It really isn't quite that simple. You see, some Muslim families are quite happy to have their daughters take part in sports. Others can make their feelings known, and we will do our best to accommodate them. It should be possible, for example, to arrange exercises for them in the gymnasium where they will not be seen by men.'

Youssuf Al-Majnooni shook his head grimly. 'This is not true. The gymnasium has large windows, and male teachers and male pupils can easily see girls taking part in exercise. It is not permissible for men to see women with their bodies uncovered. If we look at the way that men regard the tennis player Letzgetcha Nickersoff, we see why God forbids women to dress in this way in public.'

Clive Sneersly looked pained. 'So what is Marsh Mallow supposed to do? He's made clear that he would be prepared to seek a compromise. What is your position? Is any compromise possible?'

Youssuf Al-Majnooni shook his head. 'How can there be compromise with the will of God? We know the will of God because it is expressed in the Holy Koran. Those who read the Koran and reject its message will go to Hell. Nothing can save them. When this man' [Youssuf Al-Majnooni nodded contemptuously in the direction of Marsh Mallow] 'says that he is ready to compromise, he is denying the will of God.'

'No, no,' said Marsh Mallow with emphasis, 'I believe that we should simply respect each other's beliefs, or there will only ever be conflict. No one cares more about the education of our young people than General Pius Oldgit of the Salvation Army, and he speaks tirelessly of his admiration for Islam. Believe me, I will do everything in my power to address Youssuf's concerns, but I cannot simply cave in on every point. That wouldn't be compromise, that would be surrender. I have already attempted to show my goodwill by instructing the head of the History department, Boris Fartleby, to remove the Crusades from the syllabus. But I repeat, I cannot give in on every point.'

'Youssuf Al-Majnooni, are you not at least grateful to Marsh Mallow for his concession in this matter?'

Youssuf Al-Majnooni made no effort to hide his contempt. 'It is a very small detail. In the West, everyone seems to believe that religion is something in which there should be a free choice. But all Muslims know that there is only one true religion, and it is the will of God that all should follow it. That religion is Islam. All others are in error.'

Marsh Mallow shook his head despairingly. 'Well, yes, of course, I'm well aware of the strength of belief that . . .'

'Well,' said Clive Sneersly, with an air of finality several awkward minutes later, 'I don't think we're going to sort this one out here in the studio, so let me thank Marsh Mallow, who now has to leave us for another engagement, and move on to discuss some other matters with my other guest. Youssuf Al-Majnooni, if your past is nothing to be ashamed of, why do you always make such a mystery of it? Why not tell us all where you come from and what you did in your life before you came to prominence with the Farootkaik Mosque?'

'There is no mystery. I avoid talking about myself because I want to bring people close to God, not close to me. I have British nationality, but where I come from is of no importance. I am a Muslim. That is what matters.'

'Some say you were born in this country. Some say your accent shows traces of American or perhaps Irish. You admit that you are not a native Arabic speaker. Some say you may be Pakistani or Iranian.'

'It is of no importance.'

'Is it true that you fought against the Americans in Afghanistan and in Iraq? That your limp is a result of injuries received in those conflicts?'

'Jihad is a sacred duty for all Muslims, but I will not discuss my own Jihad with unbelievers.'

'So you'll tell me nothing about your background?'

'It is of no importance.'

Clive Sneersly gave a shrug of resignation. 'Very well, I'll move on. There are those who say that I shouldn't even be interviewing you, that I should not give you a platform. Can you understand their concerns?'

Youssuf Al-Majnooni smiled coldly. 'This country claims to live by the rule of law, and I have broken no law.'

'Well, let's look at some of the things you have said. You've said that this country is an enemy of God, and you've said that men who have died while committing acts of terrorism here are martyrs. Deal with those two points if you would.'

The smile on the face of Youssuf Al-Majnooni resembled, like that of Sir Robert Peel, the brass plate on a coffin. 'I have not said that this country is an enemy of God. I have said . . .'

'Well, excuse me, but I have your exact words here.' Clive Sneersly held aloft a thin sheaf of papers. 'In July this year on a visit to Birmingham, you said, and I quote "Great Britain, like the United States, is an enemy of God."'

Youssuf Al-Majnooni sighed. 'I am often quoted out of context. If you look at the context, you can see that what I meant was that the actions of the present government are against the laws of God. Muslims are persecuted . . .'

'Oh come on! Take yourself as an example. You are being given absolute freedom to speak your mind on national television. Other countries think we're crazy to allow you your freedom, let alone a public platform from which to speak. How can you say that the British government persecutes Muslims?'

'Because it is true. Muslims are discriminated against in the workplace, and the government takes no steps to prevent this. The call to prayer from the mosques is forbidden because it might disturb people. Muslim communities have been forbidden to set up Islamic schools.'

Clive Sneersly looked thoughtful. 'In Saudi Arabia, the very profession of any religion other than Islam is banned. Do you support such a policy?'

'I am not a Saudi. I do not live there.'

'No, but you are entitled to an opinion on the matter. You condemn the British government, for, you say, discriminating against Islam. Do you condemn the Saudi régime for discriminating against Christianity?'

The cold smile had left the face of Youssuf Al-Majnooni; the coffin lacked even a brass plate. 'The Holy Koran teaches us that

Islam is the one true religion. Perhaps the Saudi government does not wish to give succour to blasphemy.'

Clive Sneersly looked incredulous. 'I thought the Prophet Mohammed said that Christians, if they would not convert to Islam, should be free to practise their own religion. But let me move on, because there are other things we need to discuss. It is well known that the police have investigated your mosque several times, believing that you have given shelter to terrorists. Is this the case?'

'It is true that the police have questioned me, but they have never charged me with any crime, and they have never arrested anyone staying in the Farootkaik Mosque. They . . .'

'Forgive me for interrupting, but British police have said that they believe that a young man staying at your mosque was responsible for the failed attack on one of the factories of the arms manufacturer BOMZIZUS. He is now, they believe, sheltering in some Islamic country which is unlikely to extradite him.'

'We know that this factory was making weapons which were used against Muslims in different parts of the world. I would not myself attack it, but I can understand why others would. As for the accusation against the man who was a guest in the Farootkaik Mosque at the time, where is the evidence? I have heard this allegation, but I have seen no proof. If you . . .'

'But – excuse me again for interrupting – it is the case, is it not, that your mosque gives shelter to any Muslim who is in need of it?'

'Of course. Such hospitality is required by God of all Muslims.'

'And Muslims staying in your mosque have in fact been arrested by police – outside the mosque, of course, at the time of arrest – and found to be living illegally in this country.'

Youssuf Al-Majnooni smiled again. 'If a fellow-Muslim is in need of shelter, I do not ask him for documentation. I welcome him under my roof. This is the law of God.'

'But it isn't true, is it, to say that no one staying in the Farootkaik Mosque has ever been arrested?'

'No one has ever been arrested in the Farootkaik Mosque, and no one staying in the Farootkaik Mosque has ever been arrested for any serious crime.'

'Let me move on to the recent spate of kidnappings. No fewer than four wealthy British businessmen have been kidnapped in London of late, and a substantial ransom was paid to secure release in each case. The last of these was BOMZIZUS boss Rab McGeddon, who said just the other day that he would be prepared to meet you publicly to put to you his belief that you were deeply involved. Is it true that the Metropolitan Police have interviewed you on the matter?'

Youssuf Al-Majnooni face gave nothing away. 'The Metropolitan Police appear to believe that I am very knowledgeable about all crimes committed in London.'

'Do you know anything about these kidnappings?'

'Of course not.'

'But you are not exactly a man of peace, are you? You have not, for example, condemned those who have threatened the life of Marsh Mallow. Do you in fact condone those threats?'

'Of course not. But it is in his power to end them. He knows what he must do.'

Eighteen

It was his first day with SEXITEL, and Justin Poser looked graver than he ever had with the BBC. People remarked on it the following day. They said that the moment he began his report, they knew that this was serious. The fact that it was the lead item indicated nothing, because relatively trivial matters often made the headlines on SEXITEL. This time, though, everybody said that they knew as soon as Justin Poser's face appeared on the screen that this was serious. Sober-suited and black-tied, he was standing in the middle of a street of red-brick terraced houses.

'I have been reporting on current affairs for a decade now, but I think I can honestly say that this is the toughest assignment I have ever had. I'm not in a war zone, and there has been no natural disaster. This is just a quiet street in an English provincial town, but I still don't really want to be here.' Justin Poser paused, and pursed his lips for a moment. 'I can reveal, exclusively on SEXITEL, that *Predator* has claimed its first victim. We all knew it was going to happen, of course, and yet still, somehow, it comes as a shock.

'It's less than a week since I was in the Indian Ocean, just a few miles from Predator Island. I have to admit that somehow, I couldn't take it quite seriously. I knew, of course, that people were going to die on that island, and yet it didn't seem quite real. It was just such a beautiful place, full of such beautiful people. I knew that nothing sad, nothing tragic, could ever happen there. Now it has.

'Sharon Wonnaby is dead. The girl who has become known as the face of *Predator* was killed earlier today. If you want to know exactly how she died, and who it was who killed her, then I'm afraid you're going to have to wait for the regular helping of *Predator* at midnight GMT. But the one thing we cannot do – it would be quite unimaginably cruel – is to keep Sharon's father in ignorance of her death until he sees the programme. Can you imagine watching your daughter being killed on television without any warning that it was about to happen?

'Someone, then, has the awful task of telling Fred Wonnaby – Australian, of course, like his daughter, but resident in this country for several years now – that his daughter, his brave and beautiful 23-year-old daughter, is no more. Someone has to break the news to Fred Wonnaby, and that someone is me. Rab McGeddon of *Predator* sponsors BOMZIZUS himself volunteered to shoulder this heavy task, but we refused to take advantage of his generosity. I can tell you that I'm so glad I have you all with me, because I honestly couldn't do this on my own. Well, here goes . . .'

Taking a very visible and very audible deep breath, Justin Poser turned and walked ten paces or so down the street, then stopped in front of a somewhat shabby green door. He looked straight at the camera for a moment, squared his shoulders and set his jaw, then turned and rang the bell. He waited.

'It's all right,' he said, turning to whisper conspiratorially in the direction of the camera, 'we're quite sure that he's at home, and not having a bath or er . . . or what have you. We've been watching the hous. We . . . Ah!'

The door opened, and a middle-aged man appeared, chewing something. He was short and fat, dressed in a grubby white vest, his bald pate framed by a broken white halo of thinning hair. Brushing some crumbs from his chin, he looked at Justin Poser in evident puzzlement, then beyond him at the camera.

' . . . er, what can I do for you? Don't I know you? Aren't you . . .'
He trailed off, a look of dread suffusing his features.

'Fred? Fred Wonnaby? I'm Justin Poser from SEXITEL, the *Predator* channel. Fred, believe me, I wish so much that I didn't have to do this. I want to . . . er, trousers, Fred. Trousers? We're live on television.'

Fred looked down. 'Oh. Sorry,' he said, and pulled up his zip.

'I want to break this to you as gently as I can, Fred. Can you . . . Can you guess why I'm here?'

Fred Wonnaby began slowly to shake his head. 'No,' he said, 'No, it can't be. It can't be Sharon . . . It isn't, is it?'

Justin Poser looked down and shook his head despairingly. 'Believe me, Fred, I wish so much that it wasn't. But you know,

Fred, don't you? You already know why I'm here. You've guessed, haven't you? I'm here because SEXITEL couldn't possibly let you watch the programme tonight – midnight GMT – without warning you of what you're going to see.'

Fred's jaw was now hanging open, his head still wagging slowly from side to side. 'Oh no,' he said in a voice that was barely audible. 'Oh no, no, no. It can't be. It must be a mistake. Phone somebody. It's got to be a mistake.'

'Fred, I am so desperately sorry, but there's no mistake. Sharon died today.'

'Oh, God, no. Oh Please God, no. This can't be happening. Oh God, no, she was all I had . . . she was all I had . . .' He tried to say more, but broke into helpless inarticulate sobs.

Justin Poser put a manly hand of comfort on his shoulder. 'I know that, Fred. I know that your beloved wife Mary died last year, and this must be even worse. Tell us . . . if you can . . . Tell us, Fred, why your lovely daughter chose to risk her life on *Predator*. It's a story the world doesn't yet know. Tell the world – in your own words – just what a hero she was.'

Fred Wonnaby turned his tortured face to the sky, took a huge breath, and brought himself under some sort of control. 'She . . . You . . . you see I lost all my money to a con man in Australia just five years ago, and Sharon, she . . . she said she was going to win a million dollars, and give . . . and give it all to me . . . And she just wanted to be famous like everybody else, and she deserved it, because she was brilliant. She was . . . she was a child progeny, that's what she was, a child progeny, but . . . Oh God, God, God!'

Justin Poser turned to the camera, his face illuminated by the glow of Sharon Wonnaby's reflected heroism. 'Yes, it's true. This is what Sharon Wonnaby told us. She knew the risks, but she wanted so much to help her father, and she wanted so much to be famous. She knew the risks, but she was ready for anything, and now it has all ended in tragedy.'

He turned again to the grieving father. 'Fred, try to be brave. Try to be as brave as your daughter. She . . .'

'But how . . . how did she die? Tell me. I have to know. I just have to know.'

'Oh Fred, you know I can't do that. If you want to know how your darling daughter died, then you'll just have to watch

117

SEXITEL at twelve midnight GMT, for an hour of thrilling action from Predator Island, including the death of the beautiful and heroic Sharon Wonnaby. Who killed her? Was it the dangerous American, Paul Nekred? Could it have been Englishman Basil Wrigley, who made passionate love to her only yesterday? Tune in at exactly midnight GMT to find out.'

'Oh, why can't you tell me? Why?'

'Believe me, Fred, I am so sorry, but you know I can't do that. Fred, we agonised over this at SEXITEL, and I'm only here because we decided we couldn't let you watch tonight's programme without knowing what was going to happen. But that's all I can tell you. Now try to be as brave as your daughter was. Try to make her proud of you, wherever she is. Because make no mistake about it, Fred, she's up there looking down on you now. And she wants to see you play the man, as you always have done. Make her proud of you, Fred, and tell us some more. Tell us what you said to her when she told you that she wanted to be on *Predator*?'

'I said, Sharon, I said, I've never stood in your way before, girl, and I won't . . . I won't stand in your way now. Because when Sharon was set on something, she . . . she always went through with it. Oh why did she have to do it? Why why why?'

'And what was the last thing she said to you? Before she went, as we now know, to her tragic and untimely death on Predator Island.'

Fred Wonnaby again controlled himself with difficulty. 'She said, Dad, she said, I'm going to be famous, and you're going to be rich, I promise you. Don't worry about me. I'm a Wonnaby, and I know how to handle myself. And then . . . And then . . .'

'It's all right, Fred, it's all right. In your own time.'

'And then she just said 'Goodbye Dad. See you soon. And she . . . she kissed me, and . . . and then she was gone. Oh God, God, God . . .'

'But Fred, Fred, you can be so proud of her. Just look what she achieved. Your own golden girl wanted so much to be famous, and today Sharon Wonnaby is the most famous person in the world. Her picture's going to be everywhere, Fred, even more than it is already, and everybody's going to be talking about her.'

'WAAH! WAAH!'

With a final comforting hand on Fred's shoulder, Justin Poser, tight-lipped, turned to look straight at the camera. 'Well, as you can see, Fred Wonnaby really isn't in a condition to say anything more, but he's done very well, and I just know Sharon would be proud of him. Now SEXITEL has exclusive rights to film the funerals of all unsuccessful *Predator* competitors, and the first of these will be the funeral of Sharon Wonnaby. We'll be there in the church with Fred and other grieving friends and relatives, we'll be there at the graveside, as Sharon Wonnaby's body is committed to the earth, we . . . Or is she to be cremated? Fred . . . No, I really don't think Fred is in any condition to tell us at the moment. But if it's to be a cremation, rest assured that you will see Sharon's coffin as it slips out of sight of the mourners to be consumed by the flames. You'll miss nothing if you watch SEXITEL. We'll give you the details just as soon as we have them.

'Don't forget, tune in at twelve midnight GMT, if you want to see the death of Sharon Wonnaby, and all the other action from Predator Island. And I can now tell you that, in the case of other unsuccessful competitors, we won't in fact be repeating the experience you've just witnessed. That is, we won't in future be warning families when they are about to witness the death of their loved ones. It will be just as much of a shock to them as to everybody else, but we've arranged to be there with them to witness their reaction. Yes, for the next death, we'll have nine different camera crews in nine different homes around the world so that you'll miss nothing of the drama, the agony and the ecstasy of *Predator*. Keep watching, and you will see it all on SEXITEL.

'But now from me, Justin Poser, and the broken-hearted Fred Wonnaby, it's back to the studio.'

Nineteen

(From the *Sunday Screamer*)

Us & Them: Cassandra McRaker tells it like it really is!

Secrets and lies: Cassandra McRaker

On sale within a month will be the autobiography I said I'd never write. It's time, then, for me to honour my pledge of a month ago, and tell you why I have changed my mind.

First of all though, why did I ever say I would never write about my own life? Well, I have always thought, at least secretly, that autobiographies are monstrous exercises in self-advertisement, and never to be trusted. But in truth, as I am now prepared to acknowledge, I had another and much deeper reason. There is something in my own life that I never wanted anyone to know. I kept it hidden because I found it so shaming – and those who fail to understand this will be those who have forgotten just how easily children load themselves with guilt.

Why have I changed my mind? Well, with the passage of time doing nothing to heal the wound, I began to write about the Thing privately, with no intention of ever going public. This helped, but it was only when I decided to tell the story for publication that I began to feel that I really was exorcising the demon.

Whether or not I have succeeded in writing a good book is for others to decide. But where I have succeeded is in overcoming the trauma of what happened to me 26 years ago.

For the first time, then, here is the Thing which I was unable to mention for more than a quarter of a century:

MY FATHER LEFT US WHEN I WAS NINE YEARS OLD.

There. Said it. It was the most awful thing that ever happened to me. My father – there's no easy way to say this – was a con man, with no interest in other people except insofar as he could make use of them. If he contacted you, it could only mean that he wanted something.

With his charm, he was an excellent swindler. Women loved him, and he treated them like dirt, using them then casting them aside. Remember, though, that I was only nine when he walked out of my life. I was just too young to see through him. There is no truth whatever in the sentimental notion that children are great judges of character. I loved my father more than anyone I have ever known, and he betrayed me.

And would you believe it? Three years ago, he telephoned me in New York. He had seen my journalism, seen me interviewed on TV, and he wanted to congratulate me. I have never felt so confused. He told me how successful he had become, and how sorry he was about the way he had treated my mother and me. He wanted to meet me. He wanted to make it better. By the time I put the phone down, I was in tears.

As luck would have it, I had already arranged to be in London the following week, and we met in the foyer of the Savoy. I hadn't seen him for nearly a quarter of a century, but I knew him straight away – not by sight, of course, after all that time, but the magnetism was unmistakable.

You should have seen the smile that creased his face when he saw me. You should have seen the furtive wiping away of a tear as we began to speak. I have never been so happy. Never. We talked and talked. He seemed to know more about my work than I did. He could tell me what I thought about British schools, nuclear weapons, Islamic fundamentalism, the consumer society . . .

But no, I'm not a complete fool. I remembered it all. More than anything, I remembered the miserable November day that he left. I remembered so clearly my agony when I realised he was packing to go. I remembered my mother crying in their room. I remembered saying 'Daddy, please don't go. Please don't go . . . *Please don't go!*' And I remembered how cold he was. I remembered that he didn't say a single word to me as he walked out.

Now he explained everything. The money problems, the shame of impending bankruptcy, his absolute certainty that we would be better off without him. He told me that he had tried to kill himself. He said that he didn't want to tell me, but he wanted me to understand. He had me in tears.

He told me of how he had gradually pulled himself up by his bootstraps, how he had built a successful business, how he had wanted to contact me for years and years, but had been too ashamed to do so.

'And then I saw you being interviewed on TV, and I just had to see you again. I was actually crying, if you can believe it, to see what my own daughter had made of her life, to see just what a success she had become in spite of her father's failure. Cassie, you don't have to see me again, and I'll understand if you don't want to, but . . . but . . .'

He had to turn away, and so did I. My father, the man I loved most in all the world, had come back to me. And with him had returned in an instant a trust of human beings. Even a trust of men, who had frightened and repelled me ever since he had left. I told him that we would always be together now, and no one would ever part us. But I had to go off and do an interview – the truth was that I had fixed things so that, if it hadn't worked out with my father, at least I would have a perfect excuse to get away. We called for the bill.

My father took out his wallet. And just for a moment, I feared that he would shake his head in the way that I still remembered from my childhood, and say that damn it, he'd just forgotten to take any money with him. For a moment, my heart was in my mouth – sorry for the cliché, but it was. He shrugged his shoulders, smiled at the waitress. 'Sorry, no cash, but you'll take a bit of plastic, won't you?'

It was more than ten minutes before she returned, and I was already on my feet and about to leave. She was not alone. With her were two men, and my father went pale when he saw them. So did I. Why is it that policemen in plain clothes always look so much like plain-clothes policemen?

'We've got handcuffs here, McRaker, if we need them, but why cause embarrassment? We knew you had that credit card, and we were just waiting for you to use it. Hotels like this don't just take things on trust. I don't know, McRaker, I really don't. You've been out less than three months, and you're going straight back in.'

Three years have passed since then, but the memory seems to recede not one day, not one hour. It still hurts even to think about it, let alone write about it. But that is why I had to put it down. I had to exorcise the demons, or they would have been with me forever. I had to face the truth about my father.

In the years since he had walked out on us, he had lived in Australia and the US, and had served jail terms in both. A string of creditors had been left by his failed businesses, and some people had literally been ruined. At least one man committed suicide as a result. He explained it in the note he left for his wife.

After being released from prison in California, my father was deported to Britain, which he had not even visited in eighteen years, and he immediately took a false name, obtained false documentation, and set up a business selling a cure for cancer. He was at it for two years, and was beginning to become seriously wealthy, when the police finally caught up with him. There followed a three-year prison sentence, and then he decided to get to know his daughter again.

Why? Who cares. Undoubtedly he thought he would be able to touch me for cash, but I suspect there was more to it than that. My guess is that he thought that my reputation might be of use to him in his next phoney business venture, but who cares? I haven't even bothered trying to find out.

Anyway, this time he was given two years for fraud, a sentence he has now completed. Oh, he's written to me several times but I don't bother replying. I am in no way frightened of him. He has never (as far as I know) been physically violent, and even if he does try to meet me again, he'll have no chance. He is a seedy criminal, that's all, a con-man who has no connection with me save for the fact that he is my biological father

I'm not kidding myself. The scar is still there, and it always will be. But the writing of the book has cauterised it for me. I regret it bitterly. I find it unsightly. But it doesn't hurt any more.

So, wherever you are, you bastard, just listen for a moment. For once in your miserable life, stop talking and listen. I despise you and always will, but you are nothing to me now, because I have cut you out of my life. I won't pretend that I've forgiven you or that I feel sorry for you, because I haven't, and I don't. Forgiveness and pity are emotions which people affect when they can see no chance of revenge, of setting the record straight. But I've set the record straight with my book, which I hope you will read. You can't hurt me any more, you bastard, you can't hurt me any more.

Twenty

'Come in!'

Rab McGeddon strode in with his accustomed determination. Dan Grabbitall's office was moderate in size and severely functional, yet there was something about it that made an impact on visitors. They knew that this was the lair of a very big beast; they knew you would have to be very careful with the animal that lived in such a cage. They knew that this was a carnivore.

'Rab McGeddon.'

'Dan Grabbitall. Sit down, sit down. Are you happy with first-name terms?'

'Never been one to stand on ceremony, Dan. I come from the mean streets of Glasgow, and if you stood on ceremony there when I was growing up, you'd have got a skean dhu in the ribcage.'

'Fine. Well, I've thought about what you told me on the phone, and I've read your material. I think I've got the picture. I . . .'

'Now just before you go any further, Dan, I want you to be clear on just what it is that I'm looking for. Personal glory doesn't come into it. Couldn't care less. I'm just plain Rab McGeddon. Always have been, always will be. But it seems that to get on in today's world, you need a wee bit more of a public profile than I've got . . . I mean, than my company's got. That's what I want you to give me . . . us.'

'And you've come to the right man. First thing to say is that arms companies aren't exactly sexy. Fact is that the media is dominated by the liberals, the likes of Cass McRaker, and . . .'

Rab McGeddon growled menacingly.

'My sentiments precisely. The thing is that even the right wing people in the media don't like to support obviously unpopular causes, and arms making will never be popular in itself. That

125

means that we've got to do something special with BOMZIZUS. We're going to have to find a way of reinventing you and giving you the sort of image that you want. You . . .'

'Now don't get me wrong. It's not just popularity that I'm after. People can hate me if they like. I told you about my radio interview with Cyril Smarm after I was released from kidnap. Some of the callers were pretty unpleasant, but I can handle that kind of thing. I quite enjoyed the experience in a way, and I wouldn't mind doing a bit more like it. But only if it'll help my company.'

'You came across very well. I've heard a recording. But you see it was really only the kidnap that made you interesting to the media, and the interest was never going to last long. Businessmen in general aren't usually seen as very marketable, but I think we might be able to do something in your case. First of all, have you ever thought about politics? Always risky, and only for those that are committed, but might you be interested in standing for parliament? It would mean delegating a lot of your work with your company, of course.'

Rab McGeddon almost spat his contempt. 'I wouldn't take the safest seat in the country if you offered it to me on a plate. I'm a plain-speaking man, Dan, and politics just isn't for me. Like the men I grew up with in Govan, I say what I mean, and I mean what I say. You tell me, where would that get me in parliament?'

Dan Grabbitall held up both hands in a placatory gesture. 'Fine, we just needed to get that one out of the way. Just as well for me you're not interested in politics, as it happens, because then you'd have less need of me. But I do think that raising the profile of your company will be best done by raising your personal profile. I'd like to see your face in the newspapers, hear you on the radio, see you on TV.'

Rab looked doubtful. 'But how could you manage that? I mean, as you said, my kidnap made me, you know, famous for fifteen minutes, and that was it.'

Dan Grabbitall tapped the table with his index finger. 'It was a good start. For the time being, people still remember who you are. If you'll follow my advice, I think we could have you on, say, *Any Questions* within a year or so.'

Rab McGeddon did something he had not done for years. Rab McGeddon blushed. '*Any Questions*? Me? Oh no no. They'd never want someone like me on *Any Questions*. It's all the bleeding-heart liberals and socialist bastards – excuse my French – that they want. People like Cassandra McRaker and Pius Oldgit. You just have to listen to them. A bit of plain speaking from a plain man might be worth hearing, but they wouldn't want me. They . . .'

'They might. Do as I say, and I believe they will. Then you just need to follow a few simple rules to make sure you come across well. Don't sound pompous, always talk down to people but never let them know you're doing it, don't say *eigh* when you mean *a*, just a few things like that. You follow my advice, Rab, and the sky's the limit. How does a knighthood sound? Or . . .'

Rab McGeddon blushed still more. He squirmed in his chair. 'Oh, no, I just don't see it. Sir Rab McGeddon . . . Oh surely not. Sir Rab McGeddon . . . Och, it'd only be embarrassing. People would laugh.'

'Oh no they wouldn't. Now I know that you'd still be just straight-talking Rab McGeddon from the mean streets of Glasgow, but . . .'

'That's me. Always has been, always will be, knighthood or no knighthood. To quote my great countryman Burns, *The rank is but the guinea's stamp, The man's the gowd for a' that.*'

'But to others, you'll be Sir Robert McGeddon. Or Sir Rab McGeddon if you prefer. And even if a man like you isn't impressed by a knighthood, many are. And impressing people is what it's all about. With your charisma, you're always going to make an impact on people who work for you, and people who meet you. But what about the people who don't know you personally at all? That's what you've got to think about.'

Rab McGeddon laughed. 'All right, I'll be Sir Rab McGeddon of Govan! Sir Rab McGeddon of Govan . . . Well, you'll forgive me for not being that serious about it. But I'm still listening. What are you actually proposing to do?'

'Right. First thing is, you have to cultivate the right image. You get people who'll do anything just to be famous. They make fools of themselves on TV, they pose in daft attitudes for the paparazzi, and so on. Nobody ever takes them seriously. That's fine if it suits them, but that's not for you.'

'It certainly is not. But I just don't see how you could sell a straight-talking businessman from the mean streets of Glasgow to the sort of people that run the media today. Bastards.'

'There's always a way. Here's a little secret. If you're going to make it in PR, Rab, the most useful thing you can do is to look at the superstars of history – before the likes of me got round to creating them – and look for the secret of their success. Take . . . take anybody. Take Wagner. What was the secret of Wagner's success? Rodgers and Hammerstein meet Cecil B. de Mille, that's all. What about Emily Brontë? Mills and Boon with rabies. Now you might say that Wagner and Emily Bronte had genius, but the point is that there's always something dead simple behind a superstar's image. Understand that, and you're half way to being able to create stardom even if you can't create genius.

'Back to your case, then. We're going to have to sell you as a man of substance. Now you've got the right manner and the right look and the right voice, so we don't need to work on that. But people need to know things about you that will impress them. For instance, that you only need five hours sleep a night. You . . .'

Rab looked doubtful. 'But I need eight hours a night.'

'So does just about everybody, which is why they'll be impressed. What you've got to think about is image, and you can safely make any claim that nobody's going to be able to disprove. If you think that sounds cynical, the fact is that that's how the game is played today. Everybody else is at it, and you might as well level the playing field.'

Rab McGeddon pursed his lips, and nodded slowly. 'Well, I don't altogether like it, but if you put it like that . . . Yes, five hours sleep it is.'

'Good. But come to think of it, since Churchill started it all, nobody in the public eye ever admits to needing more than five hours a night now. So for you we'll say that four hours . . . no three hours is all you need. That should make them sit up.

'I might get somebody to have a look at your wardrobe, but that matters a lot less than many people think. What we're going to do is to take on the liberal establishment head on, and show them that an arms company isn't just a soft target for self-righteous prigs. We . . .'

'That's my kind of talk!'

'Up to now, very few people really know anything about BOMZIZUS. If they've heard the name at all, it's because you decided to sponsor *Predator*. Risky, but not a bad idea. Shows the right attitude. But have you ever done anything else to raise the profile of your company?'

Rab shifted awkwardly in his seat. This was something of a sore point with him. 'Well, not a lot, but er . . . one day a couple of years ago I was on my way to the office when I was caught short, and I er . . . just couldn't find a public toilet anywhere. Well, there was one, but it was closed because it had been vandalised. So I er . . . I put a bit of the company's money into public conveniences. Those wee cubicles made by SuperCleen, you know the ones. Our name's on the door of half a dozen of them around London, saying that we have sponsored them. Yes er . . .'

'Hmm . . . To be honest, Rab, I'd like your name off those doors just as fast as you can manage it. You don't really want your company to be associated with piss and shit, do you?'

'Er . . . no, not really. I'll see to it.'

'Good. You see, there's nothing wrong with sponsoring things, but you have to choose what to sponsor. *Predator* is risky, but still a risk worth taking, I'd say.'

Rab nodded vigorously.

'But it would be a good idea for you to lend your name to some obviously good cause, and *Predator* won't do for that. You also want something more enduring, something that will last long enough to raise your public profile properly.'

'Hospitals?'

'Maybe. Hospitals or schools. I'm still thinking about it. What we have to do first is give you and your company the right image. Now I'm going to suggest a new name and a few other things, but that's all cosmetic. PR people are always thinking that a new name and a new logo means an image makeover. Remember when the Royal Mail decided they would become Consignia? Years ago, it was. Well everybody pissed themselves laughing, and they ditched the new name as soon as they came to their senses. You see, the thing is, you've got to persuade people that there really is something completely new about you. And that demands something of substance. You need a flagship enterprise in your own line of business, and I've got just the one for you.'

Rab was enthralled. 'I like what I'm hearing.'

Dan Grabbitall looked grim. 'Well, see how you like this. Have you ever dealt with Durtapura?'

Rab McGeddon snorted his contempt. 'Not a chance. Bastards have a few old Russian weapons, and . . . Not that I'd want to deal with them anyway. Real bastards. Now don't get me wrong, Dan. Business is business, but I wouldn't do business with just anybody . . . unless . . . but why would they want my stuff anyway? They . . .'

'Ever heard of DUFF?'

'Just about. What is it? Durtapuran Union of Freedom Fighters? Biggest bunch of no-hopers on the planet. And they're all the opposition there is. That's why the government wouldn't want my stuff. They just don't need it. They . . .'

'DUFF need it.'

'*DUFF? DUFF??* They couldn't afford a claymore. The government controls the diamond mines, and that's all the wealth the country's got. I can't sell weapons to people with no money. Get real, Dan.'

'Who said sell? I want you to *give* arms to DUFF.'

Rab McGeddon's jaw fell open. Literally. 'Are you serious? *Give* weapons away?? Now you listen to me, Dan. I have never given anything away in my life. Never. And I never will . . . No, let me finish. It's not that I can't be generous, but in business, you never never give anything away. Just to look big, is that it? Well, forget it. Business and generosity don't go together. I knew a man once, ran a small company in Auchtersnochtie. Times were good, so he decided to start paying his workforce above the odds, and give them pay and conditions none of his competitors would match. Think his workers were grateful? Not a bit of it. To them, it just looked like weakness, and before he knew where he was, they were striking for more pay and better conditions. He went out of business, they lost their jobs. Generosity in business benefits no one. If this is your big idea, then we've nothing further to say.' To emphasise the point, he stood.

Dan Grabbitall was unfazed. 'I repeat, I want you to donate weapons to DUFF – free, gratis and for nothing. You . . .'

'URRGHRGH!'

'Nasty throat you've got there . . . Fine, go if you want to, but you're still going to be paying me a lot of money for the work I've already done, and you'll have got nothing out of it. It's up to you. Can't cost you anything to hear me out. Suit yourself.'

Rab McGeddon, who had begun walking towards the door, stopped. 'Go on, then, but don't waste my time. I'm a busy man. I come from the mean streets of Glasgow, and . . .'

'I know. You've already told me. Just listen. If you do as I say, then the little gesture I'm talking about – which you can certainly afford – will be no more than a loss leader. You said that the Corupcion régime has a few old Russian weapons, yes?'

'It's all they need.'

'Precisely. Because DUFF is a bows-and-arrows outfit. But you know what? They're very popular in the West – the only part of the world that really matters – because they sound like Western liberals. No doubt they'd turn into the biggest bastards you ever saw if they ever got power, but that's just the way it always is. Best of all, one of their leaders writes poetry that nobody understands, so everybody has to say it's brilliant. You give weapons to DUFF and you'll be a hero.'

'I'll be a fool. And that's exactly how my competitors will see me. No, I'm not interested.'

'I haven't finished. The government has a few old Russian weapons. And the Russians certainly aren't going to bother giving them any more, because there's nothing in it for them. It was Cold War politics, and that's ancient history now. You give good weapons to DUFF, pay for a bit of training and maybe a few mercenaries to stiffen them, and they'll be in power in no time.'

'Forget it.'

'Listen! They'll then have the diamond mines, and like all new revolutionary régimes, they'll want to upgrade the military. Who do you think they'll go to?'

Rab McGeddon began stroking his chin. 'Well . . . I see what you mean . . . Still sounds a bit risky.'

'Come back and sit down. I'm hurting my neck trying to look up at you. It's as safe as it can be. You can guarantee that neither Russia nor America nor anybody else will bother arming the government because they won't see the point. Of course, they may not want DUFF in power, but by the time they realise what's happening, it'll be too late.'

'Well, I see your point,' said Rab, as he resumed his seat. 'But it still sounds a bigger risk than I like to take. You can't actually guarantee that nobody will arm the government . . . although I can

131

see that if I move quickly enough and quietly enough . . . well . . . all right, I'll think about it. But I won't like it if it all goes pear-shaped. If DUFF comes apart before they've got power, for instance.'

Grabbitall shook his head dismissively. 'The Durtapuran government is just about the most ramshackle régime in the world. Provided you don't do things by half measures, DUFF will be in power in no time. They just won't have time to fall out with each other. The only real risk is that, for some reason, they won't then want more weapons from you. I can't give you any guarantees on that, but I'd be amazed if they wouldn't want to do you a favour. Anyway, the main thing is that you get plenty of great publicity out of it, because I'll see that you do. I . . .'

Rab McGeddon still did not look happy. 'But what sort of publicity? Publicity that says that Rab McGeddon's a soft touch? That's the last thing I need.'

Dan Grabbitall laughed coldly. 'You a soft touch? Who'd believe it? No, up to a point I can control the publicity you'll get. I know the owners of all UK national newspapers plus the big American ones, that's what counts. Forget the editors. They do what the owners tell them. Doesn't always work, but it helps. I also know a few journalists who owe me a favour, or want something kept quiet that I happen to know about. I . . .'

Rab McGeddon rubbed his palms together and grinned. 'That's my kind of talk!'

'So what it comes down to is this. You supply DUFF with enough weapons to guarantee they overthrow the Durtapuran government, and you're guaranteed big and favourable publicity. You should also make money out of it directly in the form of a substantial order from DUFF just as soon as they take power, but see that as a bonus.'

Rab McGeddon was nodding with some appearance of enthusiasm. 'You could be right,' he said thoughtfully, 'You could very well be right.'

'You see, the great thing is not just that you're supporting a resistance organisation lionised in the West, but you're doing something that no arms manufacturer in history has ever done – giving weapons away. That's bound to get you noticed. But there's more. We must . . .'

Rab McGeddon looked worried again. 'Now just a minute, Dan. Don't ask me to give anything else away. I might just take a chance on DUFF, but . . .'

'No no,' said Grabbitall impatiently, 'that's all I want you to give away. But you're also going to need a new image. Cosmetic change together with support for DUFF – plus sponsoring the hospital or school or whatever I come up with – will really get you noticed. As I've said, I want you to change the name of your company. You . . .'

Rab looked hurt. 'But it cost me a lot of money to get that name! I had a top PR firm working on it for weeks. They went out into the streets with questionnaires, they formed focus groups, they consulted and experimented. That name cost thousands.'

'Well, I'm going to give you your new name for nothing, so you should be quite happy. It's just part of the package. BOMZIZUS hasn't got the sort of street-cred you're going to need. All it means to people is bogs and the biggest TV sleazefest ever. I want you to change your name to your name, if you see what I mean. No gimmicks. Out with BOMZIZUS and in with R. McGeddon.'

Rab McGeddon nodded with grudging approval. 'R. McGeddon, R. McGeddon . . . You don't think it sounds a wee bit like attention-seeking, do you? Just using my own name for the company? R. McGeddon . . .'

'Not at all. If you want to get noticed, you've got to write your name up big. Nobody's going to think you're egotistical, provided only that you behave with conviction, as if being noticed is simply your right. People are only accused of attention-seeking if they're normally shy and self-effacing. Other people slap them down if ever they draw attention to themselves, however innocently. The poor bastards then just shut up and go back into their shell. Nobody ever accuses a major politician of attention-seeking, or a TV personality. Big people are immune from accusations of attention-seeking, little people take the rap every time.'

Rab McGeddon was nodding with sober emphasis. 'Dead right,' he said. 'Good, R. McGeddon it is. I'll redo all my signs and headed paper and so on. Register the name-change.'

'You'll need to do all that. But there's more to be changed than just the name. I've got you a new logo – also included in the whole package, of course. It . . .'

Rab looked disappointed. 'I really liked the old coat of arms thing,' he said. 'That's what it looks like, and I feel it gives people confidence. And the motto, *Bellum nec timendum nec provocandum* goes so well with it. "War is neither to be feared nor provoked." I feel that a coat of arms and a Latin motto give real confidence. I'd be sorry to change them.'

'Well, I'm afraid they both have to go. Now don't get me wrong. As with the weapons for DUFF, the decision is of course yours. But if you don't accept my advice, then my involvement is over. Certain things just aren't negotiable. So let me say right off that the motto has to go, too. Fact is, nobody knows Latin any more, so it might as well be in Martian. But back to the logo . . .' He opened a drawer, took from it a sheet of paper, A4 size, and laid it on the table.

It showed a silver shield in the middle of which stood a large bullet, dark and sinister, with a big yellow heart shining in the middle of its body.

Rab looked at it, a perplexed expression on his face.

'I haven't added the motto yet, but it'll be in English: *Bullets with hearts of gold.* Now I want you to register your new name, R. McGeddon, as soon as possible, but keep quiet about the logo and motto until I begin to get you all the publicity for the DUFF donation and the school or hospital or whatever it's going to be. Of course, you're going to have to get the signs ready, and the new notepaper and so on, but keep it low-key. Then when everybody's thinking, "Christ, imagine a weapons manufacturer who supports public services, and *gives* weapons to a cause he believes in," you reveal the logo and motto. It'll work, I promise.'

Twenty-one

(From the *New York Megatel*)

Paul is dead

The United States is in shock this evening over the death yesterday at four fifteen p.m. New York time of national hero Paul Nekred.

All America – and New York in particular – was gearing up to welcome home the *Predator* contestant, whom Americans confidently expected to dispatch British hopeful Basil 'Randy' Wrigley in what had been called the Knife Fight at the Last Chance Saloon. It is hard to convey the sheer numbness which descended on Times Square nearly five hours after the actual event, when the huge crowd, for whom several giant TV screens had been erected, saw the Brit leap from a tree to garrotte the unsuspecting Nekred.

At first there was only silence, then came the sounds of mourning as many wept openly. The fireworks never went off, the light show remained dark, New York was not, despite all the promises, deafened by the strains of *God Bless America*.

Now mourning has given way to suspicion and even anger. Many have drawn attention to the slowness of Paul's reaction to Wrigley's attack compared with his alertness in previous encounters. According to one former Marine colleague, who prefers to remain anonymous, 'That was not the real Paul Nekred. The real Paul Nekred wouldn't have had any trouble with that punk. Paul was doped in some way, and you can quote me on that.'

The White House was swift to react to rumours, which appeared on the Internet almost as soon as the news of Nekred's death was flashed round the world, that the American ambassador to London was to be withdrawn in protest. 'We have no grounds for suspecting foul play,' said the president, addressing the nation on television, 'and have no plans for any diplomatic action against London. If it should be proved that anything untoward did take place, then things might change. As of now, however, the United Kingdom remains, as it has been for so long, America's closest friend in Europe.'

(From the *New Delhi Bapu*)
Predator climax triggers riots in capital

At last it's all over. British contestant Basil 'Randy' Wrigley has won *Predator*, after leaping from a tree to strangle American Paul Nekred in the last act of a drama which has transfixed TV audiences worldwide for the past three weeks. Sadly, however, the occasion was marred by disgraceful scenes in the centre of Delhi.

The special two-hour edition of the programme ended at seven thirty yesterday morning, after which many young backpackers left their hotels in search of breakfast. Police say they are still unsure of what triggered the rioting, but local people claim that a gang of young Brits marched through Connaught Circus, shouting and singing, and looking for Americans to taunt. When they found a group of New Yorkers sitting quietly in a café, things quickly turned ugly.

A gang fight was soon in progress, and more young Brits and young Americans, initially attracted to the spot as spectators, became involved. A number of local people and others also joined in, taking one side or the other, until at the height of the disturbance, scores of people were brawling.

Bert Bovver, from the Isle of Dogs in east London, said 'We wasn't looking for trouble, but the Yanks was just unbelievable. I mean, they was saying that Baz cheated an' all, and I mean, you just can't let people say things like that, can you? So we taught them a lesson. I've never liked Americans, and I hate them now.'

But New Yorker Gary Bulligan saw things differently. 'We were just sitting quietly having breakfast when this bunch of Brits came along,' he said, as he dabbed a head wound with his handkerchief. 'They started abusing us, and when we said that Paul Nekred was doped, or he'd never have lost to a Brit, they just went berserk. But we gave as good as we got, and they won't be back for more.'

The rioting went on for over an hour before police were able to regain control of the area. A number of arrests were made, and the accused will appear in court in the near future.

(From the *Sydney Evening Digger*)

It's Bazza

'I never doubted it,' was the terse comment made by the British High Commissioner as he arrived at his office in Canberra this morning. He was replying to a reporter's question about his reaction to the triumph of Englishman Bazza (the Bastard) Wrigley in *Predator*.

It is less than three weeks since Anglo-Australian relations were severely strained by the manner in which Wrigley disposed of Melbourne's Sharon Wonnaby. Having tricked her into entering the killing zone, the Brit then stabbed her to death while making love to her. The possibility of a breakdown in relations between the two countries was averted when Sharon's father, British-based Fred Wonnaby, fought back tears to say that he thought that Wrigley had killed his daughter 'fair and square'.

On the streets of Sydney, reactions to Bazza's triumph were mixed. 'Did somebody say perfidious Albion?' asked one young intellectual, 'You can say that again. I can't believe that a Pom could have beaten both an Aussie and a Yank without some sharp practice somewhere along the way.' But there was also admiration for the British champion. 'Now that we've finally thrown off the monarchy,' said a young woman between gulps of beer, 'we can be objective about this, and say that that Pommie bastard is one tough son of a bitch.'

(From the *Morning Filth*)

Brave Bazza makes Britain great again

The spectacular victory of England's Bazza (the Bastard) Wrigley in SEXITEL's *Predator* has been greeted with jubilation up and down the land. Bazza's slaying of arrogant American Paul Nekred gave rise to a night of patriotic celebrations unparalleled in our history, though there was a mood of gloom over the border in Scotland.

London's Trafalgar Square, in the middle of which four huge TV screens were arranged in a giant cube, simply erupted at the moment of triumph. Joy was unconfined among the many thousands gathered there.

The fireworks display was the biggest in the capital since the millennium celebrations nearly a decade ago, and the patriotic fervour with which the crowd sang *Land of Hope and Glory* and *Rule Britannia* will live long in the memory. Hands covered swelling hearts, proud eyes brimmed with tears.

Rab McGeddon, executive chairman of BOMZIZUS, sponsors of the programme, proved to be one of the few Scots to react positively to Bazza's triumph, when he telephoned the *Filth* to give his opinion. 'I couldn't be a prouder man tonight,' he said, his voice cracking with emotion. 'I knew that in Bazza we had a great competitor, but he was up against very strong opposition. I think we can assume that God had a hand in Bazza's victory.'

This, however, was not the opinion of the thousands attending General Pius Oldgit's anti-*Predator* pray-in in Hyde Park, where Bazza's great victory was greeted with two minutes of silence. 'True Christians take no pleasure in the violent death of any human being,' said General Oldgit, 'and we mourn for all those who have died during this contest.'

Many TV and radio channels chose to interrupt their normal schedules in order to broadcast the Queen's reaction live. 'Basil's victory,' she said, 'has shown us that the country we so love can once again be great. God bless you all.'

Already there is mystery over the whereabouts of the winner, for Bazza has now disappeared from the scene of his triumph. Rumours abound, but the smart money says that he has been snapped up by publisher and superagent Dan Grabbitall, who is keeping him under wraps at a secret location, probably somewhere in the UK.

'This from Justin Poser.'

Justin Poser, in open-necked shirt and blue blazer, was in a house. To be specific, he was in a sitting room where he was, appropriately enough, sitting down. There with him were three other people: a middle-aged couple, and a young woman in her mid-twenties.

'Well, Cindy, this is a house you've seen before. SEXITEL has been here several times, as it has been in the homes of all *Predator* competitors, ready to catch the reactions of their nearest and dearest to the dramatic events on the island. Yes, we've come once more to the modest semi-detached in north London's Neasden where Basil Wrigley grew up, and I have here his parents Bill and Sarah, and his sister Jackie. Let's find out what they think of their hero.

'Bill, it must have been quite a moment for you when Bazza finally did it. Were you actually watching, or couldn't you bear to?'

Bill Wrigley coughed self-consciously. 'Well, Sarah and Jackie had their hands over their eyes, but I was watching, because I knew that Basil would have wanted me to. And er . . . yes . . .'

'Tell me, Sarah, if you weren't actually watching, what was the moment that you found out that your son had done it?'

Sarah shrieked with embarrassed laughter. 'Well, you see Justin, Bill just gave this great shout of "YES!" And then I opened my eyes and there he was on his feet with his arms in the air, and I just knew deep down. And then I looked at the screen, and there was Basil, with the American, Paul, lying at his feet, and I just knew . . . I mean, I just knew that . . . you know . . .'

'And Jackie, what about you? You must be very proud of your big brother.'

Jackie shook her head as if lost in an admiration which words could not express. 'Well, I mean obviously he's just fantastic, isn't he? I mean, obviously I just knew he was going to win, so that was obviously never going to be a problem, but . . . well you know . . .'

'But even so, Jackie, your father says you couldn't bear to watch the final moments.'

Jackie blushed. 'Oh, but I mean obviously I was just a bit nervous, I mean that's only natural, but I mean I just know Bazza and obviously I just knew he was going to win.'

'Sarah, I don't know if you were as confident as Jackie, but tell us, how did it feel to watch your only son, night after night for three full weeks, put his life on the line?'

'Well, I mean, it was just fantastic to see him on TV like that, but yeah, it was pretty difficult. I mean, what if he'd made some mistake and, you know, it had all gone wrong? So yeah, all right I got a bit nervous sometimes, but it's just so fantastic that it's over now, and er . . . yeah . . .'

'It must be a great relief. Bill, tell me something. Was that the real Bazza that we saw on our TV screens, or was it Bazza playing to the camera? I ask, because all sorts of people are saying, you know, nobody could be that fantastic.'

Bill Wrigley spread his arms in a gesture of total innocence. 'I can tell you that Bazza wouldn't know how to be anybody other than Bazza. That's just the way he is, and he wasn't acting for the cameras at all. I'm his father and I know him. That was the real Bazza.'

'Fantastic. And Jackie, back to you, because I think you can tell us about something that happened when you were just kids that shows us the kind of guy that your brother really is.'

'er . . .'

'The time you were nearly killed, and it was Bazza who saved you?'

'Oh yeah, right. Well I mean, obvously we were both just kids and we were just on the pavement one day, and there was this crash and obvously one of the cars came up onto the pavement, and I mean, obvously it was just, you know, going to hit me, and I just couldn't sort of do anything, and Bazza just reached out and grabbed me and pulled me away, and you know, obvously it was just fantastic.'

'Amazing. Or you wouldn't be here today.'

'No chance.'

'Bill, one last question. Everybody wants to know where your son is now, because he disappeared almost as soon as the show was over. Can you tell us?'

Bill Wrigley spread his arms again. 'I wish I knew. He's phoned us to say he loves us, but he's not saying where he is. Just that we're not to worry, and everything's going to be fine.'

'You honestly don't know.'

'I have no idea.'

'Some people are saying that Dan Grabbitall's signed him up, and has him hidden away somewhere.'

'Well, they know more than we do.'

Justin Poser smiled, nodded all round, and turned to the camera. 'So now you know. Basil Wrigley is just an ordinary guy from an ordinary family. But maybe I should say he's an ordinary British guy. He can't only kill, he can save lives, too, even at the risk of his own. He's now the most famous man in the world, and he shuns the media spotlight. What a guy. And now, back to the studio.'

141

Twenty-two

'Good of you to come.'

Cassandra McRaker raised her eyebrows. 'Not really. You said you had a story for me, and I don't turn down a fair chance.'

'Don't tell me. You thought I'd produce Randy Bastard, didn't you?'

'Who?'

'Randy Bastard. Previously known as Basil Wrigley. Didn't you read Viraga Hateman in the *Shocker* today? Some people have been calling him Randy Wrigley, and some have been calling him Bazza the Bastard, so Hateman suggested putting the two together, and calling him Randy Bastard. She was joking, of course, but I'm not. Randy Bastard is the name he'll have from now on. It's the name that will appear on the range of men's cosmetics everybody's going to buy. You thought this was about him, didn't you?'

Cass shrugged. 'You said you could guarantee I'd be interested in what you had to say, and you said it would be an exclusive. And it's an open secret that you've got him under wraps.'

'Well, Cass, I'm sorry to disappoint you, but this has nothing to do with the world's most famous man. Still, I haven't brought you here under false pretences. I promise you I'm going to interest you. You've said several times that I know nothing about books, correct?'

'True, isn't it?'

'False. I know everything about books. Everything. By which I mean, of course, everything that matters. You see, you fall into the same trap as everybody else. I tell people that I've never read a book, and they think this means I don't know about books. Thing is, if you really want to know about books, the last thing you need to do is read them. A glance here and there is enough.'

Cass McRaker yawned. 'So far, you're not interesting me at all, Mr Grabbitall.'

'I've been lucky enough to get a pre-publication copy of your autobiography, Cass, and . . .'

'But it's not even bound yet!'

'Oh, I can get hold of most things if I really put my mind to it. Well, you might be interested to know that I've read more of your book than of just about any other, I'd say.'

'I'm flattered.'

'You shouldn't be. I got hold of it to see if you'd said anything that might be useful to me. You see, over the past few years, New York and here, you've given me quite a bit of bother. You tell everybody what a bastard I am, you drag up the past, you libel my clients. You . . .'

'I never libel anyone. Too expensive. My facts are always right. I leave others to decide if they dare print them. Everything I've written about you has been true. It's also true that Letzgetcha Nickersoff is gay. I'm sorry if the truth inconveniences you.'

'No, you're sorry if it doesn't, and so far you've done me no real damage. But I still regard you as potentially dangerous. And this time you *should* be flattered.'

'I am. But if you can't tell me anything more interesting than that, then I'm afraid I'll have to go.'

'Fair enough. How interesting is this? I can tell you who Ernest Deeler is.'

Cass was unimpressed. 'Your shady business partner in Oz? Of course you can. Why should I be especially interested?'

'Well, you said that you'd been unable to identify him, which means you must have made some kind of effort. So I thought you might be interested just a bit.'

'Mr Grabbitall, you're beginning to bore me.'

'Ernest Deeler's real name is Con McRaker . . . Still bored.'

At the mention of her father's name, Cass went pale and looked down at the table.

'You know, I'd almost forgotten about Ernest Deeler until you mentioned him in that article you wrote. Good thing you did, as it's turned out, so in spite of all the nasty things you said about me in that piece, I'm quite grateful to you. Knowledge is power, Cass, and I decided I'd better get some real knowledge about Ernest

Deeler before anyone else did. There's not a lot there for stirrers like you, but that guy was so slippery that I could easily have seen him making things up about me, provided that some hack offered him enough money. So I got a private detective in Oz to follow the trail. Well, imagine my surprise when I found out that his real name was McRaker, and yes, he was Cassandra's very own daddy . . . You're not saying much.'

Cass McRaker was not, in fact, saying anything. She was still looking down, and her face was white – as were her knuckles as she gripped the arms of her chair.

'Now you could have been all right, Cass, if you'd just agreed to let me publish your book. That way, I'm sure things could have worked out between us, and I'd have been happy to print just about anything you wanted to write. But you blew it, Cass, you blew it. Still with me? Hello?'

'I'm listening,' said Cass, just audibly.

'Well, after you promised never to write an autobiography, it might have seemed a tad hypocritical to go ahead and do it anyway, but the story about your father lets you off the hook, doesn't it? You admit to all the world that you've lied about him all your life, and now you've decided to set the record straight. What's it called? Disarming candour? You were trying to make sure that nobody could attack you, weren't you? Nice try, but it hasn't worked.'

Cass looked up at last. Her colour had not returned. 'Why don't you get to the point?'

'Oh Cass, don't be so impatient. Can't you see I'm enjoying myself? I could keep you here all night, couldn't I? You couldn't walk out of this office now if your life depended on it. You have to hear me out.'

Cass looked down again in silence.

'All right, Cassie, so here's what it's all about. I knew your daddy pretty well, even if I didn't know exactly who he was, and I'd say your description of him's spot on. No conscience at all that man, not a trace. Plenty of ambition, though, and a lot of energy. His Achilles heel, of course, was always overconfidence. So often the case with con men: they find it so easy to take people in that they just can't believe they'll ever be caught. And even when they are, they just know they can beat the rap. Fair assessment, would you say?'

But Cass was saying nothing.

'No comment? Never mind, I'll go on. I could tell you all about Ernest Deeler . . . sorry, Con McRaker, isn't it? I could tell you everything about Con McRaker that anyone could wish to know, and a lot that no one would wish to know. What I've got to go on is your account, my own first-hand experience of the man, legal records in three countries, and what my gumshoe found out about him in Oz. Oh, but Cass, Cass, you didn't tell the whole story, did you? . . . Did you?'

Cass McRaker was staring fixedly ahead. A casual observer might have guessed that this was a woman about to be hanged, drawn and quartered.

'You say you've exorcised the ghost of your godawful childhood, but you haven't, Cass, have you? You say your father can't hurt you any more, but he'll hurt you forever, won't he, Cass? Nice try, in its way, putting it all down to the way he walked out on the family, but you really didn't tell the whole story, did you? It would have been something if you had. God, I wouldn't have talked about the sort of thing that you went through. I'd have shut the fuck up about it for the rest of my life.'

All the pride gone now, Cass McRaker's tortured face looked at him, pleading.

'You know what they say, Cass. You may have finished with the past, but the past hasn't finished with you. And it's true, isn't it? I've got you, Cass, I've got you. First, I know your terrible secret, and second, I know you're a fucking hypocrite for pretending to have told it when you haven't. What'll happen when I spill the beans, Cass? People will say, Christ, here's a woman desperate to tell the world how honest she is and she just can't hack it. When it comes down to it, she can't face the truth. Not that she has any trouble dishing the dirt on other people. But that won't even be the worst of it, will it, Cass? The worst of it will be that people know. That people know what happened to you. You couldn't stand that, could you, Cass?'

'Please,' whispered Cass. Tears were running down her face.

'All right, Cass, I'll come to the point. I knew your daddy very well a few years ago, and would you believe it, he was proud of what he did to you. Because, along with everything else, he's a fucking sadist, isn't he? Do you know, he's the only guy who's ever been able to shock me. Well, nearly. Oh Cass, Cass, why did you say there was no physical abuse? How do you put it in your book? "At least he wasn't a violent man, at least I wasn't hurt physically." Well, it's true he wasn't in the habit of beating the shit out of you, but sexual abuse is physical, isn't it? The doctor even got suspicious once, but old Con, he could take anybody in, and he got away with it. He . . .'

'Please stop. Please . . .'

'For a year before he walked out he fucked you whenever he felt like it. Which was often, wasn't it, Cass? Christ, imagine boasting about a thing like that! "I used to fuck my own daughter." He only told me once, when we'd had a few drinks, and he never mentioned it again. I think he realised he'd said more than he should, but I doubt if he was all that bothered. He was talking about how fucking easy it is to take people in, how you can get people to praise you to the stars even when your hand's in their pocket taking every last penny they've got.

'Well, as an example of just how easily he could get what he wanted out of people, he told me about all the things he used to do to you, and how they just made you love him all the more. He told me about the scene when he walked out, and I have to say, your account squares pretty well with his, so I believe you both. Jesus Christ, Cass, what the fuck's wrong with you that you could love somebody who did all that to you?'

By now he was talking to the top of Cass McRaker's head. She was slumped across the table, sobbing bitterly.

'Funny thing, sex, isn't it, Cass? The theory is that a kid abused as you were must grow up to hate the abuser, but old Con conned you no bother, didn't he? He fucked you whenever he felt like it, and he made you love him for it. Yes, I know it all, Cass, and like I said, knowledge is power. Now you've written your last nasty article about me, and you're no longer interested in Letzgetcha Nickersoff's sexuality, are you? From now on, Cass, you won't ever attack me, or any client of mine, will you? Because if you do, the whole world is going to find out about the real shame of Cass McRaker. And you couldn't live with that, could you, Cass? Just think about it. I'll give you a few assignments from time to time, just a few things I want said that you'll say for me, all right? . . . I said, all right?'

Cass McRaker managed to raise her tear-stained, distorted face. 'No, you bastard, no!' Her head slumped again.

'Oh Cassie, don't be like that! I'll be doing you a favour. Tell you what, here's one you can have straight away. I know you thought you'd meet Randy Bastard here today, so here's your first assignment. Don't think of it as an order you'd rather not obey. Imagine that you're a dog, and I'm tossing you a bone. I'm going to build that guy up big, and you're going to get the first newspaper interview. How does that sound?'

Cass looked up again. She was still crying silently, but there was a pathetic gleam of hope in her tortured eyes.

'Except that you won't even have to meet him. I'll tell you exactly what to write, and you'll fucking write it. Got that?'

'No! *No no no!!*'

Dan Grabbitall sighed, stood up and went over to the door, which he locked. Then he walked back to the table, and stood behind his prey. She did not look round.

'Call me daddy, Cass.'

'No!'

'I'm your daddy. Call me daddy.'

'Please!'

'I'm no different from Con. I'm your daddy. This is daddy, Cass. Daddy's standing behind you.' He grabbed a handful of her hair, and she shrieked as he hauled her to her feet, kicked the chair away, and bent her over the table. He yanked her skirt up over her waist. 'This is daddy, Cass.'

Twenty-three

The concourse of King's Cross Station always was a bleak place at eleven o'clock on a cold Tuesday night. A few people waiting for late trains, a handful of drunks, a prostitute or two there for the warmth, and one or two runaway kids about to become prey to predatory paedophiles. Even a Salvation Army officer out on patrol, looking for souls to save. A bleak place.

It was the bleakest place Virginia Greenlove, now sitting on her suitcase with her back propped up against the wall, had ever known. Unable to tell her parents the truth, she had fled to London for no better reason than that she could think of nowhere else to flee to. She had never been there before, but she knew that it was where people went when they had nowhere else to go. She had been there more than an hour, since when she had drunk two cups of coffee, and established that she didn't even have the price of a room for the night. She was in despair.

'You don't look very happy.'

Virginia looked up, her eyes registering hope and fear in roughly equal measure. Looking down at her was the Salvation Army man. He was middle-aged and slight, with a kindly face.

Virginia knew little about the Salvation Army, but she strongly suspected that she was about to be offered a bed for the night. And she was frightened. The Church of Fire warned the faithful endlessly about the wickedness of the outside world, in particular the wickedness of its men. She had once listened with horror to the story of a young female member of about her own age who had accepted a lift from a policeman who had turned out not to be a policeman . . . She opened her mouth to reply, then closed it again.

'Don't worry, I'm quite harmless. Except to the Devil, that is. He and I have never got on. I'm Captain Pius Oldgit of the Salvation

Army, and I just thought that you looked a bit lost. Now we've just opened a hostel for girls like you who come to London and find it all a bit tough at first, and . . .'

'No. Thank you. I'm just waiting for someone.' Of course, it wasn't just the story about the bogus policeman. She had had her own awful experience with a man, an experience which she preferred not even to think about.

'I see. Well, I'll be around for half an hour or so, so if your friend doesn't turn up, you can always come with me.'

'Thank you.' Virginia looked down again. She was frightened, and she just wanted the man to go away.

He did, but not very far. She kept a surreptitious eye on him as he chatted to several other people, mostly women.

Time passed, until nearly half an hour was up. She was cold and she was hungry and she was desperately tired. He had glanced back at her several times, and she was just about ready to take a chance. What would she do if she didn't go with him? And what if he did turn out to be bogus? What hope was there in her life now anyway?

'Hello, love, you look a bit lost.' A huge woman in a colourful poncho loomed over her.

'What?' said Virginia, starting. 'No, I'm all right. Thank you.' She turned away.

But the woman stayed with her. 'Look love,' she said, 'you're not fooling me. You've got nowhere to go for the night, have you?'

'I'm all right. Really.' Virginia's voice was taut as a bowstring.

The woman looked in the direction of Captain Oldgit. 'Bet he's been over, hasn't he? Well, he's probably all right if you want uniforms and a lot of religion. I reckon you'd have a better time with me, though.'

Virginia looked up at the great moon face looking down. She opened her mouth, but no words came.

'Look, why not come and have a coffee with me anyway? Can't do any harm, can it?'

'But it's closed.'

'The one in the station is. But there's a place just across the road. Come on, I'm harmless. Promise. My name's Eartha.'

Permitting herself a nervous smile, Virginia picked up her one suitcase and let herself be led to a nearby cafeteria. She had had enough. She was ready to be taken care of.

'Well,' said Eartha some minutes later, carefully placing two cups of coffee on the table at which Virginia was already seated, 'a coffee won't do you any harm on a night like this anyway. Cold for April, isn't it?' She pulled out a chair and sat down. 'I really can give you a place for the night, you know. Free and no questions asked. I'm from a women's commune near here, and whenever we have a free bed, we always try to fill it. But of course, if you already have a place for the night . . .'

Virginia looked up at Eartha's kindly face, and she began to cry.

'What's your story, love? Come on, you'll feel better after you've told me.'

In the eyes of her parents and their staid friends and relations, Virginia Greenlove had been the prefect daughter. Didn't drink, didn't smoke, couldn't even hear the word 'drugs' without visibly shuddering. And crucially, every Sunday without fail she attended church. Virginia's church kept a very tight rein on its members, and to leave it was to be cast out forever. If you left the Church of Fire, your name was struck from the records, and was never mentioned again. And when you died, you went to hell. It was that bad.

From the point of view of her parents and their church, the best thing of all about Virginia was that she had never shown any interest at all in boys. This was exactly how it was supposed to be. The Church of Fire, which did not permit its members to marry outsiders, encouraged early marriage, and would generally try to find a spouse for any single girl over the age of 21, and for any single man over the age of 23. If the couple had chosen each other, they could marry only with their parents' permission.

But the Church had been founded in the eighteenth century, and social conditions were very different by the 1980s. The first big problem had been created as far back as 1870, when the introduction of compulsory schooling made it very difficult to shield young members from the wickedness of the outside world. But it was to the 1976 lifting of the ban on television that the stricter adherents dated the Church's decline. Now that boys and girls could watch TV, they began to crave all the things that the Church had always stood against.

Virginia's parents resisted acquiring a television until 1981, by which time Virginia was eighteen. The effect was immediate and distressing. Posters of boys – film stars and pop stars – began to appear on her walls, and her parents became seriously worried. But their pastor told them they were overreacting. Times really had changed: Virginia was a good girl, and she could be counted on to make the right marriage when the time came. Until then, a little freedom would do her no harm. The Church took a more relaxed attitude to such things than it had once done.

It seemed that he was right. Her mother had a long talk with her, and agreed that the posters could stay, provided that none of them was positively indecent, and that the room in general remained tidy.

It was several months later – by which time Virginia's posters, having covered all walls, were on the ceiling too – that it happened. One of her very few friends at college, where she was studying interior design, invited her to a party. At first, Virginia said no, but then she found that her parents were to be away that night: the Church had organised a trip to Scotland to meet members of the Edinburgh congregation, and they had decided to go. They had never left their daughter alone before, but their liberal pastor, unaware as they were of the party invitation, again advised them that their daughter could be trusted: 'Don't worry. She's a good girl, and she'll never leave the Church. Don't be concerned about leaving her alone for one night. Let her spread her wings a little if she wants to.'

Had he known that Virginia, on the night in question, would end up spreading not her wings but her legs, he would certainly have taken a very different line.

The reality of the party was a shock. Now almost nineteen years old, the only real social occasions which Virginia had previously known had been Church tea parties. A party with boys and girls and thunderous pop music and alcohol and marijuana and . . . Well, it was all totally new to her. And yet she knew from television that such a world existed; otherwise, she would probably have turned and fled within the first five minutes. As it was, she was frightened by the occasion, but also intrigued. She would be all right, surely, provided only that her parents never found out.

It was quite a party – or at least, it was to Virginia. Of course, she refused to drink anything except orange juice, and she was horrified when a girl with a far-away look in her eyes offered her a half-smoked cigarette. Some of the boys were quite good-looking, though, and she was disappointed that the only one to show any real interest in her was definitely not. His name was George Slobbe. But he was at least a boy, and Virginia found that, however much she asked God for help, she was still interested in boys.

'So what do you do, Ginny?'

'I'm at college. I study interior design.'

'That's really interesting, that is. Here, have another orange juice.'

'Oh, thanks. I don't know what it is, but I'm beginning to feel a bit funny.'

'That'll be the orange juice. Stronger than you think, ha ha ha. So your parents won't be back till tomorrow, that right?'

'Tomorrow afternoon . . . This juice tastes a bit funny . . . Why do your friends call you Spike?'

'Oh, just a nickname.'

The evening went on, and Virginia was still at the party after midnight. This was quite extraordinary. Even for a Church activity, some of which took place in the evening, she had never previously been out nearly so late. By this time, she really did feel strange, which was hardly surprising considering the amount of vodka she had unwittingly drunk, and she was hardly in a position to refuse George's offer to walk her home.

He had to work for his reward, because she almost had to be carried, but they made it. When they reached the door, it took Virginia several fumbling minutes before she could locate her key.

'Oh, just in time, love. Thought I might have to search you, there. Cold night for a strip search, too, ha ha ha . . . That's it, good girl. In we go.'

No sooner were they inside than he started kissing her. Hard.

'Gerroff!' she managed to say, but without much effect.

'Come on then Ginny, let's get you tucked in. Upstairs, is it?' He half-dragged, half-carried her.

'No, wait . . . George?' Virginia was as aware as her befuddled brain would allow, that this should not be happening.

'Yeah, that's me, but you can just call me Spike, ha ha ha.'

So saying, he had opened the door with her name on it, exclaimed 'Fuck me!' at all the posters, then had fucked her.

It was nearly midday before she woke up, alone and feeling worse than she had ever thought possible. When they got back an hour or so later, her parents seriously thought of calling the doctor, but she improved gradually, and they were reassured.

George was far from finished with her. Virginia couldn't get over it. She had had sex in the worst possible circumstances, and now she was addicted. She was forever saying no, but only for the sake of form. Even Virginia was not so naive that she didn't finally realise exactly what had happened that first night, but she forgave him. She would have forgiven George anything, for her fevered spirit, denied any sexual gratification at all for so long, turned George Slobbe into what absolutely no other woman could ever have thought him: God's gift.

Her infatuation ignored the rolls of blubber, took an airbrush to the mass of pimples, sweetened the truly appalling bad breath. George Slobbe had scored in a big way. They could only meet secretly, since Virginia did not dare tell her parents that she had a boyfriend outside the Church – far less that she went to bed with him – and she found it a strain to have to lie all the time. But George lived with his mother, who never cared what he did, provided only that it did not inconvenience her. They were in his room one evening when she gave him the nastiest shock of his life.

'George?'

'What?' George, who never liked being disturbed while he was eating, was enjoying his curry and chips.

'Got something to tell you.'

'What?'

'We're going to have a baby.'

'WHAT??' George Slobbe's huge mouth swung open. Half-chewed curry and chips stared brownly at her.

'I'm pregnant.'

'Oh fuck!!'

'George, please don't swear . . . And you know I don't like you to eat with your mouth open.'

'How do you expect me to get the food in, then?' George looked down, and began disconsolately shovelling more curry and more chips into the offending orifice.

'What are we going to do?'

George looked very unhappy. 'I don't fucking know, do I?' He chewed on.

'Do you think we should . . . you know . . .'

'No, I don't fucking know!' George was getting angry.

'Get married.' When she had found just two days previously that she was pregnant, Virginia had at first been devastated. But then she had decided that everything would be all right. She was already drifting from the Church, and she knew that George would look after her. In the end, her parents would have to accept what had happened . . . And anyway, she loved George so much that she would give up anything for him, even her family.

'*Get married??* Oh fuck.'

For the first time since their night together, Virginia began to wonder if George was really such a catch after all.

She was never to see him again. When she went round the next day, his mother (who regarded Virginia as a 'spoilt stuck-up lah-de-dah little bitch') informed her that George had abruptly decided to accept a long-standing invitation to go and work for an uncle in New Zealand. 'Didn't say when he'd come back. If ever. Always did have a mind of his own, did George.'

Virginia could scarcely believe it. Her first reaction was to crave him all the more. She was like a puppy, desperate to be loved by the owner who had kicked it. But it didn't last. One night, crying into her pillow at the awfulness of her plight, she swore for the first time in her life. 'You bastard,' she said softly between sobs, 'You bastard.'

Twenty-four

'Come in, sit down.'

Taken aback by the abruptness of the invitation – or rather, command – Boris Fartleby did as he was told.

It was several minutes before Dan Grabbitall closed the file he had been reading, and put it back on the shelf behind him. 'So you're Boris Fartleby?'

'Yes,' said Boris, who had been made most uneasy by the long silence.

'This manuscript,' [Dan picked up a large sheaf of papers from his desk] 'you sent it to Clement Dormatt.'

'That's right.'

'It's me you'll be dealing with. Dormatt's dead.'

'I'm sorry?'

'He's dead. Dormatt. His body – or what was left of it – was found in the river yesterday. Suicide, it seems. He disappeared a few weeks back. It was in the papers, but it wasn't big news.'

Boris Fartleby gulped. 'Well, I er . . . I didn't see it. God . . . Well, I'm sorry, really I am. He er . . .'

'He was weak. A fool. Couldn't take the real world.'

Boris Fartleby frowned. 'That's a bit heartless, isn't it?'

Dan shrugged. 'Is it? I don't care. The fact is that he was weak, and that's why he drowned himself. Now as it happens, Dormatt was hoping to publish your novel, but that was under the old régime, when Over & Dunwith was independent. I don't know if you've heard, but I took it over a couple of months ago. Over & Dunwith is now an imprint of Sledgehammer.'

'I heard something about it.'

'According to the late and unlamented Dormatt, your novel is brilliant. Despite which, I have no intention of publishing it.'

'What?'

'I don't publish novels by nobodies. Become famous, and I might think about it. But if you do, there's no point in sweating blood over your writing, because it's your name I'm selling, not your work. It'll get rave reviews anyway, because I can always count on good notices from people who owe me a favour, or more likely want something kept quiet that I know about. That's how it works.'

Boris frowned deeply.

'Call that cheating? Of course it's cheating. Life's about cheating. You show me somebody who doesn't cheat, and I'll show you a loser.'

'But . . . why am I here, then?'

'Let me tell you something. I may be in publishing, but I have never read a book in my life. Never. It's the great secret of success in this business. Get interested in books, and you've had it. You'll spend the rest of your fucking life publishing the sort of high-brow drivel that nobody ever wants to read.'

Boris Fartleby was beginning to feel seriously hostile. 'So?'

'So you stay poor and unsuccessful. Aeons back, the publishers of coffee-table books cottoned on to the great truth about publishing: *The sort of people who buy books aren't necessarily the sort of people who read them.* Did you know that? If you want to find readers, go to libraries, not fucking bookshops. Point I'm getting at is that I'm interested only in books that will sell. Now I've got a brain, and that means it'd be dangerous for me to read books, because I might then start thinking that your sort of stuff should be published.'

Boris Fartleby had had enough. 'Look, this is all very interesting, but you still haven't told me why I'm here. If Dormatt's dead and you won't publish me, why are you talking to me?'

'Who said I wouldn't publish you? As it happens, I will. What I won't publish is your novel. Which, of course, I have not read. I never read books. Did I tell you that? But here's what I do instead: I read *bits* of books, and sometimes, I find out interesting things from them. I find that something might be worth publishing, or at least that the author might be of use to me in some way. That's what I've found out from the bits of yours that I've read. Your main character is Alex, right?'

156

'Right.'

'Successful, handsome, charming and so on. Women fall at his feet, he's good at everything. But it's all ironic, isn't it?'

'Yes.'

'You use him to point up what you think's wrong with our civilisation. The way that superficial values have taken over, and all that concerns anyone any more is the surface. Have I got you?'

Fartleby nodded. 'More or less.'

'Then there's the style you use for all the passages involving Alex. Tabloid, almost. Short words, short sentences, short paragraphs. All superficial appeal, no depth. Yes?'

'That's the idea.'

'Well, Boris, you're a very lucky man. It just so happens that Alex and the style in which you write about him is exactly what I'm going to need for the autobiography of Randy Bastard, as everybody must now learn to call him.'

Boris Fartleby twisted his mouth into a sneer of contempt. 'The guy that won *Predator*? Are you serious?'

'I don't make jokes. I haven't the time.'

'You're seriously suggesting that I should ghost the autobiography of Basil Wrigley?'

'I said I'm not joking. And please learn to call him Randy Bastard. That's the name on the range of men's cosmetics soon to appear, and it's the name you'll be using in the book.'

'Well, the answer's no.'

'What I want is Alex from your novel, but without the irony. I want Alex straight. No depth, all surface. Jazz it up, dumb it down. Works every time.'

'You've told me a lot, Mr Grabbitall. Now let me tell you something. If I had the power, I would use trades descriptions legislation to put a stop to ghosted autobiographies.'

'Normally, when it comes to ghosted autobiographies, I don't give a shit who does them, but this one's a little different. You see, Randy Bastard is on his way to becoming the biggest name on the planet, and . . .'

'Tell me, does *no* mean something different to you from what it means to me?'

'. . . and his autobiography's going to be huge. It would sell massively anyway, but even better with you writing it. You'll

157

receive no credit, and Bazza will insist that the whole thing is his work, start to finish. People can suspect what they like, but they're not going to know.'

'No.'

'No?'

'No.'

'Suit yourself. Be a teacher for the rest of your life. Of course, you'll be fucking miserable. Because all teachers are, aren't they?. All intelligent ones, anyway. The thick ones try to persuade themselves they're not, of course. When people insult them by calling them dedicated, they think it's praise. You know what I'm talking about, don't you?'

'I'm not doing it.'

'You must be so sick of it all. Jesus, the way some teachers go on. I bet you know a few of them yourself. They phone up some boring late-night radio talk show and they go on and fucking on about how the teaching's "marvellous" but all the paperwork just gets in the way and makes their lives a fucking misery. Jesus.'

'I'm not for sale.'

'Oh, I see. You teach for nothing, do you? Everybody's for sale. It's just a matter of finding the price. Which in your case is not high. How do I know? You're intelligent and you're a teacher, ergo you're fucking miserable and you want out. There's really no such thing as a happy teacher of course, but the thick ones can just about bear the misery. Am I right?'

'Quite the professional cynic, aren't you?'

'No. Quite the professional fucking realist. That's how I've got where I am today. I never get sentimental about anything. Never. There are only two human qualities that really matter if you want to be successful in the world, did you know that? There's intelligence and there's conscience. Intelligence minus conscience equals happiness. That's what I've got. Conscience minus intelligence equals self-righteousness – in which some people find a certain satisfaction, I have to admit. Intelligence plus conscience, which is what you've got, equals misery. Everything your brain tells you you really want to do, your conscience says would be wrong.'

'Very good. So you'd have been a great success under Hitler, wouldn't you? Commandant of some concentration camp, I shouldn't wonder.'

158

'Wrong. I'd have been out of Nazi Germany at the first opportunity, and taking with me whatever I could grab. I'd've seen where it was all heading. Plenty of people did, you can bet. But they were stupid. They decided they were too patriotic to leave, or that they would fight Hitler from within, that kind of thing.'

'Look, what matters is that you're wasting your time. More seriously, you're wasting my time.'

'Do you ever read Shakespeare? I don't. But I can still tell you a few things he said, because he had a fucking good brain on him did Shakespeare. If he was around today, I'd have the bastard working for me. "Conscience does make cowards of us all," Shakespeare said. It's true, you know. Somebody else, fuck knows who, said that every man would be Casanova if only he dared. Same thing. Whenever you want to do something, but tell yourself you mustn't because it'd be wrong, you're kidding yourself. You call it conscience, I call it cowardice. The only reason I'm not Casafuckingnova, the only reason I don't rape every woman who ever catches my eye is that I could get into trouble for it. If I could be rock-solid certain she'd keep her mouth shut, I'd do it. And I'd enjoy it.'

'Breath too, that's another thing you're wasting.'

'I don't see you getting up to go. I told you about my book-reading habits, didn't I? That's how I know about Shakespeare. I just got through a few pages, and I knew this guy was for me. One way or another, there was a fucking fortune in him. I was chewing the fucking carpet when I found out he was dead, but that's just the way it goes. Still here?'

'Let's just say it amuses me to listen to you.'

'Good! I like a bit of spirit in a man. Most people are scared of me, you know that? I know more about you than you think. You're head of History at Bogsworth Community . . . sorry, The School of the Torch of Learning, aren't you? Oh, there's no need to look so carefully unimpressed – I know you're amazed I should bother to find out. I always do my homework on people. Pays dividends, I find. Big dividends. You must have watched your boss Marsh Mallow on *Spotlight* a month back, trying to tell Youssuf Al-Majnooni how fucking wonderful he is. Marsh Mallow! Jesus, there's a man standing in the path of a runaway train if ever I saw one. Where in God's name do they find people like that? The school's failing, so what do they do? They bury it under a mountain of syrup and fudge. Fuck me! . . . Tell, me, has it all come to pieces yet?'

'Not yet.'

'You surprise me. Soon will, won't it? And what are you doing, Boris? Is it your conscience that keeps you there? Are you just too weary with it all even to manage the effort of handing in your notice? God, Marsh Mallow! How you must despise him! But back to Bazza. You're going to have to meet him, of course, but that can wait. You'll spend the next three weeks or so mugging up on the details of his life, and deciding which to include and which to leave out. I've had my people milking him and his family for information, and there's plenty of it. Then you'll spend a day or two with the man himself. As it happens, this isn't very important, but it'll help you to get the tone right when you actually start writing. The character is still to be Alex from your novel, tweaked as necessary.'

'You're asking me to tell a pack of lies.'

'No. Use the facts of Bazza's life. The ones that fit anyway. But the core of the character is Alex. The thing is, he's got to *smell* of sex. That's the way the cosmetics will really take off.'

'Nice meeting you.'

'I've never seen anyone get out of a chair so slowly. Oh, I nearly forgot. I've written out a cheque for you. Haven't signed it yet. I'm not prepared to do this one on a percentage basis. You get half now, and half when the job's done to my satisfaction. I'm not going to give you enough to get you out of teaching straight away, but do this well and I might put more work your way. That could get you out of the classroom for good . . . Go on, open the envelope and have a look.'

'. . . It isn't even very much.'

'That's as much as your fucking conscience is worth to me. I told you your price wouldn't be high, didn't I? As it happens, you're lucky I'm paying you anything, because I know you frustrated authors better than you know yourselves. You'd write out the London fucking telephone directory longhand for nothing if only I'd put your name on the cover. But I'm prepared to pay you just to keep you onside. Like I said, I might even want to use you again. You never know.'

'Oh God.'

'You'll also' [Dan Grabbitall opened a drawer in his desk and took from it a document which he thrust towards Boris] 'sign this. It says that you'll give me regular monthly reports of your progress, the first to include a full plan of the book, and that you'll have the thing finished to my satisfaction in six months. And that you will never admit to your part in writing it.'

'Oh God.'

Twenty-five

(From the *Sunday Screamer*)
Us & Them: Cassandra McRaker tells it like it really is!

Sex on legs: Randy Bastard

A couple of months ago, nobody could have told you who
Basil Wrigley was. And three weeks ago, nobody could
have told you who Randy Bastard was. Now the whole
world knows. Basil Wrigley, having won *Predator*, has
been reborn as Randy Bastard, the World's Sexiest Man.

Oh, please! I mean, isn't there enough hype in the world
without this? And wouldn't anybody know that it's hardly
the kind of thing that's likely to impress a hard-bitten old
hack like me? Already we're seeing him on television,
promoting the range of mens' cosmetics that bears his
name, and already the ads are boring me. So you might
imagine my surprise when, a few days ago, I got a
telephone call from my old sparring partner Dan
Grabbitall, inviting me to interview his protégé.

Well, what was I supposed to say? For the benefit of
those who have been in another galaxy of late, I would
point out that not a single journalist of any kind has seen
Randy Bastard in the flesh since his departure from
Predator Island. Dan Grabbitall has been careful to reveal
tantalising little titbits of information, and a number of
photographs of pre-*Predator* days – just enough to keep
everybody interested without truly revealing much of
anything.

What I'm getting round to is the admission that I jumped at the chance of meeting the man. I did ask Dan Grabbitall why he should single out me of all people, and his answer was interesting. He said that he wanted someone who might be considered naturally hostile both to him and to his client. He didn't, in other words, want a whitewash.

It was a strange feeling, knocking on Randy Bastard's door – he's currently holed up in an impressive country house, but I can't reveal where. Such is the man's fame that it felt a bit like going to Buckingham Palace to meet royalty. I had to tell myself not to be too easily impressed. And that's not a problem I normally have.

Well, in due course, an immaculately dressed figure came to the door and let me in. It was Jeeves, I swear it was. He led me into a sitting room – which I should probably call a drawing room, but I'm not well up on the terminology. And there in an armchair, flicking through a copy of the *Screamer*, was Randy Bastard.

With languid grace, almost feline, he rose to greet me. Casually dressed and totally at ease, while immediately recognisable as the man we saw on our screens for three weeks, he now seemed much more substantial. A heady, musky smell – which turned out to be Randy Bastard aftershave – drifted into my nostrils as we shook hands. And I may as well say it straight away. The man really does have charisma.

I pulled myself together as he invited me to sit down. You're a hard-bitten old hack, I told myself. You don't get taken in by people. Reputation means nothing to you, you always look below the surface . . . But what a surface!

Now here's an interesting thing about celebrities. Celebrities are, by definition, people you see frequently on TV. And they are all, without exception, a disappointment in the flesh. In particular, they always, always, look smaller than you expect. Take my word for it, every celebrity is bigger on television than in real life.

And that's the thing about Randy Bastard. For the first time ever, I met a celebrity who actually looked bigger in three dimensions. It threw me, I have to admit. Not only that, but he also looked more handsome, more of a hunk. All this I took in at a glance, but the effect was to put me on guard. The last thing I was going to do was yield to the temptation to be impressed simply by someone's appearance. Dan Grabbitall, I reflected, is a very smart operator. He knew that people expect me to cut celebs down to size, and he knew that his protégé's sheer charisma would give me cutting problems.

I reminded myself of the judgment of General Pius Oldgit, a man almost incapable of saying a bad word about anybody. 'In the eyes of God, Basil Wrigley is a murderer. That he should have profited so greatly from his crimes is an abomination. He should be shunned not only by Christians but by all decent human beings until he shows true repentance of his evil deeds, and gives up all the money he has made from them.'

Ah, but Pius Oldgit is not a woman, and has never met Randy Bastard. Drowning, I clutched at one last straw. Ignore the man's physical appearance and concentrate on his character – which would, please God, be awful. Well, the first aspect of Randy Bastard's personality to make an impact is his confidence. It is the confidence of a man who knows himself, and can handle any situation.

His voice is deeper and somehow richer than comes across on TV. It is the voice of a man confident that he will be listened to. I never felt the urge to interrupt him. He talked about his childhood, his schooldays, his years of unskilled manual labour, and nowhere was there a hint of pride or shame. He was simply, in answer to my questions, giving an account of himself.

Without a hint of false modesty, he made himself sound so ordinary that I had to pinch myself to believe that this was the man who, when he won *Predator* by killing American hero Paul Nekred three weeks ago, caused the biggest one-day fall in the Dow Jones in a decade. But it was.

Somehow, the facts of Randy Bastard's life fail to do justice to the man he has become. Brought up in Neasden in a small semi-detached house where his parents still live.

One unmarried sister, Jackie, two years younger than him. A sister whose life, incidentally, he once saved at great risk to his own, but he won't talk about it if you don't ask. 'It was nothing, really. This car mounted the kerb and would have hit her, so I pulled her out of the way.' A shrug.

Well, I have checked the details with Jackie, and I can tell you that it was hardly that simple. She was nine at the time, he was eleven. The car, following a collision, came at her at high speed, and she was transfixed, couldn't move. She recalls what she describes as a blur come through the air at her. It was Randy, diving, goalkeeper-style, to push her out of the way. That's all. I just thought – even if Randy didn't – that you might want to know.

He didn't do much at school, and left at sixteen with no qualifications. Between then and his application to go on *Predator* four months ago, he has travelled widely in Europe and Asia, almost always hitch-hiking, been a labourer on building sites, a roustabout on North Sea oil rigs, and a devotee of martial arts.

Interestingly for a man with no intellectual pretensions, his sitting room is lined with books. More interestingly still, two foreign languages are represented – French and Spanish. I ask him about this. 'Oh, my French isn't too bad – good enough to read Proust anyway – and I suppose you could say I have fluent Spanish, but I really should work a bit on my German.'

He didn't tell me himself, but I have established that this extraordinary man read *Madame Bovary* when he was five, Proust when he was six, and, astonishingly, *Finnegan's Wake* before he was ten.

You wouldn't think there were enough hours in the day to get through the things that Randy Bastard seems to regard as routine, but he does have one great advantage over the rest of us. He never needs more than three hours sleep a night. Up to the age of about fifteen, he needed more – up to five hours, he says – but since then he has found three more than enough.

As we chat, I become more and more uneasy with my own reaction to this man. There's no easy way to say this. I just found him irresistibly attractive. Now this is highly dangerous for someone in my line of business, which is to to reveal the feet of clay on which our idols stand.

My last throw of the dice was to bring up his reputation as a killer. This, after all, is the man who killed Sharon Wonnaby while in the very act of making love to her. Does he ever feel guilty about it? 'All I can say is that what I felt as I stabbed her was total love. She went straight to my heart at that moment, and she will always be there. In a very real sense, there can never be anyone else for me.'

No, this is no psychopath. Raise the subject of the Holocaust, and he is unequivocal ('This must never be allowed to happen again.'), mention paedophilia and he reacts with real anger ('I'd kill them with my bare hands, and I'd enjoy it.') True, he has broken countless hearts, but never because he has wanted to. He is, in fact, always vaguely surprised that he should matter so much to anybody.

Well, I may as well admit it. In the end, I just gave up looking for those feet of clay. Is Randy Bastard perfect? Surely not, nobody is. But this guy is, at the very least, by several country miles, the most attractive, the sexiest man I have ever met. And Randy Bastard aftershave only makes him more dangerous..

After I got back home, head still spinning with it all, I rang Dan Grabbitall. He found it all quite amusing, I have to say. He said he'd be most interested to read my article. Well, here it is, Dan, and I have to admit it. Game, set and match to you.

Twenty-six

'You stupid little bitch.'

Tracy Bonker's jaw fell open. She had entered Dan Grabbitall's office in high spirits. After all, when Dan asked to see her, it meant there was work for her, and work meant money. To be called a stupid little bitch came as something of a shock, and it showed. 'Dan? What . . . I mean . . .'

'Sit down and shut up. I said you're a stupid little bitch. Which you are.'

Tracy sat down, pouting. 'That's not fair. I'm not stupid and I'm not a bitch. If you're going to be nasty to me, I won't work for you any more.'

Dan Grabbitall shrugged. 'Up to you. I suppose you could always go back to your pimp at King's Cross – Hamish McSporran, or whatever his name is.'

Tracy seemed to cower inwardly. 'Jock McFleaze. Oh no, Dan, he was just so horrible, I don't ever want to go back to him. I just don't want to be insulted, that's all.'

'If I say you're a stupid little bitch, then you're a stupid little bitch. And as it happens, I'm not sure I want you to work for me any more. What have you been up to with Rab McGeddon?'

Tracy looked flustered. 'What . . ? Who . . ?'

'Come on, out with it. You and Rab McGeddon. What's going on?'

'Oh yes, I know who you mean . . . But I thought you'd be so pleased! I mean, you've told me that the secret of your success is to get hold of people who are just about to become famous, and that way you're always ahead of the field. You said that when someone is about to become big, your aerial quivers, and . . .'

'Antennae, you little fool.'

'Yes, well anyway, you see I noticed that Ra . . . Mister McGeddon was in the newspapers quite a lot now, and . . . well, I thought . . .'

'You thought? You thought?? Get this, Tray. You can't think. You're too stupid!'

'That's not fair! I thought you'd be pleased that I'd shot Mister McGeddon.'

'Targeted, pea-brain, targeted. Now you listen to me, Tracy, and you listen very carefully. I employ you to seduce certain people. There's always a reason. I may just need to know a bit more about somebody, I may need a serious hold over somebody – what the police call blackmail. Do you remember the first job I gave you? Just a couple of months back?'

'Cyril Smarm.'

'Remember what you found out about him?'

Tracy giggled. 'Oh, poor Cyril! He's just so sure that he's got a small . . . thing. He couldn't manage it at all. I just felt so sorry for him when he burst into tears.'

'Correct. And a perfect example of why I use you. I wasn't even that bothered about the guy, but I used him just to try you out, and you came up trumps. You see, I've got a real hold over him now, because he's terrified I might tell the world that he's got an undersized willie. He . . .'

'But he hasn't! It's just normal-sized!'

Dan Grabbitall closed his eyes and clenched both fists. 'Jesus Tracy, I sometimes wonder if you're real. Look, what size it really is doesn't matter. What matters is what size he *thinks* it is. He thinks it's tiny, and it embarrasses him so much that he can never get it up. What I'm saying is that you did a perfect job on him by actually getting his clothes off and finding out about his little obsession. But you only did it because I told you to. The point is that I don't use you unless I have a good reason, and I won't have you fucking everything up by going freelance.'

'That's not what I was doing.' Tracy was pouting again.

'You're a useless liar, Tray. Anybody ever tell you that?'

'If you're not going to be polite to me, then I don't think I want to stay here and talk to you.'

'Fuck off then . . . Well, what are you waiting for? It's the door you need. You came in through it not long ago, remember? . . . Still there? As I was saying, I won't have you freelancing. You got your hot little hands on Rab McGeddon, and you thought you could sell the story, didn't you?'

Tracy looked truly shocked. 'Oh no, Dan! I'd never go behind your back, you know that.'

'I know nothing of the kind. In fact, I know that you've been in touch with the *Filth* to try to sell your story. Don't try to wriggle out of it. I've got a very useful contact at the *Filth* as it happens.'

Tracy reddened, looked down at the table, then gulped and looked up again. 'But Dan, I was going to tell you, honestly. You see, I wanted to do this for you. I was going to get the *Filth* interested in the story, and then . . .'

Dan Grabbitall was yawning. 'Stupid little bitch. You couldn't lie to save your life. Lucky for you, really, that I found out what you were up to. Amongst other things, the thought of you trying to do deals with the tabloids. All on your own . . .' Suddenly, his face creased up. 'Ha ha ha . . . HA HA HA!!'

Tracy Bonker became angry. 'Don't you dare laugh at me! Don't you dare! I could deal with newspapers as well as you! Stop laughing!'

Controlling himself with evident effort, Dan Grabbitall pulled a handkerchief from his pocket and wiped his streaming eyes. 'I'm sorry, Tracy, but the thought of you taking on a tabloid editor . . . Ha ha ha . . . Jesus Christ, I'd as soon send a chicken out to hunt foxes. Ha ha ha!'

'Stop laughing! I am not stupid! Maybe I'll just decide to surprise you . . . Stop laughing! You know what you are? Do you? You're just a . . . a pimp! That's what you are! You're like Jock McFleaze. There's no difference between you, none at all. How would you like it if I really did just work on my own? Because you can't do what I do, can you?'

'I'm not built the right way. But I could easily enough find some other brainless little tart. It's just that I'm used to working with you, and if you behave yourself in future, maybe I'll keep you on. Maybe we . . .'

Tracy's face was dark with anger. 'All right, Mister Dan Grabbitall, if all I am is a brainless little tart, then you won't be needing me, will you? So I'll say goodbye.' She stood emphatically and glared down at him.

169

Dan Grabbitall yawned again. 'Don't stand on your dignity, Tray. You'll break it.'

Tracy straightened her back, lifted her head, and looked down haughtily. 'I'm leaving.'

'Suit yourself. I'd be sorry to lose you, but it's your life. McFleaze would have you back, I don't doubt.'

Seeming to grudge every movement, Tracy Bonker sat down again. 'All right, I'll stay, but only because you've said you're sorry.'

'I didn't say I was sorry. I would never apologise to a common little tart like you.'

'You're horrible!'

'Thank you. Now tell me about McGeddon. Since you've hooked him, I may as well get something out of it. Knowledge is power, Tracy, did I ever tell you that? So tell me, how did you get him, and what sort of man is he when his pants are down.'

Tracy Bonker looked chastened. 'Well, a couple of weeks ago I was with some friends just having a drink at a club, and Rabbie . . . I mean Mister McGeddon, was at another table, and he . . . well, he noticed me and he asked if he could get me a drink, and it just sort of went on from there, and . . .'

Dan Grabbitall looked at her with distaste. 'Did it indeed? More likely you spent an hour or so rubbing your crotch into his face until he finally couldn't help noticing you. Never mind, tell me about him. What's his home life like? Does he like kinky sex? Any skeletons in his cupboard that I might rattle if I need to?'

'Well . . . I don't really feel that I should tell you anything, but, . . . well, he's really a nice man. He says that he doesn't know how he ever managed without me, because his wife just doesn't understand him at all, and he says that his son's just a weakling who doesn't believe in weapons or wars or anything like that, and Rabbie says that that's just the way the world is, and . . .'

Dan Grabbitall yawned again. 'Tell me something he wouldn't want me to know.'

'Well . . . You obviously know him, so do you promise not to tell him it was me who told you?'

'Yes. Out with it.'

'There's really only one thing. Rabbie likes me to dress up as a schoolteacher and cane him. That's the thing he enjoys most. He

170

has a schoolboy outfit, with short trousers and a cap and all, and he's naughty and he has to be punished. So I have to pull his shorts down and cane him through his tartan underpants . . . But you mustn't tell him that I told you.'

'Jesus Christ, the things people get off on. I'm not surprised his wife doesn't understand him. She'd be a fucking weirdo if she did.'

Dan Grabbitall sighed. 'As it happens, that's nothing very special in today's world, but still worth knowing. Anything else?'

'No, I don't think so.'

'All right then, tell me something. You've noticed that McGeddon's getting into the newspapers these days. Any idea why?'

'Well, of course he was kidnapped, and then his firm was something to do with *Predator*, and . . . I suppose . . .'

'Wrong. Those things got him noticed. He liked the attention, he wanted more of it, but he could see his shelf-life was short. So he came to me to see if I could keep him famous, make him a real celeb. Maybe I can and maybe I can't, but he's paying me a fucking fortune just to try. That's how much he wants it. And that's why you're beginning to see his name in the papers more often. I'd hoped that even you might have noticed that he's getting a bit of publicity for giving weapons away to a good cause in Africa, but I suppose that was a bit unrealistic. Now tell me something, Tracy. How do you think he's going to react if some little bimbo does a kiss-and-tell job on him, and he finds that she works for me, hmm?'

Tracy was looking at Dan Grabbitall, shaking her head slowly. 'But . . . I'd no idea!'

'You never do. When God made you, it wasn't ideas he had in mind. Your assets are tits, ass and face, in that order. If you want to exploit them to the maximum, then you'll stay with me. I don't give a fuck who you fuck unless I'm giving the orders, but when I am, you jump to it. Step out of line once more, and it's back to King's Cross.'

'All right, but . . . but you see, you haven't given me any work to do for weeks, and I've got to live, haven't I? I mean, I don't only do it for the money, but I can't live on nothing.' She looked up at him, like a spaniel hoping to be taken for a walk.

Dan Grabbitall took an envelope from his desk and thrust it in her direction. 'See that as a retainer.'

Tracy Bonker ripped the envelope open, and began feverishly to count the contents. 'Thank you, Dan!'

'Now I'm giving you that to keep you onside, because you're valuable to me in your way. But there's plenty of other little airheads like you around, and plenty of them with tits as big as yours, too. It'd take me a little time to train a replacement, but I'd do it if I had to, so watch your step. Just at the moment, I haven't got any work for you, but something will come up soon enough. It always does.'

Twenty-seven

(From the *Daily Shocker*)
The making of a myth
Viraga Hateman

I don't do TV reviews. That's a different hack on a different page. But I would still like to say something about Justin Poser's extraordinary SEXITEL interview with Basil Wrigley – I refuse to call him Randy Bastard – last night.

You saw it, didn't you? And wasn't he great? Basil Wrigley, I mean. (For Justin Poser's greatness, his own manifest opinion is surely sufficient evidence.) He was witty, articulate, unassuming . . . In a word, he was perfect. And that's what bothers me.

Now don't get me wrong, I have nothing against the guy. Okay, so he's a serial killer, but that, it seems, is no longer a problem, provided that the killing is done for entertainment. General Pius Oldgit, it's true, thinks he should repent and give up his million dollars, but his is, as he himself might put it, a voice crying in the wilderness. Anyway, as everybody is always pointing out, all the other contestants were quite as keen to kill him as he was to kill them. He just turned out to be better at it than they were.

No, my problem with him concerns other matters entirely. Despite what you're probably thinking, I'm quite serious when I say that I have nothing against him personally. The fact is that, in himself, I don't find him even remotely interesting. What fascinates me is what he

173

has become in the hands of Dan Grabbitall. Which, incidentally, is the first time in my life that I have taken any interest in putty.

I wrote about him a month ago, immediately after his success, and I said then that I could see nothing interesting in him except his undeniable talent for killing people. I also said that I believed that his disappearance was explained by the fact that Dan Grabbitall was keeping him under wraps, and would, in due course, relaunch him as a sex symbol. Now I don't like to say I told you so, but . . . well, I did, didn't I?

For three weeks now, Basil Wrigley the sex symbol has been at large, and the image seems to be working a treat. And before I go any further, let me admit to my own part in the creation of the myth. In case you don't know, it was me who first suggested that, if half the world was calling him Bazza the Bastard, and the other half Randy Wrigley, perhaps everyone could agree to compromise on Randy Bastard. I wish to God I'd kept my stupid mouth shut. But what's done's done, so let's just accept the reality we're now stuck with, and get on with it. What are we to make of this new superstar?

The first thing to say is that the evidence is pretty thin – which is extraordinary when you consider the intensity of media interest. I mean, since his victory in *Predator* there have been thousands of press articles about him, scores of commercials advertising his range of cosmetics, but so far only that one TV interview. It was, you will recall, the second time that Justin Poser had interviewed him, the first having been on Predator Island immediately after his victory.

Poser was, of course, out to present his man in the best possible light both times, but on the first occasion it didn't really work. It was lucky for Wrigley that he was illuminated by the glow of heroism that surrounded his victory, because his arrogance and inarticulacy might otherwise have made more of an impact.

The transformation wrought in a month has been quite remarkable. Last night, everything about Basil Wrigley was positive. I said that he came across as witty, articulate and unassuming, but there was also more than a hint of danger of the most alluring kind. There was nothing boastful in what he said about girlfriends – or about anything else – but it was clear that he has had hundreds, and that he is untameable. He is, in other words irresistibly attractive to women.

Guess what? That interview was virtually scripted, start to finish. Now let's be quite clear about this. Celebrity chat shows are all the same, give or take a few details here or there. They are set up with the greatest care by the celeb's agent, who makes absolutely sure that every question is known in advance, and that every sharp and witty riposte is rehearsed. That's just how it works, and there's nothing that you or I can do about it. Basil Wrigley deserves no more obloquy than any other celeb for going through such a charade.

What gets me in his case is the manifest emptiness of the whole thing. Most celebs put at least something of themselves into their public performances, but in Basil Wrigley we look in vain for anything genuine at all. Dan Grabbitall, noticing that the Predator winner had a face, a body and a voice that could be very valuable if marketed properly, has simply created the illusion of substance from a two-dimensional image.

My guess is that he has long since established that there isn't really anything else there, and that's why we don't see the guy on TV – except when advertising his cosmetics or being led by the nose by a friendly interviewer – or hear him on the radio. Grabbitall fears, that is, that unless the whole thing is scripted for him, Basil Wrigley might make a complete fool of himself, or even (horror of all imaginable horrors) appear boring.

If I'm right, then Basil Wrigley's television appearances will remain vanishingly rare, but we'll continue to read the sort of sycophantic profile that Cass McRaker – has Dan Grabbitall got at her somehow? – did for the *Screamer* ten days ago. So far, we've established that Basil Wrigley, in addition to being a great killer, is a fine athlete, speaks four languages, reads everything, has the charisma of Lord Byron and the sexual prowess of Casanova. No woman (with the exception of ball-breaking lesbians like me) can resist him.

Well, Mr Grabbitall – there's not much point in addressing myself to your client, is there? – here's a challenge. If Basil Wrigley really can speak French, then let's hear him. But I bet we won't. If he really is so well-read and witty, let's hear him do an unrehearsed interview, or face a studio audience who haven't been told in advance what to ask. What about it?

Bet it won't happen. Dan Grabbitall will use every trick in the book to keep his protégé's market value at maximum, and that will mean giving just enough to have the media begging for more. Clever.

As it happens, I've been doing a little of my own research on the World's Sexiest Man, and I have to say that I haven't really come up with much. I haven't, for example, found anyone who has ever heard him speak any language other than English.

But here's the most interesting point of all. What really matters about Basil Wrigley is his sexiness, and we have his own word for it that he has had many many more girlfriends than he can remember. Well, why haven't I been able to find even one? Any amount of male friends, of course, and one or two of them have even hinted about girlfriends, but I haven't yet managed to find one of those. I wonder why not?

My search for an answer took me finally to *The Rainbow* in Chiswick, a pub which Basil Wrigley frequently visited in his days as a builder's labourer in west London a couple of years ago. I was a little surprised to find a well-dressed young man on the door, who told me discreetly that this was a gay bar. I told him that I would be very happy there.

Well, I won't bore you with the details, but I was able to establish that *The Rainbow* opened five years ago, and has been a gay venue from the first. I was only able to find one customer who had known Basil Wrigley at all well, and he wasn't all that forthcoming. All he would really say was the World's Sexiest Man has no prejudice against gay people, and that was good to hear.

I'm not going to duck the issue. Hype is part of our world, and if Dan Grabbitall wishes to hype Basil Wrigley, that's up to him. But while we must accept hype which exaggerates, do we really have to put up with hype which simply invents? From everything I know about him, I would say that Basil Wrigley has very little real interest in the opposite sex. Well, same here, so I don't think any the less of him for that. But at least nobody's selling me as Marilyn Monroe. I'll tell you what Basil Wrigley is. He's a man's man, and there's nothing wrong with that. Or is there?

The door of Dan Grabbitall's office was closed as he read Viraga Hateman's article. Every now and again, he smiled wryly. But as he came towards the end, his face darkened. When he had finished, he put the newspaper down, clenched both fists and breathed in deeply. 'Oh you fucking bitch!' he breathed, 'You fucking fucking bitch!' He picked up his telephone. 'Get me Viraga Hateman. Find her wherever she is. I need to speak to her.'

Ten minutes later, his phone rang.

'Grabbitall.'

'Viraga Hateman. I gather you're very anxious to talk to me.'

'I want you to lay off Randy Bastard.'

'I don't know what you're talking about.'

'Don't try that with me. I've just read your piece in today's *Shocker*.'

'I only told the truth. The man's a nonentity. Any fool can see that. His image is just something you've given him.'

'There's something specific.'

'What?'

'You say he prefers to spend his time with men. What do you mean by that?'

'That he's a man's man. I said that, too.'

'Don't take me for a fool, Hateman. I know what you were getting at.'

'I've no idea what you mean.'

'You think he's gay, don't you?'

177

'Is he? The thought had never so much as entered my head. But now that you come to mention it, perhaps it's something I should look into . . . I don't like the sound of your breathing, Mr Grabbitall. You should have your blood pressure checked.'

'Fuck you, you nasty bitch.'

'Goodbye.'

'No, no, I'm sorry. Look, stay on the line, will you? I've just been under a bit of stress. I'm sorry if I was rude. And you should know that people don't often get apologies from me.'

'I can well believe it.'

'Look, you know the score as well as I do. Randy Bastard is a very valuable commodity as a sex symbol. His cosmetics are already phenomenally successful. Now I really couldn't tell you anything about his sexuality, and I'm not especially interested. I . . .'

'Unless he's gay, in which case he instantly ceases to be a valuable commodity at all, and Randy Bastard aftershave has to be called something else and sold at a huge discount.'

'Only if it becomes public knowledge. I'd be grateful if there were no more hints in that direction.'

'Why should I oblige you?'

'I could be very useful to you. Ever thought of writing your autobiography?'

'Work in progress, as it happens.'

'Let me publish it. I'll beat any advance anyone else offers, and give it more promotion than anyone else would. That's a promise.'

'And very handsome, too. But I don't think I'll have trouble getting a decent deal without strings attached.'

'All right, you're nobody's fool, and you're no wimp. I'll go further. Have you ever thought of having your own show on TV? Have you? Because it could easily happen. It could be a chat show, it could be something investigative – about how women get exploited in this country or . . .'

'Mr Grabbitall, I'm not for sale. If I want to say something in my column, I say it. I can't be bought.'

'Can't you? I could use other methods of persuasion, you know. Less pleasant.'

'Do you know, I was expecting something like this. Our conversation's being recorded.'

'You . . . oh fuck! Look, I . . .'

'Ha ha ha! Scared you, didn't I? Of course you're not being recorded. Wish you were, though.'

'You fucking fucking bitch! You cross me again you fucking bitch, and I'll bury you. You think you're so fucking perfect, don't you? Can't be bought, tell nothing but the truth. Well, here's news for you, Viraga fucking Hateman. Everybody – *everybody* – has an Achilles heel, and you're no different. I just haven't found yours yet. But I will. Believe me, I will. And when I do, you're going to know all about it. Unless, that is, you lay off Randy Bastard. You . . .'

'Oh, God, I'm so frightened. Please please don't let the monster get me! Mr Grabbitall, you are pathetic. Goodbye. Hope you'll keep reading my column.'

'Fuck you! FUCK YOU!!'

Twenty-eight

In Londonderry – always Derry to Republicans – there had never been a problem with the pronunciation of Mhairi O'Mahony's family name. The stress in the Mahony part was on the first syllable, so that the full name sounded rather like omaany. Many O'Mahonys who leave Ireland decide sooner or later to put up with being called Oh Mahoney, but some are never reconciled. One such was Mhairi O'Mahony, who had come to London at the age of eighteen, never left, and never accepted erroneous English attempts at her surname. A considerable part of Mhairi's life was devoted to telling people – mostly social workers, doctors, nurses and policemen – that her name was 'O'Maany, fuck you, not Oh Mafuckinhoany!'

Mhairi was from a Republican family who had never accepted the 1922 settlement. 'That bastard Michael Collins sold us down the river,' as her father never tired of telling her. 'He went to London, the weak bastard, and he gave them the six counties – and we've never got them back in nigh on sixty years now – and he said to Churchill and the other Brit bastards, he said "Oh yes, sir, we promise allegiance to the fuckin' King of England." Don't youse' [Mhairi had five brothers and two sisters] 'ever fuckin' forget that either.'

Hatred of Britain and the Brits ('And the Scots are worse than the fuckin' English, don't youse ever forget that.') had been beaten into Mhairi O'Mahony and her siblings almost from birth. She could not easily have explained what it was all about, but she was vaguely aware that her father's ancestors had been from county Cork, and had suffered terribly in the potato famine of the 1840s. Like the Ancient Mariner with his albatross, she carried hatred of Britain with her wherever she went. And it was only reinforced by the arrival in Derry in 1969 of the British Army, ostensibly there to keep order, but seen by the O'Mahonys from the first as simply an army of occupation.

By this time, one thing mattered so much to Mhairi O'Mahony that she could scarcely think of anything else at all: she just had to get away from the Bogside altogether. She hated the place. And the more she thought about it, the clearer it became to her that escape from the Bogside would never be enough: she would have to leave Derry altogether. But where would she go? The prospect of living anywhere other than in a city was simply inconceivable to her. She had nothing against the countryside, nothing at all, but it was beyond her mental capacity to imagine living there. And the only other city she could think of was Belfast. Well, she had been there once or twice, because her father had two brothers who lived there. But they both lived on the Falls Road, and the Falls Road, as far as Mhairi was concerned, was only another name for The Bogside – which meant by extension that Belfast was only another name for Derry.

It was this realisation which finally broadened the bigoted horizons of Mhairi O'Mahony. It came to her that she simply had to get out of Northern Ireland altogether. She lived in a slum, her mother was a slut and her father was a drunken bully, and she couldn't take it any more. She thought of another city entirely. She thought of Dublin. At first, it seemed perfect. But then she recalled that her father had in Dublin a sister whom he occasionally visited, which meant that he would visit her too, since he would regard her as a potential sponsor of his drunken binges.

No, the only thing for it was to escape from Ireland altogether, and, with a considerable effort, she managed to think of another city. She thought of London. It was perhaps the most brilliant idea that Mhairi had had in her entire life. She would go to London! It might be full of Brits, but she knew there were plenty of Irish there too. Her father, to the best of her knowledge, had never been to London, and was highly unlikely ever to go there unless he got hold of much more money than he usually had, and made the effort of will necessary to avoid spending it all on drink.

She packed all her belongings when she went to bed one night, and at seven o'clock the next morning, terrified lest her father should awake and catch her – which would have meant an even nastier beating than usual – she crept from the house and hitched a lift to Larne. And there, with the money she had taken from the pockets of the various members of her family plus some more that she had managed to put aside herself, she bought a ticket for the ferry to Stranraer.

Having understood Scotland to be pretty well on the outskirts of London, she was dismayed at the time it took her to hitch to the capital, and by no means pleased at the price that one lorry driver demanded for taking her less than fifty miles of the way. Tired, hungry and penniless, she reached her destination late one Saturday night, smartened herself up in a public toilet, and earned the price of a bed for the night the only way she knew how. It was a start.

But her experiences since landing at Stranraer had soured her, and she went through a strange and wonderful transformation: within a few days, she saw all of Ireland – especially Derry, and most especially the Bogside – bathed in beautiful golden light. Her home was the finest place in the world, full of the finest people in the world, and . . . well, except for the Prods, of course, and the police, and the British Army, and . . . and . . . but they wouldn't be there for ever.

Mhairi quickly became in reality what she had previously been only in theory: a Roman Catholic. Gratefully she took the wafer and the wine from the priest, and gratefully she confessed her sins – though she could never, in those naive early days, get over quite how seriously the priest took them, and soon learned to be more selective, especially where sins of the flesh were concerned.

Prostitution had never been more than a means to a very immediate end, and she soon found a job in the post office as a sorter. Accommodation was not easily had, and she lived in a succession of squalid rooms which reminded her unpleasantly of the slum from which she had escaped. And then she had what seemed, at the time, like a stroke of serious luck.

Every Saturday, Mhairi went out drinking with some of the girls from work, and every Saturday, Mhairi made herself very clearly available to any man who caught her eye. For all her new-found love of her native land, she had not quite managed to rekindle her hatred of Britain, and she was any Brit man's who had the price of a few drinks and a bed for the night. But this night, at The Harp, the girls noticed somebody different: there was a black man in the bar.

'Go on, I dare you.'

'No, you go on!'

'Oh, go on!'

'Look, five pounds to whoever does it, all right? A pound each from the rest of us.'

'Okay, but you know what happens if you go with a black man? You give birth to a monkey, and that's God's honest truth.'

'Hey, look, it's Pius. Ask him. He'd know.'

Everyone looked in the direction of the door, through which a man in Salvation Army uniform had just entered. He was selling the *War Cry.*

'What? Pius? What the fuck would he know about where babies come from?'

'I'm going to ask, anyway. Hey, Pius!'

The uniformed figure, perhaps in his early thirties, picked his way through the crowded floor. 'Hello, girls, what can I do for you?'

'Listen, Pius, you're educated. Tell us, if a white girl goes with a black man, she doesn't have a monkey instead of a baby, does she?'

Pius Oldgit smiled. Well, girls, I'll tell you if you just buy a copy of the *War Cry.*'

'Yeah, all right, here you are. Now answer the question.'

'I'll do that. But don't just throw that paper away. It could be your way to salvation, you know. I'm quite serious about that.'

'I'll read it. Promise. Now tell her that a white woman doesn't have a monkey if she goes with a black man.'

'She fucking does!'

'No, she doesn't. That's just an old superstition. She has a baby which might be black or white or something in between. That's all.'

'Oh.'

'Well, nice talking to you, girls. Don't forget to read that paper now.'

With the monkey issue sorted out to everyone's satisfaction, the argument continued about who should approach the black man, who was drinking on his own. At length, for a bet of five pounds, Mhairi decided to do it. Something about him told Mhairi not to be too forward. She moved very slowly, desperate not to jeopardise her chances of winning five pounds by being too sudden. And there was something else: he was easily the best-dressed man she had ever seen in The Harp.

His name was Ahmed and he was from Durtapura – which could have been anywhere at all, for all Mhairi knew. He was a Muslim and he was a diplomat, just posted to London, where he expected to stay for three years. Mhairi was in luck.

Within a month and with Mhairi already pregnant, they were married. For the first time in her life, she had money and she had status. But it didn't last. Even before the wedding, Ahmed made clear that he objected to her going out on her own, or even with her female friends. 'I am a man, and a man looks after his woman. She must respect him and obey him, and she must not flaunt herself in public places.'

Mhairi was not bothered. Now that she had escaped from her father, no man would ever push her around again. She pleased herself what she did. But as soon as they were married, everything changed. They had tremendous rows, which degenerated into quite nasty physical violence. She was not to go anywhere ever without his express permission – which was never forthcoming, unless he was to accompany her.

The last straw was the security system. One day, he got workmen in to bar all the windows, and to put on the doors locks which could be unlocked only from the outside. She was to be a prisoner in her own home. After less than six months of marriage, she fled.

Ahmed tracked her down, and tried to kill her. He fired a total of four shots at her, one of which came close enough to put a hole through her jacket. As a diplomat, he was safe from prosecution, but Ahmed was quietly recalled to Corupcion, and that was the last that Mhairi ever heard of him.

Now heavily pregnant, she returned to her job as a sorter at the post office. She hated it. Dreadful as Ahmed had been, he had at least had money and status, and she had shared them. Now she had neither. She began to resent everything in her life, and her resentment finally coalesced around the country in which she was living.

She hated her job, she hated her squalid room, she hated being pregnant. But it came to her that these were all aspects of being in Britain. If she had never come to Britain, none of these things would have happened to her, would they? Since marrying Ahmed, she had not been to church even once, but now she started going again. And now she lived in west London's Bogsworth, with its long-established Irish community. The priest was Irish, most of his flock were Irish, or at least of Irish origin. Mhairi returned to her roots, and again, whenever she looked back on the land of her birth – which she still felt no desire to revisit ever – it was bathed in a warm golden glow.

Which Britain was not. She had an awful job, she lived in an awful room, she ate awful food. Worst of all, most of her near-neighbours were Pakistani, and Mhairi just couldn't get on with them. It was Britain all over, and she hated it.

Mhairi withdrew into her own little world, which comprised her room, her local pub, and her local church. But the latter two contained a number of people who took much more notice of the outside world, and some of them began to take an interest in Mhairi. It was an interest which she did not at first reciprocate, but they were persistent. Bogsworth's Irish community boasted an unusually high percentage of Roman Catholics from Belfast and Derry, and the roots of Republicanism were strong and deep.

'Come on, Mhairi, you can see it as well as anyone else. It's the British that's caused all the misery in Ireland.'

'So what?'

'How can you say so what? You a good god-fearing Irish Catholic girl, living in poverty in London? How can you say so what? You're from the Bogside, aren't you? You should know what the British mean to Ireland, if anybody does.'

They nagged at her, again and again, and Mhairi gradually and grudgingly allowed herself to become interested. She would meet them in the pub, and talk about Ireland, discovering in herself attitudes she had not known she possessed.

But it never quite worked out. Somehow, the better they got to know her, the less interest they took in her. After a while, she saw that they were actively avoiding her. She chose to force the issue.

'All right now, listen, all of youse. Youse think youse can just pick up some ignorant little Irish girl, tell her all about British oppression of Ireland, and then abandon her as soon as she shows any interest. Well, youse're wrong. Youse're Provos, that's what youse are, and youse can't just turn your backs on me. Youse . . .'

A hand snaked out, grabbed her arm, and pulled her down onto a seat. 'You need to watch that tongue of yours Mhairi O'Mahony. Now just you listen to me. You've heard that many are called but few are chosen, haven't you? Well, it's true. You've been called, but you haven't been chosen. We need level-headed people who know when to keep their mouths shut. You open your mouth far too wide, Mhairi, and if it's not to pour words out, it's to pour booze in. We don't need you, but if you go shooting your mouth off, you won't last. And that's a promise.'

The tone left Mhairi in no doubt that the threat was serious. It upset her much more than she would have expected. It wasn't that she was especially afraid of being murdered, more that she had decided that she wanted to belong, and now she had been told that she couldn't. It wasn't fair, and she felt the unfairness of it deeply. Anyone would have. But Mhairi knew when she was beaten. She simply gave up her Republican activist aspirations, and took refuge in dreams of a Celtic twilight rendered still hazier by alcohol.

Two weeks later, her baby was born, a boy. For some reason, she had never entertained the thought that he might not be white, but he was in fact, quite as dark as his father had been. At first she was shocked, but the moment the baby was actually laid in her arms – the baby which she had never really wanted – she felt an access of love which was like nothing she had ever known before. She was quite shocked that such feelings could even exist in her. And he did also bring certain practical benefits, in the shape of a better place to live, and a little more money.

But the place was only good enough to make her resent it for not being a great deal better, the extra money was just enough to make her want a great deal more, and little Joseph, as she christened him, was trouble from the first. She was delighted that his presence entitled her to stay at home rather than go out to work, but outraged that she was expected to stay at home with him *all the time*. Unless she could find a baby-sitter, she was not even supposed to go to the pub. She was given a formal warning: she was told that social services regarded her child as at risk, and that if she did not become a better mother, they might even take him away from her. This frightened her: not only was she, in her way, fiercely protective of him, but he had the inestimable advantage of being a meal ticket. She didn't want to lose her son.

Her tenderness towards him did not last. In her way, she always loved him, but she was keenly aware that he had succeeded where his father had failed: he had put her in prison. He was also, like any small child, weak, and Mhairi could not help despising weakness. She was determined, even so, to bring him up in a proper understanding of what mattered in the world. 'Now you listen to me, you little bastard. What's wrong with this world is that it's all part of the bloody British empire, and all decent people want to see an end to it, you hear me?'

Twenty-nine

'Baz, it's Dan. Phone me as soon as you get back, and tell me what the fuck you thought you were up to last night. It's not only Viraga Hateman we have to worry about now, because rumours are flying on the Internet. So for the second and last time: *STAY THE FUCK OUT OF ALL GAY BARS!!* And tell me, did I only *imagine* I told you to trash your hotel room on Monday? Because the manager has just phoned me to mention that you tore a sheet and broke a lamp. Jesus Christ, Baz, he actually said he was *embarrassed* that it's company policy to charge for such things. Now you fucking listen. When I tell you to trash a hotel room, I mean that it has to look like it's been hit by a nuclear fucking missile, have you got that? I want the managing director of Hilton on to me in such a fucking rage he can't even speak. Fuck me, Baz, how much publicity do you think there is in a torn sheet? Phone me when you get back.'

'Tracy, I've got a job for you. You . . .'
'Oh yes, Dan, I'll do anything, and I'll be perfect this time, I promise! I've been just waiting for you to contact me.'
'Shut up and listen. Something big has come up, and I can use you again. But any more fuck-ups, and . . .'
'Oh Dan, no! This time, I'll be perfect, I promise! I'm so sorry about Mister McGeddon, but you know what men are like with me. I haven't seen him for nearly a fortnight now, and he keeps phoning me, and he even started crying when I said I couldn't see him again. You see his wife doesn't understand him at all, and everybody just thinks . . .'
'Shut the fuck up! I've got something important for you, and I need you to listen. But on the subject of McGeddon, I didn't tell you never to see him again. I just told you never to go to the

media with anything about him. If the old fool's as upset as you say, maybe you should go on seeing him. I'll think about it. But as I was saying, I've got a real job for you this time, and it's going to pay well. It . . .'

'Oh yes, I'll do it! It's not that money matters all that much to me, but . . .'

'Fine. Then I won't pay you so much.'

'Oh no, Dan! I mean, I really do need the money. I just meant . . .'

Dan took from his breast pocket a well-filled envelope, and thrust it across the table. Tracy opened it and counted the contents, an expression of complete absorption on her face.

'That's just half. Do the job properly and you'll get the other half.'

'Yes, Dan, yes.' Tracy stuffed the envelope into her handbag, and leaned forward eagerly.

'I've got a target for you. Randy Bastard.'

Tracy squealed, and put both hands to her head. 'Oh, he's just so handsome! He's such a hunk! I just love him in that commercial, when he takes off his shirt . . . But didn't you say you don't want me to shoot anybody on your books? Because I know that you represent Randy Bastard.'

'Target, for Christ's sake, target. If I want somebody shot, it's not you I go to. You target anybody I tell you to, and I'm telling you now to set your sights on Randy Bastard. He . . .'

'But after he killed all those people! I mean, I just wouldn't feel safe!'

'He only killed two of them himself. And anyway, he's not going to hurt you, because there's nothing in it for him. He killed those people because he wanted to be rich and famous. Well, he is now, and you're completely safe.'

Tracy looked doubtful 'Well, if you say so, Dan, because I always believe you.'

'A rare example of good judgment on your part. Now listen, because this is no ordinary kiss-and-tell. I have a problem with Baz – that's what I still call him. You know Viraga Hateman?'

'Oh, she's just so awful! I mean she always looks so stern, and she's so aggressive, and she just hates men, and . . .'

Dan Grabbitall held up a hand for silence. 'Yes, yes, I know all that. Too well. My problem is that she seems to have it in for me, and she's having a go at me through Baz. In her piece in the *Shocker* yesterday, she hinted that he might be gay. Now, I can't ignore . . .'

'Oh, but that's dreadful! I just can't believe it! You must tell everybody she's wrong.'

'She's probably right. She usually is. And if Baz is exposed as a fucking woofter . . .'

'But that would be awful! Oh, I can't believe it! I mean, if everybody thought he was gay, then he wouldn't be worth nearly so much money, would he?'

Dan raised his eyebrows. 'Tracy, you astonish me. A flash of real insight. You've got it in one. Well, since you understand the problem already, I don't have anything to explain to you. Now until I find a way of buttoning Hateman's lip, I'm going to have to do a few things to protect Baz's image. I'm going to have to move fast, and I'm starting with you. You're going to spend tomorrow night at his place, and a photographer is going to be there to see you leave in the morning. That's all. Think you can manage it?'

'Oh yes, that would be so easy!'

'Now tell me, Tray, why do you think I'm paying you so much for so little?'

'Well . . . you're certainly being very generous . . . Is it your way of saying sorry for shouting at me last time?'

Dan Grabbitall laughed so hard that tears came to his eyes.

Tracy Bonker stamped her foot. 'You're horrible!'

'Fuck me, Tracy, what a fucking brain! But no, that's not it. I'm never sorry. The point is that you might find out a few things during your night with Baz – principally that he takes no interest in you whatever – and what you find out might be quite valuable. What you're not going to do is to go straight to the *Filth* with the story. Get it?'

Tracy nodded.

'That's hush money, in other words. And there's more to it than just that. You let me down in this, and I won't just drop you. I'll tie you up in a neat little parcel, and deliver you personally back to Hamish McSporran.'

Tracy shuddered. 'Jock McFleaze,' she said.

'Jock McFleaze. And there's one other small thing you might do. You still know your way around the vice scene, don't you?'

'But I never want to go back to it!'

'Correct. Which is why you work for me. But as I was saying, you still know that scene. If you really want to stay on the right side of me, you'll ask around a little, and find for me the name of some little whore who is very good-looking, and also pregnant. Think you could manage that?'

Tracy looked doubtful. 'Well . . . maybe. But it might not be easy, because the girls always try not to get pregnant, and they have abortions if they do. Why would you want to know something like that anyway?'

'Never you mind. But if you can get me the details of some decent-looking tart who's got pregnant – just a name and a phone number – I might even toss you another few quid.'

'Just listen, Letz, just listen. Your sexuality is out in the open now, and we're going to do something about it. I told you that I don't much care if you fancy women. But the fact is that you'll play better as bisexual than . . .'

Letzgetcha was pouting angrily. 'I'll play the same. My sexuality doesn't affect my tennis.'

Dan Grabbitall for a moment looked nonplussed, then his face cleared. 'Oh, I see. No, it's an expression in English, nothing to do with tennis. It means . . . it means that you'll work better . . . that I can do more with you . . . Oh forget it. It's just that your earnings are likely to be higher if people think you can be interested in men as well as women.'

Letz was still pouting. 'I don't see why.'

'Of course you don't. That's what you pay me for. To see things you don't. Now the point is this. I'm also the agent of Randy Bastard, and I've got a real problem with him. Much bigger than any problem I might have with you. I . . .'

'He's got nothing to do with me.'

'Oh yes he has. He's got plenty to do with you, because I'm telling you he has. I wasn't too bothered when that bitch Cass McRaker hinted that you might be gay, but now Viraga Hateman's hinting that Randy Bastard might be gay, and that's serious. For some reason it doesn't seem to matter too much if a bimbo fancies other women, but it matters like hell if a male sex symbol turns out to be gay. Effectively, he'd be finished.'

'It's nothing to do with me. I'm a tennis player.'

'As far as your earnings go, you're a sex symbol whose hobby is tennis. Now like I said, you'll make more money if people think you can get interested in men. But Randy Bastard . . .'

'He'll be worthless if people know he's gay, right? Nobody will buy his deodorant, and you'll lose all you've invested in him.'

'Exactly.'

'So what? You want me to have an affair with him?'

'Yes.'

Letzgetcha Nickersoff laughed loudly. 'No.'

'Yes.'

'No. You can't make me do it.'

'Refuse, and I'll drop you.'

'Do that and I'll tell everybody about this meeting.'

Dan Grabbitall stared coldly at her. 'That would be very unwise. Tell me, Letz, what do you know about Al Capone?'

'He was a gangster.'

'Do you know where he was in the 1930s.'

'I don't know what you're talking about. Chicago.'

'Wrong. Alcatraz. A prison. Very nasty.'

Letz shrugged.

'Do you know why he was there?'

'Because he was a gangster. What's this about?'

'Wrong. Tax evasion. You can go to jail for it Letz. Still. So tell me, honey, how would you like to pay back to the US Treasury all you owe in tax?'

Letz's gulp was almost audible. 'I don't know what you're talking about.'

'Oh yes you fucking well do. Your accountant's as bent as a hairpin, and you know it. Even if you didn't go to jail, you'd still lose a hell of a lot of money.'

'I don't know anything about it. You can't blackmail me.' But Letz's voice cracked as she spoke.

'Yes I can. You tell anybody what I've told you about Randy Bastard, and I'll be in touch with the US Internal Revenue Service.'

'You bastard!'

'Thank you. Now here's what we're going to do. I've got a couple of other things in mind for Randy Bastard already, but you're to be the climax. An affair between him and you will have the tabloid tongues hanging out. Saturday evening the twelfth of December you're in London, and . . .'

'I'm going to a concert at . . .'

'Cancel it. You're going to have dinner with Randy Bastard at Lukatmi's in Chelsea. You're going to arrive in a taxi with him, and the paparazzi are going to be there. They . . .'

'How do you know?'

Dan closed his eyes. 'Jesus Christ, Letz, how do you *think* I know. I know because I'll arrange it. As I was saying, you'll arrive together by taxi. You'll both be wearing dark glasses. You . . .'

Letz spread her hands wide in utter incomprehension. 'But that's what famous people do when they don't want to be recognised. I thought you . . .'

Dan Grabbitall clenched both fists and banged them down on the desk. 'Fuck me, Letz, you can be stupid at times! No, honey, it's what they wear when they *do* want to be recognised. They wear dark glasses so that everybody will say, now who the fuck's that wearing sunglasses in the middle of the fucking night? You'll both be wearing dark glasses so that everybody will notice you and know exactly who you are.'

Letz looked down and shook her head, as if amazed and saddened by the deviousness of the world.

'The paparazzi will be waiting for you when you leave the restaurant, and Baz – that's what I call Randy Bastard – will get angry, and tell them to fuck off. He'll say that he wants his privacy – which is a fucking great whopper of a lie, but that's what he'll say. And then you'll go back to his place, and . . .'

Letz grimaced.

'Just listen. You'll go back to his place, and the paparazzi will follow. They'll be snapping away like mad when you get out of the taxi, and Baz will flatten one of them. The rest will get the picture.'

'You mean he's going to hit somebody? But I don't want to be involved in violence. What good do you think that's going to do me?'

'Christ, Letz, it's not going to make any difference to your image. You're not going to hit anybody . . . Come to think of it, it might be a good thing if you're seen to stop him doing any more damage. I'll think about it. Anyway, you spend the night at his place, and the paparazzi are camped out waiting to see you leave in the morning. It's a piece of piss. It'll save Baz's reputation and help yours. Now let's sort out a few of the details.'

The ringing of his second phone always aroused mixed feelings in Jock McFleaze. Business being sufficient to require two lines without quite justifying two receptionists, he had to answer it himself. And Jock McFleaze just did not have a good telephone manner.

'Hullo,' he said, in the terrifying, grating Glaswegian voice which made him sound like a homicidal maniac even when he didn't want to. Experience told him that his voice put punters off. Some even banged the phone down in terror on hearing him. But not this time.

'Hello? I wanted to speak to Chantal.' The voice betrayed no alarm. Jock was reassured.

'She's no in. She . . .'

'So who the hell are you? Her pimp?'

Jock McFleaze's terrifying ugly face performed the apparently impossible feat of becoming still uglier. No one ever spoke to him like this. 'YUI'LL BE NEEDIN' FACIAL SURRGERRY, JIMMAH!!'

'I'll be needing nothing of the kind. What you might need if you don't keep a civil tongue in your head is another matter entirely. Now just listen. I understand that Chantal is beautiful and she's pregnant. She . . .'

Jock McFleaze bared his teeth. 'Whi' did yui say?'

'I said . . . tell me, is your name McFleaze, by any chance?'

'Mah name's none o' yuir business, Jimmah!'

'I thought so. Quite a coincidence. Never mind. Can you confirm that Chantal is pregnant?'

'If she's pregnan', she's DEID! None o' mah gurruls ge's pregnan'. She . . .'

'Hold your tongue. I understand that she is, and as it happens, her pregnancy is worth a lot to you just at the moment. You're entirely welcome to kill her after I've finished with her. But tell me, is she discreet? Does she know when to keep her mouth shut? And I need an honest answer.'

194

'Mah gurruls dui whi' ah tell them. Ah tell hurr tae keep hurr mouth shu', she keeps hurr mouth shu'.'

'Good. Now here's what I want her to do. I want her to claim that a friend of mine is the father of the child she's carrying.'

'Luik, arr yui some kind o' fuckin' time-wasterr?'

'No, but you clearly are. And I don't like having my time wasted. Now do you think she can tell the story, and then keep her mouth shut?'

Jock McFleaze stroked the huge expanse of his stubbled chin. 'I'ull no wurrk. They'll dui one o' thae fuckin DAN test things.'

'DNA. It'll work. Her pregnancy will have to be genuine, but with me pulling the strings, I guarantee that any DNA test will say that my friend is the father of the child. Now is this on, yes or no?'

'Depends on whi' ye'rr payin'.'

'Five hundred down. Another monkey when the job's done properly. Of which I will be the only judge.'

Jock McFleaze paused carefully, and spoke slowly when he answered. 'Ah'll need tae think abui' i'. Ah . . .'

'And I never bargain. Yes or no?'

Jock McFleaze looked most unhappy. 'Yes,' he said sulkily.

'Good. But before I hand over any money, I'll need to meet her, and satisfy myself that she's up to it. You're in the King's Cross area, so we'll make it the meeting point in the station at six tomorrow evening.'

'She'll be thairr.'

'She'd better be. And on time, too, because I never wait.'

'Ah said. She'll be thairr.'

'Good. Now I've no wish to meet you, though you're welcome to skulk around in the background if you're desperate to see who I am. But here's a warning. Don't you ever think you can blackmail me. Better men than you have regretted trying.'

Jock McFleaze's face darkened. His hand tightened on the receiver. 'NAEBIDDY THRAI'ENS ME, JIMMAH!'

'For the money I'm paying, I threaten anybody I like. Or in your case, anybody I don't like . . . But, come to think of it, if you look as fucking awful as you sound, I might just be able to use you. So you be there, too. On time.'

'AH DOAN' TAKE ORDERS FAE THE LIKES O' YUI, JIMMAH!'

'No promises, but you be there, and I'll see if I might be able to put a bit more work your way. Now before I hang up, here's a word of advice. Stop being so fucking mean, and employ a proper receptionist. I bet your ugly voice scares the punters off in droves. Costs you money. Goodbye.'

The face of Jock McFleaze, as he replaced the receiver, might have melted a heart of flint. He grasped the bottle of whisky from the windowsill beside him, and took from it a large gulp. He needed it.

Thirty

Once she was accepted as a full member of the commune, Virginia learned fast. Even Jack warmed to her when she found just how eager a convert the new womin was to man-hating.

Virginia had left Newcastle without a word to her parents. They had wondered why she had been so withdrawn for the two weeks before her departure, but the pastor had assured them that she was just going through a phase. She began to hate Newcastle, and all that it had ever meant to her. She even began to have doubts about God.

For Virginia, pregnancy outside wedlock was a sin of gargantuan dimensions. Still worse, it was terribly embarrassing. Of course, she knew that most people didn't much care any more. She knew that, in society at large, unmarried pregnancy no longer bore a stigma. But for her it was different. In the circles in which she and her parents moved – ever-decreasing ones, for the Church of Fire was haemorrhaging members – pregnancy outside marriage was still a terrible thing. She simply couldn't tell them.

So she prayed. Virginia always had prayed. And God did nothing. God, it became clear to her, never had done anything. Her parents had always told her that God did things, but she had never seen it. When, as a little girl, she had begun to pray, she had asked her parents why the new toys never appeared. They told her that God concerned himself with much more important matters. So she prayed for bigger and more expensive toys. And they never appeared either.

As she became more sophisticated, she ceased to pray for material goods at all. She had learned, as she now realised, to pray for things so intangible that no one could ever say whether God had granted her wishes or not. But this was the big one. She was pregnant, and she needed help. Well, where was God when you needed him? Nowhere, it seemed.

She thought about an abortion, but had no idea how to go about getting one. Her research suggested that she might have one done secretly if she was prepared to pay a lot of money and take a big risk; or she might have one done safely and free, in which case her parents would certainly find out. Then she researched a little more deeply, and found that she might manage it herself with a hot bath, a bottle of gin and a knitting needle. She succeeded in half-scalding herself, making herself very drunk and giving herself the most terrific hangover. But the unwanted foetus remained in place.

One day, she could take it no longer. She ran. She packed a suitcase, went to the station, bought a ticket to London – which she had never visited in her life – and got on the first available train. A tidal wave of misery washed her all the way from Newcastle to the capital. She was at Kings Cross Station before she fully realised what it was that she had done: penniless, jobless, friendless, homeless, pregnant, she was in a city completely new to her. Pius Oldgit almost reclaimed her for God, but Eartha Muvver swooped at just the right moment.

'Hello, love, you look a bit lost.'

Over the cup of coffee bought for her by Eartha, Virginia overcame her reticence and poured out her overflowing heart. Eartha, whose own heart was capacious, took her in. And Eartha always knew that Virginia was going to become a full member of the commune, because, whatever the communal theory, she it was who really made the decisions. If her fellow-communards ever needed a push in any particular direction, Eartha always knew how to give it.

It was a Thursday when Virginia arrived in London, and on the Sunday, for the first time since her hospitalisation with a broken leg four years previously, she did not go to church. God, she now strongly suspected, was a man, and Eartha and the other communards all had a few stories to tell about men. Her experience with George Slobbe surprised none of them.

It was that experience which was uppermost in her mind a couple of weeks later, as she thought about a name for the baby which, to her great relief, she now knew would be a girl. For her own new name, the name by which she would be known in the commune, she would choose something aggressive and spiky, as did most of the commune – Jack Ladd, Marcia Mugger and so on. But that wasn't what she wanted for her daughter, not at all. What she wanted for her daughter, she realised, was a beautiful name. She wanted a beautiful little girl – which was asking a lot for the daughter of George Slobbe – with a beautiful little name. *She wanted a girl who would break men's hearts.*

'You know,' she said to Eartha, 'if it hadn't been a girl, I wouldn't even have wanted it. I don't know what I'd have done.'

'Pre-womin,' said Eartha gently. 'Doesn't really matter when it's just me you're talking to, but some of the others could get annoyed. Girl is the word that excites men.'

'Sorry, pre-womin. Anyway, I want her to slay men dead!' she told Eartha, with a vehemence which almost shocked her. It was only when talking to Eartha that she came to understand what was going on in her own mind.

Eartha's huge moon face beamed warmly. 'And why not? Why shouldn't we have our little revenge on men, you and me?' Eartha had horrified Virginia with the story of her marriage to a violent man who had nearly killed her on two occasions. And the only crime of which he had ever been convicted was breaking a window of the women's refuge to which she had finally fled. 'I wonder . . .' she said, stroking her chins, 'Do you remember Estella?'

'Who?'

'Estella. She's Miss Havisham's ward in *Great Expectations*.' She moved a little closer to her young companion.

Now Virginia remembered. She remembered very clearly. Miss Havisham's life had been ruined when she was jilted at the altar. And she had spent the rest of her life, right up to her terrible death, living alone in a huge house, in her wedding dress, and with the table laid for her wedding feast. The memory came as something of a shock to her. But she didn't fancy the name Estella for her daughter. She was, in fact, more interested in the possibility of Miss Havisham for herself. They talked and talked. Every now and again, Eartha would reach out to Virginia, and touch her playfully.

'I'd really like the name of a flower,' said Virginia, 'or maybe a colour, but I don't want just an ordinary name for her. I want something different, something that everybody will notice. I quite like Lily, but it's just too normal.'

'Let's see, then, said Eartha, and took from the bookshelf a battered copy of *Roget's Thesaurus*. For nearly ten minutes, they discussed possibilities. And then, under yellow, Eartha found something that she liked. 'Well, there's amber, lemon . . . primrose . . . What about primrose?'

Virginia screwed up her face and shook her head violently. 'Sounds prissy,' she said.

'Okay, what about jasmine, or chartreuse, or . . .'

'Wait.' Virginia held up an urgent hand. 'Say that again.'

'Chartreuse. Well . . . I can . . .'

'No. The one before.'

'Jasmine.'

'Jasmine . . . Jasmine . . . Yes, that's it. Jasmine.' Virginia clapped her hands delightedly.

Raising her eyebrows, Eartha nodded in what seemed to be qualified approval. 'Not just a bit too . . . ordinary, is it?' She began stroking Virginia's arm.

Virginia's brow furrowed. 'Maybe. We'll just have to think of another spelling, that's all.'

Thirty-one

'Well, to be er . . . perfectly honest, things haven't gone quite as planned. I mean, I knew when I took over that it was a big job. The er . . . the government doesn't use the term failing school any more – they leave the opposition to do that, ha ha ha! But er . . . effectively, that's what Bogsworth was. Well, as I told you over the phone, I more or less reinvented the place – new name, and so on – because I wanted to give the pupils a new opportunity. You see, Dan, I *believe* in kids, and I believe in education. I believe that any kid, given a decent chance in life, can flower, can reach the stars! I believe . . .'

'Shut up. What I'm doing for you is very rare. I'm shouldering your problems for nothing. Or at least at no expense to you. That means I don't have to listen to a load of politically correct crap. If you were paying me a few million, it might be different.'

Marsh Mallow's jaw flopped open. He stared at Dan, then closed his mouth, and stared down at the desk instead.

'Quite why I'm doing this for you is something I'll come to later. From your point of view – up there nailed to a cross, that is – the important thing is that I'm offering to pull the nails out and get you down. I can help you if you'll do exactly as I say. If not, I can't. So the moment I mention something you can't agree to, tell me. That way we won't waste each other's time. Okay?'

Marsh Mallow gulped. 'All right.'

Dan opened a drawer in his desk, and took from it a file of press cuttings. He spread them out on his desk, and stared at them in silence for a few moments. 'Jesus fucking Christ!' he said at length, shaking his head.

'I know they're not very good,' said Marsh hurriedly, 'but you know what newspapers are. They . . .'

'Yes, I do know. Better than you ever will. Which is why I can help you. Now according to all these, discipline at Bogsworth . . . sorry The School of the Torch of Learning, has broken down completely. Yes?'

'Well er . . . it certainly isn't as good as I'd hoped. You see, I honestly believed that if I gave the kids respect, they'd give me respect er . . .'

'And they haven't delivered, have they, the little shits? Truancy through the roof, two arson attacks on the school, seven pupils up in court for assault, property prices hit within a mile radius . . . Jesus Christ, Marsh, what are you running? A terrorist training camp?'

'Ha ha . . . Sounds a bit like it, doesn't it? With the trainees practising on the neighbours.'

'Then there's Youssuf Al-Majnooni. How the fuck could *anybody* think that he can be brought onside by sweet reason? He's having a fucking whale of a time, him and his crazed disciples. Likewise the journalists who've been writing about him. They've all been like kids in a candy store since you turned up.'

Marsh Mallow cleared his throat. 'Well, to be fair, my predecessor wasn't able to do anything about Youssuf Al-Majnooni either. And to be honest, I doubt if even you would be able . . .'

'Shut up. I am able to do anything I want to. If I thought Youssuf Al-Majnooni was capable of depriving me of one single minute's sleep, I wouldn't be doing this. But let's move on.' Dan closed the file decisively, and put it back in his drawer. 'Tell me, how are you off for money? The school, I mean.'

Marshall Mallow shook his head in despair. 'There's never enough. When it comes down to it, no government is ever er . . . willing to spend enough on education. They make big promises, they give a bit in their first year, then they just er . . . seem to decide it's a black hole, and there's no point in it. I've looked for a bit of commercial help, because er . . . heads are supposed . . .'

'You said heads. Tell me something. Why the fuck did you decide to call yourself a SPIC?'

Marsh Mallow covered his eyes with his hands. 'Oh God, yes, that was a terrible idea. I honestly didn't know that it would upset people. I'd never heard it before. And then we had that awful demonstration by the Argentinians, when . . .'

'All right, all right, forget it. Now I know you've been trying to raise money, but it hasn't exactly worked, has it?'

Marsh's drawn face attempted a smile, but failed. 'Well, I've had some small success. You see, I've tried to avoid virtually selling the school to Coca Cola, or anything like that, because . . .'

'You had a school fête a couple of weeks ago, didn't you?'

'Well, yes, yes . . . yes, we did.'

'In November. A school fête.'

'Yes, er . . . early November. I was counting on good weather, but we were er . . . perhaps a bit unlucky. We er . . . It seemed very early for snow.'

'How much did you make?'

'er . . . I think it was about a hundred pounds . . . nearly.'

'I read about it in the local paper. Had yourself put in the stocks, didn't you? Got pelted with all kinds of things.'

Marsh tried to laugh. 'Well, you need a sense of humour.'

'Were you laughing when that kid took his dick out and pissed all over you?'

Marsh Mallow cleared his throat and looked down. 'Well . . . no, to be honest, I thought that really was taking it a bit far.'

Dan Grabbitall took a deep breath, then exhaled slowly, shaking his head. 'Well, you've really fucked up, haven't you, Marsh? Never mind, like I said, things will work out if you just do as I say.'

Marsh coughed discreetly. 'I'm certainly prepared to listen. But I retain my conscience. There are levels I wouldn't stoop to.'

'The more fool you. Now listen. What we're going to do is to create at least the illusion that your school is working. It won't last indefinitely – the illusion, I mean, and possibly not even the school – but it'll give you the time you need to work out an escape route. If you're lucky, I might be able to help you there, too. First thing is, you give me a list of all the most troublesome pupils in the school. Names, addresses, phone numbers. Can you do that?'

Marsh coughed again. 'I'd regard it as improper,' he said, 'I . . .'

'If the answer's no, then there's no deal.'

'Oh God . . . Yes, all right.'

'Next, you're going to go to the biggest toughest teacher you've got in the whole school, and you're going to put him – because it wouldn't be her, would it? – in charge of discipline. Think you could manage that?'

Marsh Mallow nodded.

'Just do those two things, and that's your discipline problem solved. You are to play no part whatever in keeping discipline. Because you can't, can you Marsh?'

Marsh Mallow said nothing.

'The same teacher is going to deal with Youssuf Al-Majnooni for the time being. Handled right, it's good publicity to be on the wrong end of religious hate, so I'm going to let it ride for two or three weeks, after which I'll bring the old lunatic into line. Just you stay out of it except for a few defiant public statements which I'll give you as and when necessary. Make sure that you avoid personal confrontation, because you'll only make a fool of yourself like you always do.

'Having said which, you're going to become a fucking hero when you're seen on TV disarming a knife-wielding pupil. You . . .'

Marsh Mallow was looking worried. 'But I really don't think . . . Well, I mean, wouldn't it look suspicious if there was a film crew there just as this fight took place? I just don't think . . .'

'Shut up. As far as I can tell, film crews are camped outside your school more or less permanently, in the hope of seeing something interesting. I'll fix it for you. You're going to be a fucking hero whether you want to be or not. What you can also do is make a half-way decent showing in a radio interview which I've already arranged provisionally. You'll get a bit of coaching, and you'll be all right. You'll learn a few tricks that will get you by.'

'Yes, well, I'm much happier with that than with the er . . . knife fight. I er . . .'

'Shut up. You'll be on *Cometh the Hour* with Cyril Smarm next week. I know a few interesting things about him, and he's terrified I might . . .'

'You mean you're blackmailing him?'

Dan Grabbitall nodded. 'Correct. Cyril always obliges me if he can. I'll tell him what to ask, and I'll see that there are a few prepared questions in the phone-in. It's not fool-proof, but again, we'll tell you how to deal with problems.'

'All right.'

'As things begin to improve, I'll get a few tame journalists to write nice things about you. Image is everything, Marsh, and you're going to be a national fucking hero in spite of yourself.

'Next thing is money. You need money, and I can get it for you. In fact, this is the whole point. This is why I'm doing all this for you. You're going to take on two very big sponsors, whose names will go on your school sign, because you're going to move outside the control of your local education authority just as soon as it can be arranged. I need good publicity for two of my clients, and your school is going to be ideal, because you and your school are about to become famous for all the right reasons.'

Marsh brightened slightly.

'You're going to be sponsored by R. McGeddon and by Randy Bastard.'

Marsh at last became animated. 'WHAT??'

'You heard.'

'No. An arms manufacturer and a cold-blooded killer. No. I'm not doing it.'

'Fuck off then.'

'There must be another way.'

'Listen. Randy Bastard is not a cold-blooded killer. He was in it with nine others, all of whom would have killed him if they could. A couple of them tried. Now he wants to do some good with the money he's won and the money he's now making from his cosmetics and other things. Who are you that you should want to stop him?'

'Oh God. All right, I might accept his sponsorship, but not McGeddon's.'

'Haven't you been following the news? About R. McGeddon and DUFF?'

'What are you talking about?'

'Fuck. I'm obviously not getting enough publicity for this yet. Listen, R. McGeddon, with Rab McGeddon himself steering, is giving weapons to DUFF, the Durtapuran Union of Freedom Fighters. The government in Corupcion is about as nasty as they come, and Rab McGeddon wants to show that weapons can be used to do good as well as harm. Now if you . . .'

Thirty-two

'Justin Poser is with me in the studio. Justin, it seems extraordinary, but this is the first kiss-and-tell that anybody has done on Randy Bastard. He's kept a very low profile.'

'Yes, I suppose so, Cindy, but remember it's only a month since he won *Predator*. It's just that we've heard so much about him since then that it seems as if he's always been around. The point is, thought, that he's not the sort of guy that just picks up any available woman regardless. Randy Bastard, if it isn't snobbish to say it, usually goes for class. He goes for the sort of woman who wouldn't go near a tabloid newspaper if you paid her.'

'But this time he did. Tracy Bonker isn't exactly a stranger to this kind of publicity. How on earth did she ensnare him?'

Justin Poser smiled knowingly. 'Yes, we've seen Tracy in the tabloids before, haven't we? Well, Randy Bastard seems to have his pick from among all the women on the planet. But looks certainly come into it, and I gather that it was half past two in the morning and he had had quite a few when Tracy made her move.'

'As I dare say any red-blooded man might to the gorgeous Tracy Bonker. Let's just have a look if we can at the picture that the *Morning Filth* have got on their front page today . . . Yes, there it is. That's Tracy Bonker leaving Randy Bastard's Hampstead pad this morning. And if you can't exactly see much of her face there, have a look at this one, taken from one of her many modelling assignments. I think we may safely say that Tracy is what is sometimes called a looker. But Justin, could this be serious? Is this the beginning of the end for the hopes of the rest of the women of this world?'

Justin Poser laughed indulgently. 'I hardly think so. I honestly doubt if this will prove to be any more than a one-night stand.

Randy Bastard has been remarkably discreet about his affairs hitherto, but you may rest assured that there have been plenty. Of all of them, this is the one least likely to lead to anything permanent. Tracy's had her moment in the limelight, but it isn't going to last. Back to the B-list for Miss Bonker, I'm afraid.'

'And Justin, a few days ago Viraga Hateman created quite a stir in her column in the *Shocker* when she seemed to suggest that Randy Bastard's sexuality might be in some doubt. I doubt if we'll be hearing any more on that front.'

Justin Poser laughed again. 'Well, Cindy, if you were writing a newspaper column six days every week, I think you might at times get a little desperate for something interesting to say. I gather that both Randy Bastard and his agent, Dan Grabbitall, regard the whole thing as something of a joke. In fact, Dan Grabbitall has been quoted as saying that his illustrious client is really quite grateful for anything that tends to discourage lovesick women and thus give him a bit of peace.'

'. . . and I make no apology for broaching that topic. It may seem bizarre to some, but many men suffer great heartache from the belief that their manhood is embarrassingly small. Those of us who have no such problem should try to show a little understanding. But it's time to move on, and to consider the latest news about a man whose virility is certainly not in question. You can't have failed to see in today's papers the pictures of Randy Bastard, whose agent Dan Grabbitall I have on the line now. Dan Grabbitall, is there anything serious between your client and Tracy Bonker . . . Hello, Dan Grabbitall, are you there? Hello?'

'Hello? Yes, I'm here, Cyril. I didn't hear your question perfectly, but I think you're asking if this is a serious relationship for Randy Bastard.'

'That's right.'

Dan Grabbitall sighed audibly. 'There's nothing personal in this, Cyril, but this is exactly the sort of thing I was dreading when I became Randy Bastard's agent. The fact is that Randy Bastard is to women what honey pots are to flies, and there's nothing he or I can do about it. I did in fact ask him to try to be discreet about his relationships, but I knew perfectly well that there would be stories. For what it's worth, I don't suppose Miss Bonker – have I got the name right? – will be with Randy Bastard for very long. I just don't think it's very interesting.'

'I see. Well, I accept that you're not much enjoying this, Dan, because we couldn't persuade you to come into the studio, and you weren't even keen to speak on the phone, but surely tales of Randy Bastard's sex life are grist to your mill.'

Dan sighed again. 'I get awfully tired of explaining this to people, but kiss-and-tell stories are just a bore. I mean, what do they amount to when all's said and done? My task with Randy Bastard, as with all my clients, is to maximise his earnings potential – I'd never deny that – but to do so in a way consistent with his development as a human being. Girlfriends are just a fact of life for Randy Bastard, even if to them he is always something special, something uniquely desirable. I can tell you that, as of now, he's far more interested in the book he's writing about his own life. And I guarantee that it won't be just another standard celeb autobiography. For a start, he's doing it himself, and how many celebrities write their own autobiographies these days? He's also taking an interest in schools, and is donating large sums of money to the Torch School in west London. You see . . .'

'All right, Dan, I take that point. But I really must return to the question of his sexual conquests. It's been rumoured that Randy Bastard has even been favoured by royalty. I wonder if you'd . . .'

'Well you can stop wondering right now. I have absolutely no intention of answering such questions. If princesses, of whatever royal house, happen to enjoy the company of Randy Bastard, that is a matter for them. As Randy Bastard's agent, I would never interfere in his personal life, or comment on it. This interview is at an end.'

'. . . Yes, well, I'm afraid we er . . . we seem to have lost Dan Grabbitall. I er . . . I think it's only fair to say that you can understand his annoyance. Here he is trying to establish Randy Bastard's credentials as a serious and substantial figure in our society, and he has to put up with all these enquiries about his client's sex life. Still, that's what hacks like me are paid for, and . . .'

The Pig and Partridge, Chelmsford
'See Randy Bastard in the paper today? Fuck me, but she's gorgeous!'

208

'Yeah, not bad, is she? See, if you're like Randy Bastard, you can have any woman in the world, that's what they say about him.'

'All right, then, answer me this. If he can have any woman in the world, why is she the first he's been seen with? That Viraga Hateman, she sort of said he might be a poof. That's what my sister said and she reads the papers.'

'A poof? Randy Bastard? Christ, if he's a fucking poof, what's everybody else? That's bollocks, that is. I mean, see the way the guy killed that Yank, wotsisname. He . . .'

'Nekred. Paul Nekred.'

'Whatever. Well, I mean the way he jumped down from that tree and just fucking strangled the cunt, are you seriously saying that some fucking poofter could have done that? Don't talk so fucking wet!'

'Oh, come on, that's just fucking naive, that is. Remember the Kray brothers? I mean, it was a fuck of a long time ago, but they were both poofs, honest.'

'The Kray brothers? The Kray brothers? Ronnie and Reggie? You've got a fucking screw loose, you have. If they gave it to people up the fucking arse, it was just to humiliate them, that's all. That's what happens in prison, see? I mean, remember George was in the Scrubs for a month, and he said it goes on all the time, and it's nothing to do with being a fucking poof, it's just dominance, that's what it is. You . . .'

'Yeah, well, look, all I'm saying is that you can't say that poofs can't kill people, course you can't.'

'Fuck off! No fucking pansy could have killed that guy Nekred the way Randy Bastard did. Fucking impossible. And what's he doing with that Tracy Bonker if he's gay? I mean, there's that picture of her leaving his house in the morning, and she can hardly fucking walk because she's been having the arse screwed off her all the fucking night.'

'Yeah, my mate says Randy Bastard can do it ten times a night.'

'Fuck!'

'Yeah, and his dick's fucking huge. I mean, if she spent half the night with that up her, it's fucking amazing she could walk at all if you ask me.'

'Fuck!'

'Fuck!'

'Tell you something, you know, my cousin reckons he saw Randy Bastard years ago. You know how he saved his sister's life that time? Well, my cousin said it would have been about then that he saw this car skid on the road cos it was wet, and then go up on the pavement. And it was going to hit this little girl, and then this lad just fucking flew across in front of the car like a fucking goalkeeper, and pushed her out of the way. He said it was fucking amazing. He said the kid was at full stretch, just sort of pushed her out of the way of the car with one hand and then he did a sort of backward flip so the car just crashed into the wall between the two of them. And the kid just sort of got up and walked off with his sister like it was the kind of thing he did all day. My cousin says he remembered when he heard Randy Bastard's sister talking about it. It just all sort of came back to him in a rush like that retrieved memory thing that everybody gets that tells them they got fucked by their fathers, that sort of thing.

'Fuck!'

'Come on, then, so you still say Randy Bastard's a fucking poof, do you? Do you?'

'Look, I never said he was a fucking poof, did I? I just said that Viraga Hateman said he might be, and . . .'

'Yeah, well she's a fucking lezzie, isn't she, and fucking weird with it.'

27 Poncy Crescent, Hampstead
'Mmm, that's a fantastic nut cutlet, really is!'

'Amazing.'

'Just unbelievable.'

'Anybody hear Dan Grabbitall on *Cometh the Hour* this morning? Now my better half and I just can't agree on this. She says that Dan is secretly delighted that Randy Bastard – you know he's Randy Bastard's agent, don't you? – that at last his client's been caught with a woman, that it'll help the sales of his aftershave and so on. But I say that his annoyance was genuine. He reckons there's more to Randy Bastard than just sex-appeal, and so he gets a bit pissed off if that's what he's asked to comment on.'

'Well, he's a fantastic guy, there's no doubt about that. But there's some crazy talk on the Net saying that he could be gay. I mean, you don't think . . .'

'Oh, God no, God forbid! No no no, that was just Viraga Hateman trying to be controversial. No, I just thought – I mean, call me cynical – I just thought that Grabbitall had to be pleased that his man was getting into the news because he was with some beautiful woman at last. Not that I don't think he's had hundreds, but he's just been a bit discreet, hasn't he? And I mean, that's not what his agent wants, surely?'

'Possibly, but you see Grabbitall wanted to talk about his autobiography, which he's working on now, and even the literary heavyweights are apparently getting quite excited about it. And he also wanted to talk about the Torch School, which Randy Bastard is sponsoring. Well, I mean, that place is just a mess, and surely it says something for the guy that he's prepared to do something about it.'

'But I mean, isn't it all hype? I mean, do we really know much about him? Aren't we just taking it all on trust?'

'Oh, come on!'

'That's ridiculous!'

'No, can't let you get away with that. I mean, all right, so there's all kinds of hype, but he's still an amazing guy. I mean, you can't deny his achievement on *Predator*. And then we know how he saved his sister's life that time. And when you get even Cassandra McRaker unable to resist him when she actually meets him, what can you say?'

'Yes, I think you should take that back, I really do.'

'All right, all right. I mean, I'm not saying he isn't amazing. I'm just saying that we're being asked to take an awful lot on trust.'

'Oh come on, if Cassandra McRaker, with her poison pen, says he speaks ten languages, or whatever it is, what can you say? He's obviously a very brilliant guy who just doesn't want to shout it from the rooftops, that's all.'

'And what about those rumours that it's really Randy Bastard who wrote Harry Potter? I mean . . .'

'What??'

'No seriously, they . . .'

'But he could only have been about ten or twelve when the first one came out!'

'So? You see the story is that J.K. Rowling was very hard up at the time, I mean we all know that, and he just tossed off the first story to help her because he liked her, and then he didn't want any publicity, and well . . . you might think it's a bit unlikely . . .'

'Actually, I'd believe almost anything of Randy Bastard, but my guess is that he just gave her a bit of help with the stories, something like that.'

'Yeah, could be.'

Refectory of the University of Middle Thames Southside North

'Well, I mean, you've got to give it to him, haven't you? Durtapura has just about the worst government in the world, and here's the kind of guy we all despise, and he's really doing something about it.'

'Oh, come on, that's just naive, it really is. My guess is that McGeddon is just using DUFF as a catspaw. You know, they'll defeat the government, and he'll get his hands on the diamond mines. I just don't believe a man like that is remotely interested in some tinpot African dictatorship.'

'Well, maybe not, but you know he's also giving money to the Torch School, the one in London that's got all the trouble with Youssuf Al-Majnooni. That's in the news just today. There's no diamond mines there.'

'Yeah, I saw that. Funny really, because Randy Bastard's supporting the Torch School, too. See they've caught him with some little bimbo.'

'Yeah, fantastic to look at, too. Some people just have all the luck.'

'Honestly, men! You just take one look at her, and all you see is her face and body. Have you any idea how insulting it is to women in general when you take that attitude? You . . .'

'Well, fair enough, but I mean, men are just like that. I mean, I can't help it. I look at a woman like her, and I just react.'

'But you *shouldn't* react like that. That's the whole point. You think she's beautiful, but you don't even know her. You . . .'

'Jesus Christ, I don't need to know her to see that she's gorgeous, do I?'

'Yes, you do! You do! Because beauty comes from within, and by your age, you should know that.'

'Yeah.'

'Right.'

'She's got you there.'

'Yeah, all right, so I'm only looking at the surface. Fair enough, I admit it. But I mean, you see, any man would fancy her, he just would. And I mean, it's always guys like Randy Bastard that get the women like that, that's all I'm saying.'

'But, I mean, do you reckon he could be bisexual, because, you know, Viraga Hateman was sort of saying he might be gay, wasn't she?'

'Not at all. If you see what she actually wrote, and don't just listen to what everybody says, all she was saying was that he's a man's man, sort of, you know, a bit of a he-man kind of thing.'

'But I mean, how do you explain the things that are getting onto the Net. I mean, you've got these guys saying yeah, you know, we used to know him, and you know, he's queer as a coot.'

'Oh honestly, you men! You're just so prejudiced! What's wrong with being gay? Gay men are the most wonderful people, they really are.'

'Oh yes, well, I mean, we're not denying that. I was just quoting what these guys on the Net are saying, you know . . .'

'Well, I don't believe it anyway. I mean, if you believed everything you read on the Net, where would you be? No, I reckon he's just a guy that gets an awful lot of women and doesn't even think about it. I bet he's, you know, totally hetero, and women just go crazy for him, that's all. I reckon he could have any woman he wanted in the entire world, I really do.'

'Well, I mean that's because he is just so fantastic, and I just totally believe he's just one of these people who can do absolutely anything. But I mean, you know, I'd be dead scared if, you know, he sort of met me, and, you know, got sort of interested. I mean, I'd just feel he could do anything with me, and that would scare me. It's like, you know, he's got supernatural powers, or something like that.'

'Oh, I wish you hadn't said that, I really do. You know Steve, who's interested in black magic, and all that kind of thing. Well . . .'

'He says it's white magic.'

'Well, the things I've seen at his place don't look like white magic to me. And I've made him promise never to do any sort of magic or spells or anything when I'm around, because well . . . it just scares me, that's all. I mean, Jesus, the Bible, the Koran, reincarnation, that sort of thing, I just totally believe, I mean, you know, the lot.'

'Yeah.'

'Me too.'

'You'd be crazy not to.'

'Yeah, but I mean, believing all that kind of thing is completely different from believing in black magic, or maybe even white magic, and . . . well, anyway, Steve was saying that he reckons it's quite possible that Randy Bastard has sold his soul to the devil, and that's how he's so fantastic. And I mean, if you just think about it, it's really quite possible. You . . .'

'Yeah, could be. I mean, I heard that some lab at Oxford or Cambridge tried to analyse his cosmetics, and there was some ingredient they just couldn't identify. One of the chemists working on it is in a coma now, but the doctors can't find anything physically wrong with him.'

'Oh God, don't. This kind of thing really scares me.'

'Well, I mean, that's what I'm saying. It scares me too, it really does. But you see, it's all quite possible. You see, Steve wants to change from Media Studies to Bastard Studies, but the problem is that the course doesn't exist yet. But Steve reckons he can persuade them, and so he's already learning all he can about Randy Bastard. What he says is that the guy's fantastically good-looking, and he's amazingly athletic and he's just brilliant, and, well, how do you explain the fact that nobody's ever heard of him till now? I mean, Steve just says that this is exactly what you would get if you sold your soul to the devil, that's all er . . .'

'Look, I just don't want to talk about this any more. I mean, maybe some people think it's okay, but I think there are dark forces out there that it's better not even to think about. I know Steve, and I've told him that he's getting himself into things he can't control, that's all. Sorry, but I really don't want to talk about it, and that's all there is to it. Sorry. I'm just like that, that's all.'

Thirty-three

'But Dan, he's just so religious! I honestly think I could manage any other man in the world, but not Youssuf Al-Majnooni. I mean, Pius Oldgit's very religious, but he would be easy.'

Dan Grabbitall laughed harshly. 'Tracy, listen. You look at Youssuf Al-Majnooni, and you see this really nasty violent guy who seems to hate everybody, and women most of all, and you think he'd be disgusted at the very idea of getting inside your pants, right? Then you look at Pius Oldgit, and you think, what a nice old boy. Likes everybody, piece of piss to get into bed. Believe me, some people really are untouchable, and Pius Oldgit's one of them. You really couldn't have him, I promise you. Youssuf Al-Majnooni, on the other hand, will be the easiest you've ever done.'

'But Dan, he's just so fierce, and I just wouldn't know how to handle him.'

Dan Grabbitall yawned. 'Tracy, you are one of life's innocents, just as I am one of life's guilties. Do you know who the randiest bastards of all are? They're the ultra-puritans. Every time. They hate the likes of you for tempting them, then rejecting them. They can't help assuming you'll reject them, because they all hate themselves so much. It's just the way they are. You do as I've told you, and you'll get the old bastard, I promise. The only difference between him and the others you've had is that with him you won't need any subtlety at all. All he wants is to fuck you, then be disgusted and hate himself and hate you for it. So don't hang about after you've got what we need, in case he decides to rearrange your face, or possibly your tits. And what we need, I would remind you, is pictures. The only tricky bit is to get the camera in the right place without him seeing you. Make sure you get it right, because there's no point otherwise.'

215

Tracy still looked doubtful. 'All right Dan. If you say so.'

'I look forward to seeing the pictures. Bring them straight to me when you've got them. All right, off you go.'

Tracy Bonker stood and made her way to the door.

'Jane? Send in the next one.'

As she exited, Tracy almost collided with Boris Fartleby.

'Boris. Have a seat. How's it going?'

Boris Fartleby coughed awkwardly. 'I'm having a few problems, I'm afraid.'

'What, with Baz? He's a pussy-cat. How could you have problems with him?'

'Look . . .' Boris shifted in his seat and rubbed his forehead. 'I just don't think I can present him as something so completely different from what I now know him to be.'

Dan Grabbitall looked evenly at him. 'Be very careful, Boris. I don't like being crossed. Our agreement says you've got less than a week to submit your plan.'

'I just feel that some sort of nod must be made in the direction of truth. I . . .'

Dan held up a hand for silence. 'Let me tell you something. You know that your school is now being sponsored by Baz and by R. McGeddon.'

'Yes.'

'My doing, in case you didn't know. I need a good cause to boost the images of Baz and of Rab McGeddon, who is also on my books. Tomorrow, Marsh Mallow is going to make headlines disarming a knife-wielding pupil. Watch out for it. And discipline is going to improve out of recognition. I promise. Marsh Mallow is going to become famous, and the images of Randy Bastard and Rab McGeddon are going to get just the boost they need.'

'Very clever. So?'

'So you'd be out of your depth if you took me on. Your school is so fucking awful that your last head tried to kill himself, and now Marsh Mallow's in despair. But I'll need just a few weeks to convince everybody that it's the finest school in the land. Without ever visiting the place, and without ever intending to. Now tell me, Boris, what do you think is going to happen if you cross me?'

For several moments, Boris Fartleby was silent. 'It won't last,' he said at length.

'I don't need it to last. I just need to create the right image for a few weeks, after which people will forget the whole thing. You'd be amazed how many image problems can be fixed simply by tarting something up short term. The attention span of the media is very short.'

'Most impressive. Thank you for telling me. I'm sure you could be a very dangerous man. But I'm still not going to tell the lies you want me to. I'm not doing it, and that's all there is to it.'

Dan Grabbitall yawned. 'Oh Boris, don't be like that. We have an agreement, remember?'

'I know that. But our agreement doesn't oblige me to write a pack of lies. I'm not doing it.'

'Oh yes you fucking are.'

Boris Fartleby, face set like granite, sat back and looked levelly at his adversary.

Who yawned again. 'Do you know, Boris, I don't get any fun out of threatening little people like you. I used to, but I've done it so often that it's become boring. I still get a kick out of threatening presidents and prime ministers and what have you. Psychopaths too, I always cheer up when I get the chance to intimidate some fucking psychopath who threatens to kill me. But the likes of you? It's just too easy.'

'You don't get it, do you? I'm not going to write a pack of lies about Basil Wrigley, and that's all there is to it. I'm not for sale, and I won't be intimidated.'

'Of course you're for sale. I've bought you already, haven't I? And like I said, you came cheap. As for intimidation, you don't have a fucking clue. If you don't come up with a satisfactory plan within a week – as per agreement – I'll have you pissing yourself. Literally.'

'Mister Grabbitall, I don't think I like you.'

'Mister Fartleby, I don't think I like myself. Let me tell you a secret, the biggest secret in the world, the secret of power. Power means control over people. Once you have that, you can do anything. Without any knowledge of finance, you can make a fucking fortune in business, because you simply get the people who do have the knowledge to do it for you. You might know nothing at all about weapons and armies, but you can still get other people to fight wars for you. All that's necessary is to know how to control people. Provided . . . in fact, now I come to think of it, let me mention that, whether you want to believe it or not, I'm behind that whole fucking revolution in Durtapura. Nothing easier. Like I said, Rab McGeddon's a client of mine, and he's taken my advice to give weapons to DUFF.

'Now of course it helps to be intelligent and it helps to have energy. But do you know what really matters? What really matters is not to give a fuck what anybody thinks of you. And that's just about the rarest human quality you'll ever find. That's it, Boris. That's the secret of power. What do you think?'

Boris Fartleby shrugged.

'You see, the moment you begin to worry about what other people might think, you're vulnerable. That's where politicians go wrong when the tabloids catch them screwing around. They wriggle and squirm and try to deny it, or get off on some technicality – the legal definition of sexual relations, or something like that. What they should say is yes, I'm a terrific stud, so what the fuck, what's it to do with you? That way they can't be attacked. But politicians are so used to being hypocrites that they can't help lying even when the truth would serve them better. Daft cunts.

'You care what other people think, and you're at the mercy of the man who doesn't. He's got you in a death-grip, and there's not a fucking thing you can ever do about it. Ever hear anybody say "I don't give a damn what other people think"? I tell you, people who say that are fucking obsessed with other people's opinions. All I care about in other people is what they do. What goes on inside their heads is their business, and I would never let it bother me. So if you don't like me, that's fine by me. But if you won't write the autobiography of Randy Bastard, that's not fine at all. That could get you into serious trouble.'

'Oh please, save me from the monster!'

'Tell me, Boris, do you know what it's like to piss yourself? Do you? Well, if you stick to your present line, you're going to find out soon enough. Of course, I could bring you back onside by just offering you more money. I could . . .'

Boris Fartleby gave a bitter laugh. 'You couldn't. You may not believe me, but you couldn't'

Dan sat back and stroked his chin. 'You know, you might be right there. Let me think . . . Yes, you're right. I know your type, you see, Boris. High-principled, that's what you are, and people like you, once they've put on their halo and admired themselves in it, really do become very hard to buy. But anyway, I never bargain, and I never raise a price after I've fixed it. That's the nearest *I* ever come to principle. No, what I do in a case like yours is just scare you. You'll write the autobiography of Randy Bastard, and you'll do it to my requirements and in keeping with the terms of our agreement. You'd find it so much easier to agree now, and just get on with it.'

Boris Fartleby leaned forward and looked fiercely at Dan Grabbitall. 'Listen. The last time we spoke, you told me very accurately what I really think of my life as a teacher. Oh yes, you were very good, and you knew it. You knew you could buy me. But that's over. I've come to my senses now, and I'm not going to lose them again. Do you know what Basil Wrigley is? Do you? He's a stupid, self-obsessed bore, and gay with it. Christ, Viraga Hateman has already said so publicly. How can you keep up the illusion that he's a superstud now? And according to his sister, he never saved her life. He just picked her up after she had to dive out of the way of a car that mounted the kerb. She's only gone along with the hero story because she's been told to. I'll write the book, just as I said I would. But I'm not going to present him as a dashing Lothario. I'm going to tell the truth. Not only that, but . . .'

Dan Grabbitall leaned back in his chair, and clapped slowly. 'Jesus Christ, Boris, this should be a scene in a movie. The little man, with nothing more than common decency, shames the powerful bastard, who . . . But this isn't a movie, Boris. This is real life, and in real life the little man who tries to make a stand against the powerful bastard gets fucked. Every time. And if you think I can't keep up Baz's superstud image, you're wrong. Watch me.'

'There's more. When I've completed the book – which will be a biography, not an autobiography – I'm going to get it published. First I'll go to Viraga Hateman, who's sure to give it the right sort of publicity, then I'll get it published. And no threat from you will stop me, so don't even try.'

Dan Grabbitall leant forward again, and rested his chin on his hands. Then he looked up, and spoke in the coldest voice Boris had ever heard. It was not the voice of a human being. 'I have never in my life made a threat without being prepared to come good on it. So you listen very carefully. This is your last chance to show some sense. Tell me now that you'll do what I say, and I'll forget about your little moment of madness. I'll put it down to a bang on the head, or low blood sugar or something. But stick to your puny guns on this one, and you'll find out what it feels like to piss yourself. That's a promise. Show some sense, Boris. I'm even offering you a literary career of sorts, because if you do the job decently and on time, then I'll probably even put a bit more work your way. But . . .'

'A literary career of the sort you have in mind, I can do without.'

'Can you Boris? Can you? What's the alternative? Oh, I know you frustrated writers. I've met so many. I know you're still hawking your novel around. If I thought anybody might accept it, I'd be a bit bothered that some reader might see the similarity to the book you're doing for me. But I know that nobody's going to publish it. Because nobody publishes middle-aged nonentities like you any more, Boris, nobody. The late and unlamented Clement Dormatt was the very last of the old school, the last editor who would even have thought of such a thing. So the only literary career open to you is the sort that I'm offering. A career as a low hack, instead of a career in teaching. I think you'll be happy enough with it in the end. If I were you, I'd get to work on that plan. You haven't got a lot of time.'

Thirty-four

'Marshall Mallow, you are the head of the School of the Torch of Learning – and as such, incidentally, the first teacher I've had in the studio. First of all, Marsh, what about the extraordinary events of yesterday, when we all saw you face down that very large and very angry pupil with the knife. Were you really as calm as you looked?'

'Cyril, I've learned a few things in my relatively short time at the school, and one of those things is that violent behaviour must be confronted. You can't make it go away by ignoring it, you can't kill it with kindness. So when I looked out of my office window and saw one pupil threatening another with a knife, I was in no doubt that I would have to intervene. But my heart was pumping, I admit.'

'Well, Marsh, it was a most extraordinary moment, when the pupil finally dropped his gaze and handed you the knife. There was sweat on my brow, I can tell you. But the fact is that the whole incident was symptomatic of much that is wrong with the Torch School, wasn't it?'

'Cyril,' said Marsh, holding up both hands in a gesture of acceptance, if not surrender, 'I've agreed to come on the programme specifically because I've acknowledged that I've got off to a terrible start at the Torch School. If I was, as they say, in denial, I wouldn't even be here.'

'Well,' said Cyril, beaming on Marsh as if on a boy scout who has just performed an especially good deed, 'if I ever hear that said by any of the politicians I sometimes interview, I'll doubt my own sanity. But this is a serious matter. I have here one of many articles about your school which have appeared in national newspapers. It was in the *Morning Filth* last week. Just to quote at random, "total breakdown in discipline . . . truancy figures through the roof . . . entire building in an alarming state of disrepair . . . toilets in a disgusting condition" . . . I could go on. How do you react to this sort of thing?'

'I'd say it's pretty accurate.'

'So you accept that things really are bad. How did it all go so wrong?'

'Well, the first thing to say is that I took over a school in crisis. That's not an excuse, just a statement of fact. My predecessor has been in hospital ever since his suicide attempt three months ago, the stress having brought on a complete breakdown. But this, as I say, is no excuse. The fact is that I underestimated the task. I turned up at the Augean Stables with a dustpan and brush. I simply . . .'

'The Augean Stables?' Cyril Smarm was not confident of his audience's knowledge of Greek mythology.

'One of the labours of Hercules was to cleanse the Augean Stables, which were incredibly filthy. Hercules did it by diverting a river through them. Well, as I say, I thought I could clean up Bogsworth Community School, as it was called when I took over, with a dustpan and brush. Now that I've seen exactly how bad things are, I'm ready to divert a river through it.'

Cyril Smarm raised his eyebrows. 'That sounds pretty dramatic. What form exactly will this river take?'

'First of all, discipline must be restored. I had thought, based on previous experience, that if I treated the pupils with respect as my equals, I would get their cooperation. That has not worked. I believe that it can and will work once discipline has been restored, but the first task is that restoration, so there will be a new behavioural unit in the school, with one staff member in charge of pupil discipline. And woe betide any pupil who steps out of line. For the time being, I'm afraid, no more Mister Nice Guy.'

'Well, we'll all watch with interest. But there's another side to the discipline problem, isn't there? Truancy. It's been suggested that some schools are in fact quite happy with a high truancy rate, whatever they might say publicly, because it ensures that some of the most difficult pupils are seldom in school. What do you intend to do about truancy at the Torch School?'

Marsh Mallow nodded soberly as Cyril spoke. Then he cleared his throat. 'I'm very pleased that you've asked me about that, Cyril, because I regard truancy as part of the problem, not part of the solution. From now on, we'll crack down hard. Parents, where necessary, will be held to account. I've also spoken to local police, and they have assured me that they take the problem very seriously, and will return to us any pupil they find at large when he or she should be in school.'

'All right, then, let's move on to something completely different. What about the problem you have with Youssuf Al-Majnooni and the Islamic fundamentalists? Another demonstration in the school grounds just the other day, police called in when things threatened to turn nasty. Youssuf Al-Majnooni seems absolutely implacable. What are you going to do about him? I mean, you didn't get far in debate with him on *Spotlight* a couple of months ago, did you, and he hasn't made life any easier for you since.'

'True. And I've learned that there's really no point in endless compromise. This is England, and we must stand up for the laws and customs of the land. I will never willingly upset any minority, but I will not allow Youssuf Al-Majnooni to dictate how the Torch School operates. General Pius Oldgit of the Salvation Army has said that he is prepared to be a one-man human shield against another invasion of our playground, but the way that things are going, that would be just too risky. Playground invasions will be dealt with by the police.'

'Well, I'm sure that this is an issue on which some of you will want to comment when we open up the phone lines. But some problems can't be solved by toughness. You can't, for example, conjure money out of thin air. Is it really true that your school has now accepted funding from R. McGeddon and Randy Bastard? An arms manufacturer and a serial killer?'

Marsh harrumphed. 'Governments always seem to think that schools are just a bottomless pit – however much money you pour in, more is always needed. Well, they're wrong. A lot of money is needed, it's true, but if the strategy is right, that money really does make a difference. I have simply accepted reality, and looked for my own funding.'

'Yes, well there was a somewhat unfortunate school fête just a couple of weeks ago, was there not? Which failed to realise any great sum, or to raise the standing of the school in the local community.'

Marsh Mallow cleared his throat awkwardly. 'We were rather unlucky with the weather on the day,' he said, 'and er . . .'

'The activity which drew most attention was the appearance of the headmaster in the stocks. Pupils pelted you with rotten fruit and vegetables, and one lad even urinated on you. It hardly seems the best way for the head to retain the respect of the local community. Sorry if anyone should find this offensive, but I really think I'd have been tempted to unzip and just show him that mine was bigger than his. That sort of humiliation can work wonders.'

Marsh cleared his throat. 'Well er . . . I couldn't really do that, because I was in the stocks at the time. In retrospect, I think I'd have to admit that the activity itself was a mistake. The idea was that pupils and others would throw water at me, and sponges and light rubber balls. Unfortunately this little entertainment was the one that was well publicised in advance, and it seems that some pupils had made plans.'

'Well now that you're tired of being peed on by your pupils, if I might put it that way, you have turned, as I said, to private sponsorship.'

'Correct. Henceforth, the money we desperately need is going to come from sponsorship. The School of the Torch of Learning is to be sponsored by Rab McGeddon and by Randy Bastard, both of whom saw all the negative publicity the school was getting, and thought that they might make a difference.'

'But the fact remains that they're both to do with killing. Is this really the sort of image you want for your school?'

Marsh Mallow shook his head impatiently. 'Of course not. And at first, when R. McGeddon showed an interest, I simply said no. But then I learned that, with Rab McGeddon himself taking the lead, the company is giving weapons – yes, giving, free, gratis and for nothing – giving weapons to DUFF, the Durtapuran resistance organisation which is fighting against one of the most vicious and repressive régimes in the world. Well, I'm proud that The Torch School should be associated with such a firm.'

'And what about Randy Bastard?'

'Well, you call him a killer. And I suppose in the literal sense, that's true. But remember that the two people he killed were both prepared to kill him. All the competitors on *Predator* were volunteers. And you know what he's done with his prize money, and all the money he's now making? Not only is he prepared to put a fair bit of it into The Torch School, but I happen to know that he's given large sums to other good causes in a less public way. I'm proud to accept the sponsorship of R. McGeddon, and proud also to accept that of Randy Bastard.'

'Well, thank you, Marsh, it's all been quite enlightening. But I'm sure there are many points which our listeners would like to raise with you, so if you just put on those headphones, we'll take our first call, which comes from . . . let's see . . . it's from Linda, who's in Taunton. Linda, you're through to Marsh Mallow.'

'Oh, hi, great show. I listen every day.'

'Yes, thanks Linda. What's your question to Marsh?'

'Right, hi.'

'Hello.'

'Hi. Well, I belong to the Temple of the Magic Twilight here in Taunton, and actually I've rung in before. I don't know if you remember, but anyway . . . It's just that the Twilighters, as we call ourselves, believe that all religions are sort of fundamentally true, and that's why we really want you and Youssuf to get together and, you know, sort of try to sort things out. We're really trying to make it happen, because we pray to the Eternal Spirit for one good cause every week, and that's it for this week, and I just really think it could happen if Marsh and Youssuf got together with our prayers behind them and er . . . I just sort of wondered what you thought about that?'

'Well, Linda, I have met Youssuf Al-Majnooni on one occasion. A couple of months ago, we debated on *Spotlight*, and I'm afraid there was no meeting of minds at all. If Youssuf is willing to make some sort of compromise, then we might meet again, but the way things stand, I honestly don't think there's much point in another meeting.'

'Yes, but like I said, this time you'd have the Eternal Spirit on your side because . . .'

'All right, thank you, Linda, I think you've made your point. Next on the line we have Dave who's in Bromsgrove. Dave, your question for Marsh Mallow.'

'Oh, hello. Well, first of all, I want to congratulate Marsh on his performance yesterday. It was just great to see him stand up to that lout with the knife, and it gave me hope for the discipline in our

225

schools if there are men like Marsh Mallow in them. But what I wanted to know is, are we just asking too much of our teachers, and head teachers in particular? They're underpaid and overworked, and I just don't see how we can get the best people for the job that way.'

'Hello, Dave, and thanks for your question. I have to say that I agree with you that teachers in general are just not getting a fair deal. I'm very lucky in that I've always been able to get by on four hours sleep a night, which means that I actually have time to get through the workload. Even if you're just a classroom teacher, if you're to stay on top of things I don't think you can get by on much less than a twelve-hour day. Not if you're going to do the job properly anyway.'

'All right, Dave, I hope that answers your question. Next on we have Graham from Glasgow. Graham, you're through to Marsh Mallow.'

'Hullo. I'm a Socialist, and I just want to say that I'm disgusted with Marsh Mallow for taking blood money to support his school. Both Rab McGeddon – I spoke to him on this programme a couple of months ago – and Randy Bastard have made their money from killing. See, what's wrong . . .'

'All right, we'll let Marsh Mallow deal with that point. Marsh?'

'Well, Graham, as I explained to Cyril just a few moments ago, both Rab McGeddon and Randy Bastard have done things that persuade me that they're decent people. I mean, would you say it's a bad thing to support DUFF in Durtapura? To give them weapons for nothing?'

'For nothing? For nothing?? I don't believe it. There's something going on there that we're not being told about. See, people like you, you just think you . . .' The voice of Graham from Glasgow gave way to wallpaper music.

'Thank you Graham, that's quite enough abuse. I remember you behaved similarly the time you talked to Rab McGeddon. Well, we won't be taking calls from you again, so don't bother trying. Sorry about that, Marsh. Let's see if we can get something more worthwhile from Delia, who is in fact calling in from Bogsworth. Delia.'

'Hello. I just want to say that I'm really angry. My son is at Bogsworth School, or whatever you want to call it now, and he just gets picked on by the teachers all the time. And just yesterday he got a really nasty phone call, telling him that if he doesn't behave better in school, somebody's going to come round to the house and break his legs.'

Thirty-five

Even in Guttersley Young Offender Institution, where anger was so normal that its absence in any inmate always caused comment, Joseph O'Mahony's temper was legendary. So ferocious was it that many preferred never even to speak to him. But Ibrahim was different. Ibrahim would speak to anybody.

'Listen, man, it's yourself you're hurting. You can't go through your whole life like this.'

'Mind your own fucking business. I hate the whole fucking world, and I hate myself. Now fuck off and leave me alone.'

'I can see inside your soul, man, and I see you're hurting.'

Joseph narrowed his eyes and lowered his voice, danger signs familiar to all. 'If you don't fuck off and leave me alone, I'm going to tear your fucking prick off with my teeth.'

But the thing about Ibrahim that made its impact on everybody was that he never lost his cool. Ibrahim's cool was more famous at Guttersley even than Joseph's temper. 'I'm not here to leave you alone, Joseph. God isn't telling me to leave you alone. He's telling me to bring you home, man.'

'Take your fucking God and fuck off out of here. All fucking love and forgiveness. I get respect everywhere because I never forgive. Never.'

Ibrahim smiled serenely. 'That's just the Christianity they teach you in this country. Your mother is Irish, isn't she? Roman Catholic. But your father was a Muslim, right?'

'My father,' said Joseph with an ugly scowl, 'was from Durtapura. He left before I was even born. Yes, he was a Muslim, and look at all the good it did me.'

'God has spoken to us all through the Prophet Mohammed, peace be upon him, and it is not the fault of God or the Prophet if some have not listened. Many Muslims stray from the path, but the error is with them, not with the path.'

'Well, I don't fucking care.'

'God sees your pain, man, and he calls you to him. Will you stop your ears forever?'

'Yes! Yes! Now fuck off and leave me alone.'

'Do you know what you have to do to become a Muslim? You get hold of two witnesses and you say "There is no god but Allah, and Mohammed is his prophet." That's all. Then you're a Muslim.'

'Look, you're a fucking weirdo, and everybody knows it. That's all that's keeping you alive when you give me fucking hassle. God doesn't even exist. Now fuck off and leave me alone.'

'Tell you something, man. It'd be so easy for you to become a Muslim as God intends. You're half way there already. When you become a Muslim, you have to take an Islamic name. My mum and dad called me Frank after Frank Worrell, who played cricket for the West Indies. There's no Islamic form of Frank, so I chose to be Ibrahim. But you're called Joseph, and that's easy. The Muslim form of Joseph is Youssuf. See? You're nearly there already, man.'

'Listen. I hate you, I hate myself, I hate God, I hate everybody. Now fuck off before I really fucking do something.'

'God has to exist before you can hate him. But I'll do a deal with you, man. You just take a few minutes to tell me the story of your life, and I'll listen. Just do that for me, and I promise I'll never mention religion to you again. After that, you can come to me if you want to, but I'll leave you alone. What do you say?'

'Fuck off.'

'I'll make it even easier. You're eighteen now, yeah? Well, all I'm asking about is the first half of your life. Just tell me about the first nine years, and I'll let you off the last nine. Then I'll never mention Islam to you again unless you mention it to me. That's fair.'

Joseph was unlucky. Had there been anywhere in the world where black Irish people were common, he might have been all right – at least he might have been all right had his mother chosen to go and live there. But in the absence of such a possibility, he was bound to attract attention, and not always of an agreeable sort. Someone whose superficial characteristics make him or her an obvious target for bullies has one possible escape route, and one only: become a leader. If you stand out from the mass by the way you look and sound, you must be either bully or victim. As a boy, poor Joseph never had the self-confidence or the physical presence to be a bully, so he was a victim almost before he knew it.

His mother, although she loved him in her way, was no help. Rejected by the Provos, and living on the margins of Bogsworth society, she knew from the moment that Joseph was born that she would spend the rest of her life on the dole, unemployment benefit, social security, or whatever 'they' chose to call it. Mhairi O'Mahony would devote the rest of her life to drinking and to maudlin assertions of the greatness of her native land. She made it the principal business of her life to see that little Joseph learned of its glory.

But poor little Joseph had so many other things to worry about that he really had no time to spare for the greatness of Ireland. In addition to the unwelcome attention which his appearance drew, he had his name to worry about: for some reason which even he could never adequately comprehend, he simply could not tolerate being called Oh Mahoney. Every time it happened, he would correct the speaker. But the result, far from being that everyone began pronouncing his name correctly, was that where mispronunciation had previously been inadvertent, now it became deliberate. Nothing was more entertaining than to shout 'Oh Mahoney' at Joseph O'Mahony.

'Oh Mahoney! Oh Mahoney!'

Eight-year-old Joseph was almost home, and he had thought that he had avoided his principal tormentors for one day at least. But they would ambush him anywhere, the pair of them: always on the way home from school, but anywhere on the way. He was never safe until he was inside his front door.

'Oh Mahoney, why are you a black cunt? How can an Irish whore be the mother of a little black cunt?'

Ears burning, Joseph tried hard to ignore them. 'Just ignore the nasty little Brit bastards!' his mother would say (cuffing him round the ear the while, like as not). 'You ignore them and they'll go away, you understand? Do you?'

Teachers noticed that Joseph was picked on, and they too had advice to give him. 'Just you hold your head up high, Joseph, and think how proud you are to be black and to be Irish. They can't hurt you if you do that.'

Ignoring bullies, Joseph found, was a sure means of enraging them, while holding his head up high served only to make it easier to hit. These and a hundred other things he was told by adults, were either useless or actively counterproductive. But they taught him one valuable lesson. When confronted with childhood problems, ignore the advice of adults: they know nothing about it.

'Oh Mahoney, I'm speaking to you. Why are you a little black cunt? Was your father a monkey?'

The pair of them roared with raucous laughter. Through tightly gritted teeth Joseph breathed with great difficulty. When he became as angry as this, he knew the feeling exactly: he knew where it was located and what it was. He was clearly conscious of his brain heating to boiling point, and expanding inside his skull till he feared it might actually burst through. And wouldn't that give the bullies something to shout about?

The larger of his tormentors – they were both older and considerably bigger than him – now danced up to him like a boxer, jabbing out his left fist now and again. 'Come on Oh Mahoney! Scared to fight, are you? Come on, you fucking IRA cunt of a coward!' He danced forward again, and this time his fist tapped Joseph on the side of the head. His friend was clapping and cheering.

Joseph could take no more. Along with blackness and Irishness, the two things which made him an ideal target for bullies were the shortness of his fuse and the slightness of his stature. Goad him sufficiently and he was guaranteed to lash out. And once you had the excuse, you could beat the shit out of him, because he simply didn't have the strength or the skill to defend himself adequately.

Within seconds, he was on the ground, rolled into a defensive bundle which his tormentors kicked as if it were a football. This went on for twenty seconds or so, then: 'Come on, you little black cunt, you got to pay up now. You lost the fight, didn't you?'

Joseph remained balled up, but it didn't help him. The victors knelt down beside him and began to tickle him. Whimpering with rage and the determination not to humiliate himself further by laughing, Joseph could not help unwinding. They went through his pockets methodically, and took from him the few coins he had.

'That's not enough, you fucking black Irish cunt! Next time you want to pick a fight with me, you see you have more money on you, you got that? . . . *I said have you got that?*' There followed another few seconds of kicking, then they left, laughing happily.

Joseph got up, wiped the blood from his nose, brushed the worst of the dirt off his clothes, and walked the last couple of hundred yards to the house. Where his mother was waiting, a glass of neat gin in her hand.

She looked at him as he entered, put the glass down and stood staring at him, hands on hips. 'Jesus fuckin' Christ, what's happened to you? You've fuckin' well been beaten up again, haven't you? By a bunch of useless Brits, too. Mother of God, but your grandfather would have been ashamed of you, so he would.'

Joseph dumped his satchel on the floor and went over to the kettle to make a cup of tea. His mother aimed a desultory blow at him as he passed. She sat down at the table with her gin. Several minutes later, Joseph joined her with his cup of tea.

'What happened in 1649?'

Joseph looked down at the table and scowled. 'Don't know.'

Mhairi put down her glass, leaned across and walloped him over the head. 'Answer me, you little bastard! You want to know why you get beaten up all the time by the bastard Brits, don't you? Well, I'm telling you why, so you'll understand, and then maybe you'll be able to do something about it when you're older. Now you tell me what happened in 1649.'

'I don't know, do I?'

'You little bastard! You answer me or I'll give you the biggest leathering of your life! Come on! 1649. Drogheda.'

Joseph sighed. 'In 1649 Oliver Cromwell invaded Ireland and besieged the town of Drogheda. When he took it against heroic resistance, he put every man woman and child to the sword, except for a very few whom he reserved for a living death in the sugar plantations of the West Indies.'

His mother took a gulp of gin and nodded. 'That's better, you little bastard. And don't you forget it either. Drogheda was a god-fearing Irish town full of god-fearing Irish people, faithful to holy mother church every one of them, and the bastard English under the butcher Cromwell massacred them, every one. Now tell me about the Battle of the Bogside in 1969.'

Joseph sighed again, and wiped some more blood away from his nose. 'In 1969 Oliver Cromwell put every man woman and child in the Bogside to the sword, except for a very few whom . . .'

Mhairi grabbed the bag of sugar from the table and threw it in his face. 'Don't you make fun of your native land, you little bastard! There's millions have died fighting the . . .'

'It's not my native land!' shouted Joseph, springing to his feet and shaking sugar from his person. 'It's yours and I hate the fucking place!' He stepped swiftly towards the door.

'Don't you fuckin' swear at your mother, you little bastard! I never learned you to swear! If I swear, it's because with all the troubles I have, God will forgive me. What have you got to swear about, you little bastard, you tell me that.'

But Mhairi O'Mahony was wasting her breath, because her son was out the door and away. She reached out for the gin bottle, and poured herself another stiff one. The little bastard had no feeling for Ireland, none at all. But that wouldn't stop her. She would go on telling him until he listened. If she said it often enough, made him repeat it often enough, it'd get through to him in the end. It had to. She took another swig of gin.

Bogsworth became too hot to hold Mhairi O'Mahony. The Provos' fear that she might denounce them – quite realistic, since there were times when she would have done anything to punish them for rejecting her – made it quite possible that she might just disappear sometime. Worse still, social services were not at all impressed by her performance as a mother: their pale and frayed young operatives were for ever threatening to take Joseph away from her. She gained some advantage from the situation by constantly insisting that she would spend more time with him if only her home were better appointed, but she knew there was little more mileage in that one. One day, they would take him into care, and then where would she be?

Mhairi was lucky. One of her drinking friends knew someone who lived in a women's commune near King's Cross, and when she heard that there might be a vacancy there, she told Mhairi about it. 'See, with social workers, the thing is that if you're poor they always want to think you're perfect. They're just like that. Now if you can get into Jack's commune, then you'll be in a different part of London, with different social workers, and they'll all start off by thinking that they can save your soul. You'll start off with a clean sheet – they even give you a new name in the commune – and nobody'll threaten to take Joseph away from you. Not for a long time anyway. Works every time.'

The idea appealed to Mhairi. Apart from anything else, she was sick of men – with her father, her husband and the Bogsworth Provos top of the list. Men had never been anything but trouble to her. And thus it was that she and Joseph came to live in the commune. It was a close-run thing that they were accepted. The main problem was Joseph, since Marcia Mugger and others feared that his presence might infringe the rule that no men were ever allowed to cross the threshold. But male plumbers and electricians had in fact been allowed in, albeit grudgingly, and on Joseph's side were his age, his dark skin and his Irishness. The final decision was that Mhairi might join the commune, and that Joseph might be admitted as a sort of honorary pre-womin. In particular, he would be required, when at home, to wear female clothes, and to pee sitting down.

It never really worked. While Mhairi did share some of her housemates' feminist principles, they were not a matter of all that much significance to her – certainly they were hopelessly outweighed by her continued Irish republicanism – and she never had the remotest intention of treating her son like a girl. She had to compromise on her name, accepting the suggestion that she call herself Harridana, but otherwise she went her own way.

Still, life in the commune was so chaotic that in practice you could get away with most things, and Mhairi and Joseph survived there for nearly six months before Mhairi found it expedient to move again. Social services were not the problem this time: her social workers in general approved of the commune on principle, and with so many people around at all times, there was never the danger that Joseph would be left on his own. The problem was that Joseph took to crime – though even that might not have mattered, had he not committed a crime against the commune itself.

Joseph hated the commune. That he should live in a house full of women struck him as shaming in itself, and that they should behave in such a bizarre manner shamed him still more. He wished that he could live in a normal home like everybody else. Many of his classmates lived only with their mothers, but none of them lived as he did in a feminist commune; none of them had to listen to their mother being called by a name that wasn't even hers.

Most of all, though, Joseph hated being poor. Television told him that the world was full of very rich people, and all of his classmates seemed to have more money than he ever did. They wore more stylish clothes, they went to the cinema more often, they could buy more in the shops. In particular, they could buy more chocolate than Joseph could, and Joseph had a very sweet tooth. In the end, overcoming the fear of being caught rather than any moral scruples, he became a skilled shoplifter. The technique was for a number of boys to go into a small shop together, one of them distracting the shopkeeper while the rest stole things.

But inevitably, Joseph was finally nabbed. This displeased Mhairi greatly, since it was exactly the sort of thing to draw the attention of social services, and she told him that if he was caught shoplifting again, she would stop even the little pocket money which he normally received. That really did it. The commune kept a store of petty cash in a tin in the kitchen, and it was always available to all. It was for emergencies, and could also be used for any purpose agreed on by a majority of the commune. That the money should be easily accessible but that no one should ever cheat with it was a source of pride to the communards, showing their essential feminine honesty in a society dominated by dishonest men.

When it disappeared, there was a witch-hunt with only one suspected witch. Marcia Mugger in particular, who had never liked Mhairi or Joseph, was quite convinced that Joseph was the thief, and said so very openly. Mhairi's impassioned defence of her son – 'a God-fearing Irish Catholic who wouldn't know how to steal, you Prod bitch!' – had led to a fight which had culminated in Mhairi's decision to leave the commune and go to join the women of Greenham Common.

They had arrived there on Joseph's tenth birthday. He was an angry and rootless boy.

Thirty-six

'. . . and we are hearing that DUFF's most advanced units are now within sight of the capital. More on this one as it comes in.

'But we move on now to what is potentially the first blot on the record of Randy Bastard. As yet, it's only fair to say, he hasn't even responded, but if he is indeed the father of Chantal Veramour's child, then he will certainly be expected to face up to his responsibilities.

'Justin, it's only a week since you last reported on Randy Bastard. That was about his affair with Tracy Bonker. Has she had anything to say about this development?'

'Well, Cindy, I gather that I'm only one of many reporters who have contacted her, and I have to say that it hasn't been easy to get much out of her. She was quite tearful when I spoke to her, saying only that she had really believed that she was special to Randy Bastard, and is very upset that he hasn't spoken to her since the night she spent at his place. As for today's development, she said that it has come as a great shock to find out that another woman is claiming that he is the father of her child.'

'And Justin, has Randy Bastard himself made any comment?'

'In fact he has. I finally managed to have a word with him within the last hour, his agent Dan Grabbitall having encouraged me to speak to him directly, and he seems quite at ease with the situation. He said that if a paternity test proves that he is indeed the father, then he will make generous provision for the child, and, as he put it, be as much of a father to him or her as he possibly can.'

'Well, that sounds fair. But what about Chantal Veramour. What do we know about her?'

'Not much is the best answer I can give you. She is 27 years old and single, lives in north London and describes herself as a model.'

'Dan Grabbitall, this is becoming something of a habit. It's just a week since I last spoke to you about Randy Bastard. But . . .'

'Yes, and I sincerely hope it's much more than a week before I'm required to talk about him again. Nothing against you, Cyril, but the fact is that stories about Randy Bastard's sex life are beginning to bore me. I mean, if half of what I hear about you is true, you don't do so badly yourself. How would you like to be asked to go on about your sex life all the time?'

'Well, if I've had a few girlfriends, clearly it just doesn't interest the general public in the same way. And I admit to being very relieved that it doesn't. But the point is, Dan, that people are simply fascinated by Randy Bastard, and I'm afraid it's part of my job to satisfy their curiosity in so far as I'm able. Briefly, then, a young woman is claiming that he is the father of the child she is carrying. Now press reports so far are confused and contradictory. Can you simply tell us, is this true, and is he admitting or denying paternity?'

'It's true that Chantal Veramour claims that he is the father of this unborn child, but my client is neither admitting nor denying anything. Randy Bastard has made quite clear that he is happy to take a paternity test, and if it proves positive, to take responsibility for his child. That's really all there is to it, and I honestly don't think it's much of a story.'

'But whatever you say, it must surely be gratifying to you that your client is getting so much attention. I mean, he seems to be the biggest sex symbol we . . .'

'Cyril, for the last time, it is not gratifying at all. Randy Bastard seems to get pursued by just about every woman who ever sets eyes on him. As a red-blooded man – very red-blooded indeed, I have to say – he can of course be tempted. But sleeping with women is so natural to him that he takes it as a matter of course. Now if you recall, when we spoke a week ago, it was about his relationship with Tracy Bonker. Well, just yesterday, she rang me up in tears begging me to get him at least to call her. The poor girl is shattered that he has, to use the old cliché, loved her and left her, and she feels she'll never get over it. Well, I felt sorry for her, so I phoned Randy Bastard and said that he might at least speak to her to try to make her feel a little better, and I gather that he's done so. But I have to say that he was quite bewildered that she should care so much. It's not that he's heartless, just that sex comes so easily to him that he can't imagine why other people take it so seriously.'

'I don't suppose today's news did anything at all to cheer her up, poor girl, did it?'

'I don't suppose it did, but life's like that.'

'And has your client really taken it all quite as calmly as everyone says? I mean, doesn't he find this sort of thing quite stressful, if only because of the massive media interest?'

'I can honestly say that he shows much more interest in other things. This morning, for example, he was so absorbed in the details of yesterday's latest round in the world chess championship that I could hardly get him to talk to me about anything else. He thinks he's spotted an opening that black missed on the ninth move, and that that could have changed the outcome of the game. It was all a bit beyond me, I'm afraid.'

'Fantastic. However, I don't mean to go into that in too much detail, since I don't think, frankly that it would interest our listeners as much as Randy Bastard's sex life, so . . .'

The Pig and Partridge, Chelmsford

'See, the thing about Randy Bastard is, he's interested in any woman that's gorgeous enough. He . . .'

'Yeah, well, I mean, me too. Any . . .'

'No, look, just listen, will you? What I'm saying is, there was that Tracy Bonker a week ago, and now there's this Chantal Veramour, right? And, see, they're completely different, aren't they? I mean, Tracy Bonker's got great big knockers and she's all kind of bouncy and . . . an' all, isn't she? And now there's this Chantal Veramour, and she looks more like . . . you know, like Audrey Hepburn, if you remember her.'

'Yeah, but I mean, like I say, any man'd go for either of them two, wouldn't he?'

'You'd be surprised. Most men go for one type or the other. It's something to do with what your mother looked like, or something like that. That's what these psycholatrist people say, but I'm only saying that Randy Bastard will go for any woman he fancies, that's all. Anyway, do you believe me now when I say he's not a fucking woofter?'

'I never fucking disbelieved you, did I? I just said, that Viraga Hateman seemed to think there could be something a bit queer about him, that's all.'

'Yeah, well he's sorted her out on that one, hasn't he? But you know what I don't get about him. I mean, what women all want is a real he-man, isn't it? I mean, doesn't matter what they say, that's what they want. I mean, not boasting or anything like that, but most women want a man like you or me, yeah?'

'Yeah, I'd say.'

'But, well, I mean, look at Randy Bastard. He speaks all these fucking languages and he plays chess well enough to be world fucking champion and he fucking reads all these books. Well, I mean, I've never met a woman who wouldn't run a fucking mile from a guy like that.'

'Fuck me, look what he did in *Predator*! If that doesn't make him a real man, nothing does. I mean . . .'

'Yeah, but since he came back, he's done nothing, has he?'

'But what you've got to see is that they all know he's got it in him, that's what matters. That and he's got all the muscles and that. So he can read all the fucking books – and a fucking gigantic dick, too, don't forget that – he can read all the fucking books he likes and it's not going to put them off, is it?'

'You could be right . . . Hey, have you tried his aftershave yet? Randy Bastard aftershave? Fucking good, I have to say.'

43 Poncy Crescent, Hampstead

'Now that's what I call champagne, really is. I mean, you get all these cheap imitations, and you get people who say there's no difference. But there is. Every time.'

'Absolutely.'

'I'll say.'

'I always say, if you can't tell champagne from some cheap imitation, you just haven't got it.'

'Did you hear that Rab McGeddon has a shipment of Bolli on ice, and he's going to fly it out personally to Corupcion the moment that DUFF finally overthrow the government? Fantastic guy, whatever you might think of arms manufacturers in general.'

'Absolutely. Some people are cynical about it, but I'd say he's quite genuine. I mean, you know, he always says he's just a plain man from the mean streets of Glasgow, and I'd say he really does just want to do the right thing. More power to him.'

'Amen to that. And more power to DUFF.'

'Well, I hope it's a good vintage they'll be drinking.'

'I bet it will be. McGeddon knows his champagne, I'm told. And so, apparently, does Randy Bastard. They say he knows as much about wine as anybody on the planet.'

'Now that I find hard to believe. I mean, until he became famous just a couple of months ago, he'd been things like a builder's labourer, a roustabout on an oil rig, and so on. Well, I'm not saying that . . .'

'Oh come on! That's just pure snobbery! Really, I'm surprised that anyone could say such a thing in this day and age.'

'Well, I mean, of course, I mean, I don't doubt that you get labourers and what have you who know a bit about wine, yes, I suppose so. I just . . . well . . .'

'You just what? If you admit that builders' labourers can as easily know their wines as people like us, then what are you on about? I heard that he's one of these guys who can tell you not only the grape and the vintage and what have you, but he can have a pretty fair shot at the vineyard, too.'

'Well, all right, maybe . . . But I mean, how would he have learned?'

'Ah, now I wondered about that. But what I've heard is that in the days when he was a labourer and so on, he did some time in France, which was where he learned the language of course. Well, I reckon that he probably worked on the grape harvest, and just got interested in wine that way. It would make sense, wouldn't it?'

'Yes, it would. But if you recall a week ago, that Tracy Bonker, I wouldn't say she'd be much of a one for wine. Alco-pops that one, I'd say. But you see this woman that's claiming he's the father of the child she's carrying? So much for Viraga Hateman's theory about his sexuality. Anyway, this one's a cut above, isn't she? I mean, I don't mean to be snobbish, but I'd say she's probably more on his level intellectually.'

'Has to be. I mean, the latest is that he's a fantastic chess player, and Dan Grabbitall is saying that he might just give up everything else for a few months to see if he can challenge for the world championship.'

'Well, of course he'd probably win it if he tried, but I don't see it myself. You see, Randy Bastard is the Renaissance Man type. You know, he's so completely rounded, good at everything intellectual and athletic, and I don't think that he could ever be single-minded enough for something like that.'

'Exactly. You see, you've got to be not just single-minded, but one-dimensional even, and I just don't think he could do it.'

'Well, for a start, he'd get distracted by all the women swooning over him all the time, wouldn't he?'

Refectory of the University of Middle Thames Southside North
'Somebody was saying yesterday that they've got real problems with the latest edition of the National Dictionary of Biography, or whatever you call it. You know, Virginia Woolf wrote the first one, but they've got to keep it up to date. Well, they can't leave Randy Bastard . . . No, really, she was just such a genius that she wrote the whole thing herself. Amazing or what? Honestly. Anyway, there's a new edition out soon, but Randy Bastard's become incredibly famous just so fast that he's not in it, and they can't leave him out, so they're going to have to kind of redo the whole thing. They . . .'

'Oh, that's just not possible. I mean, there's about fifty fucking volumes. And he'd be under B, so they'd have to change absolutely everything from there on. That's just not possible.'

'Yeah, but I heard that they've got a way out. They've decided he's so incredible that they're just going to do a whole volume on him alone, because like you say, there's dozens of volumes, and that way they can leave the rest of it as it is. It can be just like a kind of supplement.'

'Amazing.'

'Fantastic.'

'Unbelievable.'

'Did you hear that Steve has managed to get his course on Bastard Studies? We're the first to do it, but it seems that just about every university in the land is going to have one now.'

'Look, I really don't think we should be talking about this at all. I mean, like I've said before, Steve scares me, he really does. I think he's probably right about Randy Bastard selling his soul to the devil, because nobody could be that fantastic otherwise. I just think that we could get into things we don't understand, that's all.'

241

'Oh come on, all we're doing is talking about it. I don't see how that can do any harm. I mean, Steve says he wouldn't actually study Randy Bastard without knowing something of the black arts, just to be able to protect himself, but . . .'

'But it's not impossible that he's just an ordinary guy who happens to be very brilliant and athletic and so on, and . . .'

'Oh, come on, nobody's that fantastic. I mean, all those languages, and the women. That Chantal whatsit who's saying he's the father of her child. I mean, the way he can just get any woman he wants. There's got to be something going on.'

'Oh, I don't know. I mean you get men like that. You know, like Casanova and Don Juan and so on.'

'Exactly my point. Because they'd both sold their souls to the devil, hadn't they? That's exactly what they did. Everybody knows that.'

'Oh, God, stop! Stop!'

'Why?'

'What's wrong?'

'Are you all right?'

'Oh God, can't you see? Something terrible has happened. Randy Bastard has probably sold his soul to the devil, and now he's going to have a baby. I'm really scared.'

'Oh . . . Yes . . .'

'Oh my God.'

'Shit!'

Thirty-seven

'Hello?'

'Boris?'

'Speaking.'

'This is Dan Grabbitall. You haven't come up with the plan, Boris. Today was the deadline.'

'We've been through this.'

Dan Grabbitall cleared his throat awkwardly. 'Have you spoken to anyone else about this? Viraga Hateman, for example?'

'Not yet. But as I said, I'll probably take it to her when it's completed. I might even give something to the newspapers before that, though. Just to prepare the ground.'

'Look, I've been thinking. Some sort of compromise must be possible. Could we meet?'

'Well well . . . I must say, Dan, you've changed your tune.'

'I'm not a fool, Boris. I wouldn't go so far as to say that I know when I'm beaten, but I do know when to compromise. I know it's late, but I'm still in my office, and I want this sorted out. You couldn't come round now, could you? I'd come to you, but I've got a few things on my computer here that I'd like you to see.'

'You're right. It is late.'

'Believe me, I've got a good reason for making it now. Trust me. If you do, we can sort this out.'

'Well, since you no longer seem to want to do me in, yes, I'll show some goodwill. I'll be with you in half an hour . . . better say forty minutes.'

It was the last day of November, it was cold and it was late, but a hard-up mugger cannot afford to be fussy about when he does his business. Bert Bovver, recently returned from his defence of

England's honour in India, needed money, and the little man who entered the carriage just as the only other two people exited, represented just too good a chance to miss. He looked quite pleased with himself, but Bert was good at wiping self-satisfied smirks off lah-de-dah middle-class faces. It was a talent of his, and a profitable one. Having already taken the precaution of covering the lens of the inevitable CCTV camera, he would be safe for two minutes, which was more than enough time. He rose, pulling his knife from his pocket.

'Oi.'

The little man looked up.

'See this?'

'Yes. It's a knife.'

''and over your walle'.'

'Go away.'

Bert Bovver wasn't used to this kind of thing. 'I said 'and over your walle'!'

'And I told you to go away. Didn't you hear me?'

'You 'and over your walle', cun', or I'll fuckin' do you.'

'Well, just tell me something first. Have you heard of Randy Bastard? Have you?'

'Are you some kind of fuckin' nu'er?'

'Because you might be interested to know that you are talking to his biographer. I'm working on the story of his life. It's giving me plenty to think about, and I want you to go away and leave me alone.'

'I only wan' your walle'!' wailed Bert.

'I'm going to give you one chance. I can be quite a dangerous man, as a certain Dan Grabbitall has very recently found out. Now if I can deal with him, I can certainly deal with you. If you don't go away and leave me alone now, then I'll arrest you and hand you over to the police at the next stop. Well?'

To the troubled mind of Jock McFleaze, there was something immensely soothing in the feel of a broken bottle entering a human face. And quarter to eleven on a cold Monday evening was as good a time as any. If this man Fartleby was not prepared to do as he was told, so much the better . . . and then he recalled that he was not to do him serious physical harm. With a regretful sigh, Jock McFleaze took another swig from his bottle, belched loudly, and swung it appreciatively by the neck. It was almost time.

He heard him first – whistling, of all things, Rule Britannia – and then he saw him. Much what Jock would have expected – middle-aged, undersized, moth-eaten – but Jock was certainly not at all what Fartleby was expecting.

'Are yui Boris Far'leby?'

The little man started, almost jumped, as Jock McFleaze emerged from the shadows. 'er . . . Yes.'

'Ye know who sen' me.'

'I'm on my way to see Dan Grabbitall.' The voice trembled.

'I's me *yui* need tae see, Jimmah.'

'What's all this about?' Boris Fartleby was trying to sound annoyed, but Jock McFleaze knew terror when he faced it. Which was often.

'Mister Grabbi'all's no pleased wi' yuir a'itude.'

Fartleby made an effort to appear composed. 'And I'm not pleased with his. Which is why it's Grabbitall himself I have to speak to. Now I warn you that somebody pulled a knife on me just twenty minutes ago, and soon wished he hadn't. If you . . .'

'Ye'rr gan tae go tae the newspaperrs wi' some story abui' Randy Bastard, is thaa' righ'?'

'I've said I won't tell lies about him. I'm not for sale. Now Grabbitall has a choice. Either he pays me what he owes me and I wash my hands of the whole filthy business, or . . .'

Quite without warning, the huge left hand of Jock McFleaze flashed out and grabbed Boris by the throat. Jock pushed his victim back against the wall, then lifted him one handed, till he was suspended several inches above the ground. 'Or whi? . . . OR WHI'? ah said. Listen, Jimmah, if yui take one more step ou' o' line, yuir face is gan tae need mair stitches than thaa' tapestry thing o' William the fuckin' Conqueror.'

Half-strangled and wholly terrified, the teacher in Boris Fartleby, made a heroic pedagogical effort. 'Bayeux,' he squeaked.

'Whi'everr. See whi' ah've go' in my righ' haun'?' Jock held up the empty whisky bottle, drew it back, then smashed it violently against the wall a foot from his victim's terrified face. A rivulet of blood trickled slowly down Boris's forehead. Jock stared at him and twisted his grimy face into a rictus of Glaswegian hatred and contempt. He held the remains of the bottle inches from Boris's nose.

'Whi' de ye say, then, eh?'

Fighting desperately for breath, eyes wide with a terror he would not previously have thought possible, Boris tried to speak, but could not. He tried to shake his head, but could not. He couldn't even change his facial expression. His impossible terror was made still more impossible by his inability to react in any visible way. Would this horror be enraged by what he might misinterpret as dumb insolence? And at that moment, Boris Fartleby knew that he would do absolutely anything rather than be hurt. The notion that there were threats more intimidating than that of serious physical harm was garbage. This was the most terrifying thing that could happen to anyone ever, and it was happening to Boris Fartleby, and Boris Fartleby would do anything at all to make it stop. He was dimly aware of the trickle of liquid from his forehead, much more so of the flood coursing down his left leg.

Jock McFleaze was enjoying himself. If he couldn't actually do this man's face – and Mr Grabbitall had warned him not even to think about it – he would at least milk the bastard's terror for all it was worth. 'Whi's wrang? Ye go' nuthin' tae say? Ah'm talking tae *yui*, Jimmah!'

'Please!' Boris tried to say, but couldn't.

'Now yui stoap pissin' yirsel an listen tae me, Jimmah! Mister Grabbi'all says yui'rr no bihaevin' yirsel. Is thaa' righ'? Mister Grabbi'all says ye'll know whi' ah mean . . . AH SAID IS THAA' RIGH'?'

All that was needed to make Jock McFleaze's happiness complete was one thrust and twist of his right hand. Catharsis. He could almost do it. But Dan Grabbitall's voice was echoing in his head. 'Fartleby is supposed to be doing some work for me, and I still need it done. You go too far – you put him in hospital – and things may go wrong. All you're to do is scare him. Scare him as much as you like. But you put him in hospital, and I'll put you in concrete. That's all.' And Dan Grabbitall was unique: Dan Grabbitall was the only human being who had ever been able to frighten Jock McFleaze.

With a sigh of disappointment, Jock loosened his grip and let his victim fall, gasping, to the ground. Just one . . . or two or three . . .

good kicks . . . But no. He knew from experience that, like Magnus Magnusson all those years ago, if he had started then he would finish. He didn't dare.

'Now yui listen, Jimmah. Yui stay away fae the polis, an' yui dui whi' Mister Grabbi'all says, or yui'r gan tae mee' me again. An' ye wuidn' wan' thaa', wuid ye, eh? Time yui wen' home, Jimmah, because Mister Grabbi'all wuidn' be in his office a' this time o' the nigh', wuid he? Ye think he's stupid?'

Jock McFleaze tossed the remains of the bottle casually out onto the road, and crunched slowly off through the broken glass.

Boris Fartleby began to weep with a combination of relief and utter misery. At last, at long long last, Boris Fartleby knew himself.

Thirty-eight

(From the *Sunday Screamer*)
Us & Them: Cassandra McRaker tells it like it really is!

Doing the impossible: Marshall Mallow

Do you know, there are people who no longer remember Bogsworth Community School? Seems amazing to me, but there it is. I know, because I've been asking around.

But perhaps I'm being unfair. After all, I have a particular interest in the place, since it was me who first drew public attention to it. So just in case you're not sure what I'm talking about, let me make clear that Bogsworth Community School has, since mid-September, been known as the School of the Torch of Learning. With me now?

Well, you can hardly have failed to notice that it's been in the news of late, largely because of the interest taken in it by Randy Bastard. More of which in due course.

Having said so many negative things about the place, both before and after the name change, I thought I was the last person who would ever be invited on a guided tour. But I was wrong. Just last week, headmaster Marshall Mallow rang me to ask if I'd like to come and have a look round. An offer I could not, as they say, refuse.

I don't know if you heard his interview with Cyril Smarm a couple of weeks ago, but I listened to it intently. And I have to admit that I was not entirely convinced that everything was about to change, as the head claimed. Far be it from me to accuse Cyril Smarm of bias or subjectivity, but the fact is that interviewees on *Cometh the Hour* are never given a rough ride – not by Cyril, anyway. Could this be Marsh Mallow's reason for inviting me of all people to see at first hand what was really going on? If he thought my endorsement worth having, then I was flattered, but nobody was going to pull the wool over my eyes. I was going to find out what was really going on, and I was going to tell everyone.

Marsh Mallow is not a man to stand on ceremony. When you see him in his school, he reminds you of a general on campaign. Bawling out here, encouraging there, but always keeping his eye on the larger picture, always sticking to a strategy.

You can certainly see why he takes this approach, for the Torch School has been like a war zone ever since he took over. And until a fortnight ago, it was a war which Marsh Mallow seemed to be losing hands down. Then came the famous knife fight. The sight of the unarmed headmaster calmly facing down a pupil who was threatening to cut his eyeballs out made a huge national impact.

Well, Marsh freely admits that he sees this as something of a turning point. 'It was, I suppose, the moment at which I finally had to accept that there were pupils at this school who could not be reasoned with. I'd already had to accept that there were adults who could cause huge problems.' He reminded me of his notorious appearance on *Spotlight* a couple of months back, when Youssuf Al-Majnooni made clear that no compromise short of unconditional surrender would satisfy him.

How were things going on that front now, I wondered. 'Well, I wouldn't say that Youssuf Al-Majnooni and I have exactly become the best of friends,' said Marsh wryly, 'but perhaps there is a measure of respect there now which was never present before.'

I reminded him of his decision to instruct the History department to abandon the teaching of the Crusades, since it was causing offence to Islamists. Marsh laughed grimly.

'A bad mistake,' he said, 'as I now freely admit. Too late to put things right this school year, but as of next, the Crusades are back on the syllabus. We have to stand up for our liberal ideals, and be prepared to take the consequences. Too much is at stake for surrender to be an option.'

But what has really brought the Torch School into the public eye of late has been the interest taken in it by Randy Bastard, who is now pouring a substantial amount of money into the school. How did this come about?

'I've admitted that I was simply getting things wrong. I wasn't getting on top of the problems in this school at all. Well, I was beginning to see that a tougher approach could pay dividends with difficult pupils and even with difficult adults, but there was also a funding problem. Now this is common to all state schools, since no government, whatever they might say, is ever prepared to give education the money it needs. Well, I was determined to do something about it, and I recalled that Dan Grabbitall had once said that, if he didn't have so much else on his plate, he wouldn't mind having a go at sorting out the problems of British schools.'

Dan Grabbitall? The man whose projected purchase of the *Morning Filth* and SEXITEL is widely expected, if successful, to take the British media further downmarket than ever before? Dan Grabbitall? The man who has wrecked the sporting career of Letzgetcha Nickersoff? The same.

Well, Marsh got in touch with Grabbitall, and suggested that he might like to see what he could do with just one school, as an example of what might be done across the board if the will was there. Grabbitall jumped at the chance, and quickly interested Randy Bastard and R. McGeddon boss Rab McGeddon, both of whom he represents, in the project. Both have invested a great deal of money in the school, which is now effectively free of local education authority control.

Now I had a problem with this. I have always believed in state education, free to all at the point of delivery. I have always been opposed to the sort of privilege represented by Eton, Harrow, Roedean and so on. But Marsh is unrepentant. 'I believe in state education too,' he said with emphasis, 'but if the state will not fund schools adequately, what are we to do? There is no question of pupils having to pay fees, and our intake remains exactly the same as before. All that has changed is that our money now comes from two private sources. What we are attempting to do is to show just how good a perfectly ordinary school can become if only it is adequately funded. That's all.'

Fair enough. But what about the source of those funds? A killer and a weapons manufacturer. Dan is not bothered by this. 'Randy Bastard's victims were as anxious to kill him as he was to kill them. He just turned out to be better at it than they were.

'As for Rab McGeddon, I hope that everyone knows by now that the success of the DUFF rebels in Durtapura is very largely attributable to the weapons given to them free by R. McGeddon. The present régime in Corupcion is one of the most vicious in the world. Well, if its days are indeed numbered, it is Rab McGeddon who takes most of the credit. And you may have seen recently that he has spoken out very bluntly against little bimbos who seduce rich men and try to take them away from their wives. This is a highly moral man, and I am proud to accept funding from such a source.'

Marsh talks with enthusiasm of the hands-on interest taken in the school by both of these generous sponsors, one or other of whom speaks to him, it seems, practically every day. It is hard to believe that their support of the Torch School is no more than a publicity stunt. These are not just a couple of rich men who think their bleeding hearts look best when worn on their silk sleeves.

As we walk round the school, I find it hard to object to what Marsh is doing. This bold new initiative is still in its early stages, but already things are looking so much better than they ever did before. I would be very surprised indeed if the Torch School is not soon being held up as an ideal to which all our schools should aspire.

251

However strongly I feel in favour of state-funded education, I cannot in honesty expect parents to be happy sending children to schools which I would not want for my own children. The central plank in Marsh's platform is that the pupils are just the same as before. All that he is doing – with the generous financial help of Randy Bastard and Rab McGeddon – is to give them the sort of education which the state should be prepared to give all its young people.

Thirty-nine

'Dan Grabbitall.'

'Youssuf Al-Majnooni.'

The two men shook hands. Youssuf Al-Majnooni appeared wary, his host confident.

'Have a seat. So you got my letter.'

'Yes,' said Youssuf coldly.

'The photographs wouldn't win any prizes, but they're pretty clear. I thought Islam didn't allow sex outside marriage.'

Youssuf Al-Majnooni grimaced. 'Blackmail is a serious crime, Mr Grabbitall. You should be careful.'

Grabbitall's smile was at least as cold as Youssuf's. 'You wouldn't dare.'

'Are you sure?' Youssuf Al-Majnooni narrowed his eyes. 'True Muslims can be very tolerant of small indiscretions. When something happens between a man and a woman outside marriage, it's usually the woman who is blamed. If it became known that you had set me up, I think I might survive the scandal.'

Dan suppressed a yawn. 'Well, if you'd like to try . . .'

'And I may be more dangerous than you think. I know many young men who would take any risk for me, and not even ask the reason. If I told them it was the will of God, they would do it.'

Dan Grabbitall leaned forward and looked coldly at Youssuf. 'Mr Youssuf, I hope that you and I might enjoy a long and mutually beneficial relationship. But you must understand now that I am beyond your threats. If you annoy me sufficiently, it will be you who disappears, not me. That is a promise. Anyway, copies of the photographs which you have seen are in very safe places, and will be made very public should anything unpleasant happen to me. You can't threaten me, so don't even try.'

'What do you want of me?'

'Two things. And this isn't only blackmail, though I'm quite happy to admit that that's an important part of it. I have something to offer you in return. The first thing I want is easy. In future, you will attack the Torch School only when I tell you, and in ways which I will dictate.'

The dark face of Youssuf Al-Majnooni darkened still further. 'I do not compromise with the will of God.'

'Hmm . . . It wouldn't really be compromise. I have reasons for wanting the school to seem successful, for a time at least. You can still attack it, and Marsh Mallow. But I won't let you destroy it, not yet. You'll know that Rab McGeddon and Randy Bastard are now sponsoring it. Well, they are both clients of mine, and I need good publicity for them. That's all. I'd guess that you'll be free to do what you like with the place within a year or so. Blow it up for all I care.'

Youssuf grimaced. 'I don't like it.'

'And I don't care. You can go on expressing the will of God as you see it. It's just that, until I say otherwise, you don't overstep the mark. You follow my instructions. I doubt if I'll want you to do anything you would find unIslamic.'

Youssuf Al-Majnooni looked down in silence.

'Good. And now there's something else. Something much bigger. I'm having considerable problems with Randy Bastard. Never mind what they are, but . . .'

'I know what they are. I have a computer, and I have access to the Internet. The truth is that Randy Bastard is homosexual, and if everybody finds out, then he becomes worthless to you. Who would buy his cosmetics?'

Dan Grabbitall cleared his throat. 'Let's just say that I can't afford to have Randy Bastard's earning power diminished. I've already taken a few steps to protect my investment in him, but they won't be enough on their own. What's particularly worrying me at present is that Viraga Hateman is having him followed in the hope of catching him in a gay bar. If she succeeds, I could have problems. So I want him kidnapped and held in a safe place for at least two weeks while I take care of damage limitation. I'll need access to him myself, so that I can find ways of making him behave himself in future.'

When Youssuf Al-Majnooni looked up again, his eyes were narrow and cold. 'You want me to kidnap Randy Bastard?'

'Correct.'

And Dan Grabbitall saw a sight very few people had ever seen. He saw Youssuf Al-Majnooni laugh. 'Impossible. You must think I am very clever, or perhaps very stupid.'

'You're very clever. Much more so than most people realise. But I'm very clever too, so don't treat me as a fool. You've kidnapped several businessman, Rab McGeddon among them, and you can kidnap Randy Bastard too.'

'No. I know a bad risk when I see one, and . . .'

'Hear me out. You have so far kidnapped a number of rich but not very famous men, and have accepted relatively small ransoms for them. Clever. Stay away from high-profile people, and never ask for too much. Keeps public interest to a minimum so that the police aren't under too much pressure, and pretty well ensures that you get paid. Well, I know you'd never think of kidnapping anybody as famous as Randy Bastard, but I need it done. As his agent, I can give the police information that will send them off in the wrong direction entirely. All you have to do is to hold him in a safe house, allowing me full access to him until I tell you it's time to let him go. And for this I'll pay you twice what you normally ask.'

'You're wasting your time, Mr Grabbitall. This I will not do.'

'Oh but you will.'

Youssuf Al-Majnooni appeared to think for a moment. 'You would have to pay five times what I have asked hitherto.'

'I never bargain. But, as you already know, I do blackmail. And you've got more to worry about than just those photographs. Now you listen very carefully. All the mystery you make about your origins is very necessary to you. All that stuff about having no country, because your loyalty is only to God, and so on and so on. Well, any fool should be able to see that you're hiding something. I don't know what it is, but . . . Well, let me guess. Are you even a Muslim by birth? Have you ever really fought in a war? I suspect that you are really a Westerner, maybe even a Brit. I don't much care, but I know you do, and I promise I'll find out, and see that the whole world knows. I'll find out. And I never make a threat I can't come good on.'

'There is nothing to be ashamed of in my past.'

'I'm pleased to hear it. But that's the nasty bit out of the way. I said I had something positive to offer you, and it's not only the money for the kidnap of Randy Bastard. It's true, is it not, that the will of God is that all people should become Muslims?'

'It is.'

'Well, wouldn't you like your message to be heard more loudly?'

'Of course.'

'I could arrange it. If you'll take my advice, you can have a much higher public profile than you have at present, and you might even get people to listen to you with respect.'

'Some people will never be ready to hear the word of God.'

'Careful, Youssuf. Don't make God's judgments for him. How would you like to be on radio and television more often? Talking about the things you believe.'

Youssuf Al-Majnooni's laugh was quite mirthless. 'In the West, everybody hates me. They will never be sympathetic to anything I say. *You* will never be sympathetic to anything I say.'

It was Dan Grabbitall's turn to laugh. 'I won't, you're right there. But I'm not everybody. Let's say I could get you on *Any Questions* . . .'

'That would be impossible. I would never be invited.'

'Do as I say, and I can virtually guarantee that you will be. You can still preach the things you believe in, but you just have to tone it down a little. The moment that people think you have become just a little less fierce, they'll be desperate to love you. That's what happens in the rich countries of the world. The people become soft, and they're desperate to make friends of their enemies.'

Youssuf Al-Majnooni, was shaking his head, but he was unable to suppress a smile. 'Me on *Any Questions*? It's true that I could use such a forum, but . . . No, it would never be allowed.'

'Oh yes it would. If you'll only listen to me. And not only *Any Questions*. Radio and television generally could become very interested in you, and not only as a bogyman. You could become truly famous. You would still stand for the truth as you see it, but you would be heard by presidents and kings and prime ministers. People would still fear you, but they would respect you, too. Clive Sneersly would jump at the chance of having you on *Spotlight* again, and Cyril Smarm would interview you any time I told him. And ask you anything I told him to.'

'Ah, so it's not only me that you blackmail.' Youssuf stopped smiling and looked wary. 'Personal fame would not interest me, Mr Grabbitall. I would care about it only if it enabled to me spread the truth more widely. For myself, I do not care.'

'Of course. But it certainly would enable you to do much more than you do now. As I said earlier, you and I might easily enjoy a long and mutually beneficial relationship. Don't you think?'

'You could really get me on *Any Questions?*'

'I never promise what I can't deliver.'

'Perhaps also on something a little lighter? So that I can show another side of myself.'

'Perhaps.'

'I would never do this for personal glory. That would mean nothing to me.'

'Of course not.'

Forty

'Over to Justin Poser at the scene of the action. Justin.'

'Well, Cindy, there seems to be no end to the amorous exploits of Randy Bastard. Hardly has he finished with Tracy Bonker and Chantal Veramour – still no word, incidentally, on whether he is the father of her unborn child – than he is entangled with someone else. And with all due respect to Tracy and Chantal, this, I have to say, looks very much like the big one. Because you're quite right, Cindy, the figure at the edge of that picture, concealed under a hood and dark glasses, is indeed Letzgetcha Nickersoff – described in the *Filth*, with Christmas just two weeks away, as Baz's Christmas cracker.

'And as for the picture being so askew, well, the fact is that Ben Snappiter, who is here with me, took it as he was falling over, having just taken a right hook from Randy Bastard. Yes, that's right, Randy has at last shown something of the aggression that made him famous on Predator Island. I must say, Ben, I wouldn't like to annoy Randy Bastard. I'd as soon take my chances with the average famished lion. What exactly happened?'

'Well, Justin, let's just say that a little bird told me that Randy Bastard had booked a table at Lukatmi's last night, and . . .'

'Sorry, Ben, but just to explain, the rather plain facade behind us is indeed that of Lukatmi's, one of the capital's most exclusive eateries. Don't know if they'd let the likes of you or me have a table there, though, Ben!'

'Oh, I don't know, Justin, you might get in. But not me, I think, even before last night. But I was saying that a little bird had told me that Randy Bastard would be there last night with Letzgetcha Nickersoff, and that was just too good a chance to miss, so I was there with my camera.'

'Like the good pro you are. But you don't normally get beaten up for your pains, do you?'

Ben Snappiter laughed self-deprecatingly. 'Well, it's not unknown, and I have to say that I can understand it. I think I'd get on my own nerves if I was on the other end of the lens, if you see what I mean. Anyway, out came Randy and Letz, but both of them in dark glasses. Well, that was a bit of a problem, of course, so . . .'

'The point being that they were hoping to go unrecognised .'

'That's right. The more camera-shy celebs often do that, in the hope of remaining anonymous. But I was ready for them because I'd been tipped off. Well, of course, when you've got a couple of megastars together, and nobody knows they even know each other, it's a big story. But I wanted to get the glasses off so's I could get a good shot. So I gave them a shout, and tried to persuade them to oblige. Well, it must have been a bit of a bad moment, because Randy simply took three paces towards me, and floored me with that right hook. I went out like a light.'

'Wow! But you seem to have recovered. No permanent damage done, then.'

'Fortunately, no. I gather that I was out for a minute or so, but when I came to, with a few anxious faces looking down at me, the first thing I thought about was my camera, and I was very surprised that I still had it, and the film was still in it.'

'Otherwise the *Filth* wouldn't have that picture. Tell me, Ben, will you be taking any action about what was, after all, a pretty serious assault? And in front of witnesses.'

'Oh no no. Just an occupational hazard, I'm afraid. I got the picture, and I reckon it was worth it.'

'Thanks, Ben.'

'. . . and with me today, I have Dan Grabbitall, much in the news these days, with his bids for both SEXITEL and the *Morning Filth*. He says that he regards himself as a publisher first and foremost, but he also runs the PR outfit Rich & Famous, with such stars as Randy Bastard and Letzgetcha Nickersoff on his books. Dan Grabbitall, welcome to the show.'

'Thank you, Cyril. Good to be here.'

'Now I know you want to talk about other things, Dan, but the fact is that, after last night's events, everybody today is talking about Randy and Letz – both, as I've said, on your books. I have to ask, Dan, this isn't a publicity stunt, is it, a way of keeping your clients in the news in the run-up to Christmas? With all the more attention drawn to it by Randy's flooring of an unfortunate member of the paparazzi?'

'People can believe it or not as they choose,' said Dan wearily, 'but I was entirely unaware that Randy Bastard and Letzgetcha Nickersoff were even acquainted. And the notion that I could dictate to either of those two what they should do with their own time is simply laughable.'

'You can't be terribly pleased with Randy Bastard for walloping someone, then. Have you spoken to him?'

'What, to Randy?'

'Yes.'

Dan sighed. 'Yes, I've had a few words with him over the phone. I told him that this just isn't the kind of publicity he needs. But I have to say that a guy like Randy Bastard will never be tameable. It's just the way he is.'

'Well, I think there are plenty of people who would vouch for that. Not least Tracy Bonker and Chantal Veramour. Tell us, Dan, could there be something more permanent between him and Letz?'

'Don't know and don't really care. I've said it before, I'll say it again, but I'm awfully tired of it. The plain fact is that Randy Bastard is irresistibly attractive to women. He doesn't work at it, he just is. Sometimes I think he himself would be happier if he wasn't that way. He's well aware that his power over women makes many men feel inadequate, and this bothers him more than you might think. As far as I'm aware, Cyril, your virility is scarcely in question, but I think we should have some regard for men who are perhaps less successful with the opposite sex. Now I have to say that it was more than a week ago that I agreed to come to the studio this morning, and while I knew I'd have to field a few questions about Randy's sex life, I had hoped to be able to talk about other matters. If . . .'

'Fear not, Dan, fear not. I was just going to ask you about Randy's autobiography. I know you've been given a glance at it as work in progress, and you reckon it might be something special.'

'I think I can honestly say that this is one celebrity autobiography that is different. For a start, he's writing it himself.

And the fact is that the man is at once highly literate and quite unselfconscious. This is one with something for everybody, high and low brow. If you recall the diaries of Alan Clark, the 1980s Tory politician, perhaps there's some similarity there.'

'Now I should perhaps point out that in addition to being in the business side of publishing, Dan has himself been an editor, so he should certainly know what he's talking about. Tell me, Dan, will we learn more about Randy's sex life in the book? I mean, I know it's not what you think is most interesting about him, but we can be sure that a great many people will buy the book principally to read the revelations about girlfriends. Will they be disappointed?'

'Far from it. Very far from it. You see, Randy Bastard takes the sort of attitude to sex that, for example, Casanova did. That is, it really is of great interest to him, and he doesn't pull any punches. You'd be able to read the book on at least two quite different levels: as a literary masterpiece with strong erotic leanings, or – though I hate saying it – almost as a piece of porn. That's just the way it is.'

'And presumably we'll learn things about *Predator* that we don't yet know. I mean, publicly, he says so little.'

'That's right. I get so sick of the likes of Viraga Hateman suggesting that the lack of interviews is because he's boring or inarticulate. It's just that he is genuinely indifferent to publicity. No, he'll be telling all in his autobiography. Also about his sponsorship of the Torch School, of course.'

'I understand that it's beginning to show some improvements.'

'Indeed it is. As you know, Rab McGeddon is also sponsoring the school, and he and Randy, liaising closely with headmaster Marsh Mallow, mean to show that any school can be successful if only it is properly funded. They are already putting the government to shame.'

'Fantastic. But that's enough from me. Over to you, the listeners, now. And first on the line, we have Kate from Maida Vale. Kate, what's your question for Dan Grabbitall?'

'Oh, hi, how are you?'

'Fine. Your question?'

'Can I speak to Dan?'

'Yes, Kate, I'm here.'

'Oh, hi, ha ha ha, it's great to speak to you, it really is.'

'Thank you.'

'I just wanted to say, you know, it's great to see Randy getting together with Letz, because, I mean, they're just the most fantastic people, and I just wondered if, you know, it might last. I mean, wouldn't it be great if they got married? I mean, you could just fill St Paul's Cathedral or somewhere and it would be just fantastic for everybody, especially during winter, when everybody gets a bit down at times.'

'Well, Dan, what do you think? Could this one last? Might it even end with a tying of the knot?'

'The answer is,' said Dan with weary resignation, 'that I haven't a clue. I've only spoken to Randy about flooring the photographer, not about Letz. For what it's worth, I'd say he's completely untameable, and he will never be a one-woman man. As for Letz, well, she's a sweet girl, she really is, and I just hope she doesn't get hurt too badly, especially so close to Christmas.'

'All right, thank you for that, Kate. Our next call is from Harry, who is up there in Manchester. Harry.'

'Oh, hello Clive, it's . . .'

'Cyril.'

'I'm sorry?'

'Cyril. My name's Cyril. Doesn't matter.'

'Oh, sorry, I mean Cyril. Yes, it's not really Manchester, though. It's Altrincham.'

Cyril sighed. 'Well, Greater Manchester. Anyway, your question to Dan Grabbitall.'

'Yeah, well, I had to say that or my other half wouldn't like it. She always says that Altrincham's Altrincham and Manchester's Manchester. She . . .'

'Harry, I'm sorry, but we don't have all that much time. Your question please.'

'Oh. Right. Well, it's a question for Dan Grabbitall?'

'Yes.'

'Well, it's not about Randy Bastard, but about Rab McGeddon. I mean, I think Dan represents him, too, and I think he's really a fantastic guy. I mean the way that he just comes right out with it and says that it's wrong when these little bimbos seduce rich men and break up their families and all. And I mean, that's just so true, but everybody's afraid to say it, in case Viraga Hateman has a go at them, and it's really great that you get a guy like Rab McGeddon who just comes right out and says it. But it was something else I wanted to ask about. I mean, is it really true that Rab McGeddon's been giving weapons away for nothing to those people in Africa. I mean, it's obviously been in the papers and all, but is it really true, because it's fantastic if it is er . . .'

'Hello Harry. This is Dan Grabbitall. Yes, it's completely true, and it was entirely Rab McGeddon's idea. I do represent him, you're right – more accurately, it's his company R. McGeddon, formerly BOMZIZUS that I represent. Well, it took my breath away when Rab said to me one day that he was sick of just selling arms to the highest bidder, and for once he wanted to do something just because he believed in it. I told him I wasn't at all sure. I didn't want him to be seen as a soft touch, but he was determined. So for some time now he's been giving weapons to DUFF the Durtapuran resistance organisation which is up against one of the most vicious régimes on the planet. And with fighting now going on in the streets of the capital itself, it's clear that DUFF is on the very verge of victory, which will be a wonderful Christmas present for the people of Durtapura, gift-wrapped by Rab McGeddon.'

'Now I don't know if you've seen R. McGeddon's new company logo, but it shows a bullet with a gold heart in the middle, and the motto is "Bullets with hearts of gold". Well, it was when Rab told me what he wanted to do for DUFF that I came up with that idea. It's quite possible for weapons of war to do good, that's the point. I'm proud to represent R. McGeddon.'

'Thank you, Harry, for that. Next on the line we have Stuart from Glasgow, Stuart, your question for Dan Grabbitall.'

'Right, well, I'm a socialist, and I'm not taken in by any of this. Does Don Grabbitall seriously expect people to believe that he's got nothing to do with this thing between Randy Bastard and Letzgetcha Nickersoff? I mean, come on, they're both on his books, and all he wants is publicity for them so that he can make more money. What you've got to understand . . .'

'That's enough, my friend. Now I don't like it when people call me a liar. When I say that I have nothing to do with the private lives of my clients, I mean exactly that. These just happen to be two exceptionally attractive people who have got together, that's all. It's nothing to do with me, and I'm not even especially interested. It's not my fault, it's not Randy's fault or Letz's if other people are fascinated. Got that?'

'Look, Don . . .'

'Stuart, the man's name is Dan. You might at least get that right.'

'Whatever. All I'm saying is that some people weren't born yesterday. Don Grabbitall, or whatever you call him, is marketing both Randy Bastard and Letzgetcha Nickersoff as sex symbols, and bringing them together is a publicity stunt. Thing is, Mr Grabbitall's worried about the sales of Randy Bastard's lipstick, or whatever it is. If you want to know about their real sex lives, the pair of them, then have a look on the Internet at www . . .' The voice of Stuart from Glasgow faded away, to be replaced by wallpaper music.

'Yes, well, that's enough from Stuart. Whose name isn't even Stuart. We've had you on the show before, haven't we, Graham, and you're offensive every time. Well, we won't have you on again, so don't bother trying. Tough debate we welcome, abuse and bad language we do not. Next time you feel a flash of temper coming on, come down here with a pair of boxing gloves and I'll sort you out. Next on the line to Dan Grabbitall we have Linda from Taunton, Somerset. Linda, you're through to Dan Grabbitall.'

'Oh, hello, Cyril, great to speak to you. Great show, I listen to you every morning, I just wanted to say that.'

'Thanks, Linda. What's your question to Dan Grabbitall?'

'Oh, yes. Hello, Dan?'

'Hello Linda.'

'Hello. I just wanted to say that I belong to the Temple of the Magic Twilight here in Taunton, and to be honest we're a bit concerned about Randy Bastard, and how he's got to be so fantastic. I mean some people are saying that he's sold his soul to the devil like Doctor Foster, or whoever it was. And then I heard that there's this Bastard Studies course now at South Thames University, or something like that, and they really think that this is what's happened, and . . .'

The Pig and Partridge, Chelmsford

'Cor, see Randy Bastard last night. I mean, that guy's just fucking unbelievable. Don't still reckon he's a fucking poof, do you?'

264

'Look, I never said he was, did I? I just said that that Cassandra McRaker or somebody said he didn't have a lot of female friends. Didn't say I believed it, did I?'

'But you know, you got to be careful with things like this, because I mean, it's Dan Grabbitall who's the agent for both of them, isn't he? So I mean, you know, who's to say it's not just a publicity stunt? And I mean, bashing the photographer just made it even better, didn't it?'

'Made it better? How could it make it better? It just fucked up the picture, that's all. It was all at an angle, wasn't it? No, that's gen, that is, between Randy and Letz. But I heard Dan Grabbitall on the radio today saying that you can't tame Randy Bastard, and she's just going to end up with her heart broken. That's what he said, and he knows them both.'

'Cor, well if Letzgetcha Nickersoff wants a shoulder to cry on, she can have mine. I'd screw the arse off her ten times a night till she forgot about Randy fucking Bastard, that's what I'd do.'

'Ten times a night? Don't talk so fucking wet! I've heard that Randy Bastard can manage ten times a night, though. And of course, he's got a fucking enormous dick. After him, I bet she wouldn't even notice your little willie inside her.'

11 Poncy Crescent, Hampstead

'Well, of course, you are what you eat. I mean, it may be a cliché, but it's true, isn't it?'

'Of course it is. Eat junk and you are junk, that's what I always say.'

'Well, isn't that just a bit too simple? I mean, if you eat pork, does that make you a pig?'

'Darling, I wish you wouldn't say such stupid things. You know perfectly well what she means. If you want to be clean and healthy, you must eat clean and healthy food.'

'I'll tell you who's eating just a tad more than is really good for her. Letzgetcha Nickersoff is definitely carrying more weight than she should be.'

'Oh, come on, she's not carrying any more than you, and you're not fat!'

'No, but I'm not a professional tennis player either.'

'Well, whatever she weighs, it seems to suit Randy Bastard.'

'Yes, but I'd put money on it that he'll have moved on by next year – within three weeks, in other words. Apparently he's just worth the most fantastic amount of money already. They just can't turn out the aftershave and what have you fast enough.'

'Did you hear Dan Grabbitall talking on the radio about the autobiography he's working on? That's going to be worth reading.'

'Well, maybe, but, to be honest, I'm always so suspicious of celebrity autobiographies. Can we really be sure that he's writing it himself?'

'Oh come on!'

'That really is cynical beyond words.'

'I'm beginning to think you're jealous of Randy Bastard.'

'No, honestly, but I mean, Dan Grabbitall is his agent, so of course he's going to say it's a fantastic book, and it's all his own work, isn't he? But how do we actually know?'

'Look, whatever the hype, nobody has ever suggested that the man isn't brilliant and charismatic, and incredibly attractive to women. It's just got to be a fantastic story that he has to tell, and I wouldn't believe it if Dan Grabbitall said the thing was being ghosted.'

Refectory of the University of Middle Thames Southside North

'If you ask me, it's getting beyond a joke now. Steve says there's just no doubt about it. That man has sold his soul to the devil, and I'm scared.'

'Why should you be scared about it? It's not you who's sold out to the devil, is it?'

'Look, I'm quite serious about this. What about this child that he's about to have? No woman can resist him, that's completely obvious, and now Letzgetcha Nickersoff is having her heart broken. But it could get much worse than that. I heard that that Tracy Bonker has disappeared completely, and that scares me.'

'But you're nothing to do with the guy.'

'London's not far from here, and if he just looked at me, and he really is in league with the devil, what could I do about it? I think it's really scary.'

'Well, it's true that Steve says there's no doubt about it. He says that Randy Bastard is so obviously a Man of Power that only a fool could deny it now.'

'Do you know, I heard that he's working on a design for a time machine, and you know, all the best physicists in the world are really scared, because they think it might just work, and it could create all sorts of problems.'

'But I thought Einstein said you couldn't travel in time. Didn't he? Or maybe it was Stephen Hawking.'

'No, I think it was Newton, and as I understand it, he just said it could be a bit difficult. But he didn't know about black holes, you see, and if you can get into a black hole, then you come out of it at another time completely. Well, they reckon that Randy Bastard has discovered a way to do it, and it's all being hushed up because it's just so fantastic.'

'But I mean, how do you get back, if you do that? Has he worked that out yet?'

'Well, of course we don't know, because it's all being hushed up. But you can bet that if there's a way to do it, Randy Bastard would find it out.'

'God! I tell you, if it could be done, I'd go back to when Princess Diana was killed, and find out who really did it.'

'Well, we already know, don't we? I mean, it was British secret agents. Everybody knows that.'

'Yeah, but I'd really like to see them, and you know, be able to pin it on them.'

'You might even be able to stop them.'

'Yeah, that's a thought.'

Forty-one

(From the *New York Megatel*)
Randy Bastard kidnap

'I just can't believe this,' was the shocked reaction of Haleluya Nekred to the news of the kidnapping of Randy Bastard. Haleluya's son Paul died at the hands of Randy Bastard on Predator Island just two months ago, but she feels no bitterness towards the man who deprived her of her only child.

'Paul was my son, and I loved him,' she said through her tears, 'but he would have killed Randy Bastard if he could, so I can't say that Randy did a bad thing when he killed Paul. I hope that the people who are holding him will let him go, and before Christmas, because it must be so terrible for his family. I never wanted this. I am a Christian, and I will pray for them as I will pray for Randy Bastard. But they should know that God will punish them if they harm him. God will forgive almost anything, but not that. He knows what it is to lose a son.'

Haleluya's words were echoed across the land, as the shockwaves rippled across the Atlantic. The President expressed his own 'shock and horror' at the news. 'For all our grief over Paul Nekred's death,' he said, 'Americans have been generous in their admiration of Randy Bastard. I have spoken to the prime minister to express America's feelings at this most difficult time for Great Britain. All the British people should know that our prayers are with them.'

(From the *New Delhi Bapu*)
World's sexiest man is kidnapped

Randy Bastard, known as The World's Sexiest Man, has been kidnapped in London. The hunky winner of TV's *Predator*, filmed on an island off the Goan coast, disappeared from his home yesterday afternoon.

Perhaps because Predator Island is former Indian territory, Randy Bastard has been a particular hero in India, and there are concerns over the widespread belief that his kidnappers are Muslim extremists.

'If it turns out that Muslims are behind this terrible crime,' said 25-year-old Vijay Gandhi, a bank clerk, 'then Muslims everywhere can expect to pay a high price. 'I would not myself condone violence, but I would understand it in these circumstances. Randy Bastard is a great hero of mine.'

Leila Mubarak, 33, who works in a travel agency, said that she cannot believe that Islamic extremists can be guilty of the kidnap. 'Randy Bastard is a great man,' she said, 'and no true Muslim would dare harm him. It would be against the law of God.'

Fearing intercommunal violence, police have appealed for calm, saying that, even if Randy Bastard is being held by Muslims, the actions of a handful of people in another country cannot justify violence against Muslims in India.

(From the *Sydney Evening Digger*)
Randy Bastard: World holds its breath

Fears are growing today for the safety of kidnapped megastar Randy Bastard, several thousands of whose anxious fans gathered outside the British High

Commission in Canberra yesterday. The bulk of the crowd was made up of Britons and Australians, but many other nationalities were also represented. Chants of 'Randy, Randy!' split the Canberra air, drowning out even the ubiquitous roar of traffic.

Among the crowd outside was Fred Wonnaby, father of Sharon Wonnaby, the first contestant to die on the notorious *Predator* TV show which first catapulted Randy Bastard to international fame. The world watched in shock and horror as Randy Bastard, in the very act of love, stabbed his beautiful partner in the heart. The dead girl's father, however, recently returned from England, has no bitterness against his daughter's killer. 'I've said it before and I'll say it again,' he said, fighting back tears, 'Randy and Sharon took the same risk on *Predator*, and it was Randy who came out on top. I've always said that he'd be welcome in my home at any time, and I say it again now. I only hope that he lives to take advantage of the offer.'

A measure of the strength of feeling here about events on the other side of the globe was seen on national television last night, when militant British feminist Viraga Hateman, on a visit to Melbourne, said that she thought the hype over Randy Bastard's kidnapping 'ridiculous'. Several members of the studio audience rushed the platform, and security men had to intervene to rescue Ms Hateman. She was taken to hospital, but was not detained.

A spokesman for OZTV said that, while the network could not possibly condone such an attack, the strength of feeling of the audience was 'understandable under the circumstances'.

(From the *Morning Filth*)
Your Morning. Your Filth!
Randy Bastard kidnap horror

The eyes of the world are on London tonight, as anxious crowds gather outside the home of new *Filth* owner Dan

Grabbitall in the hope of hearing the first news of developments in the kidnapping of his client Randy Bastard, who has been called The World's Sexiest Man. On a bitterly cold London night, Grabbitall himself has been seen distributing sandwiches and hot drinks to the crowds.

He had earlier looked tired and drawn as he made the brief statement informing the world of what had happened. 'I can tell you very little, I'm afraid. The police are in constant touch with me, and have asked me to be extremely careful what I say. I can however confirm that Randy has been kidnapped, and that a number of demands have been made, including one for a very substantial sum of money. It is clear from other demands that the kidnapping is politically motivated. On a personal level, let me say that, while many see me as a hard-bitten cynic, in fact I have the same feelings as any other human being. Cut through the hype surrounding the name of Randy Bastard – and I accept my own responsibility for some at least of that hype – and you reveal a fine human being, a man I am proud to call a friend.'

As the world has reacted with shock to the news of the kidnapping, both the mother of Paul Nekred and the father of Sharon Wonnaby, the two *Predator* competitors killed by Randy Bastard, have called on his kidnappers to release him. Fred Wonnaby, who had watched with horror as his naked daughter, bucking and plunging astride the British contestant, succumbed to her lover's knife thrust through the heart, was unequivocal. 'Randy and Sharon took the same risk on *Predator*, and it was Randy who came out on top. I've always said that he'd be welcome in my home at any time, and I say it again now. I only hope that he lives to take advantage of the offer.'

Reactions in Britain have been equally strong. 'It is particularly distressing that this should happen at Christmas time,' said General Pius Oldgit of the Salvation Army, 'and render irrelevant any criticisms I may have made of Randy Bastard. The thought of this young and vital man spending Christmas Day in captivity is almost unbearable. I would like now to offer myself in his place, and I would stress that my offer is entirely serious. Should it be accepted, the love of God will help me to endure my suffering.'

(From *Hansard*)
Mr. Randy Bastard (Kidnapping)
3.30 pm
The Home Secretary: With permission, Mr. Speaker, I would like to make a statement about the kidnapping of Mr. Randy Bastard.

Let me say first of all that my thoughts, like those of the whole nation and indeed the whole world, are with Randy Bastard today. [HON MEMBERS: "Hear, hear."] This is no time for carping about an unfair world and how some are raised to fame and fortune above others who may be equally deserving. This is a time for us to express our common humanity and our abhorrence of the crime of kidnapping.

The basic facts of the case are well enough known, I think. Two days ago, Mr. Dan Grabbitall, Randy Bastard's agent, announced that his client had disappeared. For several anxious hours, no one knew what might have happened. And then it was revealed that ransom demands had been made. I can now tell the House that these came to Mr Grabbitall in the form of a videotape in which Mr Bastard was made to read a prepared statement. The brutality of his kidnappers I shall come to in due course.

As for their demands, they say they will release their prisoner only on payment of a sum of twenty million pounds, and the release of some dozens of Islamic militants held in custody around the world. In so far as these demands relate to this country, I need hardly say that there is no question whatever of Her Majesty's Government complying with any of them. [HON MEMBERS: "Hear, hear."]

I can also reveal that threats had previously been made against Randy Bastard by an organisation calling itself

272

Islamic Death. These were referred to the police, who advised Mr. Bastard that they were to be taken seriously. Mr. Bastard, however, made clear that he would in no way allow his life to be affected by such threats, and presented Mr Grabbitall with the following note, which he in turn has passed on to me: 'In the unlikely event of my kidnap, please ensure that no concessions whatever are made to secure my release. Such concessions could only encourage further kidnappings in future.' Mr. Speaker, this is the manner of man being held by Islamic Death.

I would not pay one penny of the ransom being demanded by Islamic Death. Randy Bastard is a personal friend of mine, and I would not insult him by doing something he would so detest. I was kidnapped myself not so long ago, and I still regret the paying of a ransom for my release. I come from the mean streets of Glasgow, and I could take it. Randy Bastard had a tough upbringing, too, and he can take it.

RAB McGEDDON, *executive chairman of R. McGeddon*

I have been threatened and even physically attacked for my views, but I still say that the hype over the kidnapping of Randy Bastard, and indeed the whole Randy Bastard phenomenon, is ridiculous. If he has indeed been kidnapped, and his life is in danger, then I sincerely hope that he will be released unharmed. But there are more important things going on in the world. The appalling treatment of women by the much-vaunted DUFF insurrectionists in Durtapura comes readily to mind.

VIRAGA HATEMAN, *journalist*

This is a sad day. I had many reservations about *Predator*, and many reservations about Randy Bastard after his victory. All these have been dispelled since I have got to know him personally. His sponsorship of the Torch School, along with that of R. McGeddon, has been a lesson to us all. The thoughts of everyone at the school are with him in his captivity.

MARSHALL MALLOW, *headmaster of the School of the Torch of Learning*

Before I met him, I was very cynical about Randy Bastard. Not any more. I have spoken to his agent Dan Grabbitall, and I know that he is doing everything that can be done . . . I'm sorry . . . I'm sorry, this is very hard for me . . .

CASSANDRA McRAKER, *journalist*

I have no admiration for Randy Bastard, but Islam does not condone kidnapping. If it is true that Islamic militants have kidnapped this man, then I call on them to release him.

YOUSSUF AL-MAJNOONI, *Imam of the Farootkaik Mosque*

I don't want to talk about it. He means a lot to me, and I've nothing to say. This will be the worst Christmas I have ever had. Please go away.

LETZGETCHA NICKERSOFF, *professional tennis player*

If they kill him, we have to be first with the news. Justin, you're on call twenty-four seven on this one. Now the moment the story comes through, we go straight to the newsroom whatever we're showing – we'd interrupt a penalty shoot-out in the England–Germany World Cup Final for this. Whoever's in the studio – and I want this practised till it's perfect – will be as solemn as fuck, and will say 'SEXITEL deeply regrets to announce the death, at the hands of Islamic militants, of Randy Bastard.' Got that? Then *God Save the Queen* and this picture of Randy Bastard filling the screen. After that it's a few more solemn words in the studio, and over to Justin. All right?

UNNAMED PRODUCER, *SEXITEL*

Forty-two

'She says her name's Chantal, and she's got something important for you. I told her you're busy, but she says you'd want to know.'

'Well, you can tell her to fuck off. She . . . On second thoughts, send her in. I wouldn't mind a quick bite.'

Dan Grabbitall put the phone down, closed the file he had been working on, and sat back. There was a timid knock on the door.

'Come in!' he roared.

The door opened slowly, and a waif-like creature entered. She had the pale skin of a pre-Raphaelite model, and the submissive manner of a geisha girl.

Dan stared at her. 'Well?' he asked loudly.

'I wanted to talk to you.'

'Speak up?'

'I wanted to talk to you.'

'Yes, well that much is obvious. Equally obvious is why. I don't know, Chantal, I really don't. For what it's worth, I actually went so far as to warn McFleaze not to try to blackmail me. I honestly didn't think it was even worth bothering in your case. You're McFleaze's property, he's been paid and your miscarriage has been arranged. I can't see what the fuck it's got to do with you. But go on, entertain me. What's the threat?'

Chantal looked at him in apparent puzzlement. 'I don't want to blackmail you. I . . .'

Dan Grabbitall yawned. 'No, I know, you only wanted to warn me about what might happen if I don't . . . But don't let me put words into your mouth. You tell me . . . I'm waiting.'

'No, really, I'm not going to threaten you. It's something else . . . The girls at King's Cross say that you're looking for information on Viraga Hateman.'

Dan's eyes narrowed. 'And what the fuck would you know about Hateman?'

'Is it true? Do you want to know about her?'

'Possibly.'

'I can tell you a lot. But I need to know what you'll pay.'

Dan Grabbitall leaned back and looked at her appraisingly. 'For your own sake, Chantal, you'd better not be wasting my time. But sit down and tell me more. When you tell me what you've got, then I'll tell you what it's worth to me. You've got one minute to get me interested.' He looked at his watch.

Chantal took the chair indicated. 'I'm on heroin. Don't think I've got long to go.'

'I could have told you that. Jock's doing, am I right? As long as you've got the habit, and he can get you the stuff, you're his.'

She nodded. 'Well, I want out. I want another chance. I've never had a chance in life yet. I . . .'

Grabbitall yawned. 'Your minute's going fast. And I warn you that, from your point of view, I have a heart problem: I haven't got one. If you've genuinely got something for me, I might find something for you. Otherwise, fuck off and die, Chantal.'

The girl looked wearier and paler than ever. 'That's not my real name. That's the name that Jock gave me. My real name's Jazmyn, and Viraga Hateman is my mother. She made me what I am today, a drug addict and a prostitute. She's nearly finished her autobiography, you know, and she doesn't even mention my existence. She thinks I'm dead.'

For a moment, Dan Grabbitall looked at her in silence. Then he picked up the telephone on his desk. 'I'm not available to anyone for any reason until I say otherwise.'

'I can prove it all. But I want you to get me away from Jock McFleaze. I want to go to the Clean Slate Clinic in Berkshire so that I can come off heroin. I want you to send me there.'

Dan Grabbitall looked down at his desk for a moment. 'Done,' he said, looking up. 'If you can prove what you've just told me, you'll get what you want. I'll book you into your clinic, and I'll cover all your costs. Now give me the detail, and how I can check it. Shoot.'

Jazmyn's face looked paler than ever, but the light of hope was just perceptible in her eyes. 'I was born in a women's commune just along the way from where I am now. My mother – her real name is Virginia Greenlove – had run away from home in Newcastle when she became pregnant. She . . .'

'Stop there. This must have been early eighties or so. People didn't run away from home for that sort of thing then.'

Jazmyn shook her head. 'It was different for her. She was in the Church of Fire, which is very strict, and pregnancy outside marriage is a terrible sin. Well, in London she became a radical feminist just like the other women at the commune. I don't remember because we left when I was only a year old, but she's told me all about it. We went to Greenham Common, where women demonstrated against the American missiles, and then we came back to London. She was very political, and she began to make a name for herself. She got into journalism, and that's how . . .'

'All very interesting, but of secondary importance at this moment. When did you leave her, why, and where does she think you are now?'

Jazmyn passed a hand wearily over her brow. 'She actually told me what she wanted me to be. She wanted me to grow up to break men's hearts. She said she was so pleased that I was beautiful . . . that's what she said, anyway . . . because that would make it easier for me. And she told me how to ensnare men. She trained me to pretend not to be interested, but then to glance up at a man from time to time, to catch his eye. She told me how to lead men on without ever quite giving them what they wanted, and she told me just when to cheat on them and how, and how to be sure they found out without openly telling them.' Jazmyn shrugged wretchedly.

'Fascinating.'

With evident effort, Jazmyn went on. 'She even told me the sort of man to go for. She said it was always dead easy to spot the men who would hurt the most, and for the longest time – the nice men, the shy men. I was only just out of primary school when she started telling me all this. And I could see how she'd been grooming me for it all my life – the clothes she'd bought for me, the coquettish manner she'd taught me. I was so unhappy, because I could see that she didn't really care about me for myself. She didn't love me, she never had. I was to be her revenge on men, on the man who had made her pregnant.' She looked away, pulled out a handkerchief and began to wipe her eyes.

277

'You're doing well. Every chance of a place at that clinic if this turns out to be true. But when did you leave her?'

'I put up with years of her bullying. She actually made me practice in front of a mirror, it was that bad. She wanted me to invite boys round so that she could see how I was coming on. I hated her. She said that it was vital that sex was nothing to me, otherwise I could get hooked by some man, and that would be a disaster. So she had me circumcised. It was horrible, but it's a good way of seeing that a woman can never really enjoy sex. Then she saw to it that I lost my virginity when I was fourteen. She got some man round, and he raped me. It was disgusting.' She began to cry again.

'So you left her?'

'Not right away. What would I have done? Where would I have gone? I was scared of her, and I'd never have gone to the police. She told me that nobody would ever take my word over hers. And she said that if I'd just be guided by her, then I'd have a really good life. She said the best way for women to have fun was to torture men. She brought back all sorts of men for me, and I got treats if I really bewitched them. When she talked to me about them, she used to call them all George. I think that must have been the name of the man who made her pregnant. Men were always Georges to her. She had a way of saying it that made it sound disgusting.'

'Very good, but I'll ask again. When did you leave her?'

'When I was sixteen. I just couldn't take any more. And I knew that that was when I was to make my debut, as she put it – you know, like debutantes in the old days. That was when she could use me openly, because it was legal. I couldn't take it, and I ran away.'

'Where to, and who can I check it with?'

'You know General Pius Oldgit of the Salvation Army? Well, I found out that he was running a women's refuge in north London. It was for women who were being abused by men, but I went there anyway. I just had to get away, and he took me in. I was there for two years.'

'Would he confirm this?'

'Yes. He'll remember me. Others will, too.'

'Hmm. And how did you come to be with Jock McFleaze?'

Jazmyn looked as if she might cry again, but she controlled herself with a couple of deep breaths. 'I had a job of sorts, and I was in a bed-and-breakfast when I left the refuge, but I was so unhappy still that when I got the chance, I tried heroin just to see . . . just as an escape. I needed it more and more, and so I had to make money somehow. I did some shoplifting, but I got caught a few times, and I found it was easier just to sell my body. Then Jock took me in . . . Don't tell him I've seen you, please. He'd kill me, he really would. You don't know what he's like.'

Dan Grabbitall laughed mirthlessly. 'I fucking well do. More to the point, he knows what I'm like. But don't worry, I shouldn't have to go to him.'

'I have to get away. I know I won't last much longer if I don't get away now. It's my last chance.'

Dan was looking thoughtful. 'Why would your mother think you're dead?'

'When I got away from her, she was terribly angry. When she found out where I was, she came looking for me, but I'd told Pius Oldgit that I didn't want to see her, so he wouldn't let her in. We haven't seen each other since I left her, but I found out not long after I left the refuge that she thought I was dead. There was another girl called Jasmine there at the same time, and she was about my age. Well, she died of hepatitis at about the same time as I left, and my mother somehow heard about it and thought it was me. I never wanted her to know the truth. I just wanted to forget about her.'

'Well well. You're right that she's writing her autobiography, but how do you know?'

Jazmyn grimaced. 'Like I said, I really don't want anything to do with her, but I'm still sort of interested, and I . . . I just found out.'

'All right, but how do you know that you're not in it? Are you saying you've seen it?'

'No, but . . .'

'That's no good to me. If there's any possibility that she talks about you, that would complicate matters. But if she doesn't even mention your existence, then we're in business. Well?'

Jazmyn shook her head sadly and looked down at the table. 'I read all her articles. It's the only thing I read. It's all there, the story of her life. Except that she never mentions being pregnant and having a daughter. She goes on about how some man raped her and she ran away to the commune, but she never tells the truth. She's changed it all to suit herself. She doesn't admit she's ever been interested in men. She says she doesn't really understand heterosexual people because she's only ever been attracted to women. She's not suddenly going to tell everybody that she's been lying, is she? And she couldn't tell the truth about what she did to me, but she wouldn't dare lie about it either, for fear that Pius Oldgit would say something. She . . .'

'Stop. If Pius Oldgit knows all about you and Viraga Hateman, why hasn't he spoken out anyway?'

'Because I've asked him not to. I've never wanted the publicity. I've never wanted her to know I'm still alive. Hardly anybody has treated me decently in my life, but Pius Oldgit has. I know everybody laughs at him, but he's been good to me, and he's never gone against my wishes. I'm only telling you this because now I can get something out of it.'

Dan Grabbitall was nodding slowly. 'If this all turns out to be genuine, then I'll get you into the clinic. If not, fuck off and die. Now just sit there quietly while I make a couple of phone calls.' He picked up the receiver in front of him. 'I need to speak to Pius Oldgit of the Salvation Army . . .'

Forty-three

(From the *Daily Shocker*)

Randy ain't no bastard
Viraga Hateman

Now it's just possible that I'm going to surprise you today. You have been warned.

Of late, I've been receiving a certain amount of unpleasant correspondence over my attitude to Randy Bastard. I tell you this only in order to emphasise that this has no bearing whatever on what I am about to say. I am used to controversy, I am used to hate mail, I've received death threats before. They haven't bothered me before, they don't bother me now. Neither, I ask you to believe, have I been intimidated by a physical assault in Melbourne a week ago.

Six weeks ago, in her column in the *Screamer*, Cass McRaker astonished readers by saying that she thought Randy Bastard was quite wonderful. Well, since she had not previously said anything against him, there shouldn't have been anything odd about that. But it was, as you probably know, the first time Cass had written in that vein about anybody. Praising to the stars just isn't her thing. Why did she do it?

What she said was that, having met Randy Bastard, she just couldn't be cynical about him. He was simply the most drop-dead gorgeous man she had ever met. Now I am in a quite different position. Because he is in captivity, I cannot meet him, and because I am gay, I could not fancy him. So why have I – hold on tight now – changed my mind about him?

In a word – or rather, in a name – Dan Grabbitall. Just as he contacted Cass McRaker a couple of months ago, in order to get a journalist of unimpeachable integrity to meet his client and write a profile, so he contacted me a few days ago, knowing that if the fiercest critic of his man could be brought onside, then the battle was surely won.

I confess I was astonished to hear from him. Did he really think that, just because Randy Bastard was in captivity and in grave danger of his life, I would be prepared to say I thought him wonderful? Did he think that, in the week before Christmas, I would not dare write anything negative? I have nothing but contempt for such sentimentality.

But Dan Grabbitall is nobody's fool. He persuaded me to come to his office, and there he showed me the notorious video referred to by the Home Secretary in the House of Commons. It is poor quality, with 'inexpertly recorded on an old tape with worn tape-heads' written all over it. But what it shows clearly enough is remarkable. Seated at a table, drawn but unmistakable, is Randy Bastard. He is reading a prepared statement.

I have been asked not to reveal details beyond what is already in the public domain, but this much I can confirm. Having completed the statement, he looks directly at the camera for the first time, and says: 'I request that no money be paid and no concessions made for my release. This will only . . .' At this point, a masked figure appears and delivers a vicious punch to the side of the head, followed by another to the jaw. Randy Bastard keels over, and the tape goes blank.

Now tell me this. Outside the world of Hollywood fantasy, how many human beings would be prepared to do such a thing while completely in the power of others who are clearly willing to do them physical harm and even to kill them? And why did his captors, who sent the tape to Dan Grabbitall, allow this to be seen? Of course, they made the recording because they wanted it to be clear that

282

they hold the man, and they wanted their demands known. But why did they not erase the brutal ending? It can only be that they actually want their brutality to be known. Chilling.

Well, I admit I was impressed. But, after all, we all knew that Randy Bastard is physically courageous. His performance on *Predator* proved that. Grabbitall, however, had not finished yet. 'You know that he's sponsoring the Torch School?' he said.

I said of course I did. Well, he said, would I be prepared to talk briefly to headmaster Marshall Mallow, just to know how much he had done for the school. Well, I admit I was pretty cynical about this. I know a fair bit about celebrity generosity, and I'm always suspicious of it. It's usually self-serving to a degree. But I said fair enough, and Grabbitall rang Marsh Mallow, who was clearly expecting the call. Now I'm not going to bother going into detail, but what the head told me was impressive. The fact is that Randy Bastard is doing much more for the Torch School than has ever been made public, and the difference he has made has been tremendous. *And he has tried to keep it all quiet.*

Grabbitall was beginning to win the battle, but he hadn't finished yet. Do you remember Fred Wonnaby, father of *Predator* victim Sharon? Well, the next phone call was to him in Australia. What would you say the chances are of a broken-hearted father praising to the skies his daughter's killer? But that's what Fred did. I can now reveal – and only because the man is in no position to prevent me – that Randy Bastard has given a substantial sum of money to the families of all unsuccessful *Predator* competitors, and that he pays regularly into a trust fund for child dependents of those competitors so that, whatever the families might do with the lump sum they have received, the children, when they reach maturity, will be well off.

Well, I hardly needed anything more, but Grabbitall's next move was a master-stroke. Just as I was putting the phone down, and trying to control the lump in my throat, he picked up his own phone and said 'Send them in.'

The door opened, and in came – you're not going to believe this – Tracy Bonker, Chantal Veramour and Letzgetcha Nickersoff. Well, these three have forgotten all rivalry over the man they so love, and simply and desperately want him to be released safe and well. Letz has even withdrawn from the tournament she is scheduled to play in after Christmas because she thinks it would be inappropriate to play tennis at such a time. 'With this on my mind, I wouldn't be any good anyway,' she said.

All three were in tears at one point or another as they talked of Randy Bastard. Chantal said how proud she was to be carrying his baby, and how, whatever happens to Randy, she will see that her son – the sex of the baby is now known – will know all about his father, and be proud of his heritage. Tracy said that she has never been much of a churchgoer, but she was in church last Sunday just to pray for the safe release of the man she loves. She was bitterly ashamed, she said, to admit that she would be so relieved if the kidnappers took up the offer of the heroic Pius Oldgit to take Randy Bastard's place..

After they had left, I asked Grabbitall about the one thing that has always made me suspicious about Randy Bastard. Why do we hardly ever see him on TV or hear him on the radio? I have suggested that he may not in fact be much good in spontaneous interview. What we get instead is an endless outpouring of newspaper articles – some of them quite sickeningly sycophantic. Surely any good agent would want his client on air as much as possible if he could be relied on to make a good showing.

Dan Grabbitall sighed resignedly. 'Nobody seems to believe me,' he said, 'but the truth is that Randy is genuinely indifferent to publicity, and that's the one real problem that I have with him. He's simply the best-informed, wittiest, most articulate man I have ever known. But being on TV or radio makes no particular appeal to him. If – please God – he is released unharmed, I hope I can persuade him to appear more often. It's just that other things interest him more – such as the autobiography he's been working on.'

As I leave Grabbitall's office, my mind is in turmoil. I always thought I was tougher than this, that I knew what was what, that I knew hype and fraud when I saw it. Could I be wrong about Randy Bastard? The truth is undeniable. I very well could. The thought that the vicious men who have kidnapped Randy Bastard might well kill him sickens me. I want to meet this man, because I have something to say to him.

It goes like this. 'Randy Bastard, I humbly beg your pardon for all the nasty things I've said about you in the past. It won't happen again.'

Forty-four

'. . . the nine o'clock news. Randy Bastard is free. For the very latest, we go straight to a news conference currently being given by Mr Bastard's agent Dan Grabbitall.'

'. . . and how and when you heard the news.'

The complex blend of strain and relief in Dan Grabbitall's face was highlighted by photographers' flashes. 'It was in fact two hours ago that I received a phone call from Randy, from a public call box in east London, saying that he had managed to escape, and that he was on his way to the nearest police station. He said he was contacting me simply as a friend who would be able to spread the news, in case, as he put it, anybody had been concerned about him.'

There was a barrage of questions. Dan Grabbitall held both hands up firmly, palms outward. 'I can only take one question at a time . . . You in the second row.'

'Where is Randy Bastard now, and will he be giving his own press conference?'

'To the best of my knowledge, he's still with the police. As for giving a press conference, I'm not at all sure that it's the sort of thing he would want to do, but I'll have a word with him and see if he might oblige you . . . No, again only one at a time . . . You in the yellow blouse . . . Yes.'

'Did he tell you anything about the conditions in which he had been held?'

'We spoke for only a very short time, because he was very anxious to get to the police station quickly in order to give the police the best chance of arresting his kidnappers. But I understand that he was held in very Spartan conditions and was chained to a radiator.'

'How did he escape?'

'He told me that he managed to get hold of a piece of metal out of which he fashioned an implement to pick the lock on his manacles. He did this when his captors were out of the building.'

'How did he sound?'

'I can honestly say that he sounded completely normal. It takes a lot to scare Randy Bastard. However, when I told him that he's been making world-wide headlines, he was speechless. I'd say . . .'

'Well, we'll bring you the whole of that press conference later. But for now, I've got Justin Poser in the studio with me, and he has, as I'm sure you know, followed this case even more closely than the rest of us. Justin, this is great news.'

Justin Poser looked as if he had just won the lottery. 'Cindy, I don't think I've ever heard better, and I have to say that I find it hard to be detached and professional at a time like this. The eyes of the world and even, as we know, the Christmas prayers of the Vatican, have been with Randy Bastard for two weeks now, and this is . . . well, this is just tremendous news. All that time, the world has watched with bated breath, desperately hoping for good news, desperately fearing bad.

'Everyone will recall that awful day when Randy was kidnapped. It was Dan Grabbitall who broke the news, and I don't think I've ever seen anyone more shaken. Dan Grabbitall the hard man of publishing and PR, the big hitter in the major league, was white-faced when he talked to the press, and I think it was his reaction that brought home to everybody just how serious this was.

'Since then, we've all been on a roller-coaster. It was just the day after the kidnap that we learned that the price of his life was a huge sum of money plus the release of a large number of Islamic militants from jails around the world.

'The Home Secretary's House of Commons statement and the ensuing contributions, made for perhaps the most riveting viewing I have ever seen from the Palace of Westminster, with the whole House united in its determination to stand up to blackmail. Speaker after speaker said that the heroism of Randy Bastard was a lesson to us all, and we must stand firm. Who can forget those TV pictures of London's deserted streets as the nation was riveted by the debate? Or the way that the world's stock markets came to a standstill as traders everywhere found that they had ears and eyes for nothing but the drama from Westminster.

287

'Then, giving way to overwhelming public pressure, the police finally agreed to release the terrifying video recording to which the Home Secretary had referred, and which so shocked Viraga Hateman. The kidnappers, clearly, were happy to let their brutality be seen, believing that this would persuade the British government to yield. They had miscalculated badly.

'The United Nations was for once truly united, unanimous in its condemnation of the people doing this terrible thing to the man memorably described by one delegate as "one of the greatest human beings who has ever lived." A Vatican spokesman said that, if the worst happened, it was quite possible that Randy Bastard would become the first non-Catholic ever to be canonised .

'Who can forget the tear-stained face of Letzgetcha Nickersoff on Christmas Eve, as she pledged her own fortune just for the release of the man she loves? And it's only three days since we feared that the worst had happened. The rumour that Randy Bastard had been murdered broke first in the Gulf on Christmas morning, and spread quickly round the world. During the six dreadful hours between its breaking and the decision of the kidnappers to prove that it was false, at least eleven young women around the world committed suicide.

'Still, the voice of Randy Bastard did at last prove that he was still alive, and now today we have the wonderful news that he is at liberty. A great day for us all, Cindy.'

'Justin, it certainly is. And, as I said, we will very shortly be bringing you Dan Grabbitall's press conference in full. But now for the rest of the news. Tens of thousands are feared dead after an earthquake in northern China . . .'

(From the *New York Megatel*)

Randy is free

There have been celebrations all round the world at the news of the dramatic escape from captivity of Randy Bastard. The man who broke American hearts when he killed US hero Paul Nekred to win *Predator* just ten weeks ago outwitted his Islamic fundamentalist kidnappers yesterday, and calmly telephoned his agent, American Dan Grabbitall before reporting to London police.

'All disappointment over the outcome of *Predator* is now forgotten,' said the President on national television last night, 'and all Americans join with the people of the United Kingdom in their joy at this wonderful news. Randy Bastard has struck a blow for freedom everywhere.'

(From the *New Delhi Bapu*)

Randy Bastard escapes

Cars around Connaught Circus in the heart of Delhi were sounding their horns in triumph yesterday as the news broke that Randy Bastard has escaped from captivity. Hindus and Muslims alike declared their delight at the news.

Forty-year-old computer programmer Mahmoud Ibrahim said 'I hope I speak for all decent Muslims around India when I say that the people who kidnapped this great man were not true believers. It is the enemies of God who do such things.'

The *Bapu* can exclusively reveal that an invitation has now been sent to Randy Bastard to visit India in the near future. Predator Island used to be Indian territory, and it is known that the British hero has spoken of his gratitude to the Indian authorities for making the territory available for the show which made his name.

(From the *Sydney Evening Digger*)

Randy Houdini

'I say the man is a hero,' was the comment of Fred Wonnaby, when we rang him to ask for a reaction to yesterday's dramatic escape from captivity of Randy Bastard. The father of Melbourne's Sharon Wonnaby, killed by Randy Bastard three months ago as he fought to win *Predator*, has never had a bad word to say about his daughter's killer. 'They were in it together,' says Fred, 'and I am proud that my daughter died a heroic death.'

Australians generally shared Fred's delight, and dissenting voices were not given a respectful hearing. There was even fighting in Perth when someone suggested that the whole thing might have been got up as a publicity stunt by Randy Bastard's agent Dan Grabbitall. 'This is not the sort of thing we want to see,' said Perth police chief Bruce Bruce, 'and although we will deal even-handedly with those we have arrested, I think I speak for all Australians when I say that decent people cannot be expected to stand idly by when a true hero is slandered in this way.'

(From the *Morning Filth*)
Your Morning. Your Filth!

Randy the Great

London was celebrating far into yesterday night. It was early afternoon when the news broke that Randy Bastard had dramatically escaped from captivity, and joy was unconfined.

'I just can't believe it,' said fourteen-year-old Daphne Duffer, throwing her empty alco-pop bottle high above her head in triumph. 'He's just the most gorgeous man in the world ever, and I just love him. If he told me to kill everybody in the world, I would. I'd do it now.'

Her friend, thirteen-year-old Susie Grockle, said that her Christmas had been ruined by worry over the fate of her hero, but that she would be making up for it on New Year's Eve. 'I'll be anybody's and everybody's,' she said, but it's Randy I'll be thinking of.' She tried to go on, but then the tears came. 'I'm just so happy,' was all she could say.

Forty-five

'Viraga Hateman, I was saving you till last on this one. Is it time to legalise prostitution?'

'Of course it is. But then again, Cyril, it always was. I don't see how any reasonable person could think otherwise. When . . . [Applause] When people react to Justin Poser's exposé by saying that the answer is for the police to crack down even harder, I just despair. Prostitution has been around throughout history, and it's not going to go away. As long as it's illegal, people like the disgusting Jock McFleaze will continue to exploit the unfortunate women we saw in the programme.

'You see, everyone seems to agree that the likes of McFleaze are beneath contempt, but it is naive beyond words to think that you can deal with the problem just by cracking down on the pimps. Until prostitution is legalised, you will never stop these parasites from making money out of it. The plain fact is that there are thousands of potential McFleazes out there. Take one out and another will take his place, it's that simple.

'I have heard nothing quite so pathetic as the story of the wretched Chantal Veramour, news of whose death prompted Justin Poser's investigation. One of the most distressing aspects of the story was that it was so sketchy, that a human life could leave so little trace. As much as could be established was that she was one of McFleaze's girls, that she had managed somehow to save the money to put herself through rehab, but ended up back with him and back on heroin. Sad or what?

'Well, she couldn't speak for herself, and Tracy Bonker may not have struck everybody as the most reliable witness, but she was the one person really prepared to talk openly about Jock McFleaze, and she takes great credit for this. She . . . [Applause] She herself was never by choice a prostitute. Who would be? She made her living that way because she had to. And she had no option but to dance to Jock McFleaze's tune.

'Well, you may say, if she's escaped, so can anyone. Not so, because the pimps are not stupid. One of their tricks is to get their women addicted to hard drugs, and themselves to supply them. Once a woman is in that position, she has no chance. Should we legalise prostitution? The choice is between that and positively encouraging the sort of abuses reported on by Justin Poser. Make no mistake about it. [Loud applause]

'And just one more point. However badly British-born prostitutes might be treated, still worse things are happening to some unfortunate women from overseas. The latest scandal concerns under-age Durtapuran girls who, with the complete breakdown of law and order under the vicious DUFF régime, are brought here – some of them sold by desperate or unscrupulous parents – by organised gangs. That such things are allowed to happen at all in a supposedly civilised country shames us all. [Loud sober applause]

'Well, we have time for just one more question, and I must ask the panel to be brief in their answers. Our questioner is?'

'Wendy Twitter. Who would the panel least like to kidnap, and why?' [Laughter]

'A question inspired, I think we can assume, by the first anniversary of Randy Bastard's kidnap. I must ask you to be brief on this one . . . Cassandra McRaker.'

'Gosh what a question! I was hoping you wouldn't come to me first. But I think I can give you an answer. She may have dropped out of the world's top hundred, but the popularity of Letzgetcha Nickersoff just goes up and up. I wouldn't dare kidnap someone with so many devoted fans, for fear of what might happen to me if I ever got caught! [Laughter and applause]

'Oh, but I haven't finished yet. I don't know how many people have got round to reading Letz's recently-published autobiography, but her description of her distress at the time of Randy's kidnap is truly moving. Some cynics have suggested that her style is so similar to that of the great man that we must assume that she has simply used the same anonymous ghost-writer. Well, if you believe that a tired old hack could have written Randy Bastard's superb autobiography, then you'll believe anything. No, the admitted similarity of style suggests rather that Randy might well have given her a few tips here and there. And if so, we can take it that they remain close, which means that, if I kidnapped Letz, I might even have Randy Bastard to deal with. Well, I can only say I'm not completely crazy.' [Laughter and loud applause]

'Youssuf Al-Majnooni. Who would you prefer not to kidnap?'

'Well, as one who was actually suspected of the kidnapping of Randy Bastard . . . [Laughter] I must be well qualified to speak on this subject. But before I answer in the light-hearted tone which the questioner is clearly inviting, let me make a serious point. Islam does not condone kidnapping, and there is no support in the Holy Koran for those militants who resort to it in order to further their aims. They must not be allowed to hijack a religion of peace. [Applause, sober but emphatic]

'Now who would I fear to kidnap? Well, he and I still do not see eye to eye on every point, but the former headmaster of this school, Marsh Mallow, is a man I have at least learned to respect. [Applause] It is true that the school was doing very badly when he took over, and the money received from Randy Bastard and Rab McGeddon was not enough in itself to turn it round. Marsh Mallow, I have to admit, accomplished a great deal. He is a man who is strongest in adversity, and that is why I would not dare kidnap him.' [Loud applause]

'Thank you. The man in question, now schools adviser to the government, is in fact sitting in the front row here in his old school, and looks, I have to say, somewhat embarrassed at the praise showered on him by his old adversary. But he needn't worry: his embarrassment doesn't come across on radio . . . Viraga Hateman, any thoughts on who it might be unwise to kidnap?'

'Well, I've jotted down a few names, but the one at the top of the list is Clive Sneersly. He's interviewed me twice, and both times I've been quite relieved to get out of the studio in one piece. The last thing I'd want is to have him on my hands 24 hours a day. No thank you! [Loud laughter and applause]

'But to be frank, I wouldn't dare kidnap anyone, for fear of the inevitable offer from Pius Oldgit to take his or her place. That would be more than I could handle. So the truth is that everybody is safe from me.' [More laughter, more applause]

'I suppose you could just kidnap Pius Oldgit. He could hardly offer to exchange himself for himself, could he? [Loud laughter] Lastly, the only panel member with personal experience of being kidnapped. Sir Rab McGeddon.'

'Well, Cyril, like Viraga, I can think of a few people I'd sooner not have to deal with in that way. But if, like Youssuf, I might be permitted a moment's seriousness, speaking as one who has been kidnapped and held hostage, I can honestly say that I would never put another human being through such torment, whatever he or she might have done. [Applause] But if I were so inclined, the one person I would definitely avoid kidnapping is Dan Grabbitall. I'd feel I would have about as much chance as Edward the Second had at Bannockburn. I come from the mean streets of Glasgow, and I never expected to meet anyone tougher than some of the characters I knew in Govan when I was growing up. That was before I met Dan Grabbitall. Heart of gold, yes, we all know that. But nerves of steel and a will of granite. If you're listening, Dan, you're safe from me.' [Thunderous applause]